ADVENTURE TALES

Publisher:
Wildside Press, LLC

Distributor:
Curtis Circulation

Editor:
John Gregory Betancourt

Associate Editors:
Darrell Schweitzer
Sean Wallace

Assistant Editors:
P.D. Cacek
Diane Weinstein

Adventure Tales is published
four times per year by Wildside Press LLC, 9710 Traville
Gateway Dr. #234, Rockville,
MD 20850. Postmaster & others:
send change of address and
other subscription matters to
Wildside Press, 9710 Traville
Gateway Dr. #234, Rockville,
MD 20850. Single copies:
$7.95 (magazine edition) or
$18.95 (book paper edition),
postage paid in the U.S.A. Add
$2.00 per copy for shipping
elsewhere. Subscriptions: four
issues for $19.95 in the U.S.A.
and its possessions, $29.95
in Canada, and $39.95 else-
where. All payments must be
in U.S. funds and drawn on a
U.S. financial institution. If you
wish to use PayPal to pay for
your subscription, email your
payment to: wildside@sff.net.

Tell us what you think!
Visit the official *Adventure
Tales* message board at:

www.wildsidepress.com

Wildside Press
9710 Traville Gateway Dr. #234
Rockville, MD 20850-7408
www.wildsidepress.com

CONTENTS

SUMMER 2006   Vol. 1, No. 3

Authors: We are looking for interesting new or classic works by authors who originally appeared in the pulp magazines of the early 20th century. No other fiction is desired at this time. We welcome proposals for non-fiction articles on subjects related to
pulp magazines.

Illustrators: All artwork is either reprinted from classic pulp magazines or commis-
sioned. We are happy to look at samples (please allow us to keep them for our files)
and will assign artwork if and when we have an appropriate project.

NEW FROM WILDSIDE PRESS!

The House of Skulls, by H. Bedford Jones
Trade paper: $19.95 Hardcover: $39.95

This new collection from the pen of H. Bedford-Jones presents five of his most exciting works from the pulp magazines of the early 20th Century, four novelets and one short story. Included are "The House of Skulls," "Written in Red," "Yellow Intrigue," "Down the Coast of Barbary," and "Skulls." Sure to please not only afficianados of pulp fiction but readers looking for some of the best adventure writing around, The House of Skulls and Other Tales from the Pulps is the latest addition to the Wildside Pulp Classics line!

Slave of Mystery, by Johnston McCulley
Trade paper: $19.95 Hardcover: $39.95

This volume presents 5 novellas by Johnston McCulley, creator of Zorro. Originally published under the pseudonym "Harrington Strong" in *Detective Story Magazine*, these mysteries showcase McCulley's lifelong devotion to the mystery field with meticulously plotted and brightly characterized stories that still hold the interest of modern readers. Presented here are "The Great Green Ring," "The Only Way," "Run to Ground," "The Obvious Clue," and "Slave of Mystery."

The Golden Dolphin, by J. Allan Dunn
Trade paper: $19.95 Hardcover: $35.00

J. Allan Dunn — one of the most popular writers for the pulps — wrote voluminously on every subject imaginable. Here are three of his swashbuckling tales of pirates, full of colorful action and daring escapades! *The Golden Dolphin*, a complete novel, tells the story of an expedition to find out what happened to a ship lost in the South Seas. "The Marooner" is the story of Long Tom Pugh, infamous buccaneer in the Caribbean, and his ship, the Scourge. "Forced Luck" tells of Barthelemy "Bart" Portuguese, superstitious freebooter, who believed a gold amulet sealed his success.

The Blotter

This issue we celebrate the work of "Murray Leinster" — the pen name of William Fitzgerald Jenkins (1896–1975) — whose writing career spanned the first six decades of the 20th century. From mystery and adventure stories in the earliest years to science fiction in his later years, he worked steadily and at a highly professional level of craftsmanship longer than most writers of his generation. He won a Hugo Award in 1956 for his novelet "Exploration Team," and in 1995 the Sidewise Award for Alternate History took its name from his classic story, "Sidewise in Time." His last original work appeared in 1967.

Here, then, are two rare Murray Leinster stories, celebrating a writer whose work has definitely withstood the test of time.

Also on board this issue are four of my personal favorites from all the pulp writers: H. Bedford-Jones, Raymond S. Spears, Harold Lamb, and John D. Swain.

Henry Bedford-Jones, dubbed the "king of the pulps" for the sheer volume of his work, always told a gripping story. Here is "Land Sharks and Others," a tale of piracy *not* on the high seas. Wildside Press recently published a collection of his stories called *The House of Skulls and Other Tales from the Pulps.* He last appeared in *Adventure Tales* #1 with "Skulls."

Raymond S(miley) Spears (1876-1950) was an award-winning author, expert woodsman, and journalist. Every story of his I've read has been uniformly good. Here is "Light on a Subject" a tale of pearl-harvesting and sales.

Harold Lamb is most famous for his historical novels. Early in his career, he penned scores of excellent historical adventure stories, and I'm pleased to include "Channa's Tabu" in this issue. (He also appeared in issue #1 with "The Make-Weight" and in issue #2 with "Yellow Elephants.")

John D. Swain, like Raymond S. Spears, is another pulp writer whose stories are always gems, often with a grim twist. His work appeared in not only general fiction magazines, but also genre fantasy and mystery titles like *Weird Tales* and *Detective Story Magazine.* He appeared last issue with "Lucifer" (from *Weird Tales*). This time we have another fantasy, "Forbidden Fruit."

We don't have room for Mike Chomko's pulp review column this issue, unfortunately. It will be back next time, as will The Morgue (the letter column). Keep writing!

This issue also introduces some "new" pulp writers to our pages. Robert Leslie Bellem, a hardboiled "spicy" fiction-writer with a prose style that raised eyebrows throughout the country thanks to an article about him in *The New Yorker.* His tale is "Kill That Headline," a two-fisted mystery. Philip M. Fisher, most famous for his creepy fantasies, appears in *AT* for with first time with "The Floating Island," a tale of high-seas military action. And George Allan England contributes a tale of the Dark Continent with "Africa."

A NOTE ON "DIFFERENT" STORIES

In the days before fantasy and science fiction became their own genres (in fact, long before the term "science fiction" or its predecessor "scientifiction" had even been coined), a "different" story was secret code for something supernatural or super-scientific. In this issue, "Forbidden Fruit" by John D. Swain was billed as a "different" story when it originally appeared. For pulp readers today, the "different" label usually means that its story is worth investigating, even if you've never heard of the author.

As always, you can find out where the stories originally appeared in the box below.

— *John Gregory Betancourt*

"Grooves" originally appeared in *All-Story Magazine.* "Land Sharks and Others" originally appeared in *Argosy/All-Story Weekly,* Sept. 24, 1921. "Light on a Subject" originally appeared in *All-Story Magazine,* Oct. 6, 1918. "Channa's Tabu" originally appeared in *All-Story Magazine,* May 4, 1918. "Kill that Headline" originally appeared in *Romantic Detective,* Feb. 1939. "Footprints in the Snow" originally appeared in *All-Story Magazine,* June 7, 1919. "Forbidden Fruit" originally appeared in *All-Story Magazine,* May 4, 1918. "Africa" originally appeared in *Cavalier,* Nov. 1908. "The Floating Island" originally appeared in *Blue Book,* May 1951.

Öwlswick Press

The Adventures of Doctor Eszterhazy

Avram Davidson

THE ADVENTURES OF DOCTOR ESZTERHAZY by **Avram Davidson**, with full-color dust jacket by **George Barr**, interior drawings by **Todd Cameron Hamilton**, and a foreword by **Gene Wolfe**.

Analog Science Fiction & Fact wrote: "Between 1974 and 1986, Avram Davidson published a number of stories of such astonishing skill, erudition, wit, and quirkiness that major markets such as *The New Yorker* and *Playboy* wouldn't touch them with a ten-foot Bulgarian. Set on the cusp between the nineteenth and the twentieth centuries in Scythia-Pannonia-Transbalkania, the fourth largest empire in Europe (the Turks were fifth) and a literal neighbor of the comic-opera realms of Graustark and Ruritania, flavored with Gilbert & Sullivan, Twain, Chesterton, and Conan Doyle (et only Davidson knows the cetera), they starred Engelbert Eszterhazy as a gentleman in search of learning wherever he might find it, unfazed by the strangest of events, cleverly combining the data that came his way to solve mysteries and ease the lots of the polyglot peoples of the empire. . . . Buy it."

In *Newsday,* Gregory Feeley wrote: "The stories are mannered, witty, and filled with the ornate archaisms of Davidson's mature style. . . . Davidson is the peer of John Collier and Lord Dunsany, and *The Adventures of Doctor Eszterhazy* is one of his finest books."

Tom Whitmore, in *Locus, the Newspaper of the Science Fiction Field,* wrote: "But what about these stories, I hear you ask. What are they about, and why should I read them? They are about Engelbert Eszterhazy, possessor of six doctorates; they are about the empire of Scythia-Pannonia-Transbalkania and its tribulations; they are about wonder, marvel, and the unexpected.

"They are Victorian tales, with a Victorian pace, with the richness of language that makes the best Victoriana so marvelous, and with modern allusions and understanding lurking just beneath the surface; to try to summarize them individually is to wreak havoc on their integrity. There are wonders here for those who know a little, and marvels for those who know a lot, about literature, history, botany, or any other subject.

"But you should read these stories because they are fun. They amuse, instruct, alert, puzzle, and challenge in the way that only great stories can. The publisher's conceit of having each story identified by an icon rather than a running title is totally appropriate. . . . A masterful performance from both author and publisher!"

Avram Davidson wrote *The Phoenix and the Mirror, Peregrine: Primus, Peregrine: Secundus,* and *Vergil in Averno,* along with many other classics of erudite, witty fantasy.

Hardcover, 386 pages: $24.50 postpaid from Owlswick Press, 121 Crooked Lane, King of Prussia PA 19406-2570

GROOVES

by Murray Leinster

The sun was pouring down heat, and the whole valley felt like a furnace. Little eddies of hot wind touched us languidly now and then, not refreshing us, not even adding to our discomfort, but merely emphasizing the heat and dryness of our surroundings. We sat on the rough-planked porch of Martin's saloon and looked up the valley, watching the trail quiver and seem to rock in the heat.

"No," said Jimmy Calton, continuing the discussion he had been carrying on entirely by himself. "Th' trouble with people is that they don't see what's just before their noses. They go round lookin' for somethin' excitin' that ain't there."

He lounged carelessly in his chair, expertly flicking the ashes from his cigarette into the floppy wide ear of a huge yellow dog that slept peacefully stretched out on the floor. When the ashes struck the dog's ear, he would lazily flick them out and go back to sleep again.

I mumbled something indistinguishable in answer to Jimmy's pronouncement. Heat always takes all the energy out of me and I revert to my normal state of utter indolence. Jimmy took my mumble as a sign of interest, however, and continued his remarks.

"'Most everybody," he said didactically, "goes around callin' himself *Sherlock Holmes* or *Nick Carter*. Everybody's got a habit o' thinkin' in a groove o' mystery. Everybody thinks the same thing every time. Nobody likes anything he can't make into a mystery."

"Don't like things they can understand?" I queried listlessly. "How's that? I don't agree with you."

"Shuh!" Jimmy flicked a bit of ash accurately into the yellow dog's ear. The dog reproachfully sat up and scratched it out with his hind foot, then lay down again.

"Shuh!" Jimmy repeated. "Why, looka here. S'pose you're ridin' on a trolley-car in Houston an' are hangin' onto a strap. Right in front of you is a pale, puny-lookin' sort of feller, pale-faced, lookin' like a girl. He's got curly hair that needs cuttin' and he don't seem never to have needed a shave. He's got small hands, an' his ears're small an' nice-lookin'. You, danglin' on a strap like they do on the streetcars in Houston, you've got a bundle in your hand. You see this guy lookin' up at you. He's got blue eyes, awful blue eyes, like you always think the girl you're in love with has got."

"I never do," I defended myself. "I always fall in love with brunettes."

"Any way you like," Jimmy conceded. "But you're standin' up there in front of this guy, an' you've got a bundle in your hand. Th' car goes around a corner sudden, an' your bundle drops in this guy's lap. Instead of closin' his knees together to catch it, he throws 'em apart. What would you think?"

"I don't understand," I said.

Jimmy pulled his bag of makings out of his pocket and tossed it into my lap. Instinctively, I closed my knees upon it to keep it from falling to the floor.

"Oh," I said. "Everybody knows a man puts his knees together to make a lap and a woman throws hers apart. That's because she wears a skirt."

"Well, what would you think if this guy on the streetcar threw his apart? Remember, he's pale, an' puny, an' sort o' hunched over."

"I'd say he was a woman masquerading in men's clothes," I said promptly.

Jimmy nodded his head.

"O' course you'd say that," he admitted. "I did hope you might have more sense, but it's all right."

"Well, what should I think?" I demanded. I was a little nettled by Jimmy's manner. He is a decent sort of fellow and has given me a lot of good stories, but there is no use denying that he is irritating sometimes.

"He might be a shoemaker," Jimmy suggested mildly. "They wear leather aprons, an' have to hol' scraps o' leather an' things in 'em, so they spread their knees to make laps to hol' things in. Ain't it true? An' wouldn't that account for his bein' hunched over, an' all that?"

I grunted in ungraceful admission of my defeat and relapsed into silence. We sat without speech for some moments. All the valley was very quiet. The heat made everything seem to dance in jerky, hypnotic motions. Inside the bar we could hear the flies buzzing dully about. Occasionally a half-strangled snore came from within. Joe, the bartender, lay peacefully behind the bar, resting against the night and the need for labor. Our two ponies dozed against the hitching-rail. Now and then one of them lazily whisked at the numberless flies with his tail, but nearly all of the valley seemed as indolent and as inert as the two of us sitting on the porch. Jimmy sprawled in his chair and fanned himself slowly with his sombrero, puffing the while on his cigarette. The big yellow dog lay soundly asleep in the strange languor of hot climates.

"It ain't to be wondered at," Jimmy said presently, referring to his former subject of conversation. "When folks had to think things out f'r themselves they diden' stick to grooves, but now — gosh! Look at Joe inside there. The barkeep that was here before him knowed every man in forty miles real intimate, an' most men in four hundred miles well enough to lend 'em money. He knowed every brand, an' every ranch, an' most Mexes well enough to keep the wrong ones out o' here. An' look at Joe. What d'you s'pose he'd do 'f I asked him where Carey Walters lives? He'd use th' telephone!"

"Not that bad," I said. "Everybody knows where Carey lives."

"Pretty near that bad," Jimmy repeated doggedly. "He'd call up somebody that knowed an' ask how to get there from here. He thinks in a groove, a telephone groove. Everybody thinks in grooves nowadays."

He threw the butt of his cigarette away and sat in disgusted silence. Without energy to stir him up again, I lay lazily back and looked out at a dazzling world through half-closed eyes. The sun-glare was terrific. The whole valley seemed to be simply baking slowly but thoroughly in the hot, pitiless sunshine. Presently, far down the quivering, baking track that through courtesy we called a road, a whirl of dust appeared, and then a darker spot in its center.

"Here comes somebody," I said without movement. "Must be Carey."

Jimmy squinted his eyes and watched the approaching figure.

"Yeah," he said. "He ought to have better sense than to travel in the middle of the day."

"I wonder," I said idly, "if his wife is standing up well in the heat."

"I saw her a couple of weeks ago," Jimmy yawned, "and she looked pretty well. He's a lucky dog. She's *una muy gallina*, believe me!"

That was Jimmy's private Spanish rendition of "Some chicken!" He had a habit of translating American slang into 'dobe Spanish and inflicting it upon his hearers. In this case, he happened to be quite correct. Mary Walters was one of the most charming little women a fool husband ever dragged away from civilization. Her husband was the manager of a tiny mine ten miles from everywhere but the saloon on whose porch we sat. With the sublime folly of an adoring husband, he had brought his wife there, to live in the manager's house, to be the only white woman in thirty miles, and to almost literally fry in the heat of the valley. There were thirty or forty Mex women attached to the village of the mine-workers, and about seventy-five or so men about the mine, but her husband was the only white man she would see for weeks on end. He usually had a white assistant, but for two months past had been without one.

"He shouldn't have taken her up there," I said resentfully. "It's ridiculous to expect a white woman to live like that."

"But he did," Jimmy said lazily. "The point isn't that he shouldn't have taken her there, but just he's got in a groove of thinkin'. He married her. Wives ought to live with their husbands. An' so —"

"He certainly oughtn't leave her there alone," I said virtuously.

"You're right there," Jimmy agreed. "We're no more'n twenty miles from the border."

"I wasn't thinking of raids," I remarked. "The rangers have pretty well taken care of them."

"I was thinkin' of raids," Jimmy was quite serious. "Every spigoty revoltoso in Chihuahua is just lookin' f'r a chanst to make a gran' stan' raid. 'F he c'n make a big splash an' get his name in all the 'dobe newspapers — like the ones that come out once a week an' say Roosevelt is headin' a revolution in the States an' the President's had to move the gov'ment to Canada — a big raid'll mean any number of men f'r him."

"But they wouldn't dare raid this far," I protested. "And no one could get any number of men this far with any hope of getting back."

"Wouldn't need many men," Jimmy persisted. "Half a dozen men 'd be plenty."

"There are seventy-five at the mine," I pointed out.

"And fifty of 'em 'd join the raiders," Jimmy replied casually. "You don't know greasers yet. I ain't sayin' there's any real danger. I'd have licked some sense into Carey 'f I'd thought there was, an' I wouldn't be loafing here, either. I just said it was possible. Those spigoties think in grooves, too. But you know the Mariposita is a dam' rich mine if it is small. It'd be worth takin' a chance on. I'd raid it myself f'r much."

Carey waved his hat to us and drew up before the door.

"Hello, people," he said cheerfully, and mounted the steps. "Come in and have a drink."

We followed him. Joe, inside, woke reluctantly and served us, then lay down again to sleep.

"I'm going to use the telephone, Joe," Carey said matter-of-factly, and went to the instrument. We heard him call his wife and give her a message to be delivered to the Mex foreman.

"Carey," said Jimmy deliberately when he turned away, "what's eatin' you, goin' aroun' in this hot weather?"

"I got a phone call that the owners are down in Dos Pasos and want to see me. They don't want to come out to the mine. I don't blame them," he added with a laugh. "It's some ride even this far, and it's going to be worse the rest of the way."

"You got a telephone out there at the mine now?" Jimmy asked curiously. "You musta had money to burn to run a wire all that ways."

Carey laughed again.

"The owners put it in, and I wanted it for Mary, anyway. She was getting a little bit lonesome, and having a phone in is almost like being in town."

"Of course," Jimmy said with a trace of sarcasm. Carey did not notice.

"You ought to see the way the mine is turning out," he said in a burst of enthusiasm. "You know what placer stuff is like, but this is a wonder! I'm carrying down some stuff that will open the owners' eyes."

"You carryin' around a lot of stuff casual like?" Jimmy asked. "An' all by yourself?"

"I've got more than I like to think about," Carey admitted. "It's all right, though. Nobody'll bother me. The men expect me to carry down the month's output next week and get the money for their pay. They'll never suspect I'm going to trot down with it today. I'll get back by tomorrow night with their pay and then I don't mind their finding out. This is the best plan, after all."

Jimmy looked a trifle queer, but said nothing. In a moment or two more Carey mounted again and rode away.

"Grooves," said Jimmy meditatively as he disappeared down the valley. "Grooves. There was a guy once wrote a thing — a story or somethin' — sayin' that the best way to hide a thing was to not hide it at all."

"'The Purloined Letter'," I suggested.

"I don't know." Jimmy's brow was wrinkled. "I ain't much on readin'. But that story thing makes more trouble than most any one other thing I know. It started a new kind o' groove. Look at Carey there. Everybody that bothers to think about it at all will know he's carryin' somethin' to show the owners. See? It's near th' time to carry the stuff, he's got a lot of it, an' he's got to go to town. He wouldn't want to leave all that unguarded at the mine anyway."

"You just said that thinking in grooves — and having a guard with him would be thinking in grooves — was the worst thing a man could do. You're contradicting yourself."

"That shows I'm tellin' the truth," Jimmy said cryptically. "When a man is lyin' he's pretty sure to be plausible. When he contradicts himself he knows what he's talking about."

He rolled another cigarette and lighted it, throwing the extinguished match at the head of the sleepy yellow dog on the porch. I lay back in my chair again, and half-closed my eyes. The valley danced and quivered in the heat. The two ponies still dozed at the hitching-rail. I was taking a vacation and had ridden over early in the morning from the ranch at which I was stopping. I had been told I would probably find Jimmy turning up some time during the day, but so far he had merely bored me with didactic reflections on life in general.

Jimmy, as a storyteller, was amusing, but as a philosopher he was dull. I found myself growing more and more drowsy from the heat. A small lizard poked his head from beneath a stumpy bit of yellow brush, heard nothing, and ventured out into the sunlight. He lay still, torpid, basking, baking in the sun. The big yellow dog gave a sigh and flopped his uppermost ear, in which Jimmy had just flicked a bit of cigarette-ash. Jimmy began to speak again, but I paid no attention. A muffled, strangled snore came from inside the house. The sun poured down. A little whirl of hot, dry air touched my face. My soft collar was damp with perspiration.

I lay back, comfortable, my arm lazily hanging down. My cigarette slipped from the relaxed fingers and rolled on the rough plank flooring of the porch. The valley danced dizzily in the heat. I slipped off into that delightful state of half-waking, half-sleeping semi-consciousness that is the true siesta.

I roused with a start. The telephone-bell inside was ringing. I had not dozed long, no more than a normal midday siesta. I heard Joe, inside, shuffle protestingly across the floor to the phone. He took down the receiver and answered it sleepily.

"Naw, he ain't here. He lef' a couple o' hours ago. Jimmy Calton's here. Wan' ter talk to him?"

Jimmy rose, stretched, and went indoors.

"Hello," he said casually into the transmitter. The next

second I had a sense of an electric tension. Jimmy's voice had changed entirely.

"You're Mendez? At the Mariposita? What's up?"

I went inside. Jimmy was pale as death. Joe, the bartender, stared at him, puzzled.

"What's the matter, Jimmy?" I asked curiously.

He paid no attention for a moment, listening on the receiver.

"Wait a minute, Mendez," he said quietly, and turned to face us.

"Felipe Mendez is at the Mariposita. He crossed th' border las' night an' made f'r the mine. His gang's in charge now, only they dynamited the safe an' foun' Carey took all the stuff with 'im. Now Mendez says if he don't come back with it, it's good-by for Carey's wife."

He stood still a moment, his fingers working nervously.

"You know what that means," he said sharply. "It'd take hours to catch Carey, an' if he came back, it'd be good-by anyway. There ain't any rangers we can get together in time. Dammit, what're we goin' to do?"

I went to the phone. Some two or three months before I had met Mendez. He was then a strong partisan of the central government, and I had interviewed him. He would remember me, I felt sure, because from motives of policy I had praised him in moderation. I told him who I was and he did remember me.

"What's this Jimmy Calton tells me?" I asked.

"I am sorree," Mendez's oily voice came over the phone. "But to conduct the *revolución* funds are necessaree. So. But reparation may be had from *el Gobernador*."

"But what's this question of Mrs. Walters?"

"My men, they are much disappointed. I cannot blame them. To hold the *señora* as a hostage is the onlee possible way to secure the funds we must have."

Jimmy suddenly came up behind me and took the receiver from my hand.

"Go get the ponies in shape," he said quietly. "You're game for a scrap? Joe, you're comin', too,"

We went out and I, for one, paced nervously up and down. Joe went to the rear of the saloon and reappeared leading a pony. I heard Jimmy still talking inside, but could not distinguish his words. He joined us in a moment and jumped on his horse. We thumped away up the valley in the blistering heat, the hot wind burning our faces. I could not understand what was wanted of me, because I am without exception the worst shot in America. Joe rode sullenly beside me.

"I don't know what we c'n do," Jimmy said wretchedly. "I said we had enough to pay him in the bar safe, an' I'd bring it if Mary Walters wasn't harmed. I talked to her, an' so far she's jus' scared. We gotta trus' t' luck."

"You mean we're goin' t' fight?" asked Joe with a groan. "Hell, I ain't no fighter."

It was very hot in the valley, but I began to feel a little chilly. Riding cold-bloodedly into a fight is not as pleasant a sensation as one would suppose. I began to think of many solemn things. The worst of them was that I would be quite useless.

"We're to ride up to a mile o' Carey's cabin, an' then a couple o' spigoties'll come an' meet me. I'm t' go on alone an' see Mary, an' bring 'er back — presumably," he added grimly. "Looka here, fellers, I got somethin' up m' sleeve, but if I don't get out with her all right —"

Joe grunted. I felt very queer.

"I think I'm goin' to be all right," Jimmy said carefully. "I'm countin' on th' Mexes thinkin' in grooves, too."

We pounded on up the trail, with the blinding dust rising all around us, soaked in sweat and with the dust turning to mud as it settled upon us. Joe rode uncomfortably and ungracefully, but he seemed vastly more comfortable mentally than I was. We were going into a tight place. Mendez was not a pleasant person to deal with. He would probably, as Jimmy had foretold only a few hours before, have only half a dozen or a dozen men with him, but to me that was far too many. It is all very well to talk about one white man being a match for several Mexicans, but — well, I was uncomfortable. In spite of the heat and the sweat that poured from every pore, I felt cold all over. I do not think I was intended to be a hero.

Jimmy seemed to be going over his plan again and again. Neither Joe nor myself knew what it was. We knew Jimmy had promised to bring a ransom for Mary Walters, and we knew he had not brought it — that, in fact, there was no sum of money to bring. Carey had the only really big sum in the locality, and he was miles away and going blissfully along, quite unconscious of his wife's danger. It was quite hopeless, altogether. I had heard some few tales of Mendez, and knew that even if Jimmy did turn over all the money Mendez demanded, Mendez was just as likely as not to shoot him casually and keep Mary Walters as his captive anyway. And the thought of a white woman in the hands of one of Mexico's *revoltoso* chieftains —

Jimmy reined up.

"I'm goin' t' try to hang on to my gun," he said to us, "but 'f I can't, after I've gone up to Carey's house you two edge up as close as you can. An' if there's shootin' — as I expec' — you two come a runnin'."

"Hell!" Joe said mournfully. "I ain't no fighter."

I confess I swallowed hard. My hands were shaking, at any rate, when I reached for the pistol in my hip-pocket. I slipped it into the side-pocket of my coat. Joe did the same. Jimmy was not wearing chaps, merely corduroy trousers above his boots, and he had a big bulge in his hip pocket. He left it there.

We came in sight of Carey's house. It stood by itself on top of a rise in the ground. The mine itself lay over the ridge. We could see one or two of the houses of the mine-workers, but most of them were hidden with the mine. Two men, apparently of Mendez's gang, loafed before the door of Carey's house.

When we appeared there was a stir. The two men before Carey's cottage called inside and the door opened. I recognized Mendez. He grinned at us and gave some orders to the pair. They started down toward us. Two or three men from the village ran up to the house, and received further instructions from Mendez. By this time the two he had first spoken to were quite near.

Jimmy rode forward to meet them. There was an angry argument. The two men were evidently insisting that he surrender his weapons before he came up to the house. At last, with a very ill grace, Jimmy gave in. He handed over his pistol. Even then, however, they were not satisfied. One of them patted his pockets to make sure he had no other weapons. Then they went on up to the house. Mendez greeted Jimmy with a flashing smile, showing his white teeth. Jimmy evidently snapped at him. The pair disappeared indoors.

Joe looked at me uncomfortably. I gripped my pistol nervously and we edged forward. Carey's house seemed to quiver a little in the heat. Our hearts in our throats, we edged our horses toward it. One of the men before the door entered, apparently in response to an order.

There was a sudden yell from the house, and an explosion. We dashed forward recklessly, scared stiff but desperate, going for the house. The men outside ran for the door. One of them stopped and fired at us, but the bullet went wild. They disappeared inside and two more shots sounded. We pounded up to the door, and Jimmy appeared, holding Mary by the arm, a little trickle of blood coming from his ear. He was facing inside with his arm leveled, and he was swearing atrociously in Spanish.

Our arrival seemed to help matters. He unceremoniously handed Mary over to me and, with Joe, went back inside. There was a slight scuffle, but then he came out again and began to wipe the blood off his neck.

"Got 'em," he said in a satisfied tone.

"But, Jimmy," I protested, "how did you do it?"

"Why, I stuck up Mendez as soon's I got inside," he said deliberately, "an' made 'im call one of his gang to come in. I'd tied Mendez up, but when this guy come in he yelled. I had to shoot 'im. Then the others come runnin', an' one of 'em nicked my ear. Th' others played my game's soon's they saw I had 'em covered."

"But they disarmed you," I protested again. "I saw them search you for a pistol."

Jimmy grinned.

"Grooves," he said sententiously. "Grooves. Mexes think in grooves jus' like other folks. You saw that feller feel my pockets?"

"I did," I said.

Jimmy stood up.

"See 'f I've got a gun now," he ordered.

I felt his pockets and shook my head.

"Grooves," said Jimmy pityingly. "You think in grooves, too. I got a gun, the same one I used on th' Mexes. You felt my right pants-pocket, an' my left pants-pocket, an' my hip-pocket, an' my coat-pockets, but you didn't never think that I might be left-handed."

"What's that got to do with it?"

"I got a left hip-pocket," said Jimmy mildly. "Nobody ever puts anything in 'em, but everybody wears 'em. Nobody uses 'em but left-handed people — an' me."

LAND SHARKS AND OTHERS
by H. Bedford-Jones

In their room in a Bush Street hotel, Captain Struthers and Mr. Hawley sat at their ease and considered San Francisco midnight from their windows. On a table between them a whisky-bottle and two glasses were flanked by black Manila cigars for the skipper and an equally black quid for the mate.

They were old men, these two, and they seemed to find San Francisco's night aspect very unpleasant. To see them, no one would suspect that they owned a line of steamers in Australia, had just bought a fine schooner, and meant to sail it home to Sydney merely to keep their hands in at a seafaring occupation, or that they had more money in the bank than they knew what to do with. No one was intended to suspect such things of them.

Mr. Hawley was bald-headed, blear-eyed, leathery of countenance, and just now suck into deepest gloom. Captain Struthers was ruddy and hearty, but he was at present stroking his whiskers — nice gray sideburns, carefully tended — with an air of frowning preoccupation. The bluff old skipper was decidedly worried.

"If you hadn't got soft-hearted in your old age," said Mr. Hawley bitterly, "I'd go down to that there ship-chandler's and lace the hide off'n him!"

"Soft-hearted ain't soft-headed, Mr. Hawley," retorted the skipper, an unwontedly acid touch to his voice. "You receipted for the stores and seen 'em stowed, didn't you?"

"How in purgatory was I to look for tricks?" snapped the indignant mate. "Hadn't you just bought 'em and sent 'em down? You'd ought to look at what you buy! What you need is new specs."

The skipper removed his old-fashioned silver spectacles and inspected them calmly.

"They ain't so bad," he observed. "The trouble was I wasn't lookin' for no tricks neither. Well, that man done us brown — all first-class cabin stores ordered and bought, and then you receipted for weevily old stock a bug couldn't eat without cramps! I don't mind the loss so much, but I do hate to be trimmed for a dinged old fool by one o' them smart-aleck waterfront chandlers. This one was smart, too — smart by name and nature. The name should ha' warned me."

Mr. Hawley kicked the cuspidor closer, and casually cut a section from his plug.

"That ain't all," he said, turning the section over in his mouth. "Where are we goin' to get a crew? There lays the *Nuvalu*, ballast all aboard, everything shipshape from truck to bottom in accordance with the United States shippin'

laws — and nobody to enjoy them comforts, blast 'em! Not even a crook!"

"Mr. Smart said he might find us a few men," hinted the skipper.

"Him!" Mr. Hawley waxed blasphemous for a moment, then continued more calmly. "All I want out o' him is satisfaction — and I'm goin' to get it if you'll keep your hands off!"

"I won't," said the skipper gently. "And where to get men I don't know! Ain't no more saloons; the Barbary Coast don't even attract tourists no more; the boardin'-houses ain't what they used to be; sailormen all goin' to the Y.M.C.A. or suchlike havens of repose where they can't be robbed or crimped —"

"And there ain't any crimps even, except in books," gloomed Mr. Hawley. "Why, I've knowed the time when you could get twenty men put aboard any hour of the day or night from any boardin'-house —"

"If you could forget half you knowed, Mr. Hawley, you'd be a sight better off," said the skipper mildly. "Trouble with us is we're old men, and folks know it. I went into that there pawnshop next door to Smart's chandlery today, and bought me a new watch-chain for ten dollars — and danged if I wasn't trimmed again! He let me cut into one link to make sure it was gold before I bought it; and when I got home I found that was the only gold link in the blasted chain!"

Mr. Hawley grinned. The skipper went on more heatedly.

"Trouble is, there ain't no way to get back at them rascals without we took a club and soaked 'em! Sometimes I've got a mind to do it, too. Where are all the sailormen gone to, anyhow? Look at them things that answered our ads in the paper today! Two drunks, a sick Chinaman, one Kanaka and a thief just out o' San Quentin!"

Mr. Hawley aimed successfully at the spittoon.

"There was a brigantine come in this afternoon when I was aboard," he observed. "Don't know who she belonged to, but she had a smart Kanaka crew. From the islands, most like. Wisht we could get hold o' them Kanakas!"

"Wishes are cheap," sighed the skipper. "Dang it! I'd like to be out to sea, away from this cussed city where you get trimmed every time you turn around and get no respect from anybody!"

"It all depends on the person," said Mr. Hawley, darkly. "That elevator boy downstairs now — he respects me a heap! I heard him call you an old foozle-head yesterday, and I hadn't the heart to disagree with him; but when he spoke of me, I clipped him one over the ear right prompt. Then there's that desk-clerk, too —"

A shocking oath burst from the apoplectic skipper. He turned suddenly to the mate to impart an item of news as yet unreported.

"Look here! D'you know what that cussed, ladylike fellow did today? I ordered me an oil-stove sent here collect from the Emporium — didn't have no cash on me, and wanted to get that stove put aboard from here tomorrow with my trunk. Well, it come all right, and that blasted, blanked clerk wouldn't give 'em ten dollars! Ten dollars! You'd ought to have heard what I said to him when I found out about it! He allowed he didn't know us and we hadn't left any money at the desk."

Mr. Hawley's face darkened. "I know that guy myself," he announced. "He short-changed me a dollar yesterday. I ain't kicked about it yet — but wait! I'd like to have him aboard that there schooner, and the elevator kid likewise, and Mr. Smart, and that there pawnshop friend of yours, and a few more I could name —"

"Ah!" said Captain Struthers, suddenly seizing his whisky-glass. "I do believe that's put an idea into my head! D'ye know, Mr. Hawley, one trouble with us is we don't flash our money! That's what these city folks respect — money! It's all they do respect. Let's have a drink, and I'll chart out a new course."

Mr. Hawley tipped the bottle expertly. The glasses clinked, and the two friends and cronies wiped their lips in unison. Captain Struthers produced a wallet from his pocket, unstrapped it, and brought to light a certified check — one of several. He pocketed the wallet again and smoothed out the check with firm fingers.

"This here's a check for twenty thousand," he observed. "First thing in the morning we get it cashed — all big bills, savvy? Then, every place we go, we pull a roll that'll make folks goggle their eyes twice when they see us in the offing! I'm goin' to produce a thousand-dollar bill on that lady-fingered clerk downstairs first crack, and see him faint, dang him!"

Mr. Hawley protested. "But I thought you were goin' to live aboard ship tomorrow?"

"How in purgatory can we live aboard the schooner," demanded the skipper, "when there ain't no one to row us back an' forth? Expect to swim, do ye? Day after tomorrow we'll be at sea; I'm goin' to get me a crew tomorrow or bust somethin'!"

"Huh!" grunted the mate. "I s'pose you're goin' to that guy Smart for a crew?"

"Yes," said Captain Struthers unexpectedly. "I am! And he ain't to know that we've found out about his sendin' us rotten stores, neither; you mind that, Mr. Hawley, if you see him! Dump that stuff in the bay, and get some more lightered aboard tomorrow — buy it yourself an' put it aboard yourself. I'll likely be busy gettin' a crew."

"You will," said Mr. Hawley acidly. "Damned busy!"

II.

Before the bank opened in the morning Captain Struthers had already performed a fair day's work, dragging with him a morose and reluctant mate.

He had not only visited the brigantine which had dropped anchor the previous day and was waiting for wharf space, but consulted with her skipper as one captain with another. Her skipper had come from the islands and was going next to Alaska; and some of his Kanakas were not anxious to go north, so when Captain Struthers offered to swap half a dozen white seamen for the Kanakas the other gladly agreed.

"Half a dozen, even Stephen," he returned. "Don't give me no cripples — s'long as they can haul a line, I'll take what you got."

"When d'ye want 'em?" asked Captain Struthers. "Better wait till ye pull out."

"I'll not be here long," said the other. "All I got is coconut oil, and I'm goin' light to Seattle to take lumber up north. Bring 'em any time — I won't lose 'em!"

"Mind," warned Captain Struthers, "they ain't likely to be sailormen! I'm tellin' you the honest truth."

"They'll be sailormen when I get through with 'em," promised the other grimly. "Anything you got will be better'n a bunch of unwilling, shiverin' Kanakas. I'll give ye six that's dead anxious to work back toward the islands — you give me six whole critters, that's all I ask."

"You'll get 'em," said Captain Struthers, and departed to his waiting launch amid gloomy forecasts from Mr. Hawley. When they reached the landing Captain Struthers called a taxicab and went to the bank.

There he cashed his check, and handed Mr. Hawley a fat wad of bills.

"Pay them accounts for riggin' and gear," he ordered, "and pay cash. Then get your stores, and pay cash likewise. Flash them bills everywhere!"

"You're makin' a mistake," said the mate dourly.

"You'll be makin' a bigger one if you don't mind my orders," retorted the skipper. Mr. Hawley departed.

Captain Struthers chartered a taxicab for the day — he was becoming partial to taxis — and steered a course down Market Street. He halted long enough to buy, for eight hundred dollars, a very decent sealskin coat that looked like twice the money; then he ordered his equipage to Washington Street.

He drew up before the rather dingy ship-chandler's establishment of Abraham Smart, and his gorgeous arrival created something of a sensation in that neighborhood. Mr. Smart came to the door of his shop with hearty greetings, somewhat tinged with relief when Captain Struthers showed no sign of having discovered the quality of stores put aboard the *Nuvalu*; and Herman Levy came to the door of his pawnshop next door with equally hearty greetings.

Captain Struthers removed his unnecessary furs and tossed them into the taxicab.

"I'm getting' a bit old," he explained loudly to Mr. Smart, "so I thought some fur would feel right good at times. I reckon seawater can't hurt sealskin, nohow! Hello, Levy! Say, I want a word with you when I get done with Smart — you ain't sold that watch I was lookin' at yesterday?"

Mr. Levy made it plain that he had not sold the watch, but was ready to; then went indoors to rub his hands and roll his eyes delightedly.

Captain Struthers entered the shop of Mr. Smart, and followed that oily gentleman to a boxed-in office amidships, where he was offered a suspicious cigar.

"No, thanks," he sighed. "I'm gettin' too old to smoke them things, I guess. Did you get them stores aboard for me like you promised?"

"All stowed, sir," returned the chandler avidly. "Got your mate's receipt right here. He's a nice old feller, ain't he now?"

Captain Struthers shook his head. "Between you an' me. He's gettin' too old, as I keep tellin' him, to follow the sea. D'you know, that man keeps all his wages for years past in a belt around his waist — he's that soft-headed, yes, sir! By the way, that was a good chronometer you showed me yesterday — I'll pay for it right now, and take it in the cab. Got it ready?"

Mr. Smart had it handy, and produced it. Captain Struthers paid for it. When he unlashed his roll, Mr. Smart nearly fainted, but heroically repressed his emotion.

"Now," pursued the skipper, after the transaction was concluded, "you made a remark yesterday to me about a crew. I'm findin' it awful to get men, for a fact! Ain't signed on a hand yet; got my papers all shipshape, all ready to pull up the hook an' go — but nobody to go with."

"Yes," smiled Mr. Smart encouragingly. "Nobody aboard at all?"

"Nary a soul but me and Mr. Hawley. Now, it occurred to me that you and Levy, next door, might get a few men between you; I was talkin' to Levy about it yesterday. I'd like about half a dozen, or more if I could get 'em. I'm willin' to pay, but I want a good crew. You see, I ain't so spry as I might be, and Mr. Hawley, he's real far gone in years, and if we got good big watches things would be a sight easier all around."

"Men are hard to get," said Mr. Smart thoughtfully. "That is, hard to hire —"

"Don't bother signing 'em on. Do that aboard ship."

"The law's the law." Mr. Smart shook his head. "You got to read articles these days, and —"

"I don't figger on coming back to San Francisco," said the skipper meaningly.

"Oh!" Mr. Smart grinned. "If it ain't legal, then —"

"It don't bother me a whoop," shrugged Captain Struthers cheerfully. "If you can deliver the men — say, at the wharf landing — I'll get 'em rowed out to the ship — I'll hire a friend o' mine to take 'em out."

"I could arrange that," said Mr. Smart in thoughtful accents. "Yes, I'm sure I could arrange that."

"So much the better." Captain Struthers rose. "Levy can send you some men — he's got lots of callers."

"Wait a minute," said Mr. Smart, then changed his mind. "No, don't wait. Where can I find you later in the day?"

Captain Struthers gave his hotel address, and Mr. Smart promised to call upon him with definite word that afternoon. So making his farewells, he left the place and passed into the adjacent pawnshop.

There he bought the watch at which he had looked the previous day. He got out his roll of bills to pay for it, and Herman Levy almost choked at sight of the size of that roll. All in big bills, too! But Captain Struthers, ruffling over the bills, seemed disappointed.

"Dang it, I got to cash another check today!" he muttered. "Got to have a little cash in the safe — well, time enough. Look here, Levy! I was just talkin' to Smart about gettin' some men aboard my schooner. He thought you might send him a few of your clients, savvy? In the course of the day you could pick up quite a few hands. I'll pay well if you and him get 'em to me. I don't want cripples, and I do want white men; there's no other hinges to it than them."

"It's illegal," Mr. Levy sadly shook his head. "It ain't like the old days no more —"

"You talk to Smart about it," advised the skipper heartily. "I wouldn't be surprised if he had a notion how to work it. Well, so-long! See you later, maybe."

Captain Struthers took himself and his glory out of Washington Street, and the waterfront knew him no more. Once back at the hotel, he bought some of his dark Manilas, and gave a thousand-dollar bill in payment. This brought matters to the attention of the day clerk — a gentleman of freshly manicured aspect with a decided *flair* for garments of colorful and ladylike prettiness.

"Oh, my gracious!" said the clerk.

Captain Struthers snorted, grabbed the large bill from the gentleman, displayed his whole amazing roll, and finally went upstairs fully conscious that he had risen away above par in the estimation of the hotel. It must have been a pleasant sensation, for he hummed blithely to himself when he entered the room and dropped into a chair, panting under the weight of his new overcoat.

III.

Mr. Smart, draped over the cage of Mr. Levy's pawn-office, displayed an unwonted excitement in his oily features. He had been conversing with the pawnbroker for some minutes, and Mr. Levy was breathing heavily and clutching at the desk before him as though before his eyes some marvelous vision had unfolded.

"It — it ain't safe!" he uttered hoarsely, yet in a tone which showed that he desired most eagerly to be persuaded that it *was* safe. "The harbor police —"

"Look here," said Smart confidently, "s'pose you leave all that to me? Remember, there won't be a soul aboard but them two doddering old men. Did you see his roll?"

Mr. Levy rolled his eyes to heaven, mutely signifying that he had seen it.

"And he's goin' to cash another check — said he didn't have enough!"

"That's his style," Mr. Smart nodded. "What'd happen at the worst, tell me that! He'd squeal to the cops, wouldn't he? Well, I'll fix it so he won't."

"How?" demanded Mr. Levy.

"He wants men bad, see? If I gets him to sign a paper relievin' us of all responsibility, that puts him in jerry, don't it? All right. I'll take Malone and Hawkins aboard about dusk; they'll play drunk. Then we'll get four real drunks an' take 'em aboard with us later. While we're chuckin' them down the fo'c's'le, Malone and Hawkins can attend to the old skipper and his mate. Then we takes the coin and blows, see? Leave the four drunks there, and nobody but you an' me, Malone and Hawkins, in on the deal. Got me?"

"The old fool won't dare holler or we'll show up the paper he signed; Malone and Hawkins can swear they was brought aboard after gettin' knockout drops and Struthers would look at the inside o' San Quentin. He won't dare let out a peep, you'll see! Why, the whole thing is safe as a church, Levy — it's a pipe! Do you want in on it or not? Speak up, 'cause we got to get them four men doped this afternoon —"

"If you can make him sign the papers, I'm on!" said Mr. Levy. "But, see here — you go get that paper fixed up by a lawyer! We don't want no mistakes."

"The law sharp will sting us," objected Mr. Smart.

"That's all right. Pay him fifty or a hundred! Ain't it worth it? Sure. We'll have to split handsome with Malone and Hawkins, too — we'll use Malone's launch."

About four that afternoon Mr. Smart arrived at Captain Struthers's hotel and was ushered into the presence of the old skipper. Mr. Hawley was absent, being still engaged aboard the schooner; in fact, the skipper was even then arranging to have all their luggage taken aboard within an hour.

"Ah, Mr. Smart!" he said cheerfully, closing the door. "Sit down and have a nip o' Scotch! How's everything?"

Mr. Smart presently wiped his lips and lighted a cigarette.

"It's like this," he stated confidentially. "Levy and me has talked it over, and we're willing to do the work for a hundred a head."

"Fair enough," said the skipper, stroking his gray tufts of whiskers. "Fair enough, all things considered."

"But we got to have protection," pursued Mr. Smart. "We got to get them men down to the docks, and run 'em aboard your ship. If the cops jumped us whilst we was doin' it, we'd be in bad, see? Of course, we don't aim to get caught, but you can't never tell. Now if you'll sign a paper sayin' that what we're doin' is by your orders an' consent, we'll go ahead. Otherwise, we dassent touch it."

"Let's see the paper," said Captain Struthers shrewdly.

Mr. Smart produced it. The skipper donned his spectacles, and perused the typed paper with careful scrutiny. He lifted his eyes to the window, and gazed for a space out over the city and harbor.

"Well," he conceded at last, "I reckon it's no more'n fair to you and Levy for me to sign it. You won't get caught if you can help it — you'd be losin' your money, because I won't pay no advance on this deal. Cash on delivery, Mr. Smart."

"That suits us," said Mr. Smart quickly.

Captain Struthers signed the paper, and his visitor pocketed it with much satisfaction. He then inquired when the skipper was going aboard.

"Pretty quick now, soon's I rustle up some grub to take," said the skipper. "Mr. Hawley and me will have to get out dinner aboard, and we ain't signed on a cook yet. I got a cook comin' aboard at midnight, I hope, soon as he gets out of a restaurant he's workin' in right now. If everything goes well, I aim to h'ist the hook and be gone with the tide about four in the mornin'."

"All right," said Mr. Smart. "We'll bring aboard two men at six o'clock, and the other four about eight. Levy and me couldn't handle too many at once."

"Sure," said the skipper.

Mr. Smart took his departure. A short time afterward the luggage went out, all except a large parcel securely wrapped, which contained the new fur overcoat of the skipper. With this in his hand, Captain Struthers left his room and sought the desk below. He had no difficulty in obtaining the ear of the ladylike clerk.

"I wonder now," said the skipper benignantly, "if you'd mind helping me out a mite, mister? When do you get off duty?"

"Six o'clock," said the clerk.

"Well, I got to go aboard my ship right now," explained the skipper, his ruddy features obscured by a look of worry. "A man promised to call here for this parcel; if he don't come I want to get it myself because it's got a val'yble coat in it. I wonder now if I paid you for it would you take care of it personally?"

"Why, I suppose I could," said the clerk hesitant.

"If nobody comes you bring this out to my schooner," directed Captain Struthers, peeling a ten-spot from his roll. "Hire a launch and come aboard. Mr. Hawley would enjoy seein' you again, I'm sure. We've had a right pleasant stay here."

"It's so nice of you, captain!" smirked the clerk, accepting the money. "I'm sure the pleasure has been all ours."

Captain Struthers turned away. His eye fell upon the elevator boy, and for a moment he hesitated as though temptation had seized upon him. Then he shook his venerable head, found a dollar in his pocket, and handed it to the boy, patting his head.

"I reckon you got a mother, ain't you?" he observed kindly. "Well, there's some things I stick at. Run along, boy, and have a good time."

So he left the hotel and entered his waiting taxicab.

Captain Struthers did not go immediately aboard the *Nuvalu*. Instead, his taxicab dodged among the wharves until it found the slip at which a certain brigantine fresh from the islands was discharging cargo. Brigantine, wharf, and longshoreman were in a glorious mess, for the casks of coconut oil stowed above the waterline had leaked, as usual, and oil was everywhere.

Amid the confusion Captain Struthers located the skipper of the brigantine and held a short but earnest talk with him. The skipper seemed highly amused by what Captain Struthers said, and the two gentlemen parted with a cordial handshake.

Captain Struthers then engaged a launch and went aboard the schooner, shaking the dust of San Francisco from his feet.

IV.

Mr. Hawley had worked like a Trojan all day long. His dour and dismal attitude changed appreciably when he viewed the basket of provisions Captain Struthers unpacked in the cabin, and only a faint remnant of pessimism clung to him over the whisky bottle.

"I got Scotch and champagne and a few other things," he announced, indicating a locker in the corner, "but the prices was ruinous. Prohibition hasn't done nothing far's I can see, except h'ist the price of a drink."

"Never mind — we'll be in Australia soon," said the skipper cheerily. "And mean time, Mr. Hawley, the only good money can do a man is to get him what he wants. Ain't that so? Well, we've got what we want, and before morning we'll be outside the headlands."

"Without a crew?"

"With a crew. I got six Kanakas coming, a cook engaged, two men comin' aboard at four bells, another man comin' at six bells or before, and along about ten tonight a round half-dozen which I'm goin' to swap for the Kanakas. The cook may bring me a couple more when he comes about midnight."

"Glory be!" ejaculated Mr. Hawley. "Did you raid a jail or a lunatic-asylum?"

Captain Struthers seized a goose-liver sandwich and bit into it. He winked one jovial old eye.

"Nope," he answered with his mouth full. "Tell you when I've et."

When Captain Struthers had "et," and had lighted a long, black Manila, he imparted as much of his scheme to Mr. Hawley as he deemed necessary.

"Now," he explained, "Smart and Levy are goin' to bring six men aboard, and I aim to keep them two friends of ours with us likewise — we ain't settled all accounts by a long shot! That's eight, six of which goes to the brigantine for the Kanakas. Then the clerk from the hotel is bringin' aboard a new coat I bought; he'll be along 'most any time now. That's nine. The cook and two friends makes twelve — all we need, huh?"

Mr. Hawley chuckled raspingly.

"D'ye know, cap'n," he observed, "I been thinking all day how much I'd like to have that there clerk in my watch! And now I'm goin' to have him — at least, I s'pose you figure on takin' him to sea with us?"

"I do," assented the skipper. "I meant to take that there elevator boy also, but my heart misgave me. He's such a young little chap, and I thought maybe he'd have a mother lookin' for him to come home of nights —"

Mr. Hawley grunted in a most expressive manner. At this instant, however, further conversation was halted by a hail from alongside.

Gaining the deck, the captain and mate found a launch coming in under the ladder. At the helm was Mr. Smart, and in his bow stood Mr. Levy. Amidships were draped two gentlemen, whose aspect was decidedly unwholesome, and who reeked of liquor; they were semiconscious, and to the eye of the skipper seemed powerful brutes.

"Glad to see you, gentlemen," said Captain Struthers. "Mr. Hawley, take these two men below and have articles signed if you please! Come aboard, gentlemen?"

"No, thanks," returned Mr. Smart from the launch, as the two hands climbed unsteadily aboard. "We'll rush back and attend to the rest of our business." He added a wink, to which the skipper waved a hand in comprehension, and the launch was shoved off.

For a space Captain Struthers stood in rapt contemplation of his schooner, as the fires of dying day lighted her fresh-tarred rigging, blazed along her tapering spars, and shone from the glittering white paint and the polished brasswork of her hull. He was absorbed in her beauty, when suddenly he was conscious of Mr. Hawley's approach, and turned.

"Them two birds," said the mate, "are snorin' down below this minute. I guess that's our clerk comin', ain't it? How do you reckon to settle him?"

Following the index-finger of the mate, Captain Struthers described a small launch cutting across the tideway toward the schooner. He stroked his whiskers for a moment, then smiled.

"I'll take him below, Mr. Hawley. You send the launch away. You didn't like them drunks in the cabin, I hope?"

"Expect me to drag 'em round by the heels myself?" demanded the indignant mate. "Of course they're in the cabin. When Smart brings the rest of the gang aboard they can chuck these two up for'ard. They signed articles 'fore they fell asleep, anyhow."

The skipper merely nodded, and said nothing in response.

Within a few moments the desk clerk was aboard with his parcel. Captain Struthers gripped his hand warmly, and insisted upon leading him down to the cabin for a friendly drink. Although insisting that he did not drink, the clerk allowed himself to be drawn below. There he gazed at the two recumbent, whisky-smelling figures of Marlow and Hawkins, and alarm came into his eyes.

"My gracious!" he palpitated. "this is terrible, captain! Are these men drunk?"

"I hope so," rejoined the skipper blithely. "If they ain't, I'm out o' luck. Wait till I get a lamp lighted now. I'd like to play ye a tune on my old accordion, but I got to fix the bellows —"

Whistling and fervently trusting that the clerk would not hear the *putt-putter* of the departing launch that had fetched him, Captain Struthers lighted the brass lamp swinging in gimbals from the ceiling.

"I'm a philanthropist," he announced as he worked. "I believe in helpin' men to right themselves, friend."

He did not see one of the two figures on the floor slowly lift one eyelid and blink at him, then nudge the other recumbent figure. He turned and looked at the clerk.

"Trouble with you," and his face became stern, "is that you're too much of a lady. Ain't that so, now?"

The clerk stuttered, smiled feebly, and then started back in alarm as the skipper came closer to him.

"Why, sir — my gracious! How fierce you look —"

"Ding my buttons!" rasped the skipper. "I can't stand it no longer —"

He took the clerk by the shoulders, turned him about, kicked him hard. Emitting a shriek, the clerk shot forward, crashed headfirst into a stanchion, and sank senseless to the floor. Captain Struthers rubbed his hands vigorously on his trousers and snorted.

"Durn him! I'll learn him something 'fore we raise the islands!" he muttered.

He cast a look at the two drunken men, then turned and climbed to the deck above. He found Mr. Hawley setting out the riding lights, and suggested a cribbage game. There being nothing further to do until the rest of the men came aboard, Mr. Hawley assented.

The two went below, unpacked some of their belongings, ignoring the figures on the floor, and fell to work with cards and pegs.

"You don't s'pose," inquired Mr. Hawley, while shuffling, "that Smart will bring along the paper ye signed?"

Captain Struthers cleared his throat nervously and seemed not to hear the query. Mr. Hawley repeated it, with dark hints as to old age affecting one's hearing faculties. Forced to take notice, the skipper merely asserted with a grunt.

"What ails ye?" demanded the mate. "If he brings that there paper, all right. If he don't — if he leaves it ashore — then we *would* be in a mess!"

Captain Struthers frowned portentously. "He'll bring it," he said. "He's got to hand it back to me before getting his money — let's see, fifteen two an' two is four, an' a pair —"

A hand, unseen, reached out from the floor and gripped one leg of the mate's tipped-back chair. A startled oath broke from Mr. Hawley, who felt himself going; he crashed to the floor and was embraced by one Hawkins, who strove earnestly to break into his bald skull with a blackjack.

At the same instant Captain Struthers's chair was cleverly jerked from under him. "Oof!" he grunted, and then sat down heavily. From beneath him echoed another but more muffled grunt — the skipper had planted himself full weight upon the head of Malone, whose brass knuckles dusted the air frantically, but vainly, beside the knee of Captain Struthers.

The skipper gazed at the thrashing figure of Mr. Hawley.

"Ah!" he observed placidly. "I warned you this morning to put that pistol in your hip-pocket —"

A slight thudding jar vibrated through the schooner; down the companionway drifted a cautious hail in the voice of Mr. Smart. The man under the skipper emitted a stifled yell, and there came a pounding of feet on the deck above.

Captain Struthers glanced at the companionway, then deftly flipped a revolver from his pocket and brought down the butt upon the writhing head underneath him. He rose to his feet, and saw Mr. Hawley in the act of getting astride his own opponent and bumping the latter's skull against the floor with vigor.

"There, consarn ye!" said Mr. Hawley as the unfortunate

Hawkins relaxed. "Gimme that blackjack —"

He seized the weapon from unresisting fingers and sprang to his feet. Just in time, too; rushing down the ladder came Mr. Smart and Mr. Levy.

"Did you get 'em, Malone?" yelled Smart, peering into the cabin.

Captain Struthers stepped forward, caught Mr. Smart by the arm, and yanked him inside. Mr. Hawley went for the pawnbroker, who turned to flee; but the blackjack landed behind his ear and put him to sleep beside the ladder.

"Wha — what's this?" stammered Mr. Smart to the skipper.

"This is what you got comin' for tryin' to trim two sailormen," answered Captain Struthers, and his fist caught the chandler under the jaw.

To do him justice, Mr. Smart put up a good fight, but in half a minute the vigorous old skipper had backed him into a corner and was hitting him almost at will.

"Thought you'd fix up a nice game to catch us, huh?" panted Captain Struthers, punctuating his remarks with two hard fists. "Thought you'd got us dead to rights and could loot us an' skip, huh? Here, try the taste of this for a change! Got your belly full, have ye? Then join your friends in the arms o' Murphy!"

He put Mr. Smart neatly to sleep with a tickling blow under the ear, and turned to the grinning mate.

"You ain't far out o' practice," observed Mr. Hawley, admiringly. "Goin' on deck?"

The skipper nodded, and stooped to go through Mr. Smart's pockets.

Together they reached the deck and investigated. Alongside rocked a launch in which reposed four unfortunate gentry, dead to the world.

"Smart planted them two thugs on us," observed Mr. Hawley.

"I thought likely he would," said Captain Struthers. "Ah! Here's the rest of our crew" — and he pointed to a boat being rowed toward them through the night — "we'll swap the four down yonder, an' the two thugs for the six Kanakas —"

"But that'll get the brig's master into trouble," protested Mr. Hawley.

"Nope." Captain Struthers waved the papers in his hand. "Smart signed them four men to a blank set of articles — well, I'm bound to admit it ain't what you'd call legal, but what of it? The skipper o' that brigantine ain't any chicken, Mr. Hawley; he knows what he's doin', and he'll do it Bristol fashion."

A boat bumped against the launch.

In ten minutes everything was done. The launch was scuttled. Six Kanakas went for'ard with Smart, Levy, and the luckless hotel clerk; the brigantine's skipper was pulling home with his prey.

"Nothin' to do but wait for that cook to come aboard," observed Captain Struthers mildly, "and take the line from the tug when the tide ebbs. I spent a bit o' money gettin' a tug to save time. We'd ought to be off the heads before daybreak."

"Yes," agreed Mr. Hawley darkly, "I think so myself — three miles off at least. Then all they can get us for is piracy! We'd better not put in at Honolulu, neither; that's United States territory. Them shanghaied men of ours ha' got the law on their side."

"Don't worry," said Captain Struthers, smiling into the darkness. "They'll need all the law they got before I'm through with 'em. Call all hands aft, Mr. Hawley, and we'll pick watches!"

LIGHT ON A SUBJECT
by Raymond S. Spears

Mr. Rodolf Lifset arrived on White River, and observed that the button-shellers were selling their pearls to a ribald mob of buyers at Newport, which was the center of the Arkansas Bottoms pearling country. Lifset went among them, keeping his tongue from disclosing his ideas, and keeping his ears and eyes constantly in service to obtain other people's ideas.

Mr. Lifset had come from Europe to teach the Yankees tricks in the pearls and gems trade, and he discovered there in the brakes and cotton fields of a far-back land some few opportunities for the practice of some of his larger ideas, without involving himself in any considerable difficulties.

He began to buy pearls cautiously, picked up three or four nice White River pinks and a hatful of baroques, and then he branched into business on a scale that pleased him very much. He rented an upstairs room with a skylight, like a photograph gallery, and a small buying table covered carefully with a clean, white paper which would reflect the light of the sky upon the under and over sides of any pearl that was being purchased.

"You see," he smiled upon his clients, "I prefer to buy pearls away from the crowd and turmoil, and where a calm and dispassionate judgment can be passed easily upon the pearls you so kindly bring to me for appraisal."

At the same time, up in one corner of the room, he fixed a six-lensed box, and ran down through a cable in the wall a multiple set of wires, and all these came up under the table and were distributed in the system of buttons on an invisible switchboard. He tried the box, and was satisfied with it.

Then he began to buy pearls on a scale according to his plans. He bought them from the secretive pearlers and button-shellers who did not want people to know that they had made a find, but wanted large prices for their pearls.

Lifset paid, at first, some enormous prices for pearls. He paid, for example, $72.50 for a pearl for which one of the mob-buyers down at the levee offered only $35. By ten purchases Lifset established a reputation which enabled him to have first whack at the finds brought to town. When he began to get first looks he easily persuaded pearlers to part with pearls at a price according to the look on the white paper of the buying table, right under the skylight.

To Pooler he showed the blemish on a nine-grain pearl.

"See," he said, "but for that yellowish stain, in this white you should have a very high price, perhaps six hundred dollars, but look at the blemish! What can I do with it? I tell you, though; I buy it for one hundred, eh? I shall make nothing at that price, no doubt; but it must discourage you to get so little for so large a pearl, eh?"

Of his purchases Lifset told nothing. He strolled out, in the twilight of the day's end, and listened to the gossip among the people who bid against one another at auctions, and who crowded around anybody who came to the river-landing, with the look of a pearler in his expression or raiment. He would watch and listen and smile — smile as he realized that in a few days he had established his fame in the river whispers. If a pearler can only be persuaded to whisper to another pearler:

"Try Lifset with the next one, Bill. He give me seventy-two fifty for that 'n' I showed you. Don't say nothin' though, for he'll likely spend all his money an' lose out, see?"

Pearl-buyers come and go; the more enthusiastic a pearl-buyer, the shorter his stay in the market. He buys and he pays big prices. The only pearl-buyers who last are pessimists. They buy with the market sure to smash next week, and they grab a customer, and they sell if only to save carrying charges, and interest mounting up on the investment!

The word had gone around that Lifset was an optimist, and that he had a bank full of money; he wasn't going to sell any till he had paid out all his money except car-fare back to Europe; thus Lifset would never know what he was doing till he had returned with his stock; of course, if he was lucky, and the market went up, perhaps he would come clear; but if he wasn't lucky — well, he'd have had his experience.

Lifset claimed to be a scientific buyer; he knew all about the chemistry of pearls, all about what gives pearls their sheen, their color, their depths, and the other things in pearl lore, interesting, but mere adjuncts to the business of pearl buying and pearl selling. The one thing a pearl-buyer must know, and have ground in his soul, is that buying a pearl at ninety dollars and selling it at one hundred dollars — quick! — is business; but buying at one hundred dollars and selling at ninety dollars is not business.

So Lifset built up a reputation. He bought pearls steadily; not very many large ones, but many little ones, many fair ones. And then he looked at a pearl from a little red-haired man from some creek unnamed. The little red-haired man wouldn't tell his name, but he had large hands, the broad shelter's back, and a blunt, reticent countenance. He had a round pearl, about twelve grains, a little lumpy on one side, and yet of a fair, pinkish color. He wouldn't sell for one hundred and fifty dollars. He went away, but returned three days later with another pearl, a nine-grain, with a slight yellowish tint on the white paper. He wouldn't sell that one at a hundred dollars, which was a bit higher price in proportion.

After that day's work Lifset walked downtown, and found the little red-haired man sitting on the levee, scowling. He joined the pearler, and began to talk to him. They sat there for four hours, and all the time the little pearler poured out a tale of woe that would have moved any heart but a cold-blooded pearl-buyer.

"I need money!" the pearler said. "No little bunch, but a big bunch — a thousand dollars now! I got to raise a stake."

"If you find three or four more pearls, likely you'll get it," Lifset suggested.

"I got to!" the little man said, and he went over the levee and rowed away in a swift, clinker-built skiff.

A week went by, and Lifset was sitting in his buying room when a woman entered through the open door and looked about helplessly. Lifset started to his feet, smiling. He enjoyed buying from women.

"Come to sell a pearl?" he asked encouragingly.

"No," she shook her head. "It's my husband. He's took bad. He's found forty-two pearls, an' — an' he said you'd remember him. He said he'd been up here — a nice little feller, my man, and he has red hair."

"I can't go away to buy pearls," he said sharply.

"You needn't to bring no money," she said. "You could bargain down there, an' I'd come back with 'em, an' then — There's a big one, that's a ball — forty grains — an' — an' some that ain't quite so big. He found a pocket. He's got to have an op'ration. He'll sell — any price, 'mos', so'f he dies — I — for cash — any price, 'mos'!"

She burst into sobbing as she spoke.

Lifset considered, and then he said he would go. Other buyers ranged up and down the river, and they carried large sums. It was a chance to buy on level terms, of course — but the man's sickness banished certain obvious chances.

"How much'll I need?" he asked suddenly.

"I — I don't know — I ain't much up on pearls. Tom always — he's had the 'sperience. He said you're liberal. Course he'd rather die 'n —"

Lifset considered. He could not guess what the pearls might be, but a pocket of forty-two pearls — it might be the business stroke of the year! He went down to the bank and drew money — drew bricks of it — and put it into his belt, and slipped his automatic into his coat-pocket, and a big gun into a holster. He was not particularly brave, that kind seldom are.

So he let the woman row him down the eddy, down the shoals, and three miles to the shanty-boat, from which the red-haired man operated up near creeks and through various lakes and dead rivers, as she pointed out by nodding her head.

"Where did he find the pocket?" he asked.

"He wouldn't tell me that," she replied, "He says women ain't got no judgment."

The shanty-boat was small and the color of brick. It had two large windows, one on each side in the middle of the side of the boat, and Lifset took his bearings by the sun. They landed just above the boat, and walked down the bank and on board. In one corner was the bunk; on the bunk was the red-haired man, querulous, groaning, and twisting about.

"Took an awful while!" He turned to her. "Thought you'd come tomorrow, maybe."

"I had to think a while, first," Lifset explained. "I don't go out much to buy pearls. It wasn't her fault."

"Is it good light?" the sick man asked. The pearl-buyer looked around him. The three-foot-square windows were clear glass, and the one to the north was at the foot of the bunk, and the little square eating-table was there, with sugar bowl, spoon-holder, salt-dish, and some humble ware. The tablecloth was a dull-gray material, and Lifset looked at it sharply with a satisfaction that showed in his eyes.

"It's good light, and I can buy by it," he said as a pearl-buyer would.

"Get 'em!" The sick man turned to the woman. "What you gawkin' at? It'll take a long time to sort them pearls an' buy 'em! Even if they is all the same kind, he's got to look at 'em."

She choked, and hurried to a trap in the floor. From the trap she drew a cigar box, and dumped it on the gray tablecloth. Wrapped in cloth were the pearls, forty-two, as she had said. He took out the first one, and put it on the cloth, and he saw that it was pink, even on that gray cloth. They were all beautiful pearls to look at.

The sick man, explosive with pain, which indicated appendicitis, was yet listening with bated breath for the buyer's expression to see whether it meant a fair price or not, and asking for bids — but Lifset made no bids. He jotted down memoranda at each pearl, and reckoned the bids all up into a lump.

"I'll make it $9,780," he snapped at last decisively. "Take it or leave it!"

"I'd hoped it'd be ten thousand!" the sick man whimpered. "I spent all my life down yeah — now I got to die, maybe." And with a sudden grimace the sick man growled: "Ten thou'! Or I mout's well die!"

The woman cried, whimpered under her breath that Tom was stubborn and willful, but tenderhearted. Lifset finally gave in.

"Take 'em!" the man grumbled, and the money was paid, the pearls wrapped up again and put into the cigar box. There were so many that Lifset couldn't very well carry them in his pocket. Besides, he would enjoy going through New-port with that box under his arm. Other buyers — wouldn't they look? Lifset had bought his pile.

He paid the woman ten dollars for rowing him back up to the landing, and she came away immediately, but not till she saw the other pearl-buyers along the levee gathering toward the successful buyer.

They strolled down casually. One of them asked, serious-faced:

"Did you get them?"

"What do you mean?" Lifset asked resentfully.

"Why, Red Nugg's set of pearls?"

"You know them?" Lifset asked.

"Not personally," the man shook his head, and two or three spectators blinked and looked away as though they had been spoken to or caught napping.

"Oh, I'm satisfied!" Lifset smiled, remembering the color.

"Ah! Then all's well!" The speaker raised his hat.

The field buyers turned and walked away. They did not ask to see the pearls, and they apparently had arrived at the conclusion of their curiosity. Lifset walked on bravely. He quickened his step, however, as he approached his own table with the white paper. There he emptied the pearls out on the table rather impatiently. He picked one out of the cloth wrapping. When he saw it he choked with indignant and disgusted amazement, though he had had an inkling of warning.

The pearl wasn't pink, and it was shallow, thin, lifeless. It was just a dull white. All the other pearls were of the same exact white hue, with only the most trifling orient in it.

"I'm swindled!" Lifset screamed, and he started out on the run clown to the levee, bareheaded and in a rage.

"What — what —" somebody asked him — "what's the matter?"

"I bought not them pearls, but—"

"Just a moment, old man!" a tall, slender buyer inter-rupted him. "You bought them at a northern exposure?"

"Yes!"

"And the light was through a nice, clear three-foot-square glass?"

"Yes!"

"There wasn't any six-light bull's-eye lantern there, each light a different color, to make the pearls look like mud?"

Lifset's jaw dropped. He blinked and stared.

"I did not see none!" he managed to whisper.

"You don't know what happened?" the man persisted. "You can't imagine?"

"No!"

"I'll tell you," the buyer said tartly. "That pane of glass in the dirty, red shanty-boat cost about three hundred dollars. We always send for Red when anybody shows up here with colored bull's-eye lights to give a pearl-seller the idea his pearl is a cloud. Red's sure some oculist, when it comes to handling a prismatic ray of pink. If you'd paid more atten-tion to that windowpane and less to Red's sick pains, you might have noticed the bottom was several times thicker than the top, that it was hung at a slant—and what you saw was neutralized, but the light wasn't, not on the pearls on the dull cloth!"

Lifset blinked. He wet his lips and looked at his watch.

"Yes, you've got time—plenty of time!" the observer un-feelingly remarked.

"Never mind about the six-eyed colored lights of yours—that's took care of, and the switch under the table. You've lots of time to pack up and catch the train. Scoot!"

THE ABSENCE OF THE MUSE

O Muse, where loiterest thou? In any land
Of Saturn, lit with moons and nenuphars?
Or in what high metropolis of Mars—
Hearing the gongs of dire, occult command,
And bugles blown from strand to unknown strand
Of continents embattled in old wars
That primal kings began? Or on the bars
Of ebbing seas in Venus, from the sand
Of shattered nacre with a thousand hues,
Dost pluck the blossoms of the purple wrack
And roses of blue coral for thy hair?
Or, flown beyond the roaring Zodiac,
Translatest thou the tale of earthly news
And earthly songs to singers of Altair?

— Clark Ashton Smith

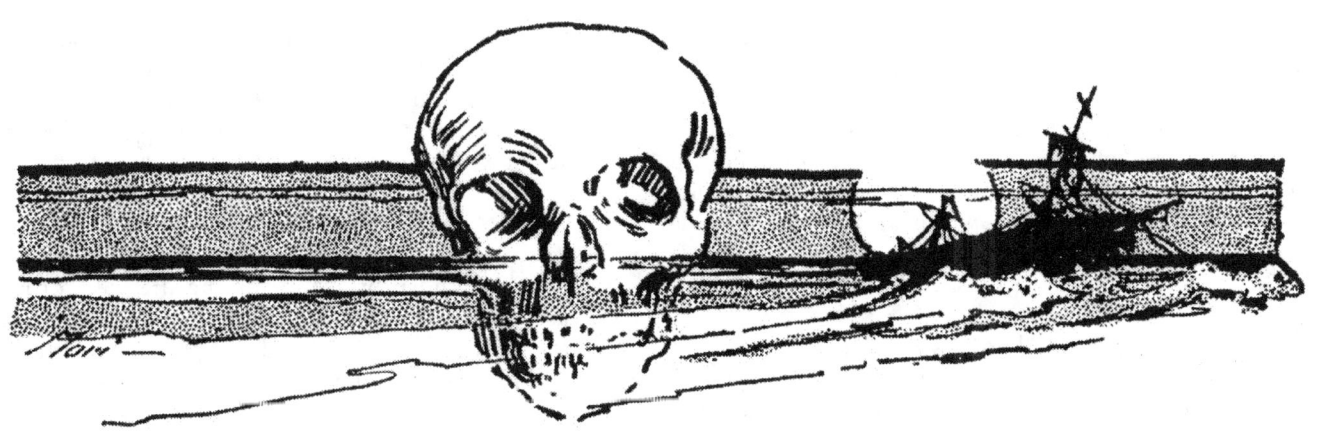

CHANNA'S TABU
by Harold Lamb

West of the Solomon Islands, in the South Seas, is the island of Savo—a three days' run in a schooner after rounding Cape Astrolabe. Savo used to be a resort for the head-hunters of those regions, and traders and missionaries still fight shy of it. The nearby islands of Malaita and Guadalcanal belonged to Great Britain, but Savo belonged to King Channa.

King Channa was a small, dark islander, who wore a white flax wig, and carried a four-foot basket shield and spear. He was expert with the spear, also treacherous, which is probably why the pile of skulls outside his hut numbered a round score instead of Channa's skull decorating the hut of one of his henchmen. He was afraid of nothing except his own tabu, which was that he must not touch fish. All his life he had dreaded the sight of fish.

Skipper William McKechnie vouches for this, and McKechnie encountered Channa during the affair of the *Sweet Alice* and the Mongava pearl.

McKechnie was master and half owner of the trading schooner *Auld Alfred*. He was a Scotchman, past copra peddler, and pearl trader, who knew the byways of the South Seas like a book. Hence it was not surprising that a few days after he heard of the wreck of the *Sweet Alice* on Savo he headed his schooner for that place.

It was late in the afternoon that the *Auld Alfred* beat up to the north shore of Savo and slipped cable in a convenient cove within bowshot of the wrecked *Sweet Alice*. Gordon, the sandy-haired mate of the schooner, joined McKechnie on the after deck after he had seen to the anchor, and together they scanned the wreck on the beach in silence.

The *Sweet Alice* lay on her port side, forty yards beyond the water's edge, where she had been driven by the force of the hurricane, which had splintered her starboard rail and snapped her foremast. Her deckhouse was crushed in, and she bore unmistakable signs of pillage by the Savo islanders. The hurricane that had wrecked her had taken the lives, apparently, of Dixon, her master, and Hallie, her mate—the only two white men aboard. At least, such had been the report McKechnie heard.

"Gordon, man," observed the weather-beaten Scotchman at length, "if ye can ease a thought out o' your sandy head, consider yon wreck, and tell me what is strange about it."

The mate puffed tranquilly at a rank pipe, and closed one eye in pretended meditation.

"She lies high, Mr. McKechnie," he hazarded, "but the surf must have topped the beach to the edge of the bush during that tempest. Hallie lost his life trying to swim the surf with a lifeline before she broke up."

Skipper McKechnie shook his head sadly.

"The good book says, Mr. Gordon, that there are them who have eyes and see not. Ye have put your muddling finger dead to the rights o' the matter; still ye see nothing strange. As ye said, Hallie, who was a decent man, was lost in the surf. Dixon, who was a scoundrel—having shot more than one harmless heathen for his amusement, besides kidnapping the brother o' Channa—stayed on the vessel with the crew. The report says that he was drowned. One o' the crew escaped to Malaita with the tale."

"Well, and why not?" demanded Gordon.

"Why not? Do ye ask me that? No doubt ye think Dixon drowned himself in the water-cask o' the cabin out o' repentance for his sins when he saw the Lord was about to take him! Cast your eye over the wreck, yon."

McKechnie pointed a blackened forefinger at the hulk on the beach.

"Will ye notice, Mr. Gordon, that the tale goes Dixon

was drowned when the vessel broke up. Ye will notice, no doubt, she is not broken up. If Dixon had stuck to his deck he would be alive this day."

"He might have been washed over the side by a comber, Mr. McKechnie," objected Gordon, who loved an argument. "Have you the testimony on oath of St. Peter that the man was not washed over the rail, which was splintered by the crash?"

McKechnie scanned the bulk of the wreck with shrewd eyes.

"Oh aye," he grunted; "I need no word from the saints. If Dixon was swept over the side did all the crew follow him? Out o' love for the man that fed them lousy tucker and strung them up by their thumbs? No, Mr. Gordon, if ye had brains instead o' ballast in your top-hamper, ye would know that if any o' her company had stuck to the *Sweet Alice*, they would have lived, for she is not broken up. And Dixon was no man to risk his life when others would serve instead."

The Scotchman swept his arm across the vista of the shore.

"What happened to him when he reached the beach? Where is he now, Gordon; where is he?"

"A look over the bloomin' tub might tell us what you want to know, Mr. McKechnie," suggested Gordon.

By way of answer the skipper pointed toward the bush. Gordon surveyed the shore through binoculars, and saw what the shrewd Scotchman had noticed—the glint of spear-points among the ferns and an occasional dark form that slipped from one palm to another. The men of Savo had sighted the schooner.

"We had best wait until the commissioner sends the *Thor* here, Mr. Gordon," said McKechnie. "The gunboat is headed this way, I heard at Malaita. The British navy is fast becoming curious about the death o' Dixon and the unlettered heathen o' Savo. Then we may do a wee bit investigating for ourselves the while."

"The curiosity of a decrepit Scotchman is a sad thing, to my way of thinking," muttered Gordon, addressing his pipe.

"Curiosity, is it, Mr. Gordon?" McKechnie eyed his mate hostilely. "Aye, it may be that. But what if I tell ye Dixon had on him the Mongava pearl?"

Gordon had heard of the pearl—a beauty of great size and purity that the native divers of Mongava had brought to the surface.

"The Malaita traders told me the tale," went on McKechnie, "Dixon bought it from the unlettered heathen o' Mongava for two pound, when he had them sweating drunk on the *Sweet Alice*. Man, it was robbery; but it cannot be proved, I'm thinking. The Mongava pearl is worth five hundred pound in Sydney and more in London. Aye, Dixon had the pearl. And we will find him or his body on the island o' Savo."

Darkness closed rapidly over the cove and the woods of Savo. A white line of gentle surf marked the shore. Between this line and the bush came forms invisible in the darkness—forms that carried shields and spears. They gathered in a group by the wrecked schooner, watching the riding lights of the *Auld Alfred*. But when dawn streaked up over the sea they were gone.

II.

Lieutenant-Commander St. George Barclay sat in a wicker-chair under the awning on the after deck of H. M. S. *Thor*, and wished that he had a better cigar than the one he was smoking. Also he wished that he could penetrate the secrets hidden behind the bush of the beautiful island of Savo.

The commander of the gunboat was a square-shouldered man of perhaps thirty-two years, with a fresh, tanned face, and mild, blue eyes. As he puffed at his cigar a frown creased his brow. It was late in the afternoon, and the heat had seeped in under the awning and into every quarter of the old gunboat. The brilliant green of the foliage that lined the beach shadowed the clear blue of the sea. A few cables' lengths away the *Auld Alfred* was tranquilly at anchor. Opposite the warship the wreck lay on the shore, some distance above the waterline.

Barclay's eyes swept the scene, which had grown familiar. Idly puffing smoke-rings at the awning overhead, he ran over in his mind the scanty fruits of his visit to King Channa.

The *Thor* had been ordered to Savo—which the trading schooners avoided on account of the evil reputation of the place—to learn how Dixon and Hallie had met their death, and, if possible, to recover their bodies. Also to salvage whatever valuables were on the wrecked *Sweet Alice*, including the Mongava pearl, which Malaita traders asserted Dixon had with him. Barclay, under orders from the commissioner, was to settle the question. Like English navy men throughout Asian waters, Barclay was an unlisted court of appeal against crime, a judge of the unwritten law. It was his task to see fair play.

Yet Barclay saw little chance of recovering the pearl. King Channa, interviewed at his village by the Englishman with a party of marines, had confirmed the story of the survivor of the *Sweet Alice*, who had come to Savo from Malaita on the *Thor*.

The *Sweet Alice*, declared Channa through an interpreter, had struck the beach of Savo during the climax of a hurricane, and the one boatman had been the only man to win ashore. The terrific wind and the high surf had prevented the islanders from giving aid to the stricken ship. Some bodies of the native crew had been washed ashore later. That was all. Nothing had been seen of the two white men of the schooner.

Channa and his spearmen had been in high good temper, plainly flattered by the visit from the warship. They admitted, when Barclay pointed out that the vessel had been looted, that they had taken the ship's furniture and fixings. But there had been no cargo, as the *Sweet Alice* was in ballast at the time, homeward bound for Sydney. No one had appeared to claim the vessel, so they had helped themselves.

Not content with this, Barclay had made a thorough inspection of the *Sweet Alice*, followed by a search of the island, which was small—being a scant ten miles around. No trace of the white men had been found. He was forced to admit to himself that there was little for him to do at Savo. He had not even found the ship's papers of the *Sweet Alice*.

Barclay knew of the evil reputation of Savo—of the headhunting spearmen. He had seen the treasured pyramid of bleached skulls before Channa's hut. But the skulls were old, and the deeds of the Savo men belonged to a time before the coming of the British.

One curious thing he had seen. In talking with Channa he had idly flicked a dead fish, which lay on the ground between them, toward the king with his foot. Instantly Channa had sprung back, his eyes wide with terror. The action had alarmed the spearmen, and for an instant there were prospects of a free-for-all fight between the islanders and the marines. Barclay had quieted the disturbance, wondering at the fear of Channa for a dead fish.

The commander of the *Thor* looked up as he saw a boat approaching the warship from the schooner. The boat drew up beside the gunboat's ladder, and a few minutes later the stalwart form of Skipper William McKechnie strode aft.

The Scotchman greeted the naval officer calmly, and appropriated a chair beside Barclay. He sniffed at the smoke from the latter's cigar doubtfully, and drew a cigar from his pocket. Barclay eyed this and the weather-beaten face of the bald Scotchman curiously.

"This is no' so bad, Mr. Barclay." McKechnie extended the cigar. "And by the smell o' the one ye have, ye might relish a change. 'Tis a failing o' my mate, Mr. Gordon, to smoke the weeds. I saw ye go up to Channa's village this morning, when I was visiting the sad remains o' the *Sweet Alice*. How did ye like the bonny island o' Savo, with its canny king?"

Barclay exchanged cigars readily, and when the new one was alight ran his eye appraisingly over the skipper.

"May I ask," he inquired, "who you are and what your business is at Savo?"

"Ye may ask," responded McKechnie agreeably, stroking his whiskers with a stubby hand, "and welcome. My name is William McKechnie, master o' the *Auld Alfred*, yon. My business at Savo is nobody else's business."

The officer turned his blue eyes to the Scotchman, who met them frankly. He had heard of the master of the *Auld Alfred*, who bore a record for honest but crafty dealing.

"May I ask," resumed McKechnie calmly, "what ye have learned from Channa about the fate o' Dixon and Hallie? I'm thinking that's why ye are here, Mr. Barclay."

"Dixon and Hallie were drowned. There's nothing fur-

ther for me to do at Savo. The *Sweet Alice* is a dead loss — can't be salvaged."

"Aye." McKechnie continued to stroke his whiskers. "No doubt ye would think that. Now, will ye tell me, Mr. Barclay, who the native was that went with ye up to Channa's village?"

"That was the survivor of the *Sweet Alice* crew."

"Aye. And did ye see the scar on Channa's cheek, Mr. Barclay?"

"Yes, I did." The commander of the *Thor* glanced at his visitor impatiently. "I say, is there anything more you would like to know, McKechnie?"

"There is." The Scotchman nodded gravely. "Do ye see nothing strange about the death o' Dixon?"

"I do not. I shall list him as drowned, with Hallie. Have you any suggestion to make, McKechnie?"

The Scotchman did not miss the mild sarcasm of this, but his expression did not alter.

"I might suggest, if ye ask it, that ye consider three things, Mr. Barclay — King Channa, who is afraid o' nothing except the tabu o' fish; also the scar on his cheek, and the man ye picked up at Malaita. Do ye know where he is, sir?"

Barclay sat up and ran his eye down the deck. When he had last seen the islander, the latter had been asleep in the shadow of a gig. The man was not there, however.

"The good book says," went on McKechnie, "that by their acts ye shall know them. The unlettered and benighted heathen is a canny man, Mr. Barclay, and will bear watching. The fellow ye are looking for saw me come aboard the *Thor*. If ye look ashore, ye will see him, yon."

McKechnie pointed to the beach. To his surprise the officer saw a dark form rise from the water and run ashore. The man ran, leaping in zigzag fashion as if to dodge possible bullets, Barclay recognized him as the survivor of the *Sweet Alice*.

"I had a good look at the boy on deck before he slid over the side," McKechnie explained. "He wore a half-moon o' pearl shells, which is a sign o' caste on Savo. That boy is one o' the Savo men, and I doubt he ever saw the deck o' the *Sweet Alice* unless he helped to loot her. He saw me watching him, and he considered it was time to slip his anchor."

"I say!" Barclay frowned. "Then the beggar was spoofing me."

"Aye. No doubt he was. 'Twas a canny move o' Channa's to send one o' his men to Malaita with the tale that all on the schooner were drowned. Now, ye marked the scar on Channa, sir. Well, I'm thinking it was a bad day for Dixon when his vessel drove ashore here. That scar was Dixon's doing, the time he carried off the king's brother to Queensland. 'Tis bad luck to speak ill o' the dead. But Dixon was over-quick to shoot when he was in the labor trade — getting islanders to work in Queensland. And Channa has a long memory. He remembers how Dixon cut a pearl from the mouth o' his brother when the poor man tried to hide it."

"Rot!" Barclay shrugged his shoulders skeptically. "Do you mean to say that Channa has taken to head-hunting again, and that he killed all the men on the *Sweet Alice?*"

"Did ye see, sir," McKechnie's burr thickened with excitement, "that a' the ship's papers was missin' from the schooner. The unlettered heathen canna read. Where did the log and papers go, if Dixon did not carry them ashore? Ye hae na dealt wi' the benighted islanders so lang as I —"

"But nothing can be proved," argued Barclay, puzzled. "I'll go ashore and find that beggar, however —"

"Ye will not find him, sir. Nor will ye find the bodies o' Dixon and the rest. Channa has taken care to put them in a canoe filled wi' stones, and sunk the lot at sea."

"Then what's to be done, McKechnie?"

The Scotchman stared thoughtfully at the woods of Savo, which were now void of sign of life.

"If ye will wait for a day, Mr. Barclay," he observed, "I will go ashore and interview Channa. The king is a verra interesting man, with his collection o' skulls — if he can be made to talk."

Barclay shrugged agreement. After all, as McKechnie said, he could do nothing, except to shell the village on suspicion, and he was not willing to do that.

III.

The village of Savo was a short distance back in the bush out of sight from the beach. Leaving their boat-crew on the beach with the gig, McKechnie and Gordon struck into the bush-trails on the following day. The mate was armed with his revolver. McKechnie carried a small bundle, but no weapon.

They had no difficulty in locating the village, where the Savo men were gathered, all armed. Their appearance took the islanders by surprise. The King of Savo was sitting in front of his hut, and he sprang to his feet, grasping his spear, when he saw the two white men. Seeing that they were alone, however, he resumed his seat.

The Savo men clustered about them as they made their way to King Channa. McKechnie showed no signs of alarm. He knew that as long as the women and children of the village were near them, the men would not annoy them.

The ruler of Savo was a small man, but muscular. One cheek bore a deep scar, and a shoulder-blade protruded where a spear had wounded him in the back. He wore his tawny wig of flax, and a woven ditty-bag hung from the pearl-shell belt at his waist. His small, bleared eyes watched the newcomers closely.

McKechnie seated himself unconcernedly by the pile of skulls beside Channa. Gordon took his stand at his back, leaning against the bamboo hut. Both men were alert for trouble, but for the present they knew that the curiosity of the natives was more powerful than any desire to attack the white men. McKechnie busied himself in turning over various presents to Channa — tobacco, knives, and a pipe. The eyes of the Savo chieftain glistened when he saw his visitor draw a pair of handcuffs from the bundle. Channa knew the use of the implements, having had dealings with the Queensland recruiters in his youth.

"You like 'em this, good fella?" asked McKechnie, holding out the handcuffs to Channa. The latter assented cordially, and extended his hand for them.

"You work 'em like this, Channa," continued McKechnie calmly. Gordon backed slowly against the hut, and his hand went to his pocket. He little liked this expedition into the Savo headquarters, but McKechnie had insisted on coming, and Gordon would not let him take the risk alone.

The natives thronged closer. McKechnie drew the key of the irons from his pocket. Channa had not withdrawn his hand. The skipper clamped one of the bracelets over his own wrist. With a quick motion he snapped the other half of the irons over the islander's wrist.

Channa started angrily, but McKechnie paid no attention to his movement. The skipper reached into his bundle. A silence fell upon the gazing spearmen — a hostile silence. In it McKechnie's hand came forth from the bundle. It held a dead fish.

As his eye fell on the fish Channa's angry yell echoed through the village. McKechnie balanced the fish near the native. His eyes wide with terror, the native strained back. But the handcuffs held him to McKechnie. Gordon had drawn his revolver, and now faced the ring of islanders.

"Listen, Channa," McKechnie growled at the struggling native; "this fish is *tabu*. You touch 'em fish, you catch 'em seven devils and die like — Don't move, or I'll rub it on your arm. Tell your boys to keep back, or Marster Gordon will shoot 'em plenty quick."

The terror that gripped Channa brought beads of sweat to his forehead. He shouted to his followers, who drew farther away, watching the scene the while with rolling eyes. Channa had been brought up from childhood to dread the sight of fish, which he was convinced would send him to immediate destruction. He had never been so near the object of his *tabu*. And his fear knew no bounds.

"Now," resumed McKechnie, "ye and I are going to have a palaver, Channa. Don't reach for that spear, unless ye want to touch this fish. First ye can tell me what happened to Dixon? If ye lie, ye will feel the fish."

Channa protested that he knew nothing of the master of the *Sweet Alice*, but a near whiff of the hated fish loosened his tongue speedily.

"Marster Dixon him plenty bad fella," he cried. "Long time him come along Savo. Him take my small fella brother along Queensland. My small fella brother him die along Queensland. Marster Dixon him give me this" — Channa pointed to his scarred cheek. So far McKechnie knew that he spoke the truth.

"Then come schooner along Savo," Channa hurried on, his gaze fastened on the fish as on a deadly snake. "Marster Dixon come along village after hurricane. Him drunk like seven bells, my word! Him tell Channa his good fella mate got drowned along hurricane. Him shoot three times at my hut. My small fella sister she catch bullet and die —"

"And ye speared Dixon, eh?" queried McKechnie.

Channa assented frankly. Reaching over to the pile of skulls, he rolled off the ones on top. In the center of the mound the severed head of a white man showed, scarred and bruised. McKechnie recognized all that remained of Dixon. He shook his head sadly. Channa glanced from the head of his enemy to the man who held him prisoner. Something like pride replaced the fear in his eyes. Pride and anxiety lest he lose his treasured trophy.

"So ye killed Dixon," McKechnie mused. "What about the crew o' the schooner?"

Channa, his gaze still fastened on the blood-stained head, replied that they had fled in a boat to Guadalcanal when Dixon was killed.

"I believe ye are telling the truth, Channa," said the white man, "especially as ye offer proof. The killing is none o' my business. But I'll take the big pearl ye found on Dixon — the Mongava pearl."

Channa's glance turned to McKechnie and traveled back to the head.

"Marster Dixon, him swallow that big fella pearl," he said slowly.

"But ye cut it out o' him, Channa!"

The king hesitated briefly. Then he put his free hand into his ditty-bag. He pulled out a pearl, large and lustrous. McKechnie took it from him silently. And, in spite of Channa's wailing protests, he took the head. On board the *Thor* that evening McKechnie told his tale to Barclay. As a climax he unwrapped the scarred head that he had brought from Savo. Barclay shuddered.

"I suppose ye'll have to shell Channa's village for him, McKechnie," he decided. "Can't let these fellows take to head-hunting again. But I won't waste many shells on him. I'm half convinced Dixon got what was coming to him. By the way, did you see anything of the Mongava pearl?"

McKechnie held out the big pearl that had come from Channa's ditty-bag.

"Channa gave up this," he said. "It must be what ye want. I'll take Dixon's head, and give it a decent burial at sea, if ye wish."

Barclay was glad enough to let the skipper attend to this task. When McKechnie and Gordon reached the cabin of the *Auld Alfred*, the former placed his grim burden on the table.

"Hard luck we had to give up the pearl, Mr. McKechnie," said Gordon, with a wry face. "It must have been worth — Man, are you mad?"

McKechnie was tugging at the jaw of the skull furiously. Gordon watched him in amazement. The teeth were clenched tightly in the rigor of death. But with an effort McKechnie pried the jaw open slightly. With a wild cry he reached two fingers inside.

The next instant he held up a round object. The bewildered Gordon saw that it was a great pearl, blood stained, but of wonderful color.

"The Mongava pearl, Gordon!" cried McKechnie. "Aye, Channa was sorry to see us take the head, especially after he had given me the smaller pearl. He lost two treasures at once. It was a verra interesting place, that skull-heap o' Channa's."

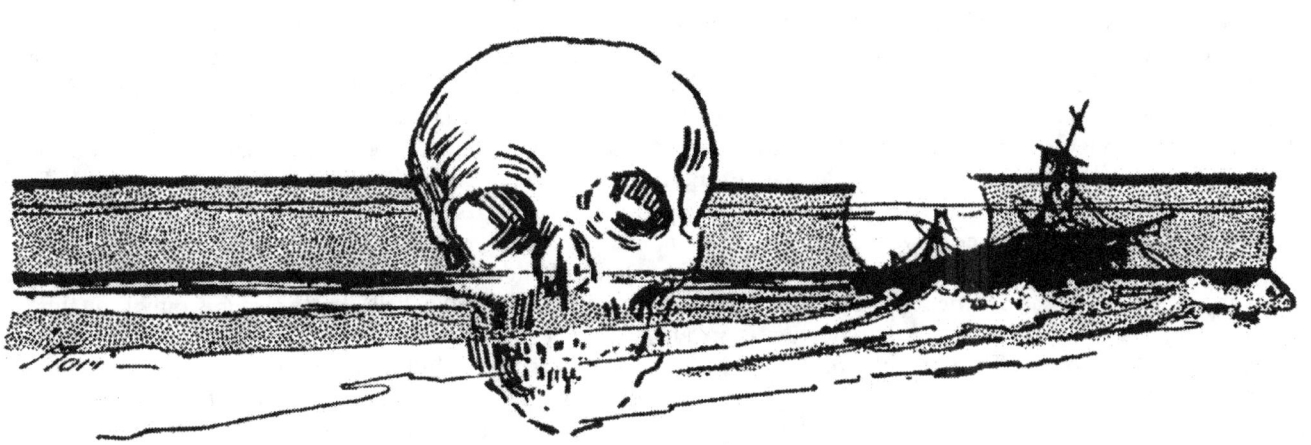

AFRICA

by George Allan England

"See there? That's Africa!"

Dr. Paul Willard gestured far across the night to where, in the vast dark, a spurt of flame glowed like a blood-ruby, died, then trembled forth again.

"Africa?" the girl questioned vaguely. A nameless awe crept round her heart, in presence of that unseen emptiness looming away to the inverted bowl of sky — a fathomless sky, spattered with great refulgent stars, among which, overhead, the funnels of the *Sutherland* traced smoky patterns. "Africa?"

"A little corner of it, anyway," the doctor answered, smiling at her tone. "Cape Roxo light. By two bells of the middle watch we'll be off the coast of Guinea, running through Bissagos Islands — a bad place at best. I never liked it, and I've surgeoned on 'old Suth' for more than seven years. Don't like it now, its reefs and cannibal wreckers and all, even with Captain Lockhart on the bridge."

The girl made no answer, but she leaned her arms across the rail, swaying as the ship rolled, and gazed out into the unknown. Steadily the Strathglass liner clove the fugitive seas, creaming them astern in surges that hissed away into the black.

He risked a side glance at her.

Never had she seemed quite so beautiful to him as under the lantern light which gleamed upon her heavy yellow braids of hair, her frost-white gown. At sight of her delicate, somewhat pale face, his smile waned. No living man — least of all Willard, in the passion which had obsessed him ever since Ethel Armstrong and her crippled uncle had set foot upon the *Sutherland*'s deck — could have felt amusement in presence of that gentle, earnest seriousness.

"Somehow, do you know," she mused at length, "I feel a bit afraid? It's all so empty! And just to know that Africa is over there." A gesture rounded out the thought. "I sha'n't quite like it till we're at the quay in Cape Town."

"When you'll immediately forget the trip, the boat, and — everyone on board?" he led along; but she ignored the opening. Her mood was far from banter. The doctor, too, repented of his speech, the clumsiness of which jarred upon the majesty and wonder of that tropic night. "Oh, well, you'll see things differently tomorrow," he retrieved himself. "Quite differently, when the big red sun rolls up over the coast and splashes gold across the sea."

"Perhaps," she half assented. "But tomorrow is so far away. I think I'll go below. This air stifles me."

He nodded.

"Yes; I understand. I used to feel it so myself, before I got quite used to it." His powers of speech had never seemed more pitifully crude.

He helped her down the steep companionway. Then, after a perfunctory good night from her, came up again to the quarterdeck.

"Great guns, what gloom!" he muttered. "Why, India ink is pale beside it. I don't half like the way these offshore swells are running, either — with Bissagos still ahead of us. Can't say I'm used to this particular bit of Africa even now. No wonder that she — Ethel — feels so shuddery."

A moment he pondered in silence.

"That's an upper-class privilege, anxiety is. A mere proletarian like me has no right to it. No, nor yet to look at an upper-class woman. For such, we aren't real men — just official objects."

He leaned upon the railing where her arms had lain, and for a long time stared off across the dark where, on Cape Roxo, winked that dim, retreating eye of flame.

II.

The doctor found no sleep till long past midnight. Even with his cabin window slid far back, the tepid land breeze choked him, and his thoughts were weft of hot rebellion, longings, and misery. He tossed wide-eyed in his berth, heard the ship's bell dole out the eternal hours, then the halves, torturing himself with images of Cape Town and the approaching separation, which (only too well he knew) must be forever. Midnight was long gone, when he lost himself in troublous dreams of distant inaccessible things, never to be reached by him.

Toward early morning something flung him back to consciousness — a grinding, raking craunch that shivered the whole fabric of the ship, and roused him to the knowledge he was struggling on his cabin floor, which slanted dizzily. He clambered up, mazed and wit-struck for a moment, groped for the electric-button, and snapped on the light.

As the glare dazzled him, the *Sutherland* pitched nauseously again; and far below he heard a hideous gnawing and rasping, as of stony Titan jaws devouring steel. Then came sharp cries, oaths, and orders hoarsely bawled, and heavy feet that ran unsteadily along the decks. The pulsing engines suddenly grew still.

"Bissagos Reef! Ethel!" These were his only thoughts.

He leaped into some clothes, snatched his revolver, jerked open the cabin door, and ran out in his shirt-sleeves to the main saloon. It was already filled with grotesque, excited passengers. A babel swelled tumultuously, with high-pitched questions, curses, and screams.

"Steady!" he shouted. "Steady, now! No danger if you all keep cool!"

Hands clutched at him; he staved them off. "Lord!" thought he. "What cattle human beings in a panic are!"

He heard the purser's voice that reinforced his own — heard other officers — knew that for a moment his presence might be spared.

"I must go!" he told himself; for in the thickening mob he caught no glimpse of Ethel or the invalid.

"I've got to find them anyway!"

He shoved by main force, along the up-tilted floor, toward their cabins. From behind him, on the aft staircase, Captain Lockhart's mellow Scotch voice boomed out: "We're good for fufteen mennets yet! No danger if ye'll tak' it easy — all han's to th' boats! *Weemen fairrst!*"

Suddenly he came on Ethel and her palsied uncle. The old man's halting steps had held her back. A flash of potent admiration lightened through Willard's soul at the vision of the girl, pale and afraid, yet not startled or hastened from her duty.

She came onward, helping the pitiful, twisted figure, step by step — a figure doubly grotesque now, in scant, disheveled clothing, with sweat of pain on the knit brow and terror staring from the widened eyes. She looked, the doctor thought, most dignified and noble in her long, loose dressing gown, over which the yellow braids hung to below her girdle. A sort of fine simplicity enshrouded her. And though he had witnessed bold, hard men in peril, he thought that never had he seen so brave a thing as that gently bred girl holding back her steps, timing her pace to the hobbling of the senile creature who now clung to her for safety.

"What is it — tell me! Are we going down?" she cried to him, her voice trembling a little, but quite clear above the uproar of the crowd or the grinding and tearing of the ship. Her look was full of confidence; even in her fear he found no trace of panic. "Are we lost? What's happened, can you tell me?"

"We're on Bissagos — probably no danger." His body shielded her from the stampeding pack that weltered past them, herded by a dozen of the officers and crew. His nerves were ice. He felt nothing save joy and high elation at this chance to save her life, at this thought that Ethel now was looking up to him, trusting him for guidance and deliverance.

"We mayn't break up — for some time yet!" he shouted, bending toward her. "No danger — lots of boats — the mainland near! Come on, though — there's no time to lose!"

He stooped and gathered the cripple in his arms, then lurched ahead through the wild mob. Ethel followed; he felt the grasp of her hand upon his shoulder, and strange, mad thoughts seethed up in him.

Thus presently, jostling and buffeted, they won through the panic and the uproar of the open lower deck, which shelved off sickeningly to the very water's edge.

The night still gloomed impenetrable round the wounded ship. The wind had risen and whipped furiously the wild, green flares which flung sick shadows over the features of the dead.

Momentarily the waves boiled in spume-vortices over the sunken reef, sweeping the bulwarks, drenching the mad throng. At every heave and slide of the impaled monster a ghastly discord rose — "She's going! Breaking up!" It mingled with the liner's sirens and exhaust, which were ripping the sky with diapasons of appeal.

A rocket screeched aloft, and by its glare the doctor saw a slashing, clawing frenzy at the rail — saw the davits rock and shudder as the boats were wrenched outboard and the horde swarmed them, bursting all constraint.

"No chance for us there — with your uncle." Willard made her understand. "They'd crush him in a second. We'll have to wait."

He saw her nod. "Talk about women being cowards!" flashed the thought through his mind.

Drawing her back into the shelter of a bulk, he put the cripple gently down. The old man, stunned, said nothing, but crouched low, with blinking eyes. Willard and the girl leaned up against the wall, bracing their feet upon the deck, which every moment settled at a steeper pitch.

Now they could look down on the hideous fight. They saw the captain's huge frame overtopping all, dominant as his voice that blared out in command. They caught a gleam of pistol steel in his hand — a spike of flame — and someone pitched across the rail.

"Bairns and th' weemen fairrst!" his brave old sea cry rang. Then, like lightning, a sudden something smote the captain's head, and he was seen no more. Hell burst its bounds; panic reaped its certain due.

III.

"Don't look! You mustn't!" Willard cried, shielding from her the tragedy of the long-boat as a tackle jammed and spilled two-score clutching, yelling creatures in the swirl. The boat flailed — a giant pendulum — and shaking loose the few that clung to thwarts or gunwales, splintered to fragments on the liner's iron skin.

An instant, black, fighting things were sown broadcast upon the roaring sea — things that shrieked, went down bubbling, rose, then, with crisped fingers, disappeared forever.

"There's been an accident — don't look!"

"I'm not afraid," he heard her answer, but the hand that grasped his arm trembled. He loved her for the very fear she knew so well to hold in leash.

A shudder ran through the wreck — a roar that boomed above the sirens' bellowing — then, where the bows had been, gaped a vast black emptiness, with death-screams choked by upswirling brine. A third of the whole ship had broken free and, with its fearful toll, had foundered like a plummet.

The *Sutherland*, eased by this loss, ground back upon the

reef more firmly than before, and settled at a safer pitch, but her survivors deemed their end was now upon them, and fought each other starkly at the boats. All but one of the green flares had burned away, and by this ghastly dim virescence Willard saw men trampled and women hurled aside.

"Safer aboard than anywhere with madmen!" he cried in the girl's ear. "Don't move! Stay where you are!"

He drove down into the wolf-pack — his duty called him there — and smote with hard fists that came back reddened from his blows, striving to scatter the crazed brutes. But in the dark and tumult he could compass nothing. A blow clipped his temple; he felt the blood run hot, but he only dashed it from his eyes and struck the harder, striving to wedge through and split the mob.

He saw foul knife-play, heard the first mate grunt and double up, got sights of hands that strangled and glimpsed blind primitive anarchy as a second boat was launched.

It foundered straightway, from gross overcrowding. Amid the drowning wretches, breaking off their handgrasps, a third boat was got away with only five oars, her gunwales shipping water at each sea. Then went the life-raft. He helped fling it overboard, aided some to jump in safety, and vainly tried to hold back others who leaped out at random — who missed and sank, with never a human hand held out to them for salvage.

"Better stay here! Safer on the ship!" he shouted to the lessening fugitives, but no one heeded him. When at last they all were gone — some to death, some to uncertain struggles with the night and the sea — when all had disappeared save a few limp figures rolling in the scuppers, he climbed back, bleeding, up the slippery deck to Ethel.

He found her in the bulkhead corner, kneeling in the gloom over a prostrate something that neither stirred nor spoke.

"What! Can I help?" he cried.

She shook her head, raising her hand silently, and he forbore. He understood. The old man's heart had lashed itself to bursting with the panic and the stress. Now, out of all the throng, only one woman and one man were left.

The doctor's wisdom kept his lips from platitudes. He turned, and left Ethel to herself a moment, gazing off landward. The ship was utterly dark now, for the last flare had burned to ash, the dynamos had stopped, and all the lights were dead. The steam-pipes' roar had dwindled to a sibilant murmur, drowned by the lash and crumble of the surges on the reef. Under the great passionless stars the wreck lay spent and weary, crushed to death, unmoved by even the heaviest seas.

Quite suddenly the doctor noticed a little speck of light far in the gloom, then another — many specks, that lay where he half guessed the shore must be. Puzzled, he knit his brows.

"It can't be that any have reached land yet. Those can't be fires. Never knew campfires to crawl that way."

Dully he watched the sparks creep, come together, then separate. They almost seemed to be advancing toward the ship.

Then the truth hit him, and he stumbled back.

"Merciful Heaven! the Guinea blacks — the wreckers of Bissagos!"

IV.

He stooped to Ethel tenderly. "Listen," said he. "We must get away from here. It's death to stay!"

She clung to him. He drew her up — away. She was only a blur in the night, but intuition told him that her face was wet with tears.

"Death?" she asked. "The wreck won't last till morning?"

"It's not that. There's something — something else. You'd better know at once. See there — off there to shoreward?"

"Those lights, you mean?"

"Lights, yes. They're torches — in canoes. They're coming. They mustn't find us here, or —"

"I understand. But can we go, and leave the — the —"

"Nobody must be left. There couldn't be a finer burial than the sea! I'll take you into the saloon, then come back here and do what must be done."

She understood, and yielded nobly. He led her off along the steep deck, after a silent moment by her uncle's body. He brought her safely to the main saloon, struck a match and found his bearings.

"All you need do is sit quite still in here. I won't be gone five minutes." Then he left her.

The work was harder than he had expected, for there was a lantern to be found and lighted, and — there were other difficulties. After a while the task was done.

When he came back to her, his pockets crammed with provisions and cartridges, a bandolier of canvas supporting revolvers and two magazine-rifles, she greeted him with a pale, thin smile. By the lantern light that glimmered sickly through the mocking splendor of the place, he saw her eyes brimming with tears, but she was calm and full of courage.

"We've got to find and launch a boat, or something, right away."

"Come, then, let's be about it," she replied. "There can't be many boats left, can there?"

"Hardly two or three. The port-side's stripped. We'll soon find out."

He helped her up across the saloon floor, which slanted like a house roof, and they issued out upon the larboard side. The wind could not strike here; and the waves, too, thirty-odd feet below, broke with less furious lashings.

Willard held the lantern high with his right hand. His left clutched the rail. Ethel steadied herself on him. Thus they worked their way slowly aft, stumbling over twisted cordage, litter, flotsam and jetsam of the tragedy.

As they neared the first boat Willard's heart died within him. What he might have guessed was true — the careening of the ship had swung the boats far inboard against their davits, so that nothing short of half a dozen men could now have got them over the rail, even had not the falls been twisted into knots and tangles.

He knew at once the prime futility of an attempt. Even to have got a life-raft over they must have rigged tackles, and time was now so short. A real fear shuddered through his veins. Too well he knew what manner of men the Guinea wreckers were. His hand slid, as by instinct, to the butt of his revolver. Before a single black should come nigh her he knew a better way.

"Impossible?" asked Ethel almost coolly. "Perhaps there's something better at the stern."

They forced a way, sliding, slipping, and clinging to whatever handholds offered. Under the counter they heard the waves run hissing. The wind whipped them as they worked out from the shelter of the after-cabin; it blew the lantern out. And as they stopped, breathing heavily in the dark, they saw once more the dancing fire sparks, heaving and tossing with the waves, and drawing very nigh. They could even see that the sparks were torches, harried by the wind; and once, in a lull, they heard a wild-pitched, minor chant that wailed and mourned across the vacant reaches of the night, with throbbings of many cadent drums.

The woman trembled at this sound, and Willard drew her close to him.

"Don't be afraid," he soothed her. "They shall never get you."

"Swear to that."

"I needn't. You know how true it is."

"No time, now?"

"No time. We'll have to hold the fort. They probably don't know we're here, so it'll be a fine surprise party. Lots of arms on board. You can shoot?"

"Try me."

Thus, on the instant, their campaign took form.

V.

"They'll board us midships on the port side," Willard planned. "They're after loot, and — and — and — well — edibles. Now we, I take it —"

"Can barricade the stern here?"

"Yes — rake 'em down by dozens. Except for knives and assegais, they're probably not armed."

"How many do you make them?"

"A good thousand. See, there must be more than fifty of those big sea-going *barracas*. But what are a thousand naked blacks against magazine rifles? They can't rush us all at once. Come, though," he added hastily, "this won't do. We've to get things ready for 'em — quick, at that."

He dragged up cordage, with her help; piled sail-cloth, debris, chains, anything that fell to hand in the port and starboard gangways. And thus they built a strong, entrenched position, whence they could sweep unmercifully the narrow approaches. By the vague light of the stars they toiled, and saw their work was good.

"We'll lie low now," panted the doctor. "If they don't see us, well and good. Otherwise a finish fight. In case they drive us, there's the aft companion to the upper deck. We can make a mighty fine killing from up there before they ever get us."

Without another word he drew from his pockets box on box of cartridges, broke the seals, and poured them out upon the deck. He set to loading all his arsenal, then laid part at the starboard barricade, the rest to port. Then, where some sailcloth touched the wooden cabin, he drenched the place with lantern oil.

"Now, let the guests arrive," said he. "Refreshment's ready."

"They're almost here," she whispered presently. "See there?"

Cautiously they peeked over the solid iron bulwark, and started with surprise. The Guinea men had loomed up almost in a moment from the night. The bulks of their long canoes were adumbrated by the guttering torches at each prow, surging upward, dipping, sliding over the hungry, lapping tongues of sea. Swarming they came. Everywhere flicked a swash of paddle-blades, everywhere swung innumerable black bodies in rhythm with the crooning plunder-song. The drums were silent, all save one that pulsed incessantly.

With a flesh-tingling wail of dissonance, the Guinea blacks teemed up about the *Sutherland*. A hum and murmur of barbaric voices filled the night. The acrid smoke from the torches stung the watchers' nostrils as they crouched, gripping their rifles.

"See," whispered Willard. "They're boarding now."

A sullen glow blurred up behind the port-rail midships. Then a blotch of flame wounded the shadows, and by this raw, wind-lashed beacon they saw the wreckers scramble in herds across the rail, their black, muscular bodies gleaming with sweat. Lights glinted from steel blades and spearheads.

"Armed for bloody work!" thought Willard, but he held his peace.

They clotted in a shifting mass, with cries like beasts; cracked, wild laughter; gibberish. And still they came, and came, and came.

"Heavens, what an onslaught!" Willard groaned. "It seems a shame to wait."

"Maybe they'll never think of coming aft?" breathed the girl.

"Heaven knows! They're in the saloon now. Hark! They're plundering — looking for the dead!"

Lights gleamed from the windows; noises rose within. The ship swarmed like a gigantic anthill, with this fetid crew. And now the watchers saw numberless black fellows crowding to the rail with loot, tossing it to waiting canoe-men. The whole scene blent and ran together like a nightmare. Ethel shut her eyes to it, bowed her head and waited.

"Ready!"

The doctor's hissed command aroused her. With sudden paralyzing dread she looked. A mob of the cursed ghouls were scouting toward them up the gangway.

Blear-faced and hideous they came, peering with brandished torches for what they might find. Ethel saw their little evil eyes; their red-dyed teeth as they grinned, jabbering; their shovel-headed spears.

"*Now!*" yelled the doctor. Night split wide-open with the fire from their rifles; crackling echoes smashed back from the cabin. Ethel looked.

She saw a struggling, screaming ruck that fled, a tangled heap jammed in the gangway — a heap that quivered.

There was no time for looking. Into her hands the doctor thrust another rifle.

"At the thick of 'em!" he shouted, and again death spouted from the barricade. Up to the sky shrilled a chorus of mad fear, so poignant, so unspeakable that they knew the rout was utter.

The wreckers made no stand. They lunged off in ripe clusters from the rail, swam for their dear black lives, and lost full many. Some reached their fellows in the boats; cries, howls, demoniac execrations dwindled as the *barracas* foamed away.

The doctor wiped his face with a torn sleeve and stood erect.

"They'll be back soon," said he. "Stay here; I'm going to investigate. If I whistle, look alive for orders."

He pressed a revolver into her hand, clambered the barricade and was gone. The darkness swallowed him.

She crouched behind the barricade, waiting, wondering, thrilling with the first imperative command which ever, as a woman, had been given her. The mastery of it steadied her, and was sweet. It almost made her forget the aching shoulder where the rifle-butt had plunged, and the dizzy swimming of her head.

The moments lagged eternal. What if some evil chance should fall and he should never come? She trembled at the thought. Suddenly and for the first time in her whole life she realized what manner of thing the comradeship of man may be, how very needful, very dear.

"Come back! Come back!" her lips formed the words there in the night — words which she dared not bring to utterance.

She heard a sudden wild noise on the sea. "They're coming back!" she shuddered.

Then, all at once, sounded a clear, low whistle on the starboard side.

"Drop a line here, and make it fast!" a voice rose up to her.

Not understanding, just obeying with a strange, new happiness in her fear, she tugged a rope from the tangled barricade, cross-looped it firmly on a chock, and flung it overboard. She heard it swish and strike the water — felt it

tauten. The voice rose again: "First-rate, so far. I'm coming up!"

She peered across the rail. From the wreckers' fleet a nearing tumult wafted. The torches now were blazing not five hundred fathoms off.

"Hurry!" she cried. "Hurry, or it will be too late!"

Staring down into the dark, she could just see a dim mass toiling up the rope. Then, quite suddenly, the doctor swarmed to the rail — was over it.

"We've got to rush!" he panted. "Found a mighty handy craft banging at the end of a liana-cord — obliging of 'em to have left it! By dropping off to starboard, they may never know we're gone; at least, not till we've made a start. You gather up the cartridges. We're apt to need 'em. I'll take the guns."

She filled her bosom with the leaden deaths, while he, with his knife, slit out a square of tarpaulin, wrapped the guns in it, and lashed them with a cord. He made a loop and slung the bundle over his head.

Then a match r-r-rasped, and eager little flames licked at the barricade, fingering the oil-soaked cabin wall.

"Good-by, old Suth!" the doctor whispered hoarsely to himself.

A moment there was silence — then the doctor faced her.

"Come!" said he. "Come, now! Are you afraid?"

"Afraid — with you?"

VI.

And it befell that, just before the breaking of the day, a man and woman, all disheveled, weary, black with powder-grime, resting on their paddles in a huge, uncouth *barraca*, turned and gazed back over the heaving ocean-breast to the distant tower of flame that bloodied the horizon.

Neither spoke. There was no need of words as the swift dawn flared up the sky. The sea crimsoned; fantom blues and opals spread abroad; luminous greens rimmed the far crescent of the western heaven as the last few watchful stars faded in the glory of another day.

"See?" said the man, pointing ahead.

The woman from her place in the bow looked far across the painted waters where a thin-drawn blur of smoke trailed slowly landward.

"See there? Two hours more and we'll be with — well, people again. Two hours more, and this will all be over, all be at an end for me — everything. I know how it will be! Just as I said last night, things will seem different to you — by the light of day. It is useless for me to hope otherwise."

"No, no," she answered, while her paddle dragged. "Not Africa — not you!"

As the full broad circle of the sun kissed the sea suddenly to gold, a song rose to the man's brave, eager lips. Strongly he plunged his paddle, urging the long *barraca* northward up the coast of Africa, over the bosom of the morning sea.

KILL THAT HEADLINE
by Robert Leslie Bellem

Deftly-applied rouge couldn't mask the chalky pallor of her cheeks. Her mouth was a tremulous crimson blossom against deathly whiteness. She walked into the *Morning Planet* city-room unsteadily, like a person drunk — or drugged.

Ken Fitch, city editor on the night side, happened to glance up from the headline he was readying — a headline that would split the town wide open. Less than two hours ago he'd had a visit from Cokey Joe Breen, who had spilled the facts behind that headline — for a cash consideration. And now, seeing the blond girl approaching, Ken Fitch stiffened with surprise.

"Letha Starke!" he muttered.

She came falteringly toward the raised platform where his desk was situated — the dais from which he could keep a watchful eye on reporters, rewrite men, and copy-desk slaves under his charge. Pendant green-shaded incandescents sent reflected glints of light shining against the oncoming girl's metallic yellow hair, revealing every perfectly-spaced wave of her artistic coiffure. Her lush curves were stressed by an expensive mink coat drawn tightly about her, so that each step she took revealed the bold, arrogant lines of her slinky figure.

"Ken — !" she whispered as she gained the platform.

He frowned. He didn't get up from his chair. A swift, roving glance informed him that every masculine eye in the room was appraisingly fastened on his visitor. Her blatant beauty always did that to the men she encountered. Typewriters had ceased clattering; there was only the steady, spaced click of teletype printers to mar the admiring hush that had fallen over the night crew.

Confronting Ken Fitch, the girl's back was turned to the others. Her pale blue eyes wavered to meet his gaze.

"Ken — !" she whispered again, pleadingly.

He flushed, conscious of the knowing grins on the faces of his subordinates. "Well, Letha, what's on your mind?" His tone pointedly lacked cordiality. He cast a look toward a desk at the far end of the room — Molly Kildare's desk.

Molly Kildare was petite, red-haired, wholesomely feminine and a crack reporter. Also, she was Ken Fitch's fiancée; they were to be married next month. He didn't like the idea of Molly seeing him talking to Letha Starke. Molly knew of his infatuation for Letha five years ago — an infatuation he had long since outgrown. Would Molly misunderstand this present meeting?

But she wasn't paying any attention. She was pawing through a desk-drawer as if searching for mislaid notes. Apparently she hadn't even noticed Letha Starke's entrance into the city room. Ken was relieved.

Again he stared up into the blue eyes of the blonde girl. Irritated, he repeated: "What's on your mind, Letha?"

"I'm in trouble, Ken. Ghastly trouble. I need you — desperately."

His lips took on a wry twist. "So you've come back to me after five years. After giving me the frigid air. After taking me for my bankroll and then handing me the gate. Now you say you need me. Rather ironic, don't you think?"

"You don't understand, Ken. This is different. I'm not asking you to forgive me for what I did to you. That's buried. I was a fool — and I learned my lesson. Too late. But now I've got nobody else to turn to. If you don't help me, they'll s-send me to the electric chair!"

He was startled. He crushed out his cigarette. "What do you mean by that?"

"Ken — *I just killed a man.*" She unfastened the fur coat and permitted it to fall open.

He choked back his sharp exclamation of surprise. She was wearing an evening gown of white satin that adhered like a caress to her lovely body. She was magnificently contoured. Her hips swelled lyrically against the clinging silk, and her snowy bosom was daringly revealed by deep-slashed décolletage. One shoulder-strap dangled, torn as if in some struggle. The front of the gown was splotched and spattered with reddish brown stains. He guessed their meaning before she spoke.

"Blood, Ken," the yellow-haired girl whispered as she closed the coat about her.

He regained composure. "So you killed a man."

"Yes. In my apartment. An hour ago."

"Who was he?"

"I — I don't know, Ken."

"You don't know? Then what the devil was he doing in your apartment?"

She reddened painfully. "I met him on a wild party this evening. He insisted on taking me home, I didn't think he'd —"

"Wait a minute, Letha. You're lying. I don't believe you."

"Oh, I know." Her smile was rueful and forced, without mirth. "You don't believe I'd ever sink low enough to invite a total stranger to my apartment. Well, Ken, you're quite wrong. I was drunk. And I thought I didn't care. The steps always lead downward — eventually. To the gutter."

He scowled thoughtfully. "What about your pal DeWitt Ragan? I thought he was footing your bills?" Asking that,

Ken casually covered the headline and the typewritten sheets on his desk — the story he'd been writing when Letha appeared. The story given to him by Cokey Joe Breen.

He didn't want Letha to see that headline — because, oddly enough, it dealt with this very DeWitt Ragan now under discussion.

The blond girl said: "Ragan? He ditched me more than a month ago — the rat."

That struck Ken as sardonically amusing. It was funny to hear her call anybody a rat for ditching her — considering how she herself had ditched Ken, more years ago than he cared to remember. He said: "So Ragan gave you the bum's rush. And since then you've been entertaining strangers. And tonight you croaked one. Why?"

"He was a b-beast. I discovered I couldn't bring myself to . . . let him maul me."

"Hm-m-m. So what happened?"

"I tried to get him to leave quietly. But he got nasty. There was a struggle. I p-picked up a brass candlestick and hit him over the head. . . ." Her knees seemed to grow wabbly under her. "Ken — Ken — you've got to help me get rid of that corpse; I d-don't want to go to the chair!"

He came to a sudden decision. "Okay. I'll see what can be done." He scribbled some instructions to Biff McQuaide, his assistant; called McQuaide to the desk and left him in charge. Ken and the blonde girl walked toward the exit.

They had to pass Molly Kildare's desk. Ken stopped for a moment while Letha swept onward. He leaned down over the petite red-haired girl. "Be back in a little while, honeysweet. Wait for me."

Molly's eyes were deep violet pools of worry. "You're going out with that Starke woman?"

He grinned and nodded. "Not jealous, are you?"

"N-no . . ." Molly's adorably piquant face wore a troubled expression; her firm little bosom rose and fell swiftly, as if with inner tumult. She laid a hand gently on Ken's arm. "No. I'm not jealous. But something tells me you're walking into danger, Ken. Intuition —"

He brushed her lips tenderly with his mouth. "Don't be foolish, sweetheart. I'll be okay." He went out.

Downstairs, Letha Starke had a taxi waiting. In the tonneau's darkness she sat close to him, so that he could feel the warm, insinuating softness of her, impinging on his own muscular solidarity. There'd been a time, long ago, when his blood would have run faster at her nearness. His arm would have stolen around her waist in a crushing embrace; he would have buried his face in the perfectly-coifed masses of her yellow hair and then searched demandingly with his lips for her waiting, sensuous mouth. . . .

But not now. That was irrevocably ended. He sat quietly, almost serenely. He paid no attention to her coquettish challenge.

She seemed to sense his indifference. "You hate me, don't you, Ken?"

"No. I passed that stage, years ago."

"Then why are you so cold to me?"

"Listen, Letha. I happen to be in love with someone else. The real thing this time. A girl named Molly Kildare. I'm going to marry her next month."

"She's the one you kissed, back in the office? The red-haired one?"

He smiled. "Yes. So you were watching?"

"I was. I couldn't h-help it. She's sweet, lovely. Oh, Ken — if only things had been different! If I hadn't been such a silly, stupid fool, five years ago . . . !"

"Forget it," he told her.

"Ken — why are you so willing to help me now, if you don't care anything about me?"

He shrugged. "Maybe because I'm a sentimentalist. Here we are at your place." He helped her from the cab and paid the tariff.

They went upstairs to the second floor of the building. She unlocked her door and switched on the living-room's lights.

"The c-corpse is in here. . . ." she whispered. She took his arm and led him into her boudoir, clinging closely to him as they stepped over the threshold. She pointed to her mussed bed.

A man lay there, face upward; his glazed eyes staring blindly at the ceiling. His skull was crushed in. Blood and smeared brains stained the pillows.

Ken Fitch drew a sharp breath. "Good God — !" he rasped. *"Cokey Joe Breen!"*

And then something smashed down on his head, from behind. Something that thudded viciously against his temple as he wheeled around. Something that sent blasting fires of agony searing into his brain.

He pitched forward. The floor seemed to come up and strike him on the face.

Over the roaring in his ears he heard a man's voice snarling: *"Got* the lousy snoop!" Then came Letha Starke's callous, amused tinkle of laughter.

Ken struggled drunkenly to his knees, felt blood running down his cheek from the cut in his scalp where the blackjack had laid the flesh open. He blinked back his daze as he stared up into a man's leering features.

"DeWitt Ragan . . . !" he mumbled thickly.

His tuxedoed attacker, president of the Ragan Construction Company, snarled: "Right. And if you start anything, I'll feed you another dose of the same."

A surging seethe of fury entered Ken's soul. He bounced to his feet as anger gave him new strength. He lunged at Ragan; bashed a knotted fist at the contractor's snarling mouth. The blow connected solidly. Ragan's gums spouted blood like squeezed sponges, and he spat out broken shards of teeth as he staggered back. Fitch followed him, battered at him —

Blam!

Another man had leaped into the room. He had a re-versed automatic in his hand. He thudded it against Ken's head savagely. And this time the lights went completely out for the newspaperman.

When he opened his eyes, he was trussed to a chair in the living-room. DeWitt Ragan was bloodily grinning at him, his arm encircling Letha Starke's supple waist. Over on the divan sat the man whose blow had stretched Ken Fitch unconscious. Ken recognized the fellow as Ragan's chauffeur.

Ragan said: "You lousy sap! So you wanted to help Letha, eh? Too bad, sucker. Because I'm dealing the cards my way from now on."

"Meaning — ?"

"You know damned well what I mean. Cokey Joe Breen spilled his guts to you tonight about my city hall contract for the new bridge across East Bay. You figured to pin back my ears by running a scoop on the graft I'm getting."

Ken blinked. "So you caught Breen and made him squeal."

"He squealed, all right. And now he's dead. Which is what you'll be — unless you kill that story about me."

Squirming against his fetters, Ken rasped: "Have another guess, Ragan. That story runs in tomorrow morning's edition. You can't stop it."

"No. But *you* can. And you will."

The newspaperman laughed shortly. "Go ahead and do your damnedest, you filthy crook. The minute you turn me loose and send me back to the *Planet* office, I'll blast hell out of you. Not only for graft — but for murder." He glanced significantly toward the boudoir, where Cokey Joe Breen's body lay.

Ragan approached the chair. He raised his fist, smashed it to Ken's jaw. He snarled: "Shut up!"

Ken shook his head jerkily to clear away the blur. Then he grinned again. "You think you can scare me by beating me up? Nuts, Ragan! You're a bigger fool than I thought you were."

The contractor's scowl was savage with wrath. "Hero stuff. Maybe you won't feel so brave when your red-haired girl friend ankles in here."

Ken stiffened. A sudden icy shock trickled down his spine. "What — !"

"Yeah." Ragan laughed triumphantly. "I phoned the *Planet* while you were knocked out. I imitated your voice. I talked to your sweetie. I asked her to come up here right away. She's on her way now."

Flooding, impotent rage churned in Ken Fitch's heart. Molly Kildare — walking straight into a trap! Sweet, unsuspecting Molly — heading innocently into murderous danger! "You wouldn't dare — !" he shouted.

Ragan's lips peeled back from his broken teeth. "No? Guess again. *I'll bet that's her now!"* he added as a knock sounded on the door.

Ken twisted ineffectually against the ropes that held him. He raised his voice. "Molly — for God's sake — *run!*" he shouted hoarsely.

But Ragan's ape-like chauffeur had already launched himself at the door, jerked it open. He reached out, made a grab — and dragged Molly into the room.

The red-haired girl went white as she clawed at her captor. She saw Ken Fitch tied to the chair, and her violet eyes widened in terror. "Ken — !"

The chauffeur slapped her viciously across the mouth, his hard palm splatting like the report of a gun. "Button your kisser, babe!" he growled.

She staggered; then she renewed her struggles. She kicked at the thug; tried to pound his face with her tiny fists. He twined his fingers in her auburn hair; jerked her head far back. He struck her again; tried to carry her across the room.

She fought him like a tigress. His hand caught in the neck of her frock, ripping it from one shoulder. She wailed and tried to cover the flesh exposed under the torn material. Her attacker forced her to the divan and bounced her against the cushions. The hem of her skirt flew up past her stocking-tops. There was a flash of smooth, ivory skin.

Beaten, cowed, she crouched shivering on the sofa as the chauffeur pinned her wrists. He grunted: "Be good or I'll sock you again, sister."

Letha Starke interrupted. "No, you needn't bother. I want that pleasure for myself. String her up to the chandelier."

Ken Fitch's throat went dry. "You damned fiends — you can't get away with this!"

Ragan snarled: "Shut up, snoop. Don't make me slug you unconscious. I want you to be awake — so you can see what's happening." He helped his chauffeur bind Molly's wrists with a length of clothesline. Then they lifted her to the center of the room; fastened the rope to the overhead lighting-fixture.

The red-haired girl dangled there, moaning; her little feet barely touching the floor. Ragan took off his leather belt and handed it to Letha Starke. "Okay, kiddo. Have your fun."

Letha stepped forward, prepared to lash Molly with the strap.

Ken Fitch shouted again. "No — for God's sake — !"

The yellow-haired woman laughed; brought the leather belt swishing venomously in a circling arc. Splat! The belt stung into Molly's smooth flesh, left a red weal on white, where its end touched her bare shoulder. *Splat!* Again the improvised whip licked out. Molly whimpered —

Ken roared: "Quit! Stop it! I'll kill that damned story! I promise!"

But Molly Kildare's voice halted his outcries. "No, Ken. Let them go ahead and whip me. If it's something that should be printed — *print it!*" Her proud eyes swept the room. She faced Letha Starke. "Go ahead. Help yourself."

Letha started to strike once more. But Ragan grabbed the strap. "Nix, kiddo. I've got a better scheme."

"What do you mean?"

He untied the red-haired girl; carried her to the divan. Then he winked at his chauffeur. "All right, guy. I've been watching you. You've had your eye on this dish ever since she ankled in. Well — she's yours!"

Helpless fury scalded Ken Fitch's soul. "You rats — you lousy, stinking swine'! You can't — you wouldn't —"

Ragan slugged him in the mouth, silenced him. He tasted the salt tang of his own blood from split lips. Raging, struggling vainly against the cords that held him to the heavy chair, he saw the chauffeur go to the divan and lean over Molly's cringing form. . . .

She whimpered — once. Then the thug had her in his arms; glued his thick lips to her averted mouth.

Wildly Ken shouted: "Stop! I give in! I swear it! I'll kill the story — I'll do anything you say!" And this time Molly gave him no contradiction. . . .

Ragan grunted: "Okay. Let up, Terry."

The chauffeur released Molly; growled sullen reluctance as he swung around.

Ragan was at work on Ken's bonds. He snarled: "Listen, Mister. I'm giving you this one chance. You're going back to the *Planet* office. You're going to destroy every bit of the stuff Cokey Joe Breen gave you. I'm sending Terry with you — in case you try any funny stuff. He'll have a roscoe, and he hasn't got any scruples about using it."

Ken Fitch was desperately sparring for precious minutes. "Your gorilla won't have to shoot me, Ragan. I give you my word I'll destroy that story. Nobody knows about it except me. All I ask is that you let Molly go —"

The contractor said: "Nuts, boyfriend. The jane stays right here — until you come back with proof that you killed that headline. I'm giving you thirty minutes to get the job done. If you aren't back here by then — well, something damned unpleasant will happen to your girlfriend. Gargle that one."

Ken stole a glance at Ragan's wristwatch; saw that he'd been away from his city-desk five minutes less than a full hour. His heart began to hammer against his chest. Five minutes to go. . . . It seemed like a bleak eternity stretching out before him. He knew that he didn't dare leave this apartment until that five minutes had snailed by . . .

Time! He had to gain it somehow. Ragan had already untied the ropes at his ankles; was now at work on his wrist-bonds. The contractor was working swiftly. Too swiftly.

And then Ken was free. He swayed to his feet. Ragan stood before him. Over by the door was Terry, the chauffeur — with his fist in his coat pocket and an ominous bulge that told of an automatic's muzzle poking the cloth. Letha Starke hovered near the davenport, keeping guard over Molly. . . .

"Get going!" Ragan rasped.

Ken Fitch took a wild, desperate chance. He tensed his sinews — and went smashing at the contractor like a stone from a catapult.

The move took Ragan by surprise; bowled him backward. Ken's fist lashed out like pistons; impacted against his enemy's jaw. He felt the jarring thud all the way to his own shoulders.

Ragan's head snapped back as if hinged. He went down.

Letha Starke screamed a gutter oath. The chauffeur came slamming across the room, his gun drawn. He yelled: "Stand back, Miss Starke — I'll plug him!"

Ken dived for the floor. He hit the carpet just beyond where Ragan had fallen. He grabbed for the unconscious contractor; used the man's limp form for a shield. "Go ahead and shoot!" he panted. "You'll kill your boss if you do!"

The thug's finger relaxed its pressure on the trigger of the automatic. He darted sidewise, seeking a clear aim at the newspaperman. Ken rolled, keeping Ragan in front of him —

But he forgot Letha Starke. She darted in, flung herself on Ragan, dragged him aside. Ken was wholly exposed to the chauffeur's weapon, now. He scrambled to his feet, zigzagging. With a blow of his fist he sent the blond woman sprawling. She went down in a flurry of white satin skirt; her chiffon legs kicked and thrashed as she landed.

The chauffeur jumped as Letha landed at his feet. He swerved around her. That was Ken's chance. He sailed full at his antagonist before the man could again raise his gun to firing position.

They met with a thumping crash of flesh against flesh, brawn against brawn.

From the divan, Molly Kildare screamed: "Ken — *look out!* Ragan's getting up!"

And then Fitch smashed his right fist square into the chauffeur's mouth. The fellow sagged; went to his knees. The automatic dropped from his hand. Ken lashed out with his foot; kicked the thug brutally. The chauffeur doubled over, retching and holding his middle.

Whirling, Ken saw Ragan coming at him — with a gun.

It was too late to scoop up the chauffeur's weapon. Too late to do anything — except brace himself for Ragan's bullet. The contractor's narrow eyes gleamed with murderous malice. He grated: "You asked for it — now take it!" He squeezed his trigger.

But even as his gun vomited flame, the apartment's door crashed inward. A knot of uniformed men came thundering into the room. Ragan's shot went wild; a slug screamed past Ken Fitch's ear. And then the police were grappling with DeWitt Ragan, disarming him, handcuffing him. They jerked the fallen chauffeur to his feet, manacled him to his employer. And they lifted Letha Starke; pinioned her.

Ken Fitch saw his *Planet* assistant, Biff McQuaide, in the thick of things. He yelled: "Biff — thank God you got here before it was too late!"

McQuaide grinned. "You should have made it thirty minutes instead of an hour, from the looks of things."

DeWitt Ragan was snarling, fighting his handcuffs. "What the hell — who — how —"

Ken's eyes gleamed bale fully. "You aren't quite smart enough, Ragan. In the first place, I knew Letha's story was a lie. 1 knew it the minute she walked into the *Planet* cityroom. I realized she was trying to trick me, trap me. That was obvious enough."

The contractor stared. "You — you knew?"

"Yes. Letha said she'd killed a man, in a struggle. She showed me bloodstains on her dress. Okay. The blood was genuine. *But there hadn't been any struggle. Because her hair wasn't mussed!*"

Ragan stiffened.

Ken went on. "You heard me. Her coiffure was a work of art. Not a single wave was out of place. So I knew her yarn about a struggle was all phony. So was her torn dress. So was everything else she told me.

"I figured she was lying when she claimed you'd thrown her over. If she was so damned hard up that she had to entertain strangers, what was she doing with that expensive mink coat? Nothing added up right. So I guessed that she was trying to lure me into a trap.

"Who'd want to trap me? Nobody but you — on account of the story I was going to run about you. Well, I deliberately walked into your scheme, Ragan. Because I wanted to find out the truth about you. I wanted to make sure Cokey Joe Breen had handed me a right steer when he gave me that information about your grafting.

"I went haywire in just one detail. I didn't expect you to conk me and lure Molly Kildare up here. You almost won out by doing that. Almost — but not quite. Because when I left the *Planet* office I scribbled a note for McQuaide, my assistant. I instructed him to wait an hour — and then, if I hadn't returned, *he was to come to this apartment with a squad of cops.*"

Ragan wilted. "I'll take a plea. They won't fry me . . ." he drooled. "I've got influence. . . ."

An officer jerked him toward the door. "Nuts, buddy. Get goin'."

Slowly the room cleared. One bluecoat was left to stand guard over Cokey Joe Breen's corpse in the adjoining boudoir. Ken Fitch slipped over to the divan; lifted Molly Kildare in his arms.

She clung to him fiercely. "Oh, Ken. . . ." she whispered.

He kissed her. He said: "Let's not wait until next month, honey-sweet. What do you say?"

She wrapped her soft arms around his neck and held up her mouth for another kiss. It was all the answer he needed.

FOOTPRINTS IN THE SNOW
by Murray Leinster

The snow was deep, but not soft. There was enough of cold to keep the snow-crystals brittle and hard. They glistened until they hurt the eyes, and as I trudged along behind my sledge they crackled with a faintly musical tinkle beneath my snow-shoes.

It was not really cold, though. I was almost hot in the heavy clothing I wore, and the dogs loafed on their job. The sled was light enough, in all conscience, but they pulled with hardly half their strength. I did not press them. There was no hurry. I was to meet Pierre Chambour at Three Mile Run that afternoon and it was still early in the morning with our rendezvous a bare dozen miles away.

I had passed the mail-sled the afternoon before and been told of a shorter trail than the one I had intended, so I had time to spare. That must explain my stop at the cabin I saw from the trail. I invented some pretext — I pretended to inquire if this was indeed the proper and shorter trail to Three Mile Run — but I felt queerly ashamed when I entered the place. I mention the cabin because what Pierre told me later made it interesting.

It was tenanted by an old man, obviously an invalid, who lay back in an improvised easy chair, and an animal that moved about laboriously on twisted and crippled limbs, The face of the old man was a proud one, with strangely scornful eyes, and I instinctively began to stammer out an apology for intruding, in spite of my knowledge that visitors are welcome in any of the French-Canadian cabins of the backwoods.

The old man looked at me scornfully, and the animal began to hobble toward me with a snarl. It was a wolf, whose body was whole and sound, and whose head and jaws were ferocious and well-muscled, but whose limbs had at some time been cruelly broken and unskillfully healed. It was barely able to progress across the floor by means of effortful contortions, and surely would not have been formidable, but I was spared the need of defending myself against its intended attack by the entrance of a girl from another room.

With a gesture she halted the wolf and bade me welcome. I completed my apology for intruding and asked if I were on the right trail.

"Yes, *m'sieu'*," she said gravely. "There is but the one trail, once you have branched from the main way."

"Thank you," I said, and hesitated. "Er — you have a queer pet," I added helplessly.

It is not customary to ask a question and depart without further words in the Canadian backwoods. One is usually expected to stay and gossip. These people, however, evidently had no such expectation. The girl bent down and picked up the cruelly misshapen creature from the floor and carried it over to a cushion by the fireplace, where it lay and looked at me steadily.

"Yes, *m'sieu'*," she said quietly. She glanced up. "I am sure," she added with perfect courtesy, "that *m'sieu'* will have no further trouble with the trail."

I found myself outside the cabin, flushing slightly. Her intimation that I was not expected to stay was unmistakable, but there had been no discourtesy in her tone. It had been rather the symbol of an invincible reserve.

When I realized that fact I remarked to myself that I had no faintest desire to pry into her affairs and mushed on along behind my dog-team. All the same, the whole thing puzzled me. That animal, crippled in that way, that proud-faced old man, and the girl who so politely showed me the door.

Thinking it over, I was struck by an expression I had noticed on her face. Once in a great while you see a face which is at once unutterably sad and quite tranquil. Most often you see that expression on the faces of women who have retired from the world for reasons which are between themselves and their Maker, and devoted themselves to prayer.

That was the expression I had seen on her face. Past agony which could never be forgotten, but palliated by later and continued peace. I made a mental note to ask Pierre about her, and continued on my way.

Pierre was waiting for me. I saw the smoke of his fire some distance away, and his dogs and mine were greeting each other with loud defiances long before I saw Pierre himself. He is a friend I value highly, in spite of the efforts of worthy people to set me against him.

His silvery hair has not been lightened in vain. He is wise in the things not taught in books, and he has taught me some of his lore. At the same time, he is a rich mine of queer fancies and occasionally grotesque superstitions. Almost the first thing he did was to show me a fresh wolfskin, which he told me he had shot.

"And it is very hard to shoot a wolf, *m'sieu*," he explained, "especially when food is as plentiful as now. They know rifles when they see them and will not show themselves."

His statement did not surprise me. I had heard many tales of wolves and their knowledge and cunning. In fact, one of the reasons I wanted to see Pierre was to get his opinion of a theory I had formed that the legends of werewolves that are found wherever wolves have been, are due to the almost or quite human intelligence of the brutes. I asked Pierre how he had shot the animal whose skin he was displaying.

He told me with great detail precisely how he came to be certain that a wolf was hiding from his rifle behind a certain copse, of how he had made it impossible for the wolf to slink away unseen, and how a supremely lucky shot had brought down the animal as it made a dash for the brushwood that would hide it.

"The merit of the shot," said Pierre humbly, "is undoubtedly due to the aid of the Virgin of Etretat, whose relic I wear. She was ever the benefactor of all travelers."

By that time I was busily arranging my camp beside his own, so he did not see me smile at the idea of heavenly intervention in favor of such a hardened old reprobate as himself. Instead, he went on to tell me wonderful anecdotes in which his reliquary figured; notably, instances in which it had aided people in danger from wolves and other wild animals, but mostly wolves.

It was a curious relic in itself, undoubtedly antique, and I knew that either from the sense of security it gave him or from some other cause he was utterly fearless where wolves were concerned. More than once he had appeared with litters of furry, snarling wolf cubs to sell to wild-animal dealers, and the securing of wolf cubs is not an enterprise to be undertaken by the nervous.

When I had fed my dogs and settled down to the preparation of supper, it had grown quite dark. I anticipated some trouble in getting my share of firewood, but Pierre had enough for both and we were soon swallowing mugs of steaming tea to top off our meal. We filled our pipes, and when Pierre had settled comfortably back and his pipe was drawing well, I started to explain my theory of the origin of werewolf tales.

Taken in itself, it sounded plausible enough. Consider an animal clever enough to attack an unarmed man and hide itself at sight of a man with a rifle. Or an animal capable of a degree of comradeship which would lead it, itself secure, to leap out of hiding and risk its life to rescue a comrade in difficulties.

Multiply those two instances by a thousand others, each evidencing an intelligence almost incredible. Think of the fact that in three years they learned what poison meant, so that it is practically impossible to poison a wolf nowadays. That they learned what rifles meant and what they did not mean.

Is it surprising that an animal displaying such cunning should in times past have been credited with possessing a human brain — of being, in fact, a human being metamorphosed? It would be astonishing if they had not.

I put forward my theory with a great deal of enthusiasm. Pierre listened with flattering attention, but when I finished he shook his head. I noticed that he reached his hand inside his shirt, and I think it was to take a comforting grasp of the reliquary suspended about his neck by a cord.

"No, *m'sieu',*" he said firmly. "I do not think your idea is right."

It nettled me a little.

"Have you a better explanation, then?" I asked, somewhat unamiably.

His face was very grave.

"I have, *m'sieu*. My explanation is that the legends are true."

My face must have expressed my amazement and amusement. At any rate, Pierre cast a glance behind him and took a fresh grasp of his reliquary.

"*M'sieu',*" he said earnestly, "let me beg of you that you will not laugh at such dangerous subjects. It is not wise. I — I assure you it is not wise. If I were not secure in the protection of the Virgin of Etretat, I would not dare even discuss it like this."

I stared at him in some astonishment.

"But, Pierre," I protested. "You don't believe that foolishness! You don't believe that there are people who turn into wolves, or wolves that turn into people!"

Pierre puffed silently on his pipe for a moment or so. He seemed to be debating something within himself, and the debate caused him a little nervousness. Suddenly, however,

he rapped the ashes out of his pipe and said decisively:

"*M'sieu'*, I shall tell you how Jean Lenoir came to his death, and you may decide for yourself what I believe. I knew Jean Lenoir, in fact, I — we — that is — there was some difficulty with the government in which we were both involved at the same time."

Knowing Pierre, I made a shrewd guess that they had both been suspected of selling whisky to the Indians, which suspicion was quite likely to be well founded. I waited for the story.

"It does not seem well, *m'sieu'*," said Pierre after a pause, "it does not seem well at all, since he is dead, to say that Jean Lenoir was an evil man, but his name was a fit description, though an accident. *Lenoir*, you understand, in our language means 'the black.'

"I do not think I should speak ill of the dead, but Jean was truly evil as no other man I have known was evil — and I have known many evil men. A huge, black-bearded man, *m'sieu'*, with arms like one of the great monkeys of which Du Challu writes. A monstrous man, with a huge chest and the neck of a bull. And most of all, the rage of a lion. Men trembled at the roar of his voice when they knew nothing of him, but they fled when they knew of his repute.

"Imagine a man always a brute, and ten thousand devils when drunk. Imagine a man whose strength was such that no man dared oppose him, and whose skill with his weapons was such that though six men had fallen at his hands there was no one brave enough to attempt to bring him to justice. Think of a man who knew no law save his own passions, and whose terrible strength enabled him to enforce that law without mercy and without respite. Sometimes, *m'sieu'*, I wonder that I risked my life to associate with him in any enterprise."

Pierre half sighed. Looking at the white-haired old sinner, with his gentle voice, one was tempted to wonder at his reputation for daring. It took closer acquaintance to reveal the cause.

"He is dead," said Pierre thoughtfully, "and the manner of his death leaves but little doubt as to the fate he met in the afterworld, but somehow I am not filled with sorrow. The good cure tells me I should pray for the souls of all that are dead, and so I do. *Le bon Dieu* knows Jean Lenoir needs prayers.

"Somehow I think of a little wolf-cub I gave him once. He admired its spirit, *m'sieu'*, among a litter I had caught to sell to the dealers, as I do sometimes. This one had pushed aside all its brothers and sisters to secure the warmest place by the fire for itself. It snarled at me when I would have moved it. And Jean Lenoir laughed hugely at it, *m'sieu'*, and asked me to give it to him.

"I gave it. One does not refuse gifts to such as Jean. He petted it for perhaps two weeks, and then he cuffed it while in drink, and it sank its teeth in his hand."

Pierre's lips tightened.

"What did he do?" I asked.

"He broke it, *m'sieu'*," said Pierre simply. "He cracked the tiny bones of its limbs in his hands until the little thing could not walk or stand, and then he cast it out in the snow. I would have shot it, but Estelle Duval found it by the side of the trail and took it to her home. It would have been kinder to have killed it, but she strove to cure it."

"Was that the crippled thing that crawled about the floor of the cabin back on the trail?"

"You stopped in there?" asked Pierre. "Yes, that is the cub, now grown. A fit companion for Marcel Duval. There is more of Jean's devilment. Not Marcel himself. A tree fell upon him and crushed him, so that he sits always in a chair and suffers. He needs drugs to make him sleep. I spoke of Estelle."

"How?" I asked. "She had a strange expression —"

"The devilment of Jean. He should have suffered a thousand deaths for that, though the death he died was horrible." Pierre shivered a little. He had seemed lost in his story, but his faint uneasiness reappeared for a moment, only to vanish again as he went on.

"I said that Jean was a brute at all times, and ten thousand devils when drunk. Only a devil would have done what he did. *M'sieu'*, you saw that household. The father an invalid, the watchdog a pitifully maimed, tame wolf, and the girl Estelle. You saw how slim, how frail, how tiny she is to bear the burden of maintaining that *ménage?*"

I nodded.

"Jean Lenoir was drunk," said Pierre, with the hurried speech of one who hastens to be rid of a distasteful incident. "He came down that trail, ten thousand devils alive in him. He saw the light in the window of the cabin.

"He entered. The father helpless, the wolf helpless, and Estelle — you saw Estelle."

"I did," I said angrily.

"That was Jean Lenoir's work." Pierre waved his hand. "When he left — he was not merciful. He did not kill her."

"And you let the man live?" I demanded furiously. "You did not kill him? And you called yourselves men?"

Pierre smiled apologetically. He is an amiable person, and as a friend I value him highly, but I would not like to have him for an enemy. There is a streak of pure, unadulterated villainy in him.

"You forget that Jean was the equal of ten men in combat, and a deadly shot with his rifle. No one dared seize him. If Estelle had had a lover, or a brother — But her father was an invalid."

I eyed Pierre with something less than my former liking. He went on imperturbably.

"I see you are not pleased with me, *m'sieu'*, but you must remember that at that time I was not in favor with the government. I was one of the few men who dared visit Jean's cabin. If I slew him, I would have been accused of murder, and to think of delivering him alive was madness.

"My sympathy was all with Estelle, as it is now —" and the old reprobate paused a moment while endeavoring to squeeze out a crocodile-tear — "but my hands were tied. I thank *le bon Dieu* that I did not stay with Jean in his cabin, but then, as now, I wore the reliquary of the Virgin of Etretat, and it is due to her that I am alive today."

"You spoke of a werewolf," I said somewhat coldly.

"But yes, *m'sieu.* A werewolf in very truth. You know the form the — the — they take?" Pierre was defiantly going on with his story, despite his knowledge of my disappointment in him, and his nervous dread of speaking of werewolves.

"They appear to a man sometimes as a beautiful woman, who smiles upon him, rousing all his passions. And when the man would seize the figure before him, it yields to his embrace until his throat is exposed. And then the man is found the next day with his throat torn out, and men say a wolf crept upon him while he slept. You have heard of such things?"

"The tale is familiar," I said grudgingly.

"Upon all nights but one they may not deceive any man who recites the charm against werewolves — which I do, *m'sieu*, at the proper times. But there is one night which is their night, and on that night, wherever they make their appearance, there is great danger.

"On that night I do not open the door of my cabin, *m'sieu*, no, not though the voice of my best friend called to me from without, for werewolves often take upon themselves the likeness of those we love and trust. On every night but one I fear nothing, but that night I tremble.

"It was on that night, three years ago, that Jean Lenoir heard a soft laugh outside his door and opened it. And there entered his cabin a woman of beauty we may only guess at."

Pierre grasped his reliquary firmly, and for once lost his assurance.

"*M'sieu*," he said desperately, "you may not believe me, but I tell you of things I saw with these two eyes. I came by the cabin of Jean Lenoir the morning after the Night of the Werewolves.

"His door was open. Leading into that door, and again leading out of it, I saw on the snow the prints of a woman's feet. A woman's feet, *m'sieu*; not wolf-tracks, but the prints of a *woman's* feet!"

"Well, what of it?" I asked.

Pierre half glanced behind him.

"Jean Lenoir lay on the floor of his cabin," he said nervously. "And his throat had been torn out by the fierce teeth of a wolf. He lay there on the floor of his cabin, and he had not struggled, for nothing was disarranged.

"There were even two glasses still on the table where Jean had sat and drunk with the thing that came to him in the guise of a woman. And in one of the glasses was the dried, caked, whitish slobber of the thing that had drunk with Jean."

"You are sure it was a wolf that had killed him?" I asked.

"I am sure that no jaws but those of a wolf could have torn out his throat like that," said Pierre. The old sinner was surely in earnest. "*M'sieu*, I swear to you that no wolf-tracks led into that cabin, only the prints of a woman's feet. I swear it, *m'sieu*. I — I swear it by the Virgin of Etretat.

"And Jean Lenoir lay on the floor of his cabin with his throat torn out by a wolf. That is how he died, *m'sieu*, and I — I believe in werewolves."

I puffed at my pipe a while in silence. Suddenly an idea came to me.

"Er, Pierre," I said irreverently. "Did you say that Marcel Duval — the invalid, you know — did you say he had to take drugs to make him sleep?"

"Why — yes, *m'sieu*. What has that to do with my story?"

"Nothing." I continued to smoke in silence. But there came before my eyes as in a vision, the picture of Estelle Duval making her way to Jean Lenoir's cabin on the Night of the Werewolves, carrying a heavy, breathing bundle in her arms.

I seemed to see her enter the cabin. I seemed to see her making merry with Jean Lenoir, drinking with him. And I seemed to see her drop a whitish powder in his drink, such as would later seem to Pierre the dried, caked slobber of the werewolf.

Then Jean Lenoir — or the picture of him I had formed in my mind — seemed to grow sleepy and tumble to the floor. And then the bundle that Estelle Duval had brought crept forward. It was a wolf, whose body was whole and sound, and whose head and jaws were ferocious and well-muscled, but whose limbs had at one time been cruelly broken and unskillfully healed.

It hobbled toward the stupefied Jean Lenoir, while Estelle Duval looked on with a fierce joy in her eyes. The vision faded, but suddenly I realized the reason of the tranquility and the peace that overlay the tragedy in Estelle Duval's eyes.

"*M'sieu*," said Pierre with uneasy insistence. "Does your theory explain the death of Jean Lenoir, or am I right? Could it have been anything but a werewolf?"

I rapped the ashes out of my pipe.

"No-o, Pierre," I said slowly. "I don't see how it could." ❊

FORBIDDEN FRUIT

by John D. Swain

Holt paused uncertainly, stepped gingerly over a pile of dusty books, and was saved in the nick of time from placing his brand-new Panama on a human brain upon the littered center-table.

"E-a-asy there!" warned Dr. Jones. "That head is done with hats! Just preparing some slides when you knocked."

He brushed a dozen dog-eared scientific reviews off a chair, hung Holt's hat on the crooked frame of Rembrandt's "Lesson in Anatomy," and invited him to be seated.

His visitor accepted and lighted a powerful *breva* to kill the rank blend of strange odors that pervaded the disorderly laboratory.

Holt and Jones had been classmates in college, and had always kept in friendly touch with one another, although having little in common save the memory of mellow undergraduate days. The advances always came from the young lawyer, who, from time to time, dropped in to chat with the physician, and endeavor to drag him out to some light form of recreation, always without success.

Even during their college years, when they had been considered to be chums, he had never got beneath the surface of the reticent Jones, whose past had been a sealed book. Jones seemed never to have had any childhood or youth. That he had been reared in Scotland by a dour couple who had adopted him, disciplined and in due time put him through Edinburgh University, was the extent of Holt's information.

"They fed me, and clothed me, and robbed me of my play-spell," Jones had explained, "and they died believing me damned. So let's forget it and live in the present! I'll sit up all night and argue with you, on either side of any question you propose. So far, I'm more Scotch than Yankee!"

And because Holt, too, liked to wrangle, a liking which had finally led him to the bar, they got on together uncommonly well.

Jones had gone in for alienism, psychoanalysis, and cerebral pathology. In his lighter moments he had written breezy sketches such as: "Jones on Suppressed Complexes," and "The Intellectual Fourth Dimension." He appeared frequently as an expert in court, was profoundly versed in all forms of mental aberration and perversion, acted as consultant to several hospitals for the insane, and remained withal an optimist and an agreeable diner-out.

Several times Holt had seriously considered having him prescribe for his wife, who was exceedingly nervous, having never recovered from a terrible experience as a child when the ill-fated *Macedonia*, now forgotten in the welter of war horrors, sank with nearly all on board. Mrs. Holt, a mere toddler, was deprived in a brief quarter-hour of parents, sister and a baby brother. Her life was saved by the fact that at the time the iceberg crashed into the *Macedonia*'s ribs, she was being held by the chief stewardess, who had taken a great fancy to her, and who had kept her head and thrust her into a lifeboat just as it slipped from the davits.

The knowledge that Jones, who was ruinously high in his fees, would charge him nothing, coupled with his aversion to meeting women, alone had prevented Holt from seeking his advice. He recalled his errand, and spoke.

"I came to book you for a ride in Seaman's quadriplane," he explained. "You remember him — a soph in our time, shark on mathematics. He has perfected a sort of super-seaplane. Great chance for us!"

Jones shook his head smilingly.

"No use, old-timer! You know me. A rathskeller, with a small *and* select party — no women — and I'll put this cerebrum on ice and go. I respect aviation in all its forms, but don't care a hoot about seeing or doing it."

Holt grunted.

"What you doing with that odious mess, anyhow?" He pointed at the specimen on the table.

"That? Oh, I forgot to introduce you. Pardon the oversight. Meet the late Lucius Treat, who suffered from locomotor ataxia, paresis, paranoia, and a few other minor afflictions, and died leaving four promising young cretins to vote for president by and by! I'm putting a section of his brain in my projector, to see if I can identify any cellular lesions."

"You're higher up in the clouds than Seaman will ever get! Why don't you do something *practical*? Who cares a hang whether Treat has any lesions or not? Whatever he had, you couldn't cure him of, and he's dead. Why don't you accomplish something we can make use of?"

"As what, for instance?"

"Well — er — you spend all *your* time monkeying with the human intellect and its repulsive envelope; why not teach us how to be prophets?"

"Oh, I don't know! Just what is a prophet, anyhow?

Whatever he is, he isn't a long-whiskered seer peering into the vapor of some witches' caldron. Did you ever stop to consider that in every great war of the past two thousand years, someone has pointed out that the prophet Daniel foretold it in the Old Testament? It is so today. Also, that in each event of world-wide import, there have been uttered predictions covering every possible outcome? And that some one of these *must*, of course, guess right? Thereupon we get that 'I told you so' stuff. It now appears that this present debacle was foretold over and over again."

"There's something in that, of course; but you're talking of *false prophets*. I'm speaking of the genuine article, if he exists."

"Very good! When you read a properly constructed mystery story, you find in the last chapter a climax the necessary elements of whose solution were all present in the preceding pages, if you had possessed the type of mind capable of reading them aright. Most editors and many observant readers do forecast the conclusion. Well, life is a mystery plot. All the clues are present — nothing is wanted but a mind capable of winnowing the chaff out and matching up the essential fragments. In other words, a prophet needs but two things: sufficient data, and the logical *a priori* and *a posteriori* intellect to utilize it."

"Ve-ry simple, learned healer! Proving either that no such mind exists in mortal born of woman, or that the data is lacking."

"Proving nothing of the sort, my egg-headed legal friend. Such minds exist, and the data is all garnered. All that is needed is to make it available."

"Then why —"

Dr. Jones silenced Holt with a bony forefinger, stained with something unpleasant, and reeking of germicide.

"Holt, I could manufacture a prophet as easily as I can make a new nose by the gentle rhinoplastic art. But who wants to be a prophet?"

"I, for one! Ever since I was a kid I've dreamed of clairvoyance, fortune-telling, the gift of prophecy."

"You've dreamed of *bunk*. I should create, not a supernatural attribute, but a perfectly normal and material function. I should simply make available to your excellent brain the store of facts it already possesses, but cannot get at."

"Talk down to me, doc! If I've got the dope, lead me to it! How do I get to bring my powerful intellect to bear on it all?"

Jones seated himself opposite his visitor, brushing aside a clutter of empty vials, stubs of pencil, fragmentary notes on old envelope backs, a piece of skull with a silver plate set in it, and other odds and ends, to make room for his elbows.

"Do you know that men are quite likely to die of the disease they repeatedly dream they've contracted?" he asked.

"Nope! Never followed the dream-book and Mother Shipton."

"Well, it is a fact! To such an extent that we of today make these recurrent dreams a part of our diagnosis. Reason why: there are a lot of little telltale symptoms too obscure to impress the consciousness, perhaps even to be noted by the family physician; but the subconsciousness takes note of them all, as of everything else, and in your sleep, they are cast up on the cerebral shore. We have hundreds of such dreams, few of which we recall. Only the vivid ones are remembered. Every persistent dream is worthy of our attention, Freud assures us, and his dictum is generally accepted by the profession."

"But this is a long, long way from the gift of prophecy!"

"No, it isn't! Consider that your subliminal mind is a vast storehouse, where every impression, however trivial, is registered and filed away. This includes the myriad of seemingly irrelevant facts that we are not aware of noting at all; every bit of color, each pebble in our paths, the faintest sound, the most elusive odor, a fragment of a dozen conversations overheard simultaneously during the intermission at a play, the meaningless sequence of numbers shouted by a quarterback at a football game you saw twenty years ago, as well as the license-number of every automobile you ever carelessly glanced at, the shape of the buttons on the coat of your great-uncle, the taste of a fruit eaten when you visited India as a child — all this lumber besides what *you* regard as *important* facts. You never forget anything; you only *think* you do. If, now, your brain had access to this stupendous mass of information covering every printed word you ever read, every spoken syllable you ever heard, why, you'd be a sort of little god, wouldn't you?"

"I'd be the original little tin god of Manhattan!"

"And inasmuch as there is no such thing as an isolated fact, each item being a link in a chain, with its own past and future, and its interrelation to other facts, the logical mind could, from its accumulated data, predict the future exactly as a professional reader can forecast the end of a novel. Thus, to make you into a very fair prophet, I would have merely to put you in touch with your own private collection of facts."

"Simple as that, eh? Mere matter of introduction, Mr. Holt, meet your own subconsciousness! Greetings, subcon, old top! Delighted, I'm sure!"

Jones grunted.

"I'm not irreligious, as you know; I suppose I'm more, or less *non-religious*. But every scientific explorer comes at times to a sort of psychic wall he recognizes as bearing the sign 'no trespassing.' In his rambles he finds a tree of knowledge, of whose fruit he knows he should not eat. Fact, Holt; I've passed up a number myself. Don't pretend to know why, but there are a few things too big for finite man to attempt. They belong to whomever you worship. Carry too high a voltage for our brains, at their present stage of development. Burn out our fuses, so to speak. Get the idea?"

"Oh, yes, as a theory. But I'd sure admire to meet up with that subconsciousness of mine!"

"That's managed easily enough. It's a shy bird — comes

out at night in your sleep, or in delirium, or the hypnotic state. But it's playing with dynamite!"

"You mean to tell me it is positively dangerous to be hypnotized?"

"Not in the least! It does not even place one in the power of the hypnotizer, as popular superstition has it. Of course, if one repeatedly submits to suggestion from another he does come in time to yield more readily; but I could not hypnotize you against your will, even if I had several times done so at your request. It's not the danger of that, but of the possible ascendancy of that subconsciousness, a sort of sleeping giant, an animal without soul or sentiment, which is normally subordinate to the mind, but abnormally its tyrant, as in the well authenticated instances of multiple personality. Good servant, poor master, you know."

"Well, I have a pretty good will, a copper-riveted digestion, and no nerves worth mentioning. I don't believe what you say, anyhow; but I'm game enough to take a chance! If you can open up that mental library of mine so I can prowl about in it and look into a few volumes, just enough, you understand, to do a few cute little parlor tricks of prophesying —"

For a long time Dr, Jones stared in silence at the faintly cynical face of Holt; so long, in fact, that the latter stirred uneasily, half suspecting that the physician was trying to hypnotize him. At length Jones shook himself and spoke.

"By George, you've no sort of business to tempt me like this! If you knew how many times I've *wanted* to try something of the sort, and was too decent to do it — afraid to, if you want to know. If your family history were not so sound, if I didn't know what a bone-headed sturdy, common sense old chap you are, I'd throw you through my window, sash and all, at the risk of ruining my crocuses planted just below. As it is — no, I'm damned if I do!"

"Quitter!" jeered Holt. "I've called your bluff!"

Jones laughed nervously. His voice actually trembled as he replied: "You win! I'll do it, and we'll see what happens!"

He rose and crossed the room to a rickety-cupboard, in which he fumbled until he found what he was after; a little upright rod with a sort of a two-bladed propeller balanced on the top, made of highly polished mirrors. This he set down upon the table, once more darkened the room and then, by means of a paper funnel, focused the light of a single incandescent upon the mirrors.

"Hypnotism, as you probably know, is produced most readily by eye-strain. If you fix your gaze upon this bright object, and relax physically and mentally, you will yield as soon as your retina is fatigued. I can produce auto-hypnosis at any time. Often do it when I'm alone here and haven't time for a real sleep. Don't think of anything in particular, or worse yet, make a conscious effort *not* to think. If I don't make the experiment now, I'll repent, and you'll lose your chance to be the only real prophet in captivity. Now look steadily!"

He turned a switch in the standard of the rod, and the little mirrors began to revolve swiftly and noiselessly.

"Didn't work, hey?" laughed Holt as Dr. Jones opened the wooden shutters a second time to the light of day.

"I didn't notice any hitch," said Jones coolly. "You were 'out' about three minutes."

"Huh! Well, I don't feel like a prophet," complained Holt, rubbing his eyes, which felt a little as they always did after following a five-reel photoplay.

"Much you know how a prophet feels! Did you expect to begin to bawl forth dire warnings before you leave the room?"

"Do you really believe you've changed a fairly good solicitor into a bum prophet just by making him stare at a silly toy in the dark for a few moments?"

"I've done *this*, my old college chum: I've roused your subconsciousness and suggested that for one week your brain shall have free access to its storehouse. One week, mind you! No longer. And if you are not glad when the seven days are past, I'm a chiropodist! I count on your mental fiber to stand the strain for that period."

"You flatter me! Meanwhile, as I propose to take in that photoplay, prophet or no, I'll toddle along. Thanking you for an interesting half-hour, *et cetera* —"

"You don't happen to feel any premonitions as to the weather for tomorrow, do you?" asked Jones, as he opened the door for him. "The reports say continued fair and warmer, but I've a particular reason for wishing to know definitely!"

"Not a premonish, doc!" Holt laughed back over his shoulder. "If I'm a prophet, I'm only a stuffed one!"

The screen-thriller put entirely out of Holt's mind the curious interview with his scientific friend. Once or twice that evening it occurred to him, but merely as a transient thought. He even forgot to mention it in the family circle, as he had intended. While preparing for bed, he had a moment of seriousness, recalling that to Dr. Jones anything relative to science was almost sacred, and that a pseudo-scientific hoax was utterly foreign to his nature. Unquestionably *he* believed what he had said.

Holt switched off the lights, and that night, if he dreamed at all, he could not recall having done so when he awakened next morning. Nor had he thought of the matter at all when he took his place at the head of the breakfast table.

It was out of a clear sky that the first demonstration of his new power came to him. There had been the usual desultory morning table-talk; references to items in the daily paper, weather banalities, grumblings because the toast was scorched, the give and take of a meal *en famille*, when in the midst of a reply to some idle query of his wife, when his eyes were resting by chance upon the serene face of his mother, there unrolled before him as a scroll the coming three years of her life.

As if he were witnessing a motion-picture, he beheld her seized with convulsions while she was knitting in her sunny chamber; saw the confusion of many distracted members of the family running to and fro, the arrival of the doctor and the administration of digitalis. She was tenderly put to bed, the nurse came, there followed weeks of anguish and a slow breaking down of her strength and courage, until the end came. Every step he followed, until they had laid her away at rest.

It seemed to him that at least fifteen minutes must have been consumed by the grievous portrayal; and yet presently he heard himself mechanically finishing his reply to his wife, beheld the very morsel of omelet balanced upon his fork, interrupted in its brief journey by his remark, and realized by a glance at the unsuspecting faces about the table, and at the dining-room clock, that time had been annihilated for him. All that he had seen had passed in a measureless flash.

Finishing breakfast as calmly as he could, he hastened from the house. The sinister feature of the strange experience he had undergone was this: he *knew* that it was truly prophetic. He realized now that while a false prophet might be deceived as well as deceiving, a true one could never mistake his message. He could not tell *how* he knew — but it was so.

Nevertheless, he proceeded directly to the office of a heart specialist well known to him socially, and requested him to accompany him back home, distant but a few blocks. He told him merely that he had reason to suspect that his mother was suffering from an organic heart trouble, explained that her health had always seemed of the best, and that she must not know the real purpose of the visit. Occasionally she had complained of flatulence; her color, too, seemed too brilliant for one of her years. It was arranged

that Dr. Young should be introduced as a stomach specialist, and that Holt had chanced to meet him on the corner, and invited him in. Something had been said about a little medicine on one occasion when her food distressed her.

It all passed off as naturally as Holt had hoped it might. There was some good-natured bantering, his mother scolded him for fetching in a strange young man without giving her time to put on her new silk house-gown, the examination was made with much thoroughness, and Holt departed with Dr. Young, after the latter had written out a prescription for — digitalis!

His diagnosis confirmed Holt's vision in every respect. His mother suffered from an incurable form of heart disease, *angina pectoris*, and was doomed to be a great sufferer.

As he stood by the entrance to Young's home, it suddenly grew dark overhead. Looking up, they noted that black thunderclouds had swept across the sun. The morning had been superb, fair weather had been indicated in the reports for the day. Yet, now, big drops began to dot the sidewalk, and distant thunder muttered. Holt found, to his surprise, that he clutched an umbrella he had taken from his rack, without knowing that he did so, or why he should. He went direct to his office now, arriving in a smart downpour.

During the rest of the day, nothing out of the ordinary occurred. It chanced to be a quiet week with him. He had just won a verdict in an important case, and for the present had nothing in hand but routine work; the reading of his mail, conferences with his associates, a directors' meeting, an office client or so. He had plenty of time to think; too much time, in fact. A knotty brief would have been a godsend. That night his sleep was uneasy, his dreams monstrous but disconnected. There was nothing in them to which he could attach the remotest significance.

The thought of his mother preyed upon him. In kissing her good-by as he left the office, her womanly intuition sensed an added solicitude which he believed he had concealed.

"What is it, Tommy?" she asked, holding him at arm's length and scanning him from her faded blue eyes. "Is anything wrong? You're not overworking, dear?"

"Fit as a fiddle, mumsey," he replied, forcing a laugh; and tore himself bruskly from her.

It came to him, his next vision, as he was boarding a trolley-car. He beheld, as plainly as if he were holding the paper before him, an account of the sensational thirty-point jump of Western Copper. Half a column there was, all told, with references to an inside ring which had kept the good thing strictly to itself, and cut a mammoth melon.

Yet, when he had finished, he was still setting one foot on the car-platform, which was not yet in motion. He could not estimate the minute fraction of time during which he had seen the future of Western Copper unfolded.

Holt did not dabble in stocks at all; but like thousands of others, he read the market reports as a matter of habit, much as he read the baseball columns without attending the games. Now, without the least uncertainty, he rode on past his office to a brokerage concern he knew by reputation, and, after telephoning his bank for his balance figures, drew a check for practically the entire amount of his deposit, and purchased a thousand shares outright. Had he been a dealer, he would have bought on margin and pyramided. As it was, he felt contented with a modest thirty thousand dollars' profit.

Returning to his office afoot, he happened to glance up the towering white facade of the new Obelisk Building, the latest skyscraper. Instantly, and in one of the mental flashes to which he was already becoming accustomed, he beheld a bulletin announcing its destruction by fire, under date of the forthcoming night at twelve.

Holt did not know the owner, nor his representatives, save by reputation. He knew nothing of the building itself save that it was the last word in "slow burning" construction — as the insurance people say — and that it housed enough concerns, with their battalions of clerks, to populate a western metropolis. He seemed to recall that a number of quasi-governmental agencies made it their headquarters, and it was possibly used by certain foreign interests, since the recollection of bewhiskered and crop-headed and ornately mustached gentlemen in frock coats and toppers, hurrying in and out of its broad portals, came to him as he paused momentarily, following the vision of the prophetic bulletin.

It seemed to Holt, distasteful as it was to do so, with no evidence whatever, his bounden duty to whisper a word of warning in the ear of whomever had the building's welfare in custody. But what on earth should be say? How introduce himself? Uncertainly he crossed over and entered, asking the starter for the agent's floor, and being ushered into a great bronze lift.

The pursy gentleman who received him at once upon

glancing at his card, looked much like a walrus, only warmer. His triple chins formed a series of rings above a low, discouraged collar, and his eyes expressed perpetual astonishment.

"Thinking of taking over one of our new suites, Mr. Holt?" he barked, his bristly mustache erecting and beating time to his syllables. "Glad to have your concern with us —"

"It's not business, Mr. Fletcher," Holt nervously began, seating himself and speaking in a conspirator's whisper. "In fact, I hardly know how to explain my errand."

He glanced at the bulging eyes and bristling lips, and plunged desperately ahead.

"You do not know me, but you perhaps know of me. I am certainly not an alarmist. It has come to me that — er — that is, I chanced to overhear a word or two — I am afraid that the Obelisk is in danger of fire this very night!"

Astonishment being Fletcher's normal mien, Holt was unable to tell whether he felt it now or not.

"Word? What word? What did you hear?"

"It was merely a fragment of talk that came to me in a crowded car," lied Holt, unable to bring himself to tell the truth. "I couldn't even see who uttered it. We — we were passing through a tunnel at the time, and though I listened, nothing more was said on the subject."

Fletcher gazed steadily at Holt.

"Well — of course I'm obliged," he said at length. "But when the Obelisk burns up, then cakes of ice will get — now — spontaneous combustion! The rate on their building is rock bottom. Mostly reinforced concrete and glass used in it. No wooden stairs or banisters or window sashes. Only the doors, and office furniture, you might say, and I leave it to you if it's easy to kindle a mahogany desk!"

"Don't seem so," admitted Holt, rising to go. "Just felt it my duty to speak of it — such a fine edifice — civic duty and all that sort of thing, you know!"

"Sure! We appreciate it — but with our force of watchmen and the materials used and everything — don't lose any sleep on our account, Mr. Holt. Have a cigar?"

Holt refused, and escaped, red of face, with the impression that Fletcher considered him mildly insane.

Nevertheless, that night when, making what excuses he could, he left home at eleven-thirty and posted himself in the deserted canyon dominated by the Obelisk, lovely in its towering whiteness as the searchlights from the harbor picked it up, he noted the pursy figure of Fletcher lurking in an office entrance across the way, and could not refrain from a grin. He was sorry that Fletcher saw him, and evidently Fletcher felt the same way about it, as he scuttled back into the shadows like a fat spider.

A policeman pounded by, trying the doors. A newsboy scampered through, empty handed and taking a short cut home. A shabby nondescript crept past, muttering to himself, possibly some former magnate, Holt reflected, haunting the battlefield of ancient triumphs. Taxicabs shot through from time to time, taking advantage of the absence of traffic.

Eleven fifty-five; and so slowly did the hands seem to move on a big illuminated dial within Holt's range of vision that twice he drew forth his watch to reassure himself by the spinning second hand. Then, almost as if the clock hand had leaped over the last three minutes, midnight boomed forth; and simultaneously Holt was hurled against a granite wall by a terrific explosion. When he recovered his wits, flames were bursting from the second and third story windows of the Obelisk.

A long time he watched the firemen at work, as they magically appeared upon the scene. Finally he returned home and to bed.

He was aroused the following morn by a message which urgently but courteously requested his presence at police headquarters.

The pop-eyed and bristling Fletcher was seated in the chief's office when he arrived, breakfast-less, in a taxi. The chief he knew slightly. After the customary desultory greetings, the police head spoke.

"Last night, Mr. Holt, the Obelisk was partly wrecked by a powerful explosive, which we have reason to believe was planted by German spies. You may not be aware that exceedingly valuable reports of their activities are kept there. Now, Mr. Fletcher, the agent naturally recalled at once your warning of yesterday. I feel sure you did not tell him all you knew. You were not obliged to, of course. Probably you dreaded notoriety, or feared lest you implicate some innocent party, I can assure you that any information, however trivial it may seem to you, is necessary to me now. You shall be fully protected, and no innocent party shall suffer even embarrassment. I have shown you my cards. Will you do the same?"

"Chief, if I could I would. But I have absolutely nothing, not even a suspicion, to voice!"

The chief smoked in silence for a moment, while Fletcher wriggled in the chair into which he was so tightly wedged that Holt irrelevantly wondered how he had got in, or could get out. A silly picture of the pursy agent hobbling out with the chair clamped to him caused him to laugh nervously.

"You were in the immediate vicinity, Mr. Holt, when the bomb exploded," suggested the chief seriously.

A sudden resolution seized Holt. He determined to tell the whole truth, no matter how ridiculous it made him appear — the whole truth save only his séance with Dr. Jones.

"I'm going to tell you everything, chief, even though you consider me ripe for a padded cell," he gasped.

"That's right!" approved the officer, settling back comfortably. "I knew you were the sort of citizen we could rely on. Shoot!"

Whereupon Holt did. He explained that he had of late been dreaming things which later came out exactly as he had been warned. He told about his mother, giving the address of the attending physician. He related his purchase of Western Copper, on a "hunch," furnishing the name of the broker, and adding that this was his first transaction of the sort. Then had followed the vision of the Obelisk fire — there had been no inkling of an explosion — and, on impulse, he had warned Fletcher. And that was all.

Even as he finished, a morning paper was thrust through the slot in the office door, and rustled to the floor, opening face upward as it fell.

The chief glanced at it, stooped over and picked it up, and after a startled look handed it to Holt. It was a marked "extra," detailing the phenomenal jump of Western Copper, and the turmoil resulting there-from.

When Holt, after leaving headquarters and snatching a cup of coffee, had proceeded to his own office, he was greeted with the news that it, with several others, had been gutted by a fire the night past. He smiled grimly, reflecting that he was a failure so far as foreseeing that particular and rather important event was concerned. Evidently a prophet had his ups and downs. His visions were not subject to call. He could conceive that Daniel himself might foretell the fall of an empire, the very end of the world, and yet never dream that he should see a live lion!

Already he heartily wished the week, of which but two days had passed, were wiped off the calendar. He was nervous as a cat, slept poorly, had no appetite. He dreaded the recurrence of his visions, and scarcely thought of the tidy fortune he had made overnight in Western Copper.

Above all, his mind dwelt upon his mother. That saintly lady, whose life had been spent in doing her simple duty, and far more; in bringing happiness to a wider circle year by year, taxing her strength and her purse to ease the lot of unfortunates she hunted up. Her creed was simple, yet world wide, her faith absolute. Religion? Holt clenched his hands. Why should God allow that pure and faithful heart, that had beat for so many all these years, to throb out in final agony? Had she not at the least earned a gentle sleep, a peaceful death in her bed — as painless as a drunkard's death, in his cups? *Was* there a God? He sought to put the torturing surmises out of his mind. But he found he lacked the power.

He tried, now, to avoid thinking of his loved ones save in the most casual way. He lived in torment lest, as he gazed in his wife's eyes, there should suddenly unroll before him another of the hated scrolls whereon he should behold, written in letters of fire, her doom. He prayed for the blessed boon of ignorance. Too late, he realized the frightful isolation of those who share the gifts of the gods, who have eaten of the Forbidden Fruit.

Deity alone could endure such a blighting burden as omniscience. And deity possessed its anodyne — omnipotence! It could change the measured and implacable march of events, fend destiny from tender souls, reach down, protecting hand to the hopeless and the suffering. Or — *could* it?

Such a record of the predestined future, which God could inscribe at will, could even He change a single link in its chain, disturb its connective tissue, without shattering past and future? Because, if He could, then no such record could be written. One was forced to deny either divine omniscience, or omnipotence. The answer of course, was that to God there is no past nor future. Eternity was not an endless line, but a circle. He visioned all in a flash, even as Holt had seen his own puny glimpse of the yet-to-be.

As if his gift increased with each recurrence, his visions multiplied to a point where his brain seemed to reel beneath the awful burden. On the cars, passing along the crowded streets, in his club or wherever men congregated, a blinding series of horoscopes danced before his eyes. People in whom he took not the slightest interest, men and women he vainly tried to recall ever having seen before, casual strangers, bared their futures to him as it seemed.

He glanced at a loutish youth leaning against an L post, a half-consumed cigarette drooping from lips too indolent to hold it; and instantly the figure straightened, the eyes cleared, the color changed to a virile bronze, and Holt beheld a lean, khaki-clad man, rifle clutched in firm hand, surging "over the top" from some far distant trench.

Or, he nodded abstractedly to a great financier, and at once his well-fitting clothes took on the stripes of prison, and he was doing a lock step for hypothecating the funds of a trust he had handled for years. In the twinkling of an eye people took on new forms, new faces, and assumed, now a tailored prosperity, again the cerements of death.

Nor were his business hours encroached upon, his time stolen. The slow tragedy of a decade defiled past him while his heart throbbed once. He was reminded of the strange experiences of drug-addicts, who lived through unspeakable epochs of world transformation during the revolution of a swiftly moving car wheel, and of the minutely detailed life-

history drowning men were said to experience.

But in sleep, troubled as were his dreams, he never received any prophetic visions. All, he supposed, must be based upon the mysterious stores yielded up by his subconsciousness; but he could not concede how, or when, the facts had touched his senses. Perfect strangers stood before him, their naked history unexpurgated to his insight; he met old friends, and received not a hint of their destiny.

His loneliness was absolute. There were none with whom he could share his burden. The few who might believe him would be alarmed and repelled; others would consider him unbalanced.

The second real shock to his spirit occurred as he was watching his little son romp on the lawn. He was a sturdy lad of ten, neither precocious nor wayward. Of a sudden, Holt beheld him lying in his casket, smelled the heavy odors of flowers, saw the sun strike through the stained glass of St. Luke's, heard the shuffle of little feet as Arthur's mates of the vested choir filed past to look upon his quiet face.

With a terrible effort of will he forced the picture to pass away. He felt fatigued, as after violent physical exertion. But at least, he had evaded the precise *date* of the death. The true horror of prophecy was now clear to him. That night as he knelt by his bed, he prayed for the boon of ignorance, for the kindly curtain which he had presumptuously rent asunder, to fall once more before the blinding future.

Late upon a murky afternoon, Dr. Jones packed his old clay pipe, and sank into a broken-springed easy chair with a grunt of satisfaction. He had succeeded in fertilizing a sea urchin's egg in a saline solution. He did not in the least need a sea urchin; there were millions of livelier, healthier ones along the Atlantic coast. But he had wished to demonstrate that he *could* do it — and he *had*.

He picked up his morning paper, as yet unglanced at, and prepared to relax. Before he had so much as run over the headlines, his door was flung open without the preliminary of knocking, and a disheveled, panting figure collapsed into a chair opposite, glaring at him from blood-shot eyes.

"Holt! My dear fellow! What on earth is the matter? Let me get you a drink of something cold and —"

His visitor stayed him with a violent gesture.

"No! I don't want a drink of anything cold, nor hot; nor a shot in the arm, nor even any soothing professional twaddle! What I want is your attention!"

The physician regarded him with a puzzled yet affectionate interest, and settled back in his chair, puffing at his pipe.

"You have it; shoot!" he said tersely.

Thereupon Holt related in detail his amazing experiences of the past few days. Jones made hurried notes on his cuff, and two or three times interrupted with a brusk question. He seemed deeply interested, and with the unfolding of the story his absorption grew.

When Holt paused, he spoke excitedly.

"This is immensely important, old man! I can assure you that when I have been able to check up your facts with absolute precision, the paper I'll write will make us both fam —"

"Fine!" interrupted Holt, gritting his teeth. "But how about *me*? What about my horrible situation?"

"Oh — that! You are, of course, in a highly nervous state; hysterical; jumpy; all that sort of thing. Perfectly natural, too. But I shall be able to point out to you that you are not to take your subconsciousness — or rather your conclusions from its memories — too literally. I shall explain —"

"How will you explain *this*?" whispered Holt, leaning forward while his hands gripped the chair arms. "I haven't told you my latest vision! Jones, as truly as I sit here before you, I saw you, at precisely six o'clock tonight hugging and — and — kissing *my wife*! Yes, damn it! And she was returning your endearments!"

A faint color flooded Jones's pale face, and astonishment gleamed in his eyes.

"What rot!" he finally gasped. "Why I never saw her! And you know about how much of a woman's man I am, even if — er — your wife could be — ah —"

"Nevertheless, true as all this is, I am so solemnly sure that it will come to pass exactly as I have seen it, and as I have foreseen other events fulfilled, that I propose at least to be in your company from now on until six. Get on your hat and come home with me!"

Jones started convulsively.

"No!" he protested. "Lock me up — lock your wife up — do anything you like; but don't bring us face to face in this preposterous fashion!"

"Jones —" Holt's voice was quiet yet surcharged with omen — "you are a doctor. You can see the condition I am in. *Don't try to thwart me!*"

With one long glance into the other's eyes, the physician nodded, rose and took hat and gloves from a table.

"Lead on!" he snapped.

It was already well past five, when the two boarded a car at the corner; and when, without another word having been exchanged, they were admitted to the house, the hall clock showed a quarter to the hour.

The maid who had opened the door detained her master.

"That long distance call you expected from Chicago, had just come as you rang, sir," she said.

Holt nodded.

"All right! I'll take it. Jones, just be seated a moment in there, and excuse me, will you? The library, Anna!"

As the caller entered the room indicated, the telephone voice of his friend came plainly to his ears.

It was some minutes later when Holt, having finished, hurriedly crossed the hall to the library, glancing as he did so at the clock, which was on the very point of striking six.

Three seconds later he stood as if frozen, in the doorway. In the very middle of the room, Jones, the old, faithful, ascetic Jones, held his gentle, modest wife in a tenacious clinch. Her arms were about his rather frowsy neck — Jones always needed a haircut — and her smooth cheek endured, nay invited, his kisses!

Somewhat to the onlooker's astonishment, he felt no resentment at the extraordinary spectacle, which above all others, spells tragedy: Pain, grief, despair, all these gripped him to the full; but anger not at all. For he perceived that fate held them all and moved them about like puppets, Jones could no more avoid what was to be, than could he, or his spotless wife. There were certain amenities to be gone through with, of course; presently he would do something; shoot Jones, or divorce his wife, or both. But not in hot blood!

The betrayer standing with his back to the door, Holt's wife presently raised herself a-tiptoe and, glancing over his shoulder, perceived her husband.

No trace of decent shame, no fear, could he descry in her eyes. Rather, she smiled sweetly upon him as he stood there, dragging at the portieres.

"Isn't it *wonderful*, dear?"

"It is!"

"But you don't seem to *realize*; it's *Frank!*"

"I *ought* to know; I brought him here, didn't I?"

Something in his voice arrested her attention. A little frown on her white brow, she added — "after all these years! My little, lost, baby brother, who didn't go down with the *Macedonia* after all!"

Something gave out in Holt's legs. He staggered two steps and collapsed on a divan. Had it been three steps distant, he would have hit the floor.

His brain spun round like a giant top. A jumble of half memories spewed up by his subconsciousness danced before him.

The unquestionable similarity between their voices, and the family nose; he was not aware of having ever noted these, yet he must have done so! A trick of lifting one eyebrow — a mutual hatred of the sea — above all —

"It's strange you didn't bring him here long ago!" his wife's slightly querulous voice broke in upon his thoughts. "You are *so* stupid! You knew my maiden name was Jones!"

THE FLOATING ISLAND

by Philip M. Fisher, Jr.

I.

The Old Man was a hellcat; and just as the leatherneck Marine port-armsing his cabin door began really to shiver at what his doom would be when the Old Man found out his delaying my entering now, the sudden scream inside froze us both. And probably every deck swab in the after part of the ship, too.

Not that it actually was a scream, of course. But the Old Man had a way of expressing himself, now purring soft, now — Why, if you've ever heard a big tomcat, starting off calm-like in the black shadows under the moon, gradually speeding up more wicked as he got het up, then climaxing with a grand blood-boiling yowl, you know what I mean. Hellcat was right.

He had funny eyes, too, the Old Man. Sort of gray, sort of green. And nighttimes he'd prowl the ship, like a scrawny hunched-over alley tom looking for a rat that hadn't ought to be AWOL from its hammock after tattoo. You might be suffocating under the signal bunting in the flag-bag up on the bridge, maybe, you and the gang, with a dowsed flashlight in your ribs, and one of the dice working back so's you had to gag or swallow. You couldn't hear his feet on the deck; but you knowed he was there. I know *I* knowed he was there — once. A little black unmoving shadow he was, al-

though you couldn't see him; bending forward, his head out and sort of cocked-like to one side. And you could almost see his stiff little gray whiskers pricked out, wriggling in the dark like trying to catch your scent and his ears running the frequencies to tune in on your very breathing. And *I* knowed his little green-gray eyes was burning green through the canvas and bunting that I thought would hide me.

And then come his voice — low, drawling, unpleasant, like when the alley prowler sights his rival from that black moon shadow, and begins to whisper his preliminary insults. With his tail slowly beginning to swish, and his claws slowly creeping in and out!

"Ah," the Old Man would whisper deep and sad-like to himself, "so there has been a little frolic up here on my bridge. With a pair of nice little ivories bought at Wing On's in Shanghai, pre-war. Yet what an inhospitable party it was, to break up just when another guest was coming along. And to hide, too!" And then his voice would begin to rise — just a trifle of a little rise. "Or perhaps they thought it was a ghost lifting up out of the sea, a ghost coming to taunt them for their sins. So they dive into the flag-bags, all five of them, if the bulges in the canvas indicate anything at all." And then he heaves a sigh, such a sad sigh it would almost make you gulp. "Ah, what a pity — tut, tut tut! Tomorrow, I see, there

will be work to do, for me and for my executive and for five new seamen, too, flang back on deck with the crows ripped off their sleeves, and packing slush buckets and swabs just like the other common sailors they so despise. And yet —" And now would come that growling sound in the dark out there: "And yet, what joy for the Bosun! Five busted petty officers to help massage his decks." And then would whip out a roar that would make your heart almost explode, and you knowed you was going to die and not easy either, and down would go that dice. "Come out of that, you !**#**! ! — ?** !!!#*!??! * — !* !**?*!!! hellions, before I sick my company of !***! #**&! — marines onto you. *Yow!*"

Hellcat? A grand fleet of them, all in that scrawny little Old Man of ourn.

Well now, when the leatherneck guarding his cabin door hears that scream, he knowed right off he'd better come out of his port arms and pass me through. So I whisper one word more as I sort of saunter by, and his face is purple as I push open the cabin door.

The Old Man is slipping up and down his cabin, his thin side-twisted nose pointing out, his tail swishing, and his head just a trifle a-cockbill to port. And when he swings next, he stops short, and still as a figurehead except for the wiggle of those whiskers, he peers at me with them gray-green eyes.

"Ah," he says. "And so our quartermaster has arrived!" He pauses; then he says soft-like: "I am sorry, but the mess attendant has cleared away the cinnamon toast and tea. But won't you have a seat?"

I look at him. And then, somehow, I just sit down.

For a minute his eyes seem to jump out. Then he gives a little grunt, and slips closer and looks down upon me, swishing his tail. And after about another minute I kind of arise to my feet again.

"Ah," he purrs. Then suddenly he snaps.

"You was ashore in the village up this river when the ship was down here before Pearl Harbor?"

I stare; and then my head jerks.

"And you saw the chief of that *barrio*, the native *datu*?"

My head jerks again, though some of the slack is coming back to my neck cords.

"Ah," the Old Man purrs. "And since a certain little incident that occurred five months and eighteen days ago, an incident on the bridge in which, Quartermaster, I believe you were involved, you may recall that orders is orders, eh?"

"Yes, sir," I says, very earnest.

"How very fortunate!" he says.

"Very, sir," I says.

"I am about to give other orders," he says, cocking his head again, and laying one finger against his nose.

"Yes, sir," I says. And a pretzel was wriggling in my stomach.

"This *datu*," he says, "changed his occupation when the Japs occupied this island. Life was too monotonous, maybe, or possibly it was the heat. Or perhaps one of his fourteen wives got somewhat on his nerves. Or even it might have been gold. For he sailed forth in his canoe of state, Quartermaster, to join the Japanese in some slight quizzling matters along this very coast."

"Piracy," I says, alert.

"A quizzling," he repeats, stroking his nose. "Compared to which mere old-time island piracy is as clean as an act of God." He paused a minute, then says: "And you, Quartermaster, because you alone might recognize him if you saw him again, are given a special detail." He looks at me sidewise. "To catch him, Quartermaster! To catch this quizzling rat!"

"To catch this quizzling rat, sir," I says. And something cold trickles down my back.

"But," the Old Man goes on, "there are not many quizzlings among the Filipinos, Quartermaster. So information comes to us that at last he is returning to his headquarters up this Rio Bontok. At the mouth of the Rio Bontok," he says, "is a low, flat mangrove swamp. To port side as you run upstream, this swamp is broad, smoothing into the main upper land. But to starboard it reaches out to sea like a long narrow tongue. With five men, Quartermaster, you will land on that tongue-like swamp to starboard. You will camouflage the motor-sailer so that it cannot be seen even by the eye of Allah. Yet — with a bayonet in his softer parts, if need be — you keep its engineer so alert he will hear the wings of a moth. And when this *datu*, this renegado quizzling rat, swings upriver after returning from his pleasant occupation of murder and looting and betraying loyal men, as he is expected to within thirty-six hours, you will capture him, Quartermaster. You quite understand?"

"Sir," I says, "I sure do understand."

"You will under no circumstances leave that point of swamp, Quartermaster, until you sight this !*!&#!*!!?!* rat."

"Under no circumstances, sir," I says, nodding hard.

"Orders," purrs the Old Man, "is what?"

II.

Maybe you think our Old Man figured he rated the blue flag with four white stars at the main truck, instead of this ancient high-waisted bucket with a lot of smokestacks and a couple eight-inch guns. Maybe you think he figured that enlisted men was just dirt to sweep around with them cat's whiskers, and to glare at with them green cat's eyes, and to pussyfoot after in the dark o' night.

But you're dead wrong if you think that.

There isn't in the whole Navy a finer, squarer, humaner officer from one stripe up, than him. And while he run that skinny old cruiser out in the Asiatic, from long before the war and then on special duty during it, they was three hundred and sixty-two and a half men — counting the top-drawer artist in the ship's writer's office — who'd 'a' flang you to the sharks if you even *imagined* to yourself that he wasn't. And they wasn't a single half of one of them men who the Old Man himself wouldn't have cat-spit in a General Court Judge Advocate's eye for, and plenty more, if he thought he was getting a dirty deal. If some dumb deck-swab on the ship done something extra handsome, even if he done it accidental, he'd jump him a grade if possible, give him extra foreign-port leave, or at very least read him a public line come Saturday inspection. He'd never fail. But if that same deck-swab done something ornery, or *forgot* something, he'd chuck him to the Bosun for enlightenment so fast the feller wouldn't come to for a couple paydays. Don't I know that!

So I hightails it to the Exec, and he and me pick out the men to go capture the *datu* with me.

We choose Bones, from my own bridge gang, a lean, thirsty slicker who took my shirt last payday, but a terrible fighter; and studying ICS on chicken farming for when war's over all the time he ain't sleeping, eating, fighting or shooting craps. And Chips, the best Nip-hater I ever see, to toss up a shelter and to use his axe if the time come. And both of us in one breath decide on Spuds, the Commissary Steward, because he still ain't popular on account of what happened in Hungry Gulf — that's Lingayen — before the Japs hit us, when we was laying around watching the old destroyers practicing their fish; and I don't have to bring him back, the Exec says, if they's other alligators in that swamp. Then the second class Pharmacist's mate, to watch the quinine and water and also just in case. And a couple hands more who had beef and guts and something better than the C-minus brains I been reading about.

"That'll make six not counting yourself, Quartermaster," Exec says.

I kind of look back at him, thoughtful like.

"The captain," I says, "he sort of mentioned only five, sir."

The Exec, he looks back at me, thoughtful like, too.

"Wait," he says.

After a while he comes back. He kind of collapses into his chair.

"It'll be all right, Quartermaster. Six, not counting you." He takes a deep breath. And then he grins. "I'll see the chief puts his best gas-engine man into Number Two motor-sailer, and gets Boats to put in a bow-hook as well as a good live, hard-hitting cox'n, so that'll make an extra man or so who'll not count on account they'll be necessary adjunks to the boat's crew." And he gives me a slow wink, which shows the good feller *he* was. "Naturally," he says then, "you will be in charge. Might be a good idea to make Chips second in command, too — older than the rest, and a level head, eh?"

"That's nice, sir," I says. "Thanks."

He looks at me kind of funny. Then he grins again.

"Yeah," he says. "Well," he says, "this *datu* skunk's got reputation, so you got yourself a job. And frankly, I don't get the captain's idea in not sending an officer along." He stops short there, and after a minute he sighs. "Well," he says then, "what exceptional orders, if any, did the captain give you?"

I kind of recalls important bits of the little palaver in the Old Man's cabin. He grins again, but is serious almost at the same time.

"I'll just add this," he says. "We shove off over the horizon as soon as you okay your landing. You'll be on your own. Not even any air snooping around. We want that bozo trapped clean. And you probably noticed the barometer's been nose-diving. Radio silence was broke this morning with a typhoon warning. So get to your spot without delay, and when you get there, get set even quicker. Right after noon chow, eh?"

"They is things worse than typhoons, sir," I says. "We'll be ready at thirteen-fifteen . . . sharp."

And we was.

III.

The sea is pushing our stern in long slick swells when finally we closes in on the *rio*'s mouth, and they're dull gray with the haze that's come over the sun. The motor-sailer just climbs up the side of one, with the engine grunting hard and smooth, and then swoops down the other side with the engine racing and every thwart a-rattle. But except for that, all in the boat is silent. Except for Spuds, who does his thinking out loud, and keeps up a continual grumble at having to leave off taking *pesos* from the war-crop lubbers of the crew playing acey-deucy. With things still ahead to plan for, this skinny shark has to bellyache about the profits he has to leave. He's got a front tooth that's a pivot and loose continual, so he has to stop every minute when he gets forgetful in his yammering and shove it up into place. But even with him muttering, it seems very silent out here.

And now as we come in to the low dark green of the shore, we could see that the Old Man had the right dope. As usual! And we could *smell* that he had the right dope, for mangrove swamps never read no Listerine ad.

To port, the land was sort of rounded out like a smooth-laying fringe of the hills. But to starboard a low-laying tongue of it crept out with the *rio*'s muddy flood. And as we come closer yet, we could see the low mangroves, each of them standing up on its spraddled roots, like they was afraid of the oozy black mud and the steaming black potholes of smelly bilge about them. And we seen them funny things hopping along the edge of the mud, kind of like tadpoles six inches long, gray gelatin sort of, and with only two legs and them right up under their bulging heads and poppy black eyes. And along the mud rim of the shore millions of little red, white and blue crabs, scuttling about sort of spangling even under the hazy sun, and then in a twinkle disappearing into their little pockmark holes so for a minute you wouldn't know whether you'd dreamed them or they had really been there.

Then Chips, standing forward by the bow-hook, hollers: "Here! Catch aholt of that log, Hooky."

The engineer jams in the reverse, and the motor-sailer shudders alongside. Chips eases for the jump, the line in one hand, his axe in his belt. But that warty mud-colored log sort of slides backwards under us, and I catch an awful cold green eye turned up at me just as it submerges altogether. And I jump near out of my socks at Spuds' yell:

"My God! An alligator! We can't land here. The Old Man's went nuts."

"We has orders to land here," I says, through my teeth. "We can land here. And we do."

Spuds sputters, shoves up his pivot tooth, but Chips cuts him off, pointing over through the roots and tangle and muck.

"There's a high place yonder."

"Aye," says I, taking over command. "Looks ideal. Elevation, drainage, a sou'west exposure. The sewers is in, though something in the air tells me they need repair. The street work kind of shows wartime neglect, too, and I doubt the water system. However," I says, "them coconut palms give us a kind of reservoy, eh?"

That's my idea right off, see? They wasn't any doubts now; like the Exec had said, they was a job ahead of us.

I glanced to seaward. The ship was still hove to, her smoke low and flat over her as if the air was too light to hold it up — like always when there's weather, real weather, in the offing. That was sort of in the background just that second, though. The thing way out in front was that I could have swore I could feel the Old Man's eyes on me — green and calculating through a long glass leveled over the bridge sill.

Well, we clambered over the side and tied up. Stepping on roots and slipping and lurching and squishing, it took us plenty of time to get our gear over to that high spot — including most of our fighting equipment, too, so's not to leave it all in the boat that night. But even that high spot wasn't half dry, with the swamp steam hanging low.

I left Chips starting camp operations, and wallowed back to the boat with the cox'n, the blackgang engineman and Bones, and we put-putted out into the middle of the stream. Just holding her there against the current, Bones, according to plan, semaphored the bridge that we was okay. We got a Roger, and that was that. Before we was tied up in that hidden little nook between the mangroves, the ship was showing her stern. We was alone. No radio, no air to look us over; just us. And a rat of a quizzling sneaking up somewheres along the coast, and with him twenty *bolo* artists with their sweet-balanced neck-clipping knives.

Chips had things as shipshape as could be. A kind of

deck smoothed under the three palms, and the tarp up like an awning. Spuds has the little gas burner hissing, and jamoke smelling good even through the swamp smell and the mosquito spray Doc has thrown out. We eats, but fast. Then I orders a footway of crisscross mangrove branches so's we could change boat watches without a light, or get to the boat fast if the lookout gives the hoot. It's about thirty yards in all, and with the whole gang pitching the job is done by the time the sun set and it was all of a sudden dark. It was terrible dark, and we was sure alone there now, on our two-by-four mound in the middle of that narrow little tongue of swamp.

"An' did you notice how the water in them black potholes would ripple when you jump hard on the ground?" says Chips through the dark.

"The whole swamp is only tied together with roots and mud," I says.

A kind of coughing grunt comes through the blackness. Then a splash. Just one.

"What's that?" whispers Spuds, like he'd heard a ghost.

"'Nother 'gator," says Chips, matter of fact.

"It's a hell of a place for the Old Man to send us to wait for a pirate in!" Then he whispers quick again: "What's that?"

"Something up the palm tree," says Doc, very calm like Chips. "Better shin up and investigate, Spuds. Probably a snake."

"Who — *me*?" Spuds yelps. "Aw, shut up." Then: "There it is again!"

It was a little squeaking chirp, right close. We all jumped. Not ten feet away has appeared a pair of little green glowing dots in the blackness. Close together, alive. Before I knowed it, I shot my electric torch.

"Huh," I says. "A monkey." But I feel kind of trembly.

And Chips says, kind of thoughtful:

"Thought it really was a snake this time. I seen one up Subic Bay country oncet. Measured nineteen feet long."

There is no talking for quite a while. We just sit there, sort of feeling things. Not even smoking, lest the *datu* glimpse a glow or even smell it way out to sea. But there is sound around us, like the heavy deep droning of the forced-draft blowers of an old four-stacker destroyer in the distance. Mosquitoes — millions of them. And the heat is heavy upon us; and the hot wet smell of rotting things.

Then a sort of shuffling sound, and then a little clicking. Then Bones' whisper, sort of hopeful-like.

"I brung 'em along," he says. "Got a blanket spread, and I'll shoot anybody for a *peso* a crack."

Kind of sorrowful I says: "Can't have no light, Bones."

"I can read 'em in the dark," he says, real alert and bright.

I just start a very opprobrious answer when they comes a sigh of wind. A moment more, a real gust of it. The little monkey in the palm tree lets out another scared chirp. Then a great whooshing rushes through the mangroves, and the canvas over us bangs like rifle rapid fire. They is a funny moment of absolute calm, with the little monk' scaring the pants off me diving into my arms and clinging tight. And then it comes: one grand roar of solid wind and water and branches and eternal blackness blacker than the plain black-

ness of the night. Rugged? In one second flat our camp simply ain't.

IV.

Hollering for the gang to leech onto our gear, I shoved the monkey over to Bones and crawled along our footway for the motor-sailer.

I had to crawl. That solid wind had already pushed the sea up into the *rio*'s mouth, and the footway was half afloat with the potholes sucking and gurgling alongside. I has to use my light now; but I wasn't worried about that. If the *datu* and his bloody playmates in their big war canoe was near enough to glimpse it, they had plenty to worry about themselves. Besides, these islanders can smell a typhoon two days off, and Chips and I had already agreed they'd of holed up in some little cove to lay up until this one had come and blowed itself out. The main thing now was if our boat was safe.

She was — so far.

When my torch found the cox'n, he was crouching and clinging in the bouncing stern, and his white face had relief on it like he'd seen the Lord himself shoving through hell's blackness to save him. Lurching and reeling and cussing and fumbling, we put out every line we had to the roots of other mangroves more protected from the direct force of the wind. We lashes down everything in the boat itself. We lash and double lash the tarp over the engine box. And now, even with the boat double secured, I has to threaten the lookout for mutiny. He hollers against the wind with his mouth to my ear, and it's only a whisper. Suppose he was tore loose, he hollers, and him and the motor-sailer go whooping out into the *rio* and then onto the raging sea.

I grabs branches, and with one foot over the jumping gunwale, feels for the runway. With water up to my chin and pure reservoys of rain bending my back in, I crawls back. They'd about give me up, and was figuring a rescue party. But they'd got most of the tarp looped around a palm tree bole, with our little ammunition dump solid and covered, and most of the grub and cans of water salvaged.

So we just hangs on — "deef, dumb, dreary and drenched" — huh! And waited. And every now and then, though you'd of thought it couldn't get heavier, the scream and roar of the typhoon would go up another number, and our bit of *terra not so firma* would shake and shudder like it needed quinine by the ton. I hear Doc's whisper; I know it's really a yell.

"How high do the numbers go on that there Beaufort Scale of Winds?"

"Twelve," I hollers.

"Then what the heck do they do when they runs out of numbers?"

"They prays," I hollers back again.

And then I hears another whisper. Spuds, coming down sudden with religion, and I reckon he's having some time of it making the good Lord hear.

Well, it was around 3-0-0 when suddenly there is peace and quiet. One minute all hell a-raging, the next you was wondering if it'd happened at all.

For the fourth or fifth time that night I crawls to check the motor-sailer again. And this time, with only the low moaning and swishing of the heaving mess under me, I hear a sort of agonized hopeless whimpering. I get words: "Oh, oh, I gotta have help. O Lord, I couldn't make them hear, an' I gotta have help. Get the quartermaster and the engineman and the rest of them to come quick. . . . I gotta —"

The *datu*? Does I hump myself then! And against the blackness I see the even blacker figure of the lookout, bending up and down, and seeming to be slinging something over the side each time. . . .

In one minute after my yell the whole gang, with coffeepot, empty ration-tins, hats, even shoes, is joining the lookout's single bucket — bailing, bailing, bailing. For the almost solid rain and the breaking seas had filled the motor-sailer almost up to the thwarts with even the engine box near out of sight.

Two solid hours, with that boat heaving like a lubber's stomach to chuck us over the side. But finally I puts the bowhook in to relieve the plumb wore out lookout, and we drags back to the mound and tries to sleep.

But a dozen times I jerk awake. And oncet with a most terrible jerk, and I shook awake the engineman, and he groans: "Gosh, don't I know that, don't I know that. But I gotta have light to do the job."

And finally comes the dawn, like they say, and whilst the others was working on the little gas burner for hot jamoke, the engineman and I make for the boat again. And me, there's one red hot question burning for an answer, and quick; and the engineman knows exactly what I mean.

Then I glimpse the bowhook's back, and it seems tense-like and him not hearing my hail I give another hoot.

He jerks about, and his face is the most perplexed you ever see. He stares at me, bug-eyed, for a full half minute, and sort of holds my eye though from the corner of it I can see the engineman tearing at the engine-box lashings and hear him cussing low and hard.

And then his arm shoots out, across the *rio*.

"Look!" he whispers, sort of hoarse. "Look!"

Well, I climbs into the boat and over the backboard separating the forward part from the engine cockpit, and I looks. Just the muddy water spreading away and away, and another island four-five mile to north'ard and west.

With his arm still out, the lookout's hand buzzes like it's a hummingbird's wing.

"No. *No!* The river — the land!"

And then I do stare, with funny prickles on my skin. *The other side of the rio's plumb gone!*

And then we jump at a yell from behind us. And here staggers Spuds, arms waving, goggle-eyed, hoarse too.

"For the love of heaven, what's happened to us now! It's the end of the world come on us, and the land all gone but ourn. Oh, why did I ever join the Navy? Oh, why did I ever leave solid ground?"

"Spuds," I says, calm-like, "as to them last questions, every man on this ship would give sixty-four dollars for an opprobrious reply. As to your inquiry Number One," I says, "it ain't the land that's gone. It's us."

V.

We'd sighted one of them things a couple of years before, down off Cebu. And as I and Chips made the rounds, with Spuds wringing his hands in our wake, we knowed doubly that I was right. We was on a chunk of land, if you could call it that, about a hundred and twenty-five yards fore and aft, by about sixty-five in beam. *And floating.*

It was only a couple weeks after a typhoon, that time our ship had sighted that one. A low, flat, dark green island it looked, about twice as big as the ship herself. I was on the bridge, and knowed the chart from going over it with the O. O. D. — that's the Officer of the Deck. And the Old Man was there, squinting one green eye through the long glass.

"'Taint on the chart," he suddenly snaps.

"No sir," nods the Exec.

"Humph," grunts the O. O. D., then new on the ship. "Then it's riz from the bottom of the sea."

"Then how," asks the Old Man, turning slow with his head out like a turtle's, "how do you account for mangroves and palm trees growing on the bottom of the sea?"

The O. O. D. kind of lays back, his face the color of a powder burgee, which is nothing but solid red.

"It's a floating island," says the Old Man softly.

"Yes sir," agrees the Exec now, "a floating island."

"Part of a swamp from some *rio* hereabouts," the Old Man goes on in a nice school-teachery voice. "The roots get all twisted and matted together, and for maybe a century the mud deposits on them when the *rio's* at high stage, and so more trees grows, and grasses and vines. Then one day three separate situations occur at the same moment: high tide, the river in flood, and a violent seaward wind. The whole mess is tore loose from its moorings and goes floating forth upon the high seas. A menace," he concludes, eying us all, "to navigation."

"A menace indeed, sir," nods the Exec, taking over the deck now and looking alert. "Ought to be blowed up." The Exec was also fire-control officer, loving his job.

"Ah," says the Old Man, very calm. "That would make forty menaces instead of one. Radio Manila, Mate, as to position, current and direction and force of wind, and have them pass he word. Only another storm can bust up that island as it should ought to be busted up. In a heavy sea it'd be weaving up and down, and rippling-like with the waves themselves. When the matted roots is parted sufficient," he says, "it will disintegrate," he says. "Radio, Mate, and forget the H. E."

And so here we was, the ten of us, on one of them floating islands. And come another blow like generally reverses back from the whirl of a typhoon, and *we* would be heaving up and down, too.

And then, suddenly, like an atom bomb has burst right clean in the middle of my brains, I sees what else has happened to us too.

And Chips, when we decide to go back to the high spot for a couple cups of hot jamoke, pulls me aside. And I know maybe the same bomb has lighted the same picture for him, too. Orders? And has I got a decision to make right now, and quick!

"So," he says, very quiet, "the Rio Bontok's up yonder now."

I only nods, for they's a kind of tightness about my head, and I'm seeing visions of things.

"With that *datu*'s home layout still upstream," Chips goes on. "And waiting for him, delayed by the typhoon."

I nods again; trying to think, and think it out right.

"And here we be," he says, "maybe five mile from the mouth of that same rio we was to guard." And then he comes out with it: "What'll the Old Man say to that, huh?"

Yeah, I says to myself, *what*? I shakes my head hard. "The Old Man's orders, Chips," I says, "was this —" I remember without a comma missing. "He says: 'You will under no circumstances leave that point of land, Quartermaster, until you sight this !%$?*! $%!*Â¿! rat!'"

"And," says Chips, persistent, "what else did the Old Man say?"

"'When this quizzling rat of a *datu* starts upriver after his pleasant occupation of murder and looting, you will capture him, Quartermaster. You understand?' I am quoting the Old Man's words exact, Chips," I says, and I almost gags. "That is what he said, too."

"Well?" Chips asks, right to the bitter end.

And then I knows what we got to do. *Knows!*

"That's the hell of it!" I holler, my insides twisting and my head busting. "Them orders don't fit, but there's only one of them that really counts, Chips, and darn you, you're thinking it just the same as me!" My stomach is now a live pretzel inside me, and I coughs all at once, and near turns inside out. But I has to say it; it's up to me to say it, being in command. "We got to — bust — one order," I sort of gasps.

"Easy, feller." I feel Chips holding me. "Let go everything, feller. So we don't stick to this very point of land, eh? We leave it to do our real job." And suddenly he chuckles, and all of a sudden my stomach is settling back. I look up at him through a blur, and by the Beard of Neptune, he's grinning.

I hollers: "Listen, Chips —"

He interrupts. "You just relieved your stomach, feller. Now I'm going to relieve your mind. They ain't no con-

flicting orders. This mess ain't that point of land any more. It's an island now. The *real* point of land is the new one up there, where we busted off. . . ."

Wow! I could have hugged Chips. I hollers:

"Let's go!"

Chips looks at me sort of funny now. "The engine?"

Holy Moses, with what had happened, I'd plumb forgot the thing I'd been worrying about there in the blackness after we'd bailed the boat. The battery! Sure, in a special-built box bolted atop the after thwart against the gunwale, and with a canvas hood all paraffined and the cable outlets too. But oh, boy, hightailing for the motor-sailer now, does I pray!

The engineman jerked when I hollers right in his ear. But he kept right on with his wrench, and made like he was reciting a list he'd gone over a dozen times.

"Generator soaked, gotta be dried. Coil may be waterproof, but better be dried.

Distributor already off, drying on the thwart back there. Spark plugs — checked two and four; no water in firing chambers, but better check others before trying to turn over. Carburetor —"

"For cripe's sake," I holler, "all them things can be done. But nothing will click without juice. *The battery!*"

He looks up at me sort of astonished-like. "Would I be doing this? Weak," he says, "but we get a spark."

I sort of sit down. After a while, with the engineman whistling soft-like, I says: "How long?"

He shrugs. I says: "Some of the boys was handy with cars . . ."

"If we aim to get that pirate," he says slow and hard, "this engine's got to mote, and mote right. I was," he says, "just initiated into Auto Mechanic Local 1546 in Oakland, Cal, when the Japs hit Pearl. This job is mine."

I took a deep breath. I wasn't reminding that feller what time meant; not me. I says: "I'll send the cox'n to be your wiper and makey-learn." And was I singing when I hit the high spot again.

VI.

Boy, did my gang whoop it up then! Christening our divorced chunk of swamp the "U. S. S. *Floating Island*," putting her into commission with flags from the boat-box! Speeches and congratulations from my old shipmates, with me taking over as skipper. Inducting into service the little monkey, with the rating of Marine Corps corporal, heh!

And more folderol than you used to see at the initiation into the Order of the Exiles of the Earth up in Cavite, where you had to learn the Language of the Lizard and plenty more, and have to sleep it off three days handrunning.

Mid-morning come, and that danged tangle of roots and mud and potholes, the good ship *Floating Island*, was swimming along before the wind right handsome. Farther away, yeah; now about seven-eight mile off shore. But what the heck — that good little engineman, all sweat and grease whilst we was playing, was sending the cox'n with hourly reports.

Maintaining morale, while waiting, was my job now. And discipline, too, I figures must be held, even if I sort of ties it in with the folderol. I reorganizes personnel.

I was captain already; I makes myself Navigator now. Chips I made my Executive First Lieutenant, Ship's Carpenter. Bones, out of my own bridge gang, took over as Code and Communication Officer, Signal Officer and Chief Watch Officer. The cox'n I made Bosun, with rank as Chief Warrant, and to act as Second Watch Officer. Doc, he was Third, Gunnery, and naturally Medical Officer. The engineman, he was a natural for Chief Engineer. Finally I looks at Spuds, the only other rated man. After a minute I appoints him Commissary and Supply — and also cook. And immediately I makes a short speech.

Like this:

"To assure prompt action in all departments," I says, slanting my eye on Spuds, "I appoint the following officers and rated personnel as a standing GCM — that's General Court Martial, if you don't know them initials: My Executive, my Surgeon, my Bosun. Mr. Bones here," I says, real formal and grave, "will act as Judge Advocate. Any man coming before the court, or any officer, can choose his own Counsel for Defense from the remaining complement of the ship. I will be Convening Authority and the Last Court of Appeal."

And that left Mr. Spuds with his mouth sagging — and suddenly shoving up that loose pivot tooth.

Right off I issues the orders of the day.

"Mate," I says to Chips, "as First Lieutenant it's your duty to check condition of the ship. See that the Carpenter makes a thorough inspection of all bilges, double bottoms, wells and the like. Go with him yourself, Mr. Chips, so's there's no mistake. And I wish to see the Hull Book each watch, Mr. Chips. Any questions?"

He salutes very solemn, but when he shoves off, he has a grin.

I turns to Spuds, looking wary at me from the corner of his eye. I gives him a look, and he salutes, right brisk.

"You want me, Captain?"

"No," I says, kind of pitying-like. "I want grub."

"Oh." He kind of jumps. "I mean, aye-aye, sir."

"Also," I says, "bring me a report on all food and water supplies on the ship. I would also appreciate," I says, "your initiating procedure as to procuring fresh food from the sea. And kindly send me the Bosun."

He salutes, right brisk again.

"Aye-aye, sir. Grub on hand, fish from the sea, and the Bosun for the Captain. Aye-aye, sir."

Now that was a little bit *too* much.

"Leftenant," I says, low and soft, "Leftenant, what is orders?"

"Orders?" Sidewise he kind of pops them washed-out eyes. And then I reckon he remembers my standing GCM. "Why," he says in a funny voice, "orders, Captain, is orders."

"Ah," I says. "Even from a sour onion them words is sweet. Shove off."

And off he shoves, and a-pushing up that tooth again.

And in a minute, teetering hasty over the repaired runway from the motor-sailer, here comes the skinny little cox'n, with his shiny sunburned forelock.

"Boats," I says, still sitting in my cabin on the rounded hump at the foot of the coconut palm, "how many men have you available for deck duty?"

"Four," he says prompt. "Counting the bowhook. And five," he says, "counting the monk' — I means the Marine Corporal, sir."

I kind of let that pass for the time.

"The First Lieutenant is off taking soundings," I says. "Get your gang to massaging these decks. Rig that wrecked tarp over the quarterdeck here. Wash and scrub down all footways, including the one to the captain's gig. Got any sooji-mooji?"

He shakes his forelock, but they is a twinkle in his eye.

"Not a Gold Dust twin 'board ship, sir," he kind of races. "And no washing soda unless the Supply Department's holding out on the deck. I ain't complaining none, sir, but I believe the Captain understands the Supply Officer?"

Well, I see now something has to be done here, too. Sure, none of us is forgetting as how Spuds fed us Spanish rice sixteen days handrunning up at Lingayen that time, but I cannot allow my officers to criticize each other before me. I kind of lean my head toward him and cocked to one side.

"Ah," I says, low and smooth. "You indeed seem to show faint signs of intelligence. It is still a strange thing to me, after long weary years with moron deck-swabs aboard this and countless other idiot-crewed vessels of this man's navy, how every now and then, when a man least expects it, a tiny gleam of intelligence does emerge like a little bright light over yon horizon. Sometimes it maybe ain't quite human," I says, "but it's there. And it is most *re*freshing, my lad, most *re*freshing. It makes a man feel that after all there is something worth while in this onsecured-like life of ourn spent on the broad un-fathomable deep. So you believes the Captain understands the Supply Officer, does you? Ah." I suddenly snaps out my head, glaring. "So also does the Captain understand the Chief Bosun. Shove off!"

Well, sir, to see his face, you'd of thought I was the Old Man himself, in person. And after a while of his standing there, stiff and eyes mystified, I says in a sweet, kind voice:

"Tell the Signal Officer I want him, if you will, please."

"B-B-Bones, sir?" he stutters.

"The gleam of intelligence becometh a flame," I says.

And I turn up my eyes at the blue sky, then duck quick as the white-hot sun near blinds me.

VII.

"Bones," I says, passing off his snappy salute, "you danged cross between a zero pennant and a loaded ivory, we're floating on the deep briny on a hull that's not a hull, and we got to stay with it until we motes and can go after that ding-blasted *datu*, or until the good Lord in His wisdom throws a miracle and lets this blankety-blank *datu* come by. But meantime we got to work like this was as near a ship as possible, and pass the time that way or go nuts. I got all the others hopping to their jobs, with threats of a rope on that palm tree heavy on their souls. And when we finally gets back to the ship," I says, "if we ever does alive, and *stays* alive once we're aboard, I'm going to catch hell from most every man in this crew, and most probably more than hell from somebody else, and you know just who I mean. You got to stand by me, Bones, same as Chips and Doc. Any suggestions, Bones, besides the usual about shooting a little game?"

"Aw, now —" he starts. But I put up my hand.

"Sit," I says. "You're just visiting the captain in his cabin, friendly-like, for a little cup of tea." Huh!

"All right," he begins right off, "if we get weather again, how long will she last?"

I shrug that one off.

"Even this hump in the middle has the jiggles now," he says.

I looks about us, and swabs some of the sweat which isn't altogether from the heat. And then I arises. "We will now leave the monkey, even if he is a Marine, standing by the quarterdeck," I says. "Which ain't so onusual these days — though gosh knows some of 'em aren't doing a half-way bad job of it, considering they been lawyering and selling insurance and swabbing windshields not so far back. Let us make, Mr. Bones, a grand tour of the ship. An' here comes Doc, too. Ah there, Sarge," I hails him. "What's in the wind?"

Doc steps up most respectful snapping a salute that would have knocked the Old Man for a row of pink pagodas. Then he dumps out some pills into his hand.

"Mosquitoes," he says. "The typhoon blowed most of them away, but some of them had their proboscusses in so deep they was stuck with us here." He holds out a pill between his fingers. "If the Captain will just open his mouth — wide."

We make thwartship for the motor-sailer.

"My compliments on the engine work, Chief," I says. "But I'd like a report on the fuel."

He swivels a greasy thumb at a mangrove twig on the engine cockpit thwart, by that battery box.

"Eighteen measured gallons in the tank," he says.

"What reserve?" I ask quiet, drawing on my pipe as my eyes light on the two cases under the thwart.

"Twenty gallons, for cripe's sake," he says, and he makes to duck back to his engine.

"Ah," I says, "and how much does that make altogether, Chief?" And I emphasizes that "*Chief.*" And he sort of stammers then:

"Why — thirty-eight gallons." And he adds quick: "Sir."

"Ah," I says. "An' what speed do you estimate we can make, Chief?" I goes on.

"Speed, sir?" He kind of looks at me funny, and now stands up.

"Towing, Chief," I says, very solemn. "Towing the ship, if need be?"

"Oh," he says, and starts rubbing his hands on the rag. "Towing." He takes a deep breath.

"Well, Captain," he says, "I reckon if we run with tide and wind, we can make about four mile to the hour. With tide alone, no wind, about three. With tide at slack, and no wind, about one mile. With tide at slack and wind against us, sir, we'll lay about dead in the water. With tide against us, and no wind, maybe about the same. But with tide and wind both against us, sir, we'll tow with sternway of about two mile. And with tide and wind against us, and the motor busted down again — gosh knows."

"Enough," I interrupts, fanning my face. "Keep me posted. But I commend you, Chief. I — like men about me who have alert minds."

We turns away, Bones giving a little grunt. And we come on Chips kneeling by one of the potholes.

"I never see such a ship, Captain," he sings out. "The water in this well is plumb flush with the gun-deck, but my lead don't even find bottom. How deep is these bilges, anyway?"

"The blueprints was throwed away," I says, dry-like. "But where did you get that sounding line?"

"Bummed it off the Supply Officer," he says. "And he got it from the boat box. According to orders, I suspect. Fish line."

I turns to Bones.

"Learn from the Executive what it means to have them officer-like qualities of initiative, efficiency and et cetera, Mr. Bones. I do like men about me who have alert minds."

"Aye-aye, Captain," says Bones, with a most noble salute.

"Initiative is only wrong, Mr. Bones," I says, "in a crap game."

Bones jerks a sort of startled look at me.

"I wasn't saying nothing," he yelps.

But then we hears *clang-clang, clang-clang, clang-clang, clang-clang* from the fry pan the boys has rigged between the palm trees. Eight bells — noon already. And the pretzels jittering inside me again. But I sit with my brother officers, and Spuds has either really got religion or is polishing apples for the rest of the gang, for the chow is really good. I gets my pipe drawing sweet, then takes another sight for position. We've drifted maybe another mile away. And then, with a sort of shock, I see we've been drifting in the direction the ship ought to be. I start to shin the fore — then recollects my position and hails a seaman. But in a minute he slides down. Nothing in sight.

I put it to my Exec, aside, quiet.

"Well," Chips whispers, "just like we agreed during the typhoon, the Old Man probably run for a lee, feeling we was safe on the beach. And anyway he said they'd steam back to the *rio* in about two days, didn't he?"

"He told me," I says, "he'd be two mile off the point of land on which he told us to land, at exactly four-fifteen, I mean sixteen-fifteen new style, on the afternoon of the second day, which is tomorrow. Two mile to the inch, Chips, an' sixteen-fifteen to the split second."

"Yeah," nods Chips, dry-like, "off that point. All right But he may have had to run plenty. He may even have lost a funnel or two, and half his top hamper. May even be stove in. These damn coral reefs —"

I feel a little jump inside of me, at that.

"Not him, Chips!" And I reckon maybe I get a little mad, with this idea bothering me deep, too. "Nor the Exec of that old bucket, either. They knows navigating, Chips, and dang your liver, you ought to know they does. That's no way to talk about the Old Man, nor the Exec either, you sawdust-stuffed woodchopper!" I begins hollering, and can't help myself. "What the hell do you mean by insulting the Old Man like that anyways! Why blast my $%!&? %$&! hash-marks, if you say anything like that again, or even hint at it, I'll knock you for a row of pink pagodas! You hear me?"

Then I kind of recollects. And I shove out my hand; and Chips, he shoves out his.

"Still," he whispers, "we ain't there yet."

Aye. All this christening and coconut juice, all this fiddlesticks over the monk', all this jackasserie over Chips sounding the double bottoms and calling this two-by-four high spot the captain's cabin, all this ordering about I been giving! Why, hadn't I noticed every man jack of 'em taking every chance to sneak over to see how the engineman was making it? And maybe praying, under all the kid stuff they was talking, that he really could get the engine turning so we could shove for the *rio* — yeah, and that *new* point of land — in time for when the feller come about to make upstream? Lord, them jittery pretzels!

When six bells in the afternoon dragged up, a breeze sighs through. No, not a heavy wind, just a good Number Two. And then I catch something. It's from s'uth'ard. I send a watch to the pointed end, which is still to south, to look for ripples. If they show, then we're being pushed north again. But, I says to myself, eying a pothole, we don't want the wind *too* heavy.

Then of course Spuds suddenly comes to and suggests rigging up the tarp as a sail. Well now, just think of putting up a nine by sixteen canvas, half shreds at that, to sail a chunk of swamp three hundred and seventy-five feet long by a hundred and sixty thereabouts wide. And the sharks only knowed how deep, with roots maybe five fathom long trailing the keel. But he'd give us one good meal at noon; so, with no off words, I just says:

"Thank you, Mr. Spuds. The Executive and I will look into your idea. For the time, however, I wonder if you won't just try your luck with that fish-line Mr. Chips was using for sounding the wells. Chow's due at seventeen-thirty," I says. "Exact."

VII.

Eight bells drags up. The watch is changed. But the wind is now reaching Number Three, and ripples, by gosh, showing at the stern. . . .

Middle of the first dog approaches; the pretzels is beginning to work hard inside me again. But likewise approaches Spuds, his face as long as Neptune's whiskers.

With him, so to speak, is a opticus. This opticus is about four feet acrost, and four of its feelers is clamped about Spuds' chest, over his shimmy shirt, thank the Lord, and three of them is clamped along his bare bony arms, and one is waving, looking maybe for a hold.

It takes three men and Chips with his razor-edge carpenter's knife to peel them away, leaving the Commissary and Supply Officer cussing in a low sick voice at the red sort of welts its suckers has raised. Well, he's caught a couple fish, too, sort of eels. So I says as how opticus is most succulous food, the Chinks calling it first chop, and that he can have it all to himself, and we'd struggle along on just the eels.

And boy, the *report* then coming from the motor-sailer! Everything's dry, all parts near in place, and not long before the Chief'll be set to turn her over — if she'll turn.

And so, at seventeen-thirty, prompt, we dines. With the ship heaving and wriggling with the rising breeze, but we forgetting that, just praying we can make a night run up to the *datu*'s *rio*. In time.

And it was half through the second dog watch and darker than an opticus' cave, when a yell that's nothing but plain frantic alarm cuts through.

"Hey! Hey! We're busting apart. Help! *We're busting apart*!"

Was they action then!

Flashlights? Still seven-eight miles from that *rio*? I'll say. And they showed up a crack already about ten foot wide, running sort of jagged down the starboard side and then thwartship clean acrost the whole ship. Fore and aft is simply two parts, and the black water between is widening as we look at it.

Then comes another yell. And suddenly I realize that the motor-sailer is tied to the broken off end, and it's the engineman a-yelling. And suddenly, too, comes a low sputtering and then a crack like a pistol shot, and then sputtering again, and a couple more bangs. Then another yell.

"Call away the fire and rescue party!" I hollers to the

Exec. "The engine's shooting and the engineman's got to have a hand!"

"Away the fire and rescue party!" sings Chips.

"I won't go," groans Spuds, he being in charge of it.

"Away the fire and rescue party!" hollers Chips. "On the jump!"

"I ain't agoin' to swim over to that boat," weeps Spuds. And I don't hardly blame him, but I has to hold control.

"Leftenant Spuds," I says, real calm but watching that widening band of black water, "it would tear at my heart to have to put an officer in my command under hack, and an old shipmate at that, particularly in wartime. And I have strove to be sympathetic, and patient, and just. But they's a fine brig in one of them potholes, and if a man was sunk into one with just a line holding his shoulders out so's only his bare feet is down among the brother opticuses to the one you just et, Leftenant," I says, "they might get a trifle curious about them ten little wriggly pink tootsies all of a sudden jiggling amongst them — even if *on*cooked, Leftenant. Mr. Spuds," I says, low and firm, "what is orders?"

But now, as I use them words, I can see the Old Man hunching toward me in the black, looking at me with them green eyes and drawling them same words. We was going at last to leave this very point of land. Even if a new point was up yonder. Lord help me if I wasn't right!

Well, Spuds peers at me, and me at him. Slowly his mouth comes up sort of grim. He yanks away the line Chips holds ready, bends it to his belt, gives a hitch to his pants, shoves up that pivot tooth, holds his nose. They is an almighty big splash, and a trail of blue phosphorescence as he claws for the other bank, getting farther and farther away.

The Bosun, who a deck swab had relieved at the boat, I just taps on the shoulder, and there's another splash.

It ain't long before we hear the engine really put-putting, snapping another backfire or two, then purring smooth. And I hear Boats' order through the dark:

"Shove her off, Mr. Spuds. The engineer says we can make a trial run. And don't worry about the seas; she can take 'em. Back her slow, Chief."

The gears grind, and they is a crashing of mangrove branches. Then the quick order:

"Stop her."

We hear the engine running free. "Ahead easy," we hear Boats sing out. "I'll watch the seas and swing when I can for the part the boys are on."

"Bring her around to the lee side," I hollers. "Don't chance coming through the break."

"Aye-aye, Captain," comes from Boats, pretty well away. Then comes a wild yell:

"Put that down, you %0$#!& &) !%$ idiot!"

And then, while something cold is trickling down my shoulders, Spuds' voice, shrill and excited:

"I got you covered, every danged one of you! We got the boat going now, and we'll leave those blankety-blank fools to play along with their monkey boy friend on that blasted mess of roots. You hear me? Swing her north'ard, for the main island, and we'll get the Old Man's job done by ourselves."

"I will not!" we hears Boats holler. But then he yells frantic: "Captain, Captain, they's mutiny aboard. He wants to —"

Bang!

Good Lord.

And then before we know what's actually happened with that one pistol shot, the motor starts purring soft and deep through the swooshing wind, farther and farther into the blackness beyond the piece of our ship that's floating away.

Well, Chips and me and the others stand there, staring into the dark. Then we slip and flounder back to the quarterdeck, the six of us left. Not talking. And somehow a sort of gulp comes up in me, and I hopes the boat, even with Spuds doing what he's doing, makes it safe. And I breathes a sigh, too; thanking the good Lord we hadn't brought all our fighting gear ashore.

Then me and Chips and Doc, carrying another line between us like mountain climbers, makes a tour to inspect just what we has left. About a third of the good ship *Floating Island* is gone. Chips gives a grunt; he says in a low, sort of tired voice:

"Some of the watertight bulkheads seem to be holding, Captain."

"Yeah," I says, knowing how he means it.

"We had ten men to handle the entire ship," Chips says. "Now we got six to handle two-thirds of it. Not bad arithmetic." Then he says something that strikes me crazy enough, and he sort of coughs first. "So," he says, "we are sticking to this very point of land."

Me, I don't answer right then. The pretzels are twisting again. But a minute later a sort of dull whisper comes up out of me:

"Hell of a skipper I turned out to be."

"Nuts!" hollers Doc, by my side.

Then Chips says, quiet:

"Tough on Spuds."

I don't answer. But Doc suddenly busts out:

"You mean because he's going up there with only four men?"

"Nope," says Chips, as if thinking aloud to himself. "I am just sorry for Spuds. When the Old Man hears this — well, I guess you know what'll happen. Time of war. And Spuds is really half nuts with too long in the Asiatic. And maybe got just a little *vienta de cabeza*, too, as they used to say in Manila, with having Chink compradores kowtowing to him, and greasing him up with all them *cumshaw* chow dogs and parrots and canaries down in Hong Kong, and loquats and silver and silk in Shanghai, and bolts of pongee, and four goats chop pongee at that, up in Chefoo. He told me once, that time he was peddling the bum chow to us up at Lingayen, that he'd like to get back to the States, but somehow every time he'd made up his mind to ask for a transfer, he'd find himself re-applying to stay out here. Just couldn't leave. You fellers know what it does sometimes — when you do finally go home, old-timers, I mean: it's either in a box or a straitjacket. We been maybe kind of hard on the Commissary and Supply Officer, Captain," Chips concludes his long talk. "And I sure am sorry for him when the Old Man hears."

Maybe it's just everything that's happened tying into one jittery knot — I don't know, but something sure busts in me then.

"Sorry for hell!" I hollers. "Soon as the engine's fixed so we can all shove off up there, he deserts, don't he? An' didn't you hear him layin' into us for being a monkey's brother and wanting to stay here? Here? With a job to do up on that *rio*? And him taking it? Sure he's been out here for too long a time. Two hitches before the war even. I know that. But dang it all, he's still a Navy man."

Chips kind of sighs. And then Doc hollers:

"Look out for that open hatch!"

I jumps the porthole just in time.

I slugs around for balance, for the mass under me is humping like a camel. Then, just as we is about to turn in to the high spot to try for a catnap, there being nothing else to do, we hear the lookout sing out, startled-like:

"Halt! Who the hell's there?"

And the next minute, whilst I'm just beginning to pray it's Spuds changed his mind:

"Bang!"

And this time it ain't a pistol-shot.

IX.

Another yell from the lookout, and desperate and shrill:

"Captain! For the love of Mike!" And then even shriller, and he just a kid: "Repel boarders! Repel boarders!" And vicious and loud and frantic, out sputters his tommy gun.

For one half-second we freeze.

Then, grabbing up our own tommies and grenades, and Chips hollering he can't loose his axe from his belt, and falling into potholes and slipping all over ourselves, and knowing our torches was making us swell targets for whatever's trying to break onto our ship, we hits for the bow. And did I thank the Lord again we'd brought most of our fighting gear ashore when we'd first made our landing here!

The lookout's still banging away, and we hears deeper, heavier banging as we come out to the fo'c's'le head and in the clear more or less of the tangled mangroves.

"A boat!" The lookout yells as if he thought he was still back on the quarterdeck "A sailboat and a bunch of pirates! Help! Help! Repel boarders! Repel boarders!" And *uck-uck-uck-uck* went his tommy gun.

We got to him just in time to see a dark shape loom up alongside, cutting a big triangular bite out of the stars, and hear the crunching of roots and the squishing of mud as the craft, spitting fire and heathen cusswords, hits us half-beam on.

In a minute more out jumps what looks like a hundred black figures which I can't tell anything about on account now of my lost flashlight. And then they *is* a fight.

Their shrill, howling, monkey yells kind of whooped along with the gale, and the cussing of my own men cracked hard.

My tommy gun yelped and jerked, and the screams yowled like the spirits of the dead. The whole hundred of them, seems to me, just sort of descended upon us in one big wave. I was throwed to the ground, with my nose sucking mud, and a dozen knees shoving me deeper, and a dozen arms, slick and oily, trying to jerk my gun away. I hear Chips yell.

"Give 'em hell, boys! Give 'em hell! Save the Captain! There, dang yuh!"

And then another tommy gun hollers so close to my head I can feel the ejected empties rattling against the back of it. And then suddenly they was nothing but low grunting, with occasionally a ear-cracking *"Bang!"* and another howl about me, and over me, in the darkness. And the deck heaved and waved, and I could hear feet come out of the mud with a kind of "plop!" most ugly to hear.

Finally I heave over on my side, and let go my own tommy gun again, thanking the Lord I'd been able to keep it out of the mud. And they is another wild yell. And I shove them off and grab a greasy arm here and a gee-string there in the dark, and haul myself to my feet, and drop my gun, and start in with the good old American right-and-left *two*, stuff the Old Man made us practice continual out on the little old bucket.

"Chips!" I hollers when I has a clear chancet.

And the way he sings it out makes my heart jump. "Giving 'em hell with the little old tommyhawk!" he yells.

"Doc!" I hollers next, and then jerk out my forty-five and let go again.

"Here!" And Doc's voice has a laugh in it between gasps. "Giving 'em medicine they don't like," he sings. And from the direction of his voice I hear the blunt cracking of his own forty-five.

I holler for the other three. And only two of them answer, and I feel a sort of sinking inside me as I duck and dodge and fumble for reloads.

"Get together!" I holler. "Here. Get together."

"They're using their knives," sings out somebody's warning *"Bolos!"*

Good night! Them damn big heavy neck-choppers. And I cusses Spuds again for deserting and leaving us in the pinch. A couple more tommies to back us up, or a couple more forty-fives. . . . Why, the forty-five was invented just to

knock the everlasting hell out of them running-amok natives in the southern isles. Old — but what a wallop! They
was one to every man on our ship; the Old Man had insisted they be kept.

We got together at last, only five of us now, and that
black mob jumping and screaming and stomping the roots
and mud into a tangled muck that sucked continual at our
feet. Doc still belched his forty-five, and Chips now is
swinging his axe again. But on they come. And it looked to
me, crazy enough, as though they wanted us alive, and the
knife-swinging was to scare us into hollering "Enough!" I
know I must have knocked a dozen of them clean into
dreamland, with their noses in the black ooze underfoot,
but still they come.

I remembers the Exec saying he wished he could come
out here with us, and I sure now wished he had. And the
Old Man — he'd have just et it up, talking to them all the
time, and peering with his green eyes. And then I get a clip
alongside the shoulder with a club or something, and my
right arm goes numb. And then I hear a groan beside me,
and something falls heavy against me, and I go down
again. And it's blacker than inside a dead boiler, and the
wind roaring through it all, and the stink of the sloshed-up
mud, and the sea surging over, and the deck, if you call it a
deck now, weaving and lurching and sucking like its appetite was hot to swallow us all down. But then I get a kick in
the other side, and I reckon that knocks me up again, and I
hear a yell like from the distance, and then a rifle shot. And
then another, a regular volley of them, and the bullets
kechugging into the mud, and into other things, I hoped,
too.

T here's a scream of rage from our attackers, and they
break for the side of the ship. I stagger like a drunk, and
swab my eyes with my arm — and there is the glowing red
light not twenty feet from the side, and there is the roar of a
engine and the screeching of gears. I never heard such sweet
music.

And in another minute we're stampeding them black
rats right back into their own craft. And in two minutes
more after that we got the eight of them left alive all triced
up neat and shipshape with good old Navy knots, wet at
that, that *they* won't savvy how to get loose, though it takes
only a jerk here and a yank there and it's done.

And then a flashlight moons out a face that certainly *I*
didn't even dream was within ten miles by now, and I yells
out one word:

"Spuds!"

Yes, sir, it's Spuds. He salutes me, grinning with that
potato face of his and his washed-out eyes kind of warm-like
and twinkling in the beam of the light.

"Aye-aye, sir," he says.

"But my God, Spuds! Dang yuh, I thought —"

He grins sort of a funny grin.

"I been starving for a fight, I guess, Cap," he sort of whispers. "Besides, look out there."

And there, by the Beard of Neptune, is the black silhou-
ette of the old bucket herself, not a quarter-mile off our
bows. Well, I just sort of sits down in the mud.

"I made her out there just as we was about to swing back
to you, Cap," says Spuds. "And also I seen the sail of this
here craft black against the sky. And I shoots into the air to
get the cox'n's attention to what I mean. And then I goes for
help. But when we hears that first gun crack back here, I
orders the boat around. The ship, I figured, would hear it
too, and would shove off a couple of boatloads." He grins
sort of embarrassed-like. "I — I reckon I'm kind of glad we
got back when we did, sir, I reckon I am that."

W ell, sir, they was almost tears in Spuds' voice. I stares.
They might be something fishy in his yarn of why he
left in the first place, but that could be checked up later.
What he had done, though, was enough for me. He heard a
fight going on, and he had come back.

I slither to my feet, and shoves out my hand.

"Shake, Commander," I says.

"Commander?" he says, looking wary at me again.

"Aye," says I, grinning kind of foolish, I reckon. "Pro-
moted for heroic conduct on the field of battle, sir."

And then we all has a whoop, slapping each other on the
back, and punching each other's chests, and acting like fool
kids.

And then we examines the fellers we've captured. And
when I flash the light on one of them's face, I stare, hardly
believing. I just stare, with my throat sort of cramping tight.
And then out I go, like a light. And I sort of dreams there

comes a soft-like voice through the darkness and the wind, just hearable; and the steady thrumming of a heavy-powered boat. It is a voice that give me a shiver clean from my bumped up head to the mud lumps that is my feet.

"Ah," it purrs, and a light plays upon me from this new boat of which I dream. "I see it is the Quartermaster and his gang that was to stay by the Bontok Rio and capture the *datu* pirate all nice and shipshape according to orders. What a fortunate meeting — what a very fortunate meeting this is indeed! Is it not a fortunate meeting, Quartermaster? Ah, but I see you cannot speak. Perhaps later then — in my cabin. Or even before the mast. Come, Quartermaster. Surely you understand who is speaking to you, greeting you thus so pleasantly." Then the voice screeches like a leaping tiger's: *"Speak up!"*

X.

There wasn't a man of our outfit but come through that scrap. Bunged up, sure; and needing collision mats, and bracing, and plugs. Bones was the worst, maybe. And he's complaining yet that he can't get his old-time grip on the ivories. But I reckon he means that he can't *switch* ivories on us any more up there in the dark corner of the bridge when the Old Man ain't on the prowl. And that's his hard luck. Yeah. Specially considering what happened in the Old Man's cabin.

He was slipping smooth-like up and down in his cabin there, the Old Man was, with his tail swishing and his head thrust out as usual, and them gray-green eyes of his peering, peering at me every time he swung about.

And finally he stops not three feet from me, with them cat's whiskers a-twitching, and just a glint from his eyes.

"Ah," he says, and this time it wasn't no knocked-out dream. "Ah, I believe, Quartermaster," he says, "that some five hours and twenty minutes before you shoved off from this ship on the day before yesterday I gave you certain instructions, did I not?"

"Yes, sir," I says, standing straight.

"And," he says, "I believe that you agreed with me, did you not, Quartermaster, that orders were — ah, just what did we agree orders are, Quartermaster?"

"Orders, sir."

"Just so," says he. "And yet I fear that I discover you some seven and one quarter miles from the point on which certain orders specifically instructed you to stand by, did I not, Quartermaster?"

And then, for the first time I ever done such a thing in my whole life in the U.S.N., I contradicted the Old Man.

"No, sir," I says, firm and right out, "you did not."

For a whole minute his head is still, like it was frozen. And then it stretches closer, them green bits of his eyes boring into me. And I imagine his tail is beginning to swish very nervous; very.

"Ah," he says. "Perhaps I am becoming slightly deaf."

"No sir," I say again. "You are not deaf, Captain."

Again there is silence, and I feel my heart thumping like a drifting log might thump against a small boat.

"Ah," he says then, still kind of calm. "Then perhaps it is my eyes."

"Not your eyes, either, Captain," I says.

"Ah," he begins. "Ah." And then he explodes like I been waiting for all the time — just praying for him to do, for I had a secret I hadn't told yet to a single soul. The Old Man explodes: "Then !*&$!? *%*!! my !&$!**?! my soul, *what in hell* do you mean by this?"

And then I says, kind of soft-like and sweet too, from practice on my own ship:

"My orders, Captain, was to stand by that point of land and not to leave it until the *datu* come by — and then to capture him."

He takes two cat leaps for the cabin table, and his fist comes down on its green cover so hard that the deck jerks underfoot.

"But I have found you seven and one quarter miles from that point of land, Quartermaster!"

I interrupts, soft and easy as before, though there is something inside me a squirming.

"On that point of land, Captain," I says. "And not leaving it, Captain, until we had captured that *datu* quizzling rat."

His fist raises for another pound at the table; and then, still holding it up, he stares.

Lord, I had him, and I knowed it then. I reckon I'd never have such a chancet again with the Old Man, but I had it then, and it sure was grand.

"If you examine the prisoners we took, sir," I says very calm, but with my heart flopping like a fish in the bottom of a boat, "you will find that the one with his ear fresh cut off, and shreds of a kind of green turban still hanging over the other, is *the* datu you ordered me to capture. You will remember, Captain," I goes on fast, that you sent me in charge because I'd seen the *datu* a few months before the war busted out, and was the only member of the crew as knowed him, sir. And we didn't leave the point of land, Captain, even to get him. Because in the dark he sailed plump into us, not knowing it was part of the mangrove swamp that had been tore loose by that typhoon and shoved off to sea with us aboard."

I could hear him breathe now, kind of rasping and deep. And for a while neither of us says a word, just kind of looking into each other's eyes. And his fist drifted slow-like down to his side, and them cat's eyes opened wide. And his gray cat's whiskers twitched. And I almost felt sorry for the Old Man then, he was so disappointed-looking at not having found me in a corner. At least for that half second I thought he was.

Because then he straightened. And in another minute I like to have cried, I don't know why.

He stepped close to me and clamps one hand on my shoulder, and says:

"Quartermaster," he says, kind of hoarse, "I'm getting to be an old, old man, and maybe sometimes too —" He breaks off. For a moment his eyes glue onto mine; and then after a while he goes into his bunk compartment and comes out with a bottle which still has tissue paper on it, and some of this here rattan netting. And he starts tearing the paper off the bottle top. And when he has it off, he upends the bottle and bunts the butt of it with the palm of his hand, to start the cork.

"Quartermaster," he says, kind of soft, "this bottle of special forty-year-old brandy was given me by a Limey friend in Hong Kong two years before the war. I haven't touched it yet, as you can see, saving it for when that Limey and I next met. I do not drink on shipboard; I do not condone drinking on shipboard," he says, still pounding the bottle, careful now, for the cork is beginning to swell out at the end. "But here," he says, is one occasion where I shall break the Navy code myself, Quartermaster, just between you and I." The cork comes out with a *plop!* and a most glorious sweet smell sort of drifts forth into the cabin air. The Old Man half fills two tumblers he has fetched from his stateroom. "Here," he says, clinking his glass to mine, "is to *orders*."

Down goes his half-tumbler. And down goes mine.

Then he pours again, but just his own.

"And here," he says, "and I'm sorry you can't drink this one yourself, is to the best !*%$! *$%#!* quartermaster in this !*?$! !$#*! navy or any other !*$!&!** navy! Good luck!"

And he makes one swallow of that one, too, like it was water, which I knowed it ain't. And then, before I knows it, I had the bottle in my own hand. And I plumb fills my own

glass; and I raises it, and I says:

"And I'm sorry, Captain, sir, that you can't drink this one," I says. "But here's to the best captain in this or any other !$%#* *!%$!* navy, sir, and I thank you." And I wipes my lips on my sleeve.

And in another minute he laughs, and then so do I. I just bust out with it someways, not being able to hold back. And then he says:

"Ain't there some little thing I could do, Quartermaster? Any special thing 'board ship here, beside the new ribbon you're going to wear there. A flight back home for thirty days? Something?"

But I just shake my head. I don't want to take advantage now. You know what I mean.

He stares at me until I begin to feel creepy again. Then there comes a little kind of twinkle into his eyes and he leans close and whispers in my ear. And I give a little jump, then grin. And we drink on *that*, by thunder! And off I shove, feeling like the world has nothing but sweet dreams and sweet air and sunshine, and all the decks colored clouds.

And I reckon if I'd of stayed one second longer with the Old Man, I'd of kissed him.

Outside, just beyond the stiff Marine at the cabin door, is Spuds, peering nervous-like, his Adam's apple wobbling fierce. I leads him to the deck. I kind of liked the poor guy, some reason. But they was things to be just cleaned up, and made clear.

"Spuds," I says, up in the open, "I just left the Old Man, and I had a hell of a time getting you off."

"Off!" he kind of yelps. "Off from what?"

"Desertion," I says, "I know danged well why you left my own ship out there, Mr. Spuds. And in time of war, too. Now, you brung that monkey back to the ship, didn't you?"

He nods, staring.

"I have a friend back in the States," I says, "who for long has what you might say yearned for just such a little monkey."

"It's yourn!" Spuds almost yells.

"Thanks," says I. "And up on the bridge tonight, Spuds, at exactly one bell after the shift to midwatch, a little session will be held, its membership very, very select. It gives me great pleasure, Mr. Spuds, to invite you to join in."

A fierce whisper busts in. It is Bones, who's been apparently hanging around, and had listened in.

"But good night, Chief!" he gasps, nursing his bandaged hand. "We just got out of one jam. Why climb right into another with the Old Man —"

I stops him with a gesture like when I was captain of my ship.

"Mr. Bones," I says, "we need never again fear that. Don't ask me how I know, but, brother, I do!"

※

BONUS MATERIAL FOR THE BOOK PAPER EDITION

Each issue of *Adventure Tales* is issued in two states: the newsprint version and an expanded version on book paper. This is the special book paper edition with additional content . . . in this case, two more Murray Leinster short sto-ries ("Nerve" and "The Street of Magnificent Dreams") another John D. Swain ("The Moon Calves"), and "Pirates' Gold," a short novel by H. Bedford-Jones. Enjoy!

— John Betancourt

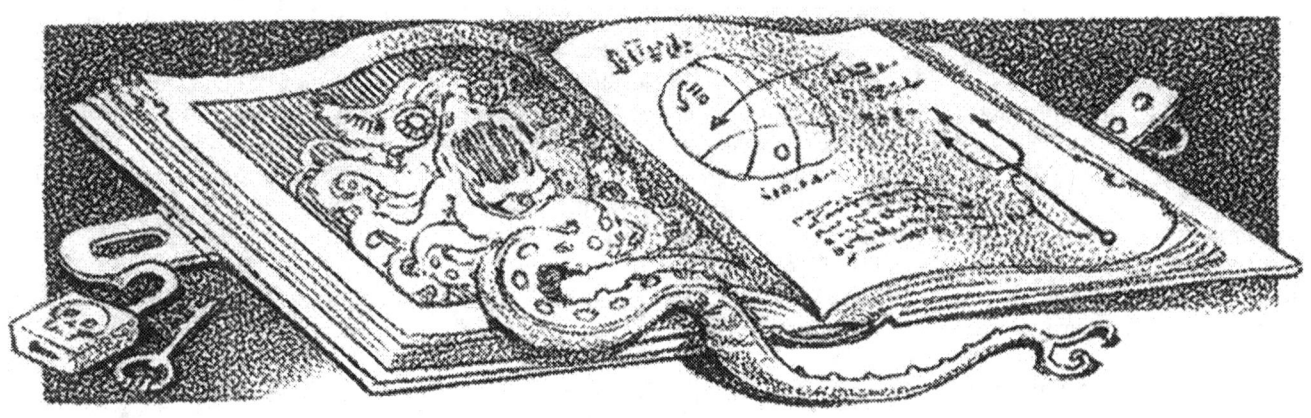

EXTRA CONTENT

THE STREET OF MAGNIFICENT DREAMS

by Murray Leinster

There is a certain street in Burkton which might be called a street of magnificent dreams. There is in every town just such a street, or perhaps it is a park, and in the city of New York it is a curious mixture of bus tops and sidewalks that takes the place of a vantage point. But in Burkton it is a street — a quiet, elm-shaded thoroughfare with a white roadway in the middle, and plank sidewalks, and modest, comfortable homes on either side.

To look at it in the daytime, it seems quite an ordinary place, merely a succession of more or less well-kept lawns, with picket fences and occasional hedges, small houses, and — after school hours — playing children. But at night it is a pathway of dreams. At night the trees cast a deep, dim shadow. They meet above the roadway and darken it completely, and they shadow the walks to a dense and gentle gloom. From the flowerbeds and the lawns come the scent of growing things.

From the darkness of the porches may come the red glow of an after-dinner cigar, or a girl's laugh, or perhaps a flood of inconsequential melody may tinkle out into the night. Fireflies flash their blue flames among the trees, possibly pursued by small and grubby hands, to be captured and imprisoned in glass bottles for some of the unknown purposes of childhood.

But on the walks — there are dreams and visions. Slender young girls in summery, white dresses walk shyly there with their sweethearts. Some of them talk gaily. Now and then those upon the porches will hear a little ripple of utterly carefree laughter. Some of them talk softly. Some of them pass slowly through the gloom with shining faces and gently intertwined fingers. And sometimes the young men will be speaking eagerly, confidently. They will be describing the visions they see.

The young girls, too, are seeing visions, but they do not speak of them. They look with soft eyes into the future and see the happiness that will infallibly come to them, and they see homes, perhaps, which are not quite as imposing as the visions of the young men beside them, but are vastly more desirable. And then, too, they may see other things, which are just a little more vague but infinitely to be hoped for. Very small things, pink and white, and miraculously alive.

These are the visions that are seen upon the street of magnificent dreams in Burkton.

Alicia Blake had walked upon that street, years before, and now she lived upon its edge, but the dreams were gone. Dreams have a way of fading. She sat upon her porch, feeling the cool of the summer night. Before her gate passed two of the dreamers — carefree dreamers, these. The girl was laughing at some jest of her escort. Alicia listened with a troubled brow. She could see what would come to those two who walked in the gloom, and it might be good fortune or it might be bad, but inevitably it would not possess the beauty of those radiant phantasms of lovers' dreaming. There was always disillusionment. She knew.

Her husband was sitting but a little way from her, his feet propped luxuriously upon the railing of the porch, smoking his after-dinner cigar and gazing at the strollers with an untroubled brow.

"I like to watch them, Alicia," he said presently, as a dim white figure passed slowly before the gate. "It's rather — it reminds me of old times. We used to walk like that."

"Yes," said Alicia slowly, "we did."

She lay back in her chair, curiously unhappy. No one had ever known such dreams as they had had. Harry was to become an important man in Burkton. The road was clear before him to the presidency of his firm. In five years, they had devoutly believed, they would be well-to-do. In ten years they would be wealthy. And in fifteen years, they foresaw infallibly, they would be spending their summers abroad. Harry would be one of the big men of the town. There was nothing to hold him back. He was ambitious, he was capable, and — he would have Alicia to help him. It had seemed very certain, in those days.

A young man's voice came from the obscurity beneath the trees.

"And in five years —" he was saying earnestly, confidently.

His tone dropped to a murmur. There was a little speck of grayish white beside him — a girl, of course.

Alicia closed her eyes. The fragrance of her husband's cigar came faintly to her nostrils. That, after all, was the measure of their success. Now he could smoke cigars. When they were first married he had smoked a pipe and doled out his tobacco sparingly. Now they owned their home. They would never have to fear poverty. Bat for the rest —

Harry grunted suddenly.

"Forgot to tell you, 'Lecia," he said idly. "I heard from Tom Kerry today. He's been taken into partnership."

Alicia did not answer. Harry expected none. Her unhappiness increased just a little. Harry had had the chance that Tom Kerry had taken. The opening for which he had commended the other man had been offered first to him. If he had taken it —

Instead, he was sitting upon his front porch, smoking quietly, quite untroubled, while the business for which he had been working for ten years was changing hands. It was being bought in by a larger concern, a million-dollar house, and Harry might be kept on, or he might be dropped.

She asked a sudden question. "What about the office, Harry?"

He shifted his position easily. "The papers were to be signed tonight, I understand. The deal's gone through. By tomorrow I'll have a new set of bosses."

He smiled to himself in the darkness.

Alicia felt a curious uneasiness. "How about changes, Harry?"

His tone was casual.

"There'll be a few, I suppose. We've got some good men."

Alicia clenched her hands, unseen. That was Harry's way. He did not push himself. Three or four times he had been consulted on details of management. More often than that he had been consulted on promotions. He had commended other men — even younger men — for advancement over his own head. True, they had invariably made good, but Harry could have done the same. He had became a plugger, a steady, dependable man, instead of a brilliant one. And there was no reason for it.

"No danger of my being out of a place long," he added suddenly, smiling. "No need to worry."

"I know."

But the unhappiness persisted. It was quite true that he need not fear unemployment. He had helped too many men now in positions of power. Tom Kerry was but one of many whom Harry had given a boost, and Tom Kerry was now making easily twice what Harry earned.

The procession on the street of magnificent dreams continued. Always the dreamers walked in pairs. They walked beneath the overhanging trees, and some of them talked gaily, and some talked softly, and some passed slowly along the way with shining faces and gently intertwined fingers. All of them saw visions of the future, a radiant future, most marvelously certain to be achieved.

There was a little pause, and a young man and girl walked alone.

The young man's voice came, strained a little, bitterly unhappy.

"But — but what can we do?" he asked despairingly. "What can we do?"

The girl was silent, but her head was bent.

They passed on in silence. Only the faint murmur of the young man's voice came back despairingly.

"That's Jack Grahame," said Harry suddenly, "and I suppose that's little Milly with him."

Alicia nodded.

"She lives with her aunt, you know, and her parents are dead. Her aunt makes her do all the housework. She doesn't have a very pleasant time."

Harry puffed at his cigar for an instant, "I rather imagine they feel pretty badly," he said reflectively. "Jack has a rather poor job. He couldn't possibly marry on his salary. And Milly isn't in very happy surroundings. If they're in love with each other it must be pretty hard on them."

Alicia meditated an instant.

"No, they can't marry now, but it would be splendid for them if they could."

She felt a certain vague sympathy for the pair, but soon dropped back into her own depressed musing. She and Harry had walked along this street of dreams, and had dreamed of the future. Harry was to be a big man in Burkton. He was to be a success. It had looked so perfectly certain. He was young and ambitious, and had Alicia to help him.

But he had helped other men instead. There were a dozen of them, in different lines, that he had helped to get their start. He had got Tom Kerry the position that had led up to his present partnership in the firm he worked for. He had

loaned another young man the money to start in business —
and the business was now a big one, A third he had urged for
promotion over his own head, and that man was a vice-presi-
dent of the Amalgamated Wood Products Company, the
firm that was buying out his own company now.

There were others — many others. They had been clerks
under him, and he had trained them and shown them the
path.

And they had all outstripped him.

There was no reason for it. Harry was as good as any of
the men he had assisted, though they were successes and he
was a failure. Alicia winced a little at the branding word.
There was no escaping it, though. Harry was a failure. The
others had gone ahead, and he had stayed behind. They
could afford European trips, if they chose, but Harry could
not. In justice, Alicia did not wish for foreign travel as a
thing in itself. She wished for it as a symbol of success, as a
fruition of those radiant visions they had seen when they
walked together in the dusk.

Harry was puffing thoughtfully upon his cigar.

"Tom Kerry said," he remarked suddenly, "that he'd heard
our firm was being bought out. He told me they could use me
in his line, if I cared to come. Said they had a vacancy."

Alicia felt another little pang. Tom Kerry had been a
clerk under Harry, and was now offering to become his employer. It was a symbol of Harry's failure. And it would be a
good position, too. Tom Kerry would be grateful. The thing
that rankled was the reversal of places. Harry had once been
above Tom Kerry. Now their relative importance was neatly
inverted. Harry had been outstripped, and the fault was all
his own. He had failed of self-assertion. He had failed of ambition. Despite Alicia, he had failed.

II.

Those who walked along the way saw visions. Heart-
breakingly sure of the future, they faced it eagerly. A
young man and a young girl. A young girl and a young man.
Always neatly paired, always eagerly confident, they strolled
together in the dusk and talked gaily, or softly, or walked in
silence with fingers intertwined.

All but two of these strollers. Jack Grahame and little
Milly returned, slowly, unhappily.

Milly was crying quietly, trying not to make any noise.

"They make Milly do all the housework, eh?" said Harry
suddenly. "I know that aunt of hers."

They saw a little movement, as if Jack had clumsily tried
to comfort the girl by his side.

"Loving each other," went on Harry whimsically, "and
unhappy, and not able to marry. Jack!" He raised his voice a
little. "Jack! Come here a moment."

The two figures halted. There was a moment's murmured
conference, and then Jack came up the path alone.

"What is it, Mr. Blake?"

They could not see his face from the porch, but his tone

was weary and forlorn and full of a youthful despair.

"Wanted to talk to you a minute, Jack," said Harry. "Isn't
that Milly by the gate?" He added the question with a diplo-
matic air of casualness.

"Y-yes." The young man hesitated. "She's not feeling very
cheerful," he explained with something of defiance. "She
doesn't want to talk, just now."

"Bring her up here, Jack," said Harry gently. "I want to
speak to her, too."

The young man stood irresolute for a moment, then
went down to the gate, and presently returned with Milly reluctantly in his wake.

"You know the plant's being sold tonight, Jack," announced Harry.

He nodded gloomily,

"That means new bosses," he said desperately, "and no
chance for a raise for me."

Harry smiled a little in the obscurity.

"It isn't the best thing," he observed, "to think of your
work in terms of wages, but let it pass. Jack, aren't you engaged to Milly?"

"Y-yes, I am," said Jack defiantly.

Harry nodded.

"You can't marry on your present pay, Jack, and you
really aren't worth more where you are. It isn't your line.
Jack, how'd you like a new job?"

Jack stared at him.

"I'm going to be fired?" he asked unsteadily.

Harry shook his head.

"I got a letter today from a man I know," he went on.
"He has a vacancy in his business. I can get you the place, if
you like. It won't pay you as much as it would me, but if you
make good —"

Jack drew a deep, quick breath.

"Would it — could I —" He stopped.

Harry stood up.

"Come in the house, Jack. I'll show you the letter."

They went indoors. There was silence for a long minute.
Milly stood there in the dusk, her head bent a little, struggling
to keep back the tears. She had not really heard what had been
said. A sudden wave of sympathy swept over Alicia.

"Come here, Milly," she said quietly. "And if you want to
cry — I won't listen."

III.

Out on the street of magnificent dreams the couples
went by, dim shadows in the gloom, while in the darkness of the porch little Milly wept in a sudden passion of
despair. She had been walking upon the street of visions,
and had not been able to see the marvelous panoramas that
the street contained for others. She and Jack had been
walking there, and could not imagine rose-tinted castles, nor
iridescent dreams. They could see only the shadows, and it
had disheartened them.

And then Jack came out quickly, and took Milly incontinently in his arms. His face was glowing. He was almost incoherent with happiness. Harry came more slowly after, and watched with a whimsical smile as Jack babbled out his marvelous tidings.

"Why — why, it means everything, Milly!" he said breathlessly. "I'll tell you all about it. Mr. Blake —" He was anxious to be alone with Milly, so he could point out to her the marvelous thing that was before them. He hesitated upon the step of the porch.

"I — I — you understand, Mr. Blake?" He fumbled for words, and crushed Harry's hand. "I feel as if I'd like to say — God bless you, sir."

He finished shamefacedly, and went down the path with Milly. His voice was hurried now, in explanation. It was exultant. And as they passed slowly along the street of dreams it came back to them, eager and confident. "Milly — in five years —"

Harry nodded, smiling, as they passed from view.

"And he'll make good," he commented. "He'll fit in where Tom Kerry'll put him."

Alicia was silent. A sudden unworthy thought occurred to her, Harry might need the position he had just given to Jack. His firm was being sold. With the new management he might lose his position. They need have no fear, but still —

Harry reached out his hand and found Alicia's.

"How about it, 'Lecia?"

"I'm — glad you did it," she said uncertainly. "But, Harry, when the new management comes in —"

He smiled obscurely to himself.

"We'll worry about that when it happens," he told her.

Unhappy, she let him hold her hand. She could never feel that she did not love him. It was only that she felt that he had failed. He had showed so many others the way to success. He had made so many successes for others, but none for himself.

A white, brilliant light swept suddenly down the tree-lined avenue, silvering the lower branches and etching vividly the tree trunks. A couple just before their door was outlined sharply. For an instant Alicia saw the line of a girl's throat and chin. The girl was laughing. And then as the motorcar moved she was dropped back into darkness again.

Curiously speckled, the edges of the headlight glow moved and wavered as the car drew nearer. It slowed, as if the chauffeur were looking for an individual house. It stopped, and there was the faint murmur of voices, above the soft purring of a throttled-down motor. And then it came on, slowed again, and stopped before their door. The light within the limousine was snapped off. A door clicked and then slammed, and their front gate squeaked a little as a figure came into their yard.

He came up toward the house, a small, wispy man whose features were hard to make out in the darkness.

"Mr. Blake?"

Harry rose and extended his hand.

Alicia was bewildered.

"Told you I'd probably want to see you tonight," said the strange voice. "How do you do?"

Harry turned to Alicia.

"'Lecia, I want you to know Mr. Grover. He's the president of the Amalgamated. My wife."

The wispy man acknowledged the introduction. Harry motioned him to a chair.

"Would you rather talk indoors?"

"It's better out here." Harry's new employer sat down and stared out at the soft dimness. He sniffed at the scents of growing things, and at Alicia's flowers near the porch. "I wish I had a place like this. By James, I do! I begin to understand you now."

Alicia was growing more and more confused. The man was a (millionaire, several times over, and envying Harry his house.

"You know why I came, Blake," he said abruptly. "I hinted at it today. Didn't know when we'd finish with those silly papers, so I thought I'd drop by. Going early tomorrow morning. We've closed the deal. The Amalgamated takes over your firm, lock, stock and barrel."

Alicia felt utterly bewildered. Harry was no more than a department head in his firm. Why was the new owner —

"Now you know, Blake," went on Grover quietly, "why we bought you people out. Your plant hasn't been dangerous to us, but it was getting along a little too well. And we found out why. It has probably the best set of executives in the country. We wanted those men — but more than that, we wanted the system that made 'em. And you know what that system was."

"I'm afraid I don't," admitted Harry, smiling,

"By James!" exclaimed the visitor indignantly. "If you don't, I don't know who does! Look here! One of the vice-presidents of the Amalgamated says you're the greatest man in the United States for picking out and developing good timber for high-priced men. It probably isn't modest of him to say so, because you picked him out. Remember?"

"Pretty good man," admitted Harry.

"We've got one or two more men who worked under you. They're good men. We're paying the least of them five thousand a year. We're short of five thousand a year men and we're shorter of ten thousand a year men, and we're in howling, crying need of some twenty thousand a year men. There aren't enough men who're really good! And we need 'em!"

He settled back in his chair and waved his hand.

"Now, you can pick them, and you can develop them. That's why I want you. There are a dozen ten to twenty thousand a year men who swear that you set them on their feet. If you can do it for them, you can do it for some others, and I can use half a dozen men right now if they're good enough for salaries like that. If they can earn it I'll pay it to 'em, but I can't find 'em!"

"We've got some pretty good men —" began Harry,

"Piffle," muttered the millionaire inelegantly. "I know what I'm talking about. That's why you're going to manage this plant for me."

Alicia drew in her breath sharply. Harry to manage the plant!

"I'm going to run this place as a college," continued Grover. "This plant I've bought tonight is going to be a supply station for men for big jobs. If I hit on a likely man I'm going to send him to you to be polished up — though he won't know it. You've made a dozen successful men. I need successful men.

"You're going to run this place and develop every bit of worth-while timber you see. And as fast as you develop 'em I'm going to take 'em away from you. You know what a man's good for — how, I don't know. You picked out most of the men who're above you now. They're good, but you're better. So — I expect to find vice-presidents and executives coming out of this plant. And in the meantime your salary will be multiplied by four and you're in charge of the place. That suit you?"

Harry debated.

"I don't know that I can do anything special," he answered tentatively. "Only, now and then, when I find a good subordinate — "

Grover chuckled and stood up.

"That's just the trick," he said enthusiastically. "When you find a good subordinate — Have you any bad ones now?"

"No-o," admitted Harry. "They're all pretty good."

"Which may be an accident," retorted Grover, holding out his hand, "but may not. It's just possible that you make 'em good. I'm banking on that anyway. You take charge of the plant Monday week."

Harry went dawn to the car with him. Alicia was almost afraid to believe what she had heard. Harry — her Harry — to be in absolute charge. He'd be one of the big men of Burkton. He'd be — he'd be —

He came up the pathway whistling.

"Had a hint of that yesterday, 'Lecia," he said apologetically, "but I didn't want to mention it. It might not have worked out."

Alicia was breathless.

"But, Harry!" she exclaimed. "It's wonderful! Why — why —"

"I've been sort of a failure up to now," said Harry reflectively. "I haven't made much of a success. But in five years —"

A sudden light burst on Alicia. Down before her front gate couples were walking upon the street of magnificent dreams. They saw the future laid out before them, marvelously beautiful and radiant, and most infallibly certain to come about as they desired. And Alicia smiled.

"You a failure, Harry?" she repeated. She put her hands in his. "If you haven't made a success of yourself, it's been because you were making successes of other men. And you've surely made a success of that!"

But Harry still rubbed his chin reflectively. "In five years —" he began. "I say, 'Lecia, let's take a little walk up and down the street."

And then they, too, slipped out beneath the trees. And Harry's voice became eager and confident. They were walking for the second time upon the street of magnificent dreams, and Harry was describing the visions he saw there. They were radiant and beautiful visions, and Alicia listened with soft eyes. She felt very proud, for she was marvelously sure that *these* dreams were infallibly certain to be fulfilled.

HAS WORSE LUCK THAN "THUBWAY THAM"

"Thubway Tham" the clever little pickpocket of Mr. McCulley's invention, would probably say that it served "Immune Mickey" Franks right for doing his work on a street car. True it is that Immune Mickey, a famous "dip" of Chicago, Illinois, made a fatal blunder, if the police reports of what happened are correct.

Immune Mickey was riding in a streetcar with two of his pals. In the same car was James Stone, a Y. M. C. A. worker, who suddenly felt some one remove his wallet from his pocket. Stone gave the alarm, and several persons immediately rushed toward the rear entrance of the car. Among them was Mickey.

At that moment a patrolman in civilian clothes entered the car and felt a wallet being forcibly deposited in his pocket. Immune Mickey, it seemed to the policeman, was the man who had placed it there.

The pickpocket's associates beat a hasty retreat and escaped, but Mickey was not so lucky. He was escorted by the guardian of the law to a police station, where he protested his innocence and declared that he had never been arrested before. His identity as a well-known dip was, however, soon established.

— from *Detective Story Magazine*

NERVE
by Murray Leinster

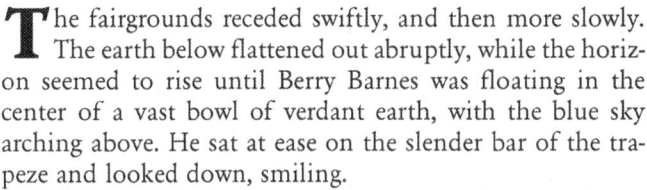

The fairgrounds receded swiftly, and then more slowly. The earth below flattened out abruptly, while the horizon seemed to rise until Berry Barnes was floating in the center of a vast bowl of verdant earth, with the blue sky arching above. He sat at ease on the slender bar of the trapeze and looked down, smiling.

He had a passion for the heights. To look down, down, down at the earth held a sort of fascination for him — a fascination that was wholly different from the suicidal vertigo so many people experience. Over his head a huge cotton bag billowed in ungainly bulk. It stank of the gasoline fumes of the fire that had inflated it. From where Berry sat he could look up through its narrow neck into a cavernous, smoky interior.

He loved the whole thing, the whole game of his daring ascents and parachute jumps, from the first laying out of the sooty bag on the green grass — with the center buoyed up between two poles at the sides — through every phase of the inflation and flight of the dirty-gray balloon. He loved the furnace that inflated his pet. He loved his last, always dramatic leap for the trapeze bar as the great bag was released and shot upward into the air. He loved the peace of the heights, the stillness broken only by the increasingly faint blaring of the band that always played "Up in a Balloon, Boys," as he rose, dangling on that slender, ineffective looking trapeze bar.

But most of all, he loved to look down from the heights at the earth below, swinging back and forth as he watched for a favorable landing-place. When he had selected his spot, there was the slender rope, the knife-cord, by his side. A pull, the cord was cut, and then — a breathless rush downward, fifty, a hundred, sometimes two hundred feet, before the parachute opened and his fall was stayed with a slight jar. After that he floated down beneath the suddenly blossomed flower above him. It was life, the quintessence of life. The thrill of danger, the intoxication of the heights, and that rapturous dash earthward at the end — those were the most perfect moments of Berry's life.

Only Anne knew how he loved it all, but only Anne knew how her heart constricted when he shot downward from the cooling balloon. Perhaps the parachute would not

open. Perhaps some rope would give way. Perhaps — perhaps — She lived in an agony of fear for him.

He laughed at her. He had made two hundred ascents before she married him, and nearly as many since, but she never saw him rise into the air without a terrible fear taking possession of her. Her greatest dread was that the parachute would not open. Some day that quick downward rush would not be checked. The little black dot that meant her husband would fall with the trailing bud of canvas behind it, and the bud would not blossom out. Swiftly and more swiftly he would fall, and the parachute would not open. She awoke sometimes in the middle of the night, crying out in terror. Berry could hardly comfort her.

He never told her of his own chief anxiety. Down beside him there ran a slender rope, connecting above with a sharp knife. When he pulled the rope the knife severed the cord that held his parachute and himself to the smoking, stinking bag. If ever that knife failed him, and the parachute was not released —

It was the one appalling thought in his mind. The bag above him would slowly cool, then more quickly. It would shrivel a little, and begin to droop toward the earth. He would sink, at first slowly, then swiftly. The bag above him would cease to be a bulging, ungainly object. It would become a slim, writhing, snake-like thing. He would drop.

Once he had seen that happen to another balloonist. The man had jumped clear two hundred feet up. When they came to him he was not a pleasant sight to look upon. Berry resolutely thrust that thought from his mind, only examining the knife in person before each ascent.

The big tents of the fair had grown small and toy-like. The blaring of the band was indistinct. The only noises he could hear were faint cheerings and the more penetrating sound of auto horns. He estimated his height with a practiced eye. Twelve hundred feet; fifteen hundred feet; eighteen hundred feet. He began to look down for his landing-space.

A big, clear field caught his eye. In a moment or two he would be over it. He waited, swinging back and forth on the trapeze bar and watching the earth flow slowly by beneath him. He smiled unconsciously. No one could tell what this meant to him. Even Anne only guessed. If she knew how he loved these moments up aloft she would never again beg him to take up some less dangerous trade.

The field he had selected was below him. He watched a moment, allowing for his drift during the parachute drop. His hand was on the rope that would cut him free from the balloon. He looked to the left. The sand-bag that would overturn the bag when he had deserted it swung free. He glanced up. The parachute was in its proper position, not tangled, in every way as experience dictated. He pulled the knife-cord. Nothing happened.

He still swung below the bag. A quick cold sweat broke out on his face. He pulled again and again. The rope did not part. His heart seemed to stop beating. Eighteen hundred feet up, under a cooling balloon, and unable to free himself. He craned his neck upward, but could not see the knife that should have released him.

In a flash he visualized the bag shrinking, then finally collapsing, then the dash downward the parachute opening fitfully, only to be crushed and tangled in the flapping bag, and finally Anne being brought to where he would be lying crushed on the ground. The pictures snapped before his eyes like the scenes of a movie. He groaned and shut his eyes. Then, quite suddenly, a vision came before him.

It was that morning. Anne and he were sitting at breakfast in the rather dingy hotel that was the best the county seat afforded. The waitress served them with a little awe in her manner. He was that reckless daredevil who made the parachute jumps at the fair, and she always felt that perhaps this would be the last meal he would eat on earth. The other people in the dining room looked at him curiously. They all knew who he was and wondered at his daring. They did not know how he loved every bit of the game. They wondered what queer trait made him so reckless.

Anne was pale. She had waked in the middle of the night, crying out in fear for him.

"What's the matter, Anne?" Berry asked. "You look as if you didn't feel well."

"I don't," she said reluctantly. She looked at him, and her eyes filled with tears, though she tried to smile bravely.

"Frightened again?" he asked.

She nodded.

"I never stop being frightened," she said in an oddly quiet voice.

"Oh, piffle, Anne!" he exclaimed. "There isn't anything to be worried about. I'm careful. You know I'm careful."

She shook her head wordlessly. She tried not to bother him about her fears, but she did wish she had not this constant prospect before her, of his horrible death at any time.

"Carefulness isn't much of a comfort, Berry."

"Now listen, dear," he said coaxingly. "I've made nearly four hundred ascents without a serious accident. One time I

sprained my ankle in landing. Once I went up when the wind was high and was dragged along the ground a bit by the parachute when I struck. A broken rib that time. Look at that record, Anne. Think of the people who are killed in every big city by automobiles and streetcars. I'm almost afraid to go into a big town!"

He stopped, hoping she would smile. Instead, she only looked at her plate and halfheartedly tried to eat.

"Lord, Anne," he went on cheerfully, "when I think of the perils to which people in cities are exposed — I'm positively a danger dodger! And anyway," he added pleadingly, "you know how I dote on the game. You know how I love the whole business, from the stink of the furnace that inflates the old bag, to the last least littlest thrill of the jump. You wouldn't have me lose that, would you?"

"You know how I love you," said Anne softly. "Do you think I like to be afraid I'm going to lose you?"

"But you aren't," protested Berry with a laugh. "I'm safe as can be, Anne. I never take any unnecessary risks."

"I know," said Anne. "But, oh, Berry, if there weren't any 'necessary' ones!"

The vision vanished, and Berry was again sitting high in the air beneath his old gray balloon, that had carried him aloft so many times, and now seemed to be holding him up for a last few moments before dropping him to his death. The vision of himself and Anne at breakfast had been instantaneous, merely a flash of memory that carried him back to the talk at the table. He jerked agonizedly at the knife-cord. The rope that held him fast remained unparted. The balloon was rising sluggishly now. The air within was still hot enough to carry him a little higher, but was cooling steadily.

Berry ground his teeth together. He was not afraid. He had faced death too often to feel a touch of cowardice now that it had come so close. It was only that a glimpse of what his death would mean to Anne had suddenly swept over him. He had married her a year before.

She was clerking in a store in New York, one of the shops that show such startling values for their prices. It was known among thrifty shoppers as the cheapest store at which to buy. Anne knew why. The advertisements said it gave great values because of the reduction of overhead expenses and the consequent decrease in the cost of goods to the purchaser. Anne knew that "overhead expenses" included, among other things, the salaries it paid to its clerks.

They were young girls mostly, and they hated the store with a consuming hatred. To cut down the cost of operation it paid them salaries on which they could barely keep body and soul together — this was in the days before the war, remember — and sometimes it did become a question of keeping body or soul alive. Berry had married Anne from behind a counter.

Sensing the growing sluggishness of the balloon above

him, Berry remembered with a groan the story she had told him after their marriage, of the terrible, monotonous struggle with poverty, with the ever-present problem of getting enough to eat and still maintaining the standard of neatness the store required. She had no relatives to help her out. She had to fend for herself. She could not be a stenographer or a typist — she had no training. And the store was a deadly grind, a monotonous torture.

With Berry dead, Anne would have no one to care for her. They had saved a little money, a very little. Berry earned it so easily it hardly seemed worthwhile to save. Anne might live on their savings for a year — perhaps. Then the store again, no friends, no family, and a grinding poverty, lasting until she gave up.

Berry seemed to see her coming out of some employees' entrance, buffeted by the other clerks, tired out, her clothes shabby.

A great rage swept over him, rage at himself. He had been so absorbed in the joys of his work that he had neglected to provide for her. He had thought of the fun he was having, glorying in the thrill of his flight and the breathless dash downward in the parachute, thinking only of himself while she had been fearing for him constantly. Berry still was not afraid for himself. He was as good as dead, and he knew it. He ignored that, thinking only of Anne.

He glanced up at the balloon. It was cooling noticeably. Long wrinkles began to appear in the lower part of the bag. Berry jerked automatically at the knife-cord, his face deathly pale and his forehead beaded with sweat. Anne. Only Anne. His own death was nothing, but Anne would care. He remembered how she had looked when he was in the hospital with those broken ribs of his.

The utter pallor of her face while the doctor poked investigating fingers about his chest had distracted Berry's attention even from his pain. The agony of apprehension that was reflected in her expression had fascinated him. Berry had felt a little awe when the doctor pronounced the triviality of his injuries. Her face had been radiant beyond any radiance he had seen before.

The balloon was cooling. Somehow, Berry sensed the loss of buoyancy even before it began to droop sluggishly toward the earth. It would not be more than a minute or so more now. The long wrinkles in the lower part were more prominent. Berry's arm automatically jerked and jerked at the knife-cord. The balloon sank slowly, and then more quickly. Berry was not afraid for himself, but only for Anne; for what his death would mean to her. He had been selfish, utterly so. For his own part, the joy he had had in his ballooning was payment even for the death he was now to meet, but Anne —

The balloon had ceased to be globular and was sinking rapidly. Berry looked up for the last time. It was a wrinkled, emaciated object. It began to flap back and forth, heavily and awkwardly. Berry groaned and closed his eyes. One arm

held fast to the side rope of the trapeze. The other jerked unconsciously at the knife-cord. Down, down, the bag flapping more loudly and violently. Suddenly he began to fall with a rush. This was the end. Anne —

He gasped. His drop had been checked with a soft jar. He looked up, unbelieving. The parachute was open, blossomed out above his head. He no longer saw the flapping balloon. Incredulously he saw that every bit of the open parachute was bathed in sunlight. He was free of the huge bag that had threatened him! The knife, failing to cut, had at last chafed its way through the holding-rope.

For an instant Berry was faint with the revulsion, then he recovered and looked down. An open field, small, but amply large for his needs, lay directly below him. He made his landing skilfully.

Forman, his helper who inflated the balloon, greeted him with a grin and an outstretched hand.

"Gee, boss," he said thankfully, "I thought you was a goner then. When the old bag begun to flap I says to myself I'd seen you go up for the last time."

"You have," said Berry briefly.

"What's that?" demanded Forman incredulously. "You ain't goin' up no more?"

"I'm cured," said Berry with a smile. "No more."

A puzzled look came over Forman's face.

"Lost your nerve?" he asked.

Berry shook his head. Forman could not be made to understand. He would never be able to grasp that Berry had already devised a new type of parachute-release that simply could not fail — and never intended to use it. He would never understand that Berry, in spite of his recent extraordinarily narrow escape, still felt that in giving up his ascents to make sure that Anne would always be cared for and happy he was giving up the thing he cared most for in all the world.

"No, I haven't lost my nerve," he said with a half smile at Forman. "I —" He shrugged his shoulders slightly. "Where's my wife?"

THE MOON-CALVES
by John D. Swain

Perry Hughes occasionally ate in the Getabite cafeteria; but only during the last week of each quarter. From this significant fact, even Dr. Watson would readily have deduced that he was a remittance man, and the Getabite cashier was a far keener observer than the satellite of Sherlock Holmes. She knew a surprising lot about the cafeteria patrons. Her final judgment of them was formed after she had learned just what classes they did or did not belong in.

For instance, Hughes belonged to that very limited cafeteria group which eats its eggs from the shell. And he did it deftly, and without self-consciousness. Next, he belonged to another small unit whose members prop reading matter against the sugar bowl while eating. The cashier did not count newspapers; she meant what she termed "lit'rachoor." To the much larger group which helped itself from the toothpick bowl on the cigar case, Mr. Hughes did not belong.

Her knowledge was even more specific. She knew his name, having seen it stamped in gold on his pigskin billfold when he paid his check; and the distended condition of the wallet, with the very few greenbacks it held, indicated infallibly that he had it in bales, but was now up against it.

In one respect alone he did not classify at all. He was sui generis. To the cashier's positive knowledge, he was the only male patron of the Getabite who could not have told the color of her hair or eyes. He apparently looked upon her as one does on a nickel-in-the-slot machine. She had purposely delayed in handing back his change, and he had merely glanced up in a bored way, as one does if a slab of chewing gum or box of matches does not instantly materialize when one drops a coin into the proper slot.

She had even spoken to him. Nothing fresh, of course. Tessie Desmond was not that kind of a girl! But she had said, "Thank you, Mr. Hughes!" once or twice when he paid, and he had not seemed gratified or even surprised that she knew his name. Probably he took it quite for granted that everybody knew it. Conceited puppy!

Even as the words formed in her mind, she was honest enough to repudiate them. He wasn't that. No one could be less self-conscious, more abstracted than this quietly yet "swell" dressed young man of thirty, with rather sad, twinkling brown eyes, if you get the idea. It wasn't conceivable that he was a hermit; but she had to confess that he might as well be, so far as she was concerned.

There is an excellent plating which looks more like refined gold than gold itself does, just as there are wax flowers more perfect than nature can produce, and extemporaneous hair which is blonder than anything in Scandinavia. Tessie was a natural blonde; hence her tresses held glints of amber and red as the light, sun or arc, played over it, and her brows were darker instead of being perfectly matched as they would have been in any beauty shop. There was mingled gold and black in her eyes, and a dimple at the right of her red, smiling lips was cunningly balanced by a faint freckle on the left of her short nose.

Eighteen, slender but well-rounded, and breathing such perfection of health and vitality that one sensed at once a clean, if not aristocratic ancestry, Tessie's instinctive taste led her to follow the prevailing mode of dress with reservations. She wore her heels and skirt at least two inches lower than her more extreme friends did, and she refused to roll her near-silk stockings; and nearly half of her pretty, close-set ears were visible, unless her hair became unruly.

She felt certain that Mr. Perry Hughes would feel repaid could she but once manage to catch his eyes. In the end, it was a profound sigh which attracted his attention. Glancing up, he beheld all that has been detailed, with every feature and attitude denoting extreme dejection.

"What seems to be the trouble?" he asked.

He had a nice voice; virile, but low-pitched, and with what Tessie, with memories of stock-company Britons, would have called an English accent; but which was really Harvard grafted on to West Pennsylvanian.

"It's thinkin' about that gold tooth I gotta have put in," she sighed.

The young man regarded her parted lips, disclosing teeth as nearly perfect as anything except an artificial set can be.

"I can't imagine such a necessity," he commented, his eyes straying from her mouth to other delectable features. He was conscious of a faint surprise that he had not noticed her before.

"Oh, it ain't *necess'ry*," Tessie reassured him. "But all my friends have got a gold tooth! They tell me mine look kinda monotonous; that a gold one would go well with my hair an' eyes."

"Oh, I say! That would be a terrible pity," Perry Hughes protested. "I have a gold crown, but am thankful to say it is back out of sight on a wisdom tooth. Nothing would tempt me to have one in front."

The cashier wriggled contentedly on her high seat. The conversation was pleasantly personal and informal.

"Do you honestly wish I wouldn't, then?" she speculated, tilting back her head and regarding him thoughtfully through narrowed lids.

The occasional patron of the Getabite looked both puzzled and amused.

"Why, I should hardly consider it to be any of my business!"

"Oh, I don't feel that way, Mr. Hughes, a-tall! I know you have good taste."

"I don't see how you know anything of the sort."

"I've seen you eat eggs," she candidly explained. "An' other things about you. I guess I'm a quick study, sorta."

He felt that the situation was rather getting out of his hands, and stalled by purchasing a brand of cigarettes he would never dream of smoking. He even lighted one. This seemed to restore his aplomb. It was probably why actors always did it in the mimic crises of the stage. He turned as he was passing out, and touched his hat brim.

"Think it over a day or so, at least," he urged.

As a matter of fact, his quarterly check was due today, and he had anticipated several weeks of real dining before the wolf chased him into the Getabite again.

II

Perry Hughes, Sr., had sold out his little foundry to a syndicate, they had gouged him pretty deep. He never contrived to get back on his feet again, and although all during young Perry's Harvard days the motherless household was maintained on a rather lavish scale, there wasn't much left when the old gentleman suddenly died. He had regarded his son's business instinct with deep abhorrence, and had frankly told him that he was atavistic; a throwback, or "sport," on the family tree, which, through many generations of hand-picked marriages, had become anemic.

"There's nothing positively bad about you," Perry remembered hearing him state, not a month prior to his death. "Sometimes I wish there was! I don't know anything that will save you except to marry some intelligent country cook who never smelled gasoline or sat up later than nine o'clock in her life!"

Things went well enough, on the whole. The only trouble was, there was just one week too many in each month, Perry decided. His allowance was ample for three weeks, but not for four. That was why he ate at the Getabite, as Tessie Desmond had easily guessed. There were much better cafeterias; but Perry's sole idea was to pacify his hunger as cheaply as possible, and he had wandered into the Getabite by chance, and gone back to it by habit. He read while eating, to forget where he was.

He belonged to two good clubs, and lived in one of them; but he was apt to be posted for dues there, and no food was served at the other. As he left the Getabite after his first chat with its cashier, he planned to go at once upon receipt of his quarterly check, cash it at the club and pay up his dues, and dine luxuriously that evening. He did, in fact, get his name removed from the delinquent list, but most surprisingly, with the pigskin billfold stuffed full once more,

he found himself heading, at six o'clock, for the cafeteria.

Tessie had thought much and tenderly about him during the afternoon. Like himself, she was an orphan; but she had no family tree. This was not because there had been anything to conceal in the lives of her ancestors, but that there had been little to record. She knew that the first Desmond had been a Huguenot refugee, who settled in Delaware, where the family had always lived. Her father, employed in a munitions factory, had risen high — along with a ton or so of T. N. T. — and much of him had never come down. At least, they never found much. Then her mother had married a market gardener, and Tessie's youth was spent in going to a village school, and weeding onions and transplanting lettuce during vacations. Stepbrothers and stepsisters came, and Tessie's mother died. She found herself edged out of the nest, and fluttered to New York.

In time the tan and calluses of the outdoor life wore off, and all but one of the freckles. There remained an exuberant vitality, and a prettiness notable even on Broadway. Several times she had been obliged to resign because of temperamental employers. On such occasions her sharp tongue reduced their stature by at least a cubit. She always found it easy to get a new place. Her present one was untroubled, since the owner of the Getabite was a middle-aged failure without ambition or vices.

III

Tessie was just leaving the cafeteria as Perry Hughes arrived. It was her short day, when she was on duty from noon until six. On alternate days she worked until noon, returning at six to remain until midnight. Lomasney, the owner, alternated with her, and had just seated himself beside the cash register as the girl, attractive in blue tricotine and darker blue straw toque, passed out to the street.

Hughes paused on seeing her. He knew nothing about her hours; had not thought of them. His return to the Getabite on this night, when he might have eaten wherever he chose, had been solely on her account. All the afternoon her gold-black eyes had followed him, and her ridiculous notion about a gold tooth had caused him many smiles. He had made no plans for improving the acquaintance; nothing beyond securing a table from which he could observe her, and see if she really was as distractingly pretty as she had seemed.

Now, seeing her on the point of leaving, he stopped uncertainly, not wishing to have her see him turn away for no reason, but unable to think of anything to say.

Tessie, who knew perfectly well why he hesitated, took matters in her own hands in order to give him time to collect himself. It was highly gratifying to her to know that he did not care to go inside now that she was off duty; and as it was evident that he must go somewhere, and the same was true for herself, it was possible that, with a little encouragement, he might ask her to dine with him, and perhaps go to a movie later.

This was not at all her custom. She sometimes went with a party to dinner, and now and then to the pictures with some nice boy; but not to dinner with him. There was a young Greek who kept a fruit store near the Getabite — a suave, black-eyed man of uncertain temper, who had pestered her for the past six months with all sorts of invitations; but Tessie did not like him, and resented his fits of jealousy. But she knew that if Perry were to invite her, she would go anywhere he suggested; and she stopped and spoke to him, to give him time to feel at ease. It would have amused the sophisticated Perry to know that a little nobody like Tessie felt that he must be put at his ease.

She smiled at him and said: "The goulash and noodles is good tonight, if you're real hungry. But lay off the Irish stew; not enough Irish in it!"

Perry smiled back at her.

"You're not going for that gold tooth, are you, Miss — er —"

"Desmond. *Tessie*. No — I'm going to put my own teeth into something hearty. I can't eat in a place I work in, after smelling the cooking all day!"

"I'm not keen about goulash and noodles," confided Perry.

Tessie waited, calmly surveying the throng of clerks and stenographers, and bobbing her pert turban in greeting from time to time. She was in no hurry; there was nothing to do till tomorrow.

"I say — why not come and have dinner with me?"

The man looked anxiously at her unconcerned and very perfect profile. "We've both got to eat. Why not together?"

She turned slowly toward him, her long lashes masking the triumph in her gold-black eyes.

"Uh-huh. Sure! We'll make it Dutch."

"We'll do nothing of the sort, I have oodles of money tonight. We'll eat in a regular place — not meaning to knock the Getabite!"

"O-oh!" She prolonged the vowel, and her gaze. "Then your allowance came today?"

His own eyes widened.

"How did you — what do you mean?"

Tessie laughed. She had a nice, gurgly laugh that began deep in her round white throat, and it ended by a thrust of the extreme tip of her tongue between her teeth.

"Why else would you eat at our place on the last few days of the quarter, and no other times? Don't you s'pose I been broke, too? Only with me it's at the end of the week, instead of the quarter."

"You're a regular little sleuth! That reminds me that you know my name, too, though I do not recall mentioning it, or signing I.O.U.'s at the Getabite? Just how much do you know about me, anyhow?"

"Enough so I'm accepting an invitation to dinner, Mr. Hughes."

"Then you don't know the worst, for which I'm grateful. Haven't you a coat or something, to wear over that thin suit?"

"Sounds like Coney," she speculated.

"But isn't. Not with me! We're going to fly high tonight."

She nodded, and darted back into the cafeteria to take a blue cloak which hung on its hook back of her cage.

"Whassa matter?" the despondent Lomasney asked, looking up from his nearly empty cash register. "Change in the weather?"

"I'm elopin'," she flung back at him with a smile.

"I'll be doin' it all by myself, if business falls off much more!" Lomasney grumbled.

Perry threw her cloak over his arm, and signaled a passing taxi.

"To the Moon-Fixers!" he said to the chauffeur.

"Where's that?" Tessie queried, wrinkling her nose.

"To tell the truth, I've never been there; but some of my friends have. It's the latest jazzery, and about the most expensive. I feel in the mood for it tonight."

It was a good ten-mile drive up the Hudson before their car drew up at the end of an already fairly long line of waiting taxis and roadsters. They alighted, and walked a short distance beside a high brick wall to a wide entrance beyond which was a roomy lawn dotted with elms, from whose boughs Japanese lanterns cast a varicolored glow over many little tables gleaming with linen and cut glass and silver. Behind a syringa a Filipino orchestra drowned out the more musical katydids and crickets.

A dancing pavilion bounded the lawn at one side, and its far end overlooked the Hudson, a silver roadstead in the moonlight. But there was nothing in all this to distinguish the place from dozens of other roadhouses. What set the Moon-Fixers apart, and gave it its name, was a novelty in the presence of half a dozen captive balloons, tethered to earth by a stout hempen cable wound on a drum. In each basket, which was reached by a short rope ladder, was a little *table à deux*. The successive courses were sent up in a wicker service container; and the couverte charge for the privilege of dining above the earth was twenty-five dollars.

It was toward one of these swaying monsters that Perry guided his pop-eyed little companion.

A waiter wound up the drum, and the basket slowly descended until its rope ladder touched the dew-drenched lawn. Tessie nimbly clambered up and inside, with a whip of skirts and a flash of silken ankles. Perry followed, and seated himself across the diminutive table from her in one of the two wicker chairs. There wasn't a foot of space to spare.

The waiter scribbled the order on his pad, and placed olives and salted almonds and celery hearts on the table. Then he began to unwind the drum, and foot by foot they rose, level with the swinging Japanese lanterns, up among the elm boughs, clearing their tops, to come to rest gently swaying a hundred feet in the air.

Directly below them, the lanterns formed a misty screen of colored light through which rose the softened wails of ukulele and steel guitar, the laughter and chatter of those dining al fresco on the lawn, the shuffle of pumps on the pavilion floor. As they were the first to dine in the air tonight, they were as much alone as if they had taken refuge in the fourth dimension. Far below, and a little to one side, the Hudson lay in a ribbon of dull silver, the mists clinging to its surface.

Tessie sighed.

"I'll say we're on the top of the world!" she declared. "I don't believe there is any such place as we're in. Don't wake me up!"

"Thought you'd like it," Perry nodded at her. "Pretty clever idea somebody had, what?"

A buzzer sounded beneath the table, and there appeared at the outer rim of their basket a little cage containing their oysters. Perry removed them, touched the button which sounded another buzzer down below, and the container descended.

There was quite a little air stirring, and the two-inch guardrail on the table was needed to keep the dishes out of their laps. A great tureen of *purée Mongols* followed their oysters; a sizzling hot lake trout came next. The cool night air whipped their healthy young appetites; and for a space they devoted themselves to the dinner, speaking only in fragments.

By the time they had finished the trout, another balloon joined them, just far enough away to avoid danger of collision. They exchanged jovial greetings with the intruders, a fat, bald gentleman, rather nervous, and a slim girl ostentatiously at ease.

"I knew you were worth knowing," said Tessie as her host served a ruddy cut of beef a full inch thick. "But I certainly thought you'd never sit up and take notice!"

"You brought me to life with that awful gold tooth idea. Hope you have changed your mind?"

"Well — I had to do *something* to get you to talk!"

"You mean you were not in earnest?"

"Who — me? Not so you'd notice it! I just made that up as I went along."

Perry grinned.

"I fell for it all right! But why I never noticed you before I can't imagine. Suppose it was because I was always broke, and low-spirited when I went to the Getabite. Used to wish I could sleep through the last week of the quarter."

"I know the feeling," Tessie nodded. "But at least you didn't have to work. It's bad enough to have to eat at the Getabite — let alone work there!"

He patted the firm little hand that held her water glass. She looked reflectively at it, but made no move to withdraw it.

"Seems to me you don't show much business sense, Mr. Hughes."

"Please say Perry — at least, till we get back to earth!"

"Well, then, Perry, I don't know what it costs to eat in a balloon, but I can see you hitting a one-arm chair more'n a week to pay for this spree."

"Righto. But isn't it worth it? You are not the first to observe that I am no young Napoleon of finance. That's why my dad left everything in trust. Trouble is, there are too many weeks in a month. If there were only three, I'd live like a lord!"

Tessie shook her head vigorously.

"No, you wouldn't. You'd spend twice as much in the first two weeks, and go broke the third. And if you got your income once a year, you'd starve along about November."

Perry for the third time sounded the buzzer on the table.

"That waiter must have forgotten he has a party in the sky," he grumbled.

"There's a lot of this dinner coming yet — and it's getting cool up here."

He leaned over the basket edge and peered down through the darkness, shading his eyes from the electric candelabra over their table. Then, an astounding thing happened. Japanese lanterns, elm trees, all the dimly visible earth seemed to drop away from them, leaving them resting in space.

Tessie saw things differently. She was looking idly at the couple fifty feet away, and as usual with her, placing them in their proper classes. Suddenly she shot above them. She had the briefest glimpse of the fat man's face, mouth open, and a large portion of sweetbread arrested on its journey. She heard the shrill diminuendo of the girl's scream, noticed that the Filipino band seemed to die away to the mere ghost of syncopated melody. She leaned across the table and seized Perry's arm.

"We're off!" she shouted to him. "Our balloon's broke away, and we're going up a mile a minute!"

IV

From his fruit store two doors below the Getabite, Demetrius Pappas had beheld with deep resentment the encounter of Tessie and her young "gentleman friend."

He was a passionate man, with a glossy black mustache and a jealous nature. Often he had tried to induce the pretty cashier to dine with him at the Marathon or Minerva coffee house; and she had always replied that while she might go with a feller to a picture, maybe, that was her limit. Now, observing intelligently that the man with whom she was talking was far above him in class, a gentleman and presumably rich, he knew that at this hour she would be going out to eat; and he watched them narrowly to see what might happen.

When the girl re-entered the cafeteria to appear an instant later with her cloak, while her companion signaled a taxi, Demetrius suspected the very worst. He edged up to them, mingling with the six o'clock throng, and for once the sharp-eyed Tessie, absorbed in her conquest, failed to notice his proximity. So it was that he heard his rival direct the chauffeur to drive to the Moon-Fixers' restaurant.

He had never heard of this place; but he found it listed in the telephone directory. He slipped a sharp banana knife with an ugly curved blade in his pocket, left his fruit stall in charge of his assistant, and set out to follow. He had no definite plan in mind. He was given to brief fits of violent rage, although in general a sunny child of the Levant.

He did nothing so foolishly extravagant as to hire a taxi; but having learned where the Moon-Fixers was, he was able to get a surface car for nearly half the distance, and set out to walk the rest of the way. He argued that his prey would spend a couple of hours, at least, over their dinner, and that there would be plenty of time.

On arriving, he strolled about the grounds, observing each table, looking on at the dancers in the pavilion, making a careful survey of the entire place. He had about made up his mind they were not there, when his sharp ears detected Tessie's laughter floating down from somewhere above the Japanese lanterns.

When he had satisfied himself that the two were alone in the balloon, far above him and out of reach, his rage, which had been gradually cooling in the night air, flared up afresh. He observed the waiter sending up expensive food by a pulley, heard above the whining of the Filipino orchestra snatches of laughter and talk from the gently swaying basket above the tree-tops.

While the waiter was engaged in seating some fresh arrivals, Demetrius Pappas edged up to the wooden drum, to which was attached the cable. It was now quite dark, and nobody paid any attention to him. There were many, singly and in pairs, strolling about the spacious grounds.

It was but the work of a second to whip out the banana knife, and with one slashing stroke, sever the hempen cable. An instant later Demetrius had slipped around an elm tree, crossed over to the pavilion, and passed out through the entrance just as the place began to hum with the news that one of the captive balloons had worked loose with a party of diners.

There was, in fact, more excitement among those left behind on earth than in the runaway balloon itself. The great bag shot straight up at first, but the occupants of the basket were not conscious of any violent motion. Low-hanging clouds hovered over the valley of the Hudson, and in a few moments they passed through these and found themselves bathed in moonlight. The balloon ceased to rise, and, borne along by a steady easterly breeze, it swept over the fleecy cloud floor, across which their black shadow pursued them. Overhead fled the golden phalanx of the stars, while the full moon, seeming to have doubled in size, raced with them in playful rivalry.

The two refugees were still seated. There was no room to move about. They clasped hands, straining toward one another across the table.

"It's incredible that such a thing could happen, but it has," said Perry, his voice sounding hollow in the great void. "Your people — they will never forgive me —"

Her fingers moved ever so slightly in his.

"I have none."

"There must be *somebody* who cares?"

"Old Lomasney will be peeved if I'm not in my cage at six sharp. There's nobody who counts. No one I'd rather be alone with up here than you!"

He tightened his grip on her little hands.

"And you're not afraid?"

"I don't think so. Somehow, looking at this" — she lifted her face to the moon-shot sky — "we seem sort of unimportant. Awful small, if you get the idea."

He inclined his head in sympathetic understanding. Below them the clouds lay as solid as a sea. One might conceivably drown in them; but it seemed impossible that one could fall through to the vanished earth beneath. Here and there were rents, like deep wells at the bottom of which glimmered faint lights, representing sleeping towns over which they were drifting.

Tessie shivered a little, and released one hand to draw closer about her neck a small fur piece.

"That's effective," approved Perry, seeking to distract her mind by compliment.

"Huh!" She scorned. "Monkey fur."

"And isn't that worn this season?" He laughed.

"I s'pose it is — by monkeys! But not by regular folks. It's all the fur I got. Which goes for monkeys, too."

Before they realized that they were descending, they found themselves smothered in cold, clammy mist. Then the earth burst into view, a patchwork of moonlighted spaces spangled on ink-black shadows.

"A lot depends on where we land," Perry worried, "I believe balloonists toss overboard one of their fifty-pound bags of sand when they want to rise."

He had a vague notion that these bags were heaved over bodily — not realizing the effect this would have on whomever a fifty-pound sand bag might drop from a distance of a mile or so!

"Hold tight to the ropes," he warned, and held her shoulders until she did so. "I'll try tossing over the table. It's in the way, anyhow. Here goes!"

First the dishes, then the table itself. So rapid was their own descent that at first the table seemed to hang suspended in air beside them. Then, as they leaped upward, it shot out of sight.

They now sat down in the basket, peering over the rim. They did not again pierce the cloud belt; and as no broad fields suitable for a landing appeared below, and after a time they began to descend once more, the chairs were thrown over.

By good luck no one was injured. It was very late — long past midnight — and few were astir in the rural section over which they were passing. An Italian truck gardener was amazed the following morning to discover a perfectly good set of tableware, each piece bearing an embossed half moon, in his onion field. As there were no footprints anywhere about save his own, it was manifestly a miracle. A mile away a farmer speculated on the strange vision of a wrecked table lodged on the ridgepole of his barn; but by noon the story of the runaway balloon had spread over the country.

For a long time after discarding the chairs, the derelict swept steadily south and east, very gradually sinking earthward, until Perry became alarmed as the tallest trees thrust upward at them with menacing boughs. There was nothing more to throw overboard, and it was evident that before long they would make a forced landing.

"Ought to be a rip-cord, somewhere; but I don't see any. Just as well, perhaps. I might let out all the gas at once, and drop us like a sinker," he thought.

Once they swung perilously near a white village steeple, just as its solemn bell struck the hour of two. Twice they missed a hillock by yards; and for a long time they skimmed along a marsh, from which millions of frogs jeered at them.

Perry reached out and gathered Tessie into his arms in the shelter of their basket. She snuggled warm and fragrant there, her head against his breast. Presently her own arms stole up and about his neck, and her lips were on his. Traveling with the wind, there was no sense of motion, no discomforting breeze. They seemed suspended in a golden flood of moonshine. It was as if they were alone in the firmament, companions of the planets, and floating in the midst of dead worlds.

He was the first to recall their peril. Glancing over the basket edge he was horrified to see that they were a scant ten feet above ground, and hurtling toward a row of long, narrow white buildings.

"Hold tight!" he bawled, wrenching her arms from his neck, and guiding her hands to the supporting ropes. "Don't jump, whatever happens!"

Hardly were the words spoken than with a shock like the end of the world, their basket struck. As they were hurled out, there came a ripping crash, and in an instant they were in the midst of a multitude of fluffy white, flapping, and frantically squawking creatures. Then, with a spine-jarring bump, they sat on Mother Earth.

Minds and bodies were stunned for the moment. They were roused by the sound of voices, and the winking of lanterns.

"Head the varmints off, Jawn! We'll try what a load of double-B'll do to the pesky hen thieves!"

The lights separated, and heavy footfalls became audible. Perry rose unsteadily to his feet. He cautiously raised Tessie.

"Anything broken?" he whispered.

"Everything, I guess! But I don't seem to mind it."

"We must have lighted in a chicken-run; let's go while the going's good."

At this instant an amazed cry startlingly near at hand arrested them.

"Pa! Looka here! They've gone an' ripped off the hull roof of the white Orpingtons' roost!"

A deeper voice answered from somewhere to the left:

"They couldn't! There wasn't time. It'd take a couple o' hours to do that."

"You just come an' see for yerself! I tell ye they *hev*!"

A consultation followed, and the trespassers took advantage of it to steal away. They fetched up several times against chicken wire, and disturbed numbers of outraged Orpingtons rendered homeless by the sudden snatching away of their rooftree; but at length they found a gate, and slipped through, and across a field to a well-traveled road.

Their balloon, lightened of its passengers, had leaped high in air, and was doubtless several miles away by now.

"Here's where we count the ties back to Broadway," sighed Tessie. "The show's over."

She smiled up at him, and put her hand in his. They swung gaily up the white highway, not much caring where they were.

"This road must lead somewhere, and I've the price of gasoline!" Perry declared. "We'll breakfast in town yet."

In fact, a scant mile brought them to a sizable village, and at its garage they awakened a night man, and learned that they were in Long Island.

"Broke down a mile back, and want to get carried to New York," Perry explained.

The man rubbed his eyes and grumbled. Although his sole reasons for staying at the garage nights was to profit by just such mishaps, he seemed sore at having his nap spoiled.

"'S a long ways. Cost ya twenty," he said.

Perry promptly peeled off a couple of tens and offered them. "Hurry up, then!"

The car was rather shabby, but in good condition; and shortly they were speeding toward home.

"No more work at the cafeteria, Tessie," said Perry Hughes, drawing her close to him in the darkened rear seat.

"How do you get that way? We're back on earth now — not up in the clouds with the moon!"

"I'm serious! I don't want anything in the world but you, now. The license and the ring are my first errands after we have some coffee."

Tessie laughed contentedly.

"It listens pretty in the moonlight," she admitted. "But how about that last week in the quarter? You can't stretch your income for one, now. It'd crack, trying to feed two. Wait!" As he started to protest, "I got a lot better plan than that. My boss is all ready to quit cold. He's got a three-year lease, and a trade that's falling off every day. Why? Because he's a simp! The Getabite oughta show a clear profit of twenty beans a day. It did once. But he's got no sense. Hires a chef that can't cook fish decent — and blooey! goes our whole Friday business. Skimps his coffee four ounces to the gallon, and it tastes like tea. Boils his tea, and it tastes like coffee. Nothing served warm — except the ice water."

"Well — what of it? What's it all to me? I don't intend to eat there after you are Mrs. Hughes!"

"You don't have to; but if you will show a little courage I'll make you like it! And bring your friends, too. As I say, the old man is all in. He'd jump at any kind of an offer. A thousand dollars would buy the Getabite. Say three hundred down, and give my boss notes for the rest. Couldn't you fix that?"

"Why, yes; I suppose so. I could even pay that much cash. Of course! But what do I want of a cafeteria?"

"Ain't I telling you? So's you can have twenty a day to add to what you got — and a place to eat in for nothing the last week of each quarter! And speakin' for myself, so's the future Mrs. Hughes can buy herself a trousseau befittin' her silk-stocking fiancé!"

It took quite a bit of argument to convince Perry, but he had capitulated before Brooklyn was reached.

"It's horrible to think of having you go to work after such a night, without one wink of sleep!"

"Never you mind me; reading the newspaper accounts of the missing balloon, and making change at the same time, will keep me awake till noon. Then the hay, till six. My bad time will come between ten and twelve tonight."

"I'll be there to stay awake with you," he promised.

"We'll drink black coffee and yawn in each other's faces," she prophesied.

It was quarter to six o'clock when the shabby car was dismissed a few blocks from the Getabite.

Perry bought an armful of morning papers, the headlines of each featuring their mishap and hinting at the worst.

"I'll never go back to pay that dinner check," he said. "Their own fault. Could sue them if it wasn't for the notoriety. Must find out who that chicken-breeder was, though, and send him a bank note."

Considering their thrilling night, they parted in very matter-of-fact manner. It wasn't Perry's fault. The street was too crowded.

Tessie, looking as fresh as if she had had a ten-hour sleep, tripped into her cage five minutes ahead of time. Perry turned toward his club. He yawned and passed a hand over his chin. It rasped sharply.

"I need a shave and bath, and a lot of coffee, and a sleep," he reflected. "Outside of kiting all over Long Island and ruining a perfectly good hen house, and agreeing to buy a cafeteria, and getting myself engaged to the greatest little pal in the world, I spent a quiet evening!"

Demetrius Pappas watched him go.

His fit of jealous rage had passed quickly, and all night he had sat in the Minerva Cafe, consuming endless cups of syrupy-black coffee. He was filled with remorse, and dreaded to look at the early papers lest he read news that would convict him, in his soul, as a murderer.

He beheld the arrival of the two at six o'clock, afoot, and unconcerned. His simple soul was puzzled, but vastly relieved. He turned to an early customer, and with a clean sweep of his knife — the selfsame one that had severed the balloon cable — he removed six nice yellow bananas from the parent stalk.

"Fif-a-teen cent!"

He smiled and forgot all about his blighted affections.

PIRATES' GOLD
by H. Bedford-Jones

I

It was past six bells and growing on to noon, and I was a homesick man as I stood on the quay below London Bridge and watched the *King Sagamore* swinging on her hawser out in the tideway. For she was Virginia-owned, and I, George Roberts of Virginia, knew her well, so that the sight of her was like a touch of home to me.

Also, I had a vile headache, and my memory of the previous night's events was very hazy. I had met a number of other captains, and I think some ship-owners, at the Royal Arms, though I could remember only Ned Low and the dark man, Russel, because I liked the one and disliked the other. I seemed to remember that Low had promised his interest to try to get me a ship, or else a chief mate's berth, but I could recall little of what he had said, except that he told some gorgeous yarns of the Guinea trade.

"Good morning, Captain Roberts!" came a voice, and I turned to see Russel himself approaching.

I greeted him without pleasure, for there was a sneer in his eyes, and I did not like his gold-laced hat and jeweled fingers, or the look in his dark face.

"You seem mighty busy," he went on, his heavy-lidded gaze searching me. "The cap'n put you under the table, I hear! Well, what think you of the *King Sagamore*?"

"Out of trim," I responded. "She's down by the head, or I'm a Dutchman!"

"Oh!" said Russel, eying me. "But you're a Virginian, sir — and a seaman to boot! I never heard of seamen coming from Virginia or the other colonies."

This angered me, as it also puzzled me. Why on earth the man should want to pick a quarrel, I could not see. But, knocking out my pipe and smiling, I obliged him swiftly.

"Plenty you never heard of, I imagine! Particularly here in England."

"Eh?"

He bent his black brows upon me, scowling.

"How mean you?" he added.

"Why, just this: What was your name before you made it Russel?"

At that, his white teeth showed. He clapped hand to belt as if feeling for a pistol, and I laughed at him.

"Aye, try it with a Virginian!" I told him, and chuckled again. "Think you're on the high seas, my bucko? Russel, forsooth! If you're not a Portugee, I don't know my business! Aye, snarl all you please — and ladies' rings to your fingers. You cursed fool, don't you know they hang pirates in London town? How long since you were on the Account, as the gentry of that profession term it?"

That reached him between wind and water, as it were. I really meant to taunt him into action, since I wanted to feel my fist in his dark face; but I went too far. His hands dropped. He stood motionless, his eyes eating into me, and they become bloodshot.

"On the Account!" he repeated the phrase, a thickness in his voice. "You speak glibly of it! Perhaps you've been on the Account yourself, my fine Virginia sailor?"

"Why, perhaps I have," said I cheerfully. "And what of it?"

He looked at me for another moment, then turned on his heel and strode away very swiftly, as one who goes of set purpose. I looked after him, frowning. He had been at the tavern with Captain Low the previous night. Ned Low was an engaging rascal of the sort that men love, had been master of a Guineaman, and had traded at the Indies. Russel was of a very different stripe; a sinister man, certainly no Englishman, and I wondered that Ned Low would keep company with him.

However, I dismissed the matter, filled my pipe afresh and turned to watch the ship out in the stream. She was making ready to sail, and to a seaman's eye she presented some uncommonly interesting aspects.

That homesick feeling grew on me as I looked. My first voyage had been made in her, under old Andrew Scott — a cold and hard master he was, too! Anyone who had sailed with Scott had tales to brag of. But Cap'n Scott was dead and gone these two years, thanks to a drinking bout with Sandy Fisher aboard the *Margaret* at Barbados; for Sandy craftily mixed some rare claret in the rum, and Cap'n Scott never rose from under the table.

Well, Scott was dead, and here was I a captain, and yonder the old *King Sagamore*! Heartily did I wish that I were commanding her or at least aboard of her, since I was down to my last guinea, with no hope of a ship except I took out a slaver, for which I had no stomach.

Gossip along the quay told me that she was bound for Virginia, but I doubted this. She was in ballast, and no ship went to Virginia in ballast these days. Also she had bent a new suit of canvas and was fresh-varnished; and I, knowing how stingy were her owners, realized that this was something like a miracle.

What was more, I perceived a featherbed being put aboard her from the lighter alongside. A featherbed, indeed! No wonder all the Thames boatmen jeered her as they passed, and the crew of a fishing-lugger tied at the quay began to bawl comments which set the river in a roar of laughter. I wondered who was going to use that featherbed.

One cannot deny that the *King Sagamore* has a certain roll to her in the best of seas; an uneasy and fretful roll, as if endeavoring to shake loose of the bloodstains that have sunk into her teak. Even old Cap'n Scott had groaned and left the deck at times.

Just now I heard a voice calling out:

"There 'e be, sir! That's 'im a-smoking of the 'bacca!"

I glanced about, to see a quay loafer pointing me out to a gentleman approaching rapidly. I faced about to meet this stranger in some surprise.

He was a man in a hurry; a small fellow of forty-odd, wizened and thin in the cheeks, his eyes very sparkling. From his heaving chest and awry wig, he had lately been running. As he strode up to me he produced a snuffbox with a great air of grandeur.

"Your pardon, sir," he addressed me, his words rapid and with authority. "You are Captain Roberts, the Virginian?"

"I am," was my response.

"My name is Dennis Langton, merchant and goldsmith, living at the Wheatsheaf in Lombard Street. I had word this morning from Low that you'd be sailing with us."

He rattled this all out in a breath. Then he flung a glance over his shoulder and suddenly thrust the snuffbox at me.

"Here, take this and fetch it aboard wi' you — move sharp now! Tell Ned that I'll come aboard as he drops downstream. Give it to him and no other. With you this side Gravesend — Devil sink me! The dogs have caught the trail — hide it, lad —"

Leaving the snuffbox hidden in my fist, the spry little man darted away from me and ran for cover like a hunted rabbit. I gaped after him, thinking him a madman until the burst of shouts went up from the running men.

"Stop thief!" went up the yells, shrill and sharp with the hunting fever. "Escape! Trip him up — 'scape! 'Prentices out — stop thief — king's name! Pirate and thief —"

Upon and past me swept a shrilling throng in a mad rush, two constables in the lead. Langton vanished in among the buildings, and they after him, and the chorus of yells was swiftly drowned in the noise of the city.

I stood there staring after the rout, until the whimsicality of it all drew a laugh from me. The swift change from the pompous manner and address to the wild flight was ludicrous. The incident was strange and unreal — a merchant of Lombard Street pursued as thief and pirate!

Pirate! Dennis Langton! Suddenly the name flashed across my consciousness and startled me. Three years previously, or rather four, since it was early in 1720, I was mate aboard the ship *Susannah*, owned by a merchant of Southwark Side, near London. There had been much talk aboard her of how she had fallen prey to a brace of pirates near Madeira last voyage and had later escaped. Spriggs was one of the rovers, the same who was lately hanged at Tyburn and still hangs there.

And the other one — Now the name came back to me clear enough! Langton, and none other; Dennis Langton, a soft-spoken man, who was reputed to have murdered many with his own hand.

Could the pirate Langton be the same man as this merchant and goldsmith? Most unlikely, and yet all things are possible in this world!

Now came suspicion that he had stolen the snuffbox which he forced on me, and that I might be taken for a thief. This vanished when I opened my hand. The box was a small one of black wood, absolutely worthless. Nor had the little man the look of a cut-purse.

And what was it he had said about Captain Low? A message for Low, too. And what was that about my shipping with Low? I felt bewildered.

Thrusting the snuffbox into my pocket, I drew again on my pipe, frowning over this singular incident. I was still turning it over in my mind perplexedly, when there arose a new and more singular matter which drove it completely out of my head; and no wonder!

Hearing my name called, I looked around to see Captain Low himself coming toward me, bravely puffing at a pipe and laughing to himself over some inward joke.

"Ha, Roberts! A fine morning to you, George! Damn me, but we had a pretty rouse last night! Why are you standing thus idle in the market place?"

"Why, for lack of work!"

Smiling, I gave him a grip of the hand.

"It seems to me that you said something about looking you up today — but I confess that last rum punch we brewed put a stopper on my brain! Sink me if I can remember a thing."

"What!"

Low gave me a singular yet whimsical look.

"Come, lad! You don't mean to say that you can't remember our discussion?"

"Not a thing," I said ruefully. "I've lost even the name of your ship, Ned!"

He broke into a roar of laughter, dropped his pipe and smashed it, roared again, then clapped me heartily on the shoulder and swung me about.

"There she lies, Roberts, damn me, this is a creamy jest! Wow! Wait until I tell John Russel about this! And you entered with me as chief mate, too! Oh, lad, ha' pity on me! Yonder's the *King Sagamore* with poor Gunner Basil loading the last aboard; and me sleeping abed all morning thinking you stood on her deck!"

"Good Lord!" I stammered. "D'you mean to say that I, George Roberts, shipped as chief mate with you —"

He fell to roaring again with laughter, and I chimed in, helpless to withstand it. We stood there like two fools, holding our sides and sending up shouts of mirth that drew curious folk about to stare and wonder if we were loose from Bedlam.

At length I came out of the fit of laughter, and we walked apart down the quay, discussing matters. When I told Low how I had been homesick for the *King Sagamore*, he began to bellow again.

His news struck me with incredulity, but a glad man I was for the carouse of the night before, since I appeared to have landed a good berth with a man I liked. Ned Low was fully as tall as I, and even wider in the shoulder; a lean man, his face brown and hard as if carven from mahogany, but ever ready to slip into the cheeriest laughter man ever heard. He had a whimsical touch about him, and I think had run away from Oxford for love of the sea, since he could quote the classics by the hour and spoke sometimes of Magdalen Towers.

Well, he speedily made it clear to me that I was signed with him, and that he had all morning supposed me to be aboard, at which we laughed again.

"Russel came back and dragged me from table just as I was sitting down to breakfast with word that you were standing on the quay like a man in a dream," he concluded with a final chuckle. "So I came along to see —"

"Russel!" I said, and frowned. "Does he sail with us?"

"Aye."

Low took my arm frankly and turned me eye to eye with him.

"Listen, Roberts! We've scant time to talk — I must get aboard and see to things. But you're a man after my own heart; I drank you under the table last night to make certain, since rum brings out the worst of a man!

"I know you and Russel must fall out. That's as it should be; but look out that Russel doesn't slip a knife into you. Understand? I have to take him as second mate, willy-nilly, and as we explained last night — Well, run along and get your things, and don't miss the tide on your life! I must aboard."

He turned, calling to a wherry just leaving the landing-stairs and made her with a swift run and a leap. I marveled at his catlike agility, responded to his wave of the hand, and turned to seek my own clothes at the Hare and Hounds, fortunately close by.

For all that I was a happy-go-lucky young devil this morning's affair left me in somewhat of a daze. Or perhaps the rum punch contributed to that effect. However, I was gradually coming to an understanding of things. Russel had come up to me in an evil humor, thinking that I was shirking my duty by loafing ashore; which would well account for his attitude.

Not until I had nearly reached my lodgings did I recall that extraordinary meeting with the man Dennis Langton, and clapped hand to pocket with an exclamation. I had clear forgotten to speak of him to Ned Low!

However, no matter now. It was evident that he must have seen Low that morning, or have heard from him that I was in charge of the ship.

I packed my trunk and stepped in to the ordinary to pay off my landlord. Just then a number of men came crowding in with much high talk, amid which I caught the name of Langton. At that I turned and listened, while the landlord gaped likewise.

"And to think that Langton has all this while been a merchant in Lombard Street!" cried one man with a volley of oaths. "A pretty pass we're coming to in London town!"

"They say," chimed in another, "that he has already sold out his business and was in shape to skip the city —"

"All by accident he was betrayed," spoke up another, a late comer. "You've not heard? Zounds, a ripping story! In Lombard Street itself, only this morning, gentlemen! He came face to face with a shipman whom he'd plundered years ago, was recognized, dodged the hue and cry and broke clear away. Now the constables are searching the city for him, and the waterside as well. A pirate at loose — zounds!"

I paid my score, engaged a man to carry down the trunk and went my way somewhat thoughtfully.

This Dennis Langton, known for a pirate, was a friend of Low and was hoping to get aboard the *King Sagamore*. I was going as mate aboard that ship. So was John Russel; and my words had stung Russel that morning. Russel like Langton, had been on the Account, as those who take to piracy term the profession.

What about Ned Low? He was one of them; no use shirking the fact. This fine Virginia ship was going a-sailing on a mighty queer cruise, in ballast at that!

And what about me, George Roberts of Virginia?

Why, that was simple enough! Duty lay clear and straight before me — inform the authorities, have everyone aboard the *King Sagamore* laid by the heels, and become a popular hero! The ship would be saved to its owners and everybody happy.

Against this there balanced Ned Low's frank and keen blue eyes, the clap of his hand on my shoulder, the comradely liking I bore him. Aye, because I liked him I laughed at duty! Besides I was never a great hand at informing. If I want a thing done, I go do it; this running to catch-polls and constables is not to my mind.

So we came down again to the quay, and as I pocketed my pipe my hand touched the black snuffbox. I drew out the thing and looked at it, pressed the catch and opened it. Inside there was no snuff, but a folded, bone-hard bit of vellum. I put the thing away once more.

"Let sleeping dogs lie!" I reflected. "Dennis Langton may be caught. If he's been posing as a merchant here in London, he'll be well known and should be caught in an hour's time. That may simplify matters a bit.

"As for Ned Low, I trust him more than a little, and he should have sense enough to know that I'm not going on the Account. Perhaps that's not his own intention, either! I may be wronging him."

I called a wherry and was taken out toward the ship. As we approached her I fell to laughing again; for I had not the least notion whither she was bound or on what errand. And I remembered that featherbed going aboard, so that the whole affair struck me afresh with such whimsical humor that I could not refrain from laughing. Captain Low looked over the rail as we drew near, and he caught the infection and began to roar again with mirth, and was still grinning as I came over the side.

"Welcome!" he cried, and struck hands again, a hearty grip. "What's so merry?"

"Why, I can't remember where we are bound for," I said. "Guinea or the plantations?"

"It wasn't mentioned," and Low chuckled. "The Verde Islands, if you want to know, and then Barbados or elsewhere."

"Then we stow salt at the islands, do we?"

Low glanced around, saw that we were alone and gave me a straight look.

"Nay, Roberts — we stow gold! Art satisfied? And not on the Account neither."

I nodded, and once again forgot about Dennis Langton's message.

II

After stowing my duffel away in one of the stern cabins I came on deck again and inspected things. Captain Low had everything shipshape, and now there was little to do save to await the tide. Russel had not come aboard as yet, either.

Truly a sweet ship was the *King Sagamore*! Built originally for the India trade, she had much of the black teak in her making, and this was ever kept oiled and waxed, in neat contrast to her white deck and varnished spars and the new canvas stowed aloft. At her bow the torso of a feathered savage was set for figurehead; glass eyes the Sagamore had in his painted visage, and I have heard said that the evil eye was entered into him.

The men were clumped in groups forward. And to my disgust one of them was standing on the rail, exhorting several around him with a voice of wild fervor; a tall, thin man, hair flying in the wind, cheeks like yellow parchment and a godly eye. Gunner Basil was this, who had a true preaching whine to his Puritan voice.

"No place for you, gunner!" I said when I understood who he was. "Get you aft!"

He rolled his eyes at me and shook his head.

"Nay, nay, sir! It is time that one officer of this ungodly heathen vessel should be able to think for the souls o' these poor men!"

"Your argument may be sound, gunner," I said, "but you had best learn that your place is to obey first and argue later."

With which I clipped him under the ear and took his place at the rail.

"Douse him with a bucket, lads," I said to the men, "and look alive! Where's the bosun? Ah! Damn me if it isn't Bosun Pilcher out of the *Merry Thought*! Bose, remember our voyage in the Guineaman, do you? Glad to find you here, old friend. Watches made up, are they? All taut?"

"Aye, sir, all taut," and Pilcher grinned. A savage brown fellow he was, with golden earrings dangling against his cheeks; short and squat, powerful of build, he was worth dozen men in a pinch.

"What are these preachers we have aboard, bose?" I demanded, looking at he men who stood about. A long-haired lot, with sanctimonious faces and rolling yes.

"Puritans," said Pilcher, and spat over the rail. "Damned if they ain't, sir! It was Mr. Langton shipped the lot. I said 'twas no luck to let a crew be shipped by a Lombard Street merchant, nor is it. Not an oath all mornin', and us a-working like blacks!"

The crew shipped by Langton! I whistled at that. Obviously no one aboard knew anything about Langton's adventures of the morning. Leaving my perch, I took Pilcher's arm and led him forward into the bows, where we might have a quiet word.

"What's this, bose?" I asked. "Say no word of it, but the merchant Langton is being hunted through the city for a pirate. Russel has been on the Account, or I'm a liar! And I'm not so sure about the master —"

"Cap'n Low is the bloodiest of the lot," said Pilcher gloomily. "I'm not s'prised to hear about Langton; not me! Low was piratin' around Madagascar last year. Oh, I'm a wise man, I am! But nobody aboard knows it, d'ye mind, sir! If 'twas not for what we've got stowed aft I'd ha' jumped ship."

"Eh?"

I stared at him.

"What's stowed aft, then?" I asked. He gave me a grin.

"Oh, you don't know, sir? Well, I'll not tell ye. Why Langton went and shipped these here psalm-whining fish I don't know, but that bleedin' Gunner Basil ain't the soapy fool he looks nor acts, Mr. Roberts! You and me are honest men, and the score up for'ard are honest fools; but Gunner Basil ain't one or t'other. D'ye know where I heard tell of him? Far and away it was, last v'yage —"

We leaned against the rail, filled and lighted our pipes, and Bosun Pilcher told me what he knew about our zealous gunner. It was worth the telling.

"D'ye mind, sir, last v'yage 'twas in a Bristol brigantine, to Madeira and the Verde Islands, and back with wine and salt, and a weary time it was, for she leaked like a sieve all the while. We hove out o' Funchal and made for the Isle o' Sal to take our salt aboard, that was in the making; and got safe into the north end of Palmera Roads, and anchored with the palm-trees east-and-by-north, in that spot o' clear sand bottom, five fathom.

"A man came off to us, a white man, marooned there, he had been, by a Frenchman named Maring or some such name, a pirate it was. He told us of a great fight there had been aboard o' the Frenchy six months back, and how there was a famous gunner aboard of her, a gunner by the name o' Basil, full of all pirate learning and a very law-shark for all them that were on the Account. And he said the Frenchy had shot off the lobe of this gunner's ear with a pistol and had set him ashore, all from some dispute over a woman.

"And sink me if this here preacher ain't the identical scoundrel, sir! You look at his ear, and there it be.

"Well, that's not the whole of it neither. This chap told us a long story, which I disremember in the main, but 'twas all about this here Gunner Basil and some wild tale that lay along of he. D'ye mind the pirate Avery? Gunner Basil had sailed with him, and talked in his cups about Avery's treasure that lay buried at one of the Verde Islands; he knew where the place was, and there be not another living man knew of it, and he was all for going after it. A wild tale enough!"

"Wild, but it might hold truth," I commented. "Avery burned down one of the towns in those islands, and cruised about there. However, what matter to us? This Gunner Basil, you think, is pretending to be a preaching Puritan just now?"

"Aye, to save his neck, belike."

Pilcher shook his earrings.

"Folks do call me a pirate because I wear hoops, and have a roll to my legs on dry land, and have use for an honest oath or two; but zounds! You know me, Master Roberts. I had liefer be me than this cutthroat devil of a Gunner Basil, with his Scripture and Psalms and whine!"

I had to laugh at this, which was true enough. Bosun Pilcher had the looks of a pirate and the life of an honest man; a wife and six children in Jamestown, and a sober, careful record. Gunner Basil, on the other hand, with all the earmarks of a fanatical blue-nosed Puritan, was by repute a devil on the leash.

"Well, bose," I said, knocking out my pipe, "keep a close tongue and wait for what turns up. You'd best look over the capstan and hawse and be ready to up anchor. Tide's almost at the turn, and I see a boat yonder with Mr. Russel coming aboard."

I turned and started aft, having now remembered something mighty important. As I went I encountered Gunner Basil, who touched his forelock to me as I passed and made no comment on my lesson in obedience. Russel's boat was hailing us, and at the break of the poop I found Captain Low waiting for me. I was up the ladder and had him by the arm, fumbling in my pocket.

"Ha, cap'n! I met a friend of yours ashore, and he charged me with word for you —"

Before I could say more, Russel was over the rail and leaping up to us, his dark face all ablaze with fury and excitement.

"The word's out after Dennis!" he cried, but low-voiced that the men might not hear. "Devil's luck, Ned, devil's luck! Some fool recognized him this morning; put the catchpolls after him! Zounds, if we don't get up the hook and into the Channel they'll twig the whole affair! Up and away, I tell you!"

Ned Low flung a glance at the after companion. His eyes were suddenly stricken.

"Damn me, this is bad news!" he murmured. "And at the last minute!"

"Up and away!" snarled Russel, still panting.

"No, no, I'll not run and leave him!" exclaimed Low warmly; but I intervened.

"Langton isn't nabbed, and won't be," I said, coolly enough, while they stared at me. "I met him ashore, and he had time to give me a message for you, cap'n, before the constables set him running afresh. Said for you to drop downstream with the tide, and he'd come aboard — this side Gravesend, most likely."

"Good!" cried Low.

He snapped erect as if this news had put fresh life into him, and his smile leaped out once more.

"Trust Dennis to come clear! Mr. Russel, be ready to shake out those topsails in five minutes; the tide's nearly at the turn. Mr. Roberts, take charge for'ard and see the anchor's well stowed."

Russel gave me one look that was like a stab; then his white teeth flashed in a laugh.

"So you know Langton, Mr. Roberts!" he said, and nodded. "Good enough. We'll pull together after all."

Oddly, it seemed that his ill will toward me had vanished; this was all seeming, however, because he thought that I was a friend of Langton, and bore this latter some well-founded fear. He was soon enough snarling again.

I went forward while the bosun's whistle shrilled and the men jumped to stations. Everything was shipshape; the men began to stamp about the windlass, capstan bars of dark teak all ashine in the sun, pawls clinking as the ship walked up on her hook, and the canvas aloft beginning to loose. A sweet ship was the *King Sagamore*! Every little detail of her was sweet and natty. Even the fife-rail was of red teak, and the belaying pins of black, heavy as iron.

Now she leaned over to wind and tide and began to slip through the water, while Cap'n Low himself conned her through the river traffic; six bells was struck from the brass bell, and I minded the cabinboy struck them; a slim lad, a guttersnipe of the town, his face pinched and marked with deviltry beyond the ken of most men.

And I noted an odd enough thing. Shoving on the black capstan bars of teak, or hauling on the lines, there was no singing from those men of ours. Instead, not a sound from them until we were bracing the yards a bit, and then one long-nosed rascal began to chant out a psalm, in which they all joined. Damn me, but I can still hear the roar of mirth that went up as a barge passed us and caught the words!

I sent the gunner down to see that all the ports were closed; she carried four guns to a side and six patteroes — a well armed jade! Or, should I say, warrior? The matter of sex is all a jumble when it comes to the *King Sagamore*. Pocahontas would have been a better name for her. This psalm singing was too much for me, however.

"Belay that singing!" I ordered at length. "Bose, pipe 'em the old bowline! Join in, you Newgate rascals, or you'll taste trouble!"

So presently Pilcher led them, and the voice of Gunner Basil boomed up the words from below, and the rascals stamped the deck to a right tune:

> *"Oh, haul upon the bowline, the fore and maintop bowline!*
> *Oh, haul upon the bowline — the bowline, haul!"*

And so we had everything snugged down for the present, and I joined Cap'n Low on the quarterdeck, while Russel and the gunner stood at the rail, watching the riverbanks slide past us. Now I went up to Low, who stood at the wheel, and spoke to him softly.

"Ned, I said nothing of it before Russel, but Dennis Langton gave me more than a word for you. Hold out your hand and take the little box."

He dropped a hand to his side, and I put the little black snuffbox into it; and, not taking his eyes from the water ahead, he nodded.

"Good, Roberts!" he said quietly. "So Dennis is playing fair with us, eh? Fine. Ah! Look there, behind those fishing-smacks — is that a boat? Here take my glass."

I took the spyglass from his pocket and leveled it.

"Aye! Two oarsmen and Langton himself in the stern. Now they've seen us —"

"Stand by with a line, Russel!" cried out Low, "Roberts, stand by those braces and be ready. We'll pick him up on the jump."

Pick him up we did, nigh swamping the wherry in the attempt. Langton came up and over the rail, nimble as a cat; but he had not been on the escape for nothing, since his clothes were torn and muddied and his wig clean gone, leaving him bald and shiny.

Nor was this all; for no sooner was he on deck than he staggered and collapsed into the arms of Russel with a choked cry, and I glimpsed a smear of blood across the mate's shoulder. Ned Low saw it too, for he turned to me with a quiet word.

"*Habet!* Lead in the lungs, and that's one of us gone to hell. Crack on all sail, Mr. Roberts! I leave the deck to you. Get us out o' this cursed water and to sea before they send a man-o'-war to stop us. This is a sad business — the poor girl!"

What he meant by this last, I had no idea, for I was already calling all hands, and Pilcher piped the men to the weather braces and aloft on the instant. Russel and Ned Low carried the figure of Langton to the quarterdeck, and I saw nothing more of them for the time, being mighty busy alow and aloft. Gunner Basil I sent to the helm, needing a good man there if we were to race out of the river. The sails were loosed already, and the men piping down from aloft.

"Haul aboard! Get your tack well down, bose! Tend braces, you lads — set taut! Sheet home — sheet home and hoist away, there! Lead along and man the flying-jib halyards — clear away the downhaul — hoist! All hands main braces —"

So it went, with Pilcher's pipe whistling shrill and the canvas fluttering out. Much to my surprise I perceived that these long-nosed dissenters forward were good enough seamen; and in no long time we were bowling away for dear life, our new canvas straining in the wind and Gunner Basil handling helm in sweet fashion.

Then, with all clear, I turned to the quarterdeck — and stood thunderstruck.

Russel, sitting under the weather rail, held the head of Dennis Langton in his arms, while Ned Low knelt beside and talked to Langton, who was coughing blood. The man had a bullet through the body, and it needed no surgeon to know that his hours were numbered. It was not this, however, that held me transfixed, but the person kneeling over Langton's hand; for this was a woman!

She had come from the after cabins obviously; a straight, slim slip of a thing all yellow golden hair and sober gray gown and long hands. Her face I could not see, but judged that she was young.

A flutter aloft caused me to look at the helmsman. Gunner Basil was staring at the scene, and being down the wind was probably hearing their words. With an angry shout I leaped to the wheel, shoved him away and ordered him to take charge forward. He went, but with a sour snarl in his yellow parchment face.

Indeed, standing in the wheel-box I found that the wind brought me snatches of talk from the group. The girl was sobbing, and Dennis Langton was speaking to her between his terrible coughs. The words reached to me clearly.

Even as I listened, even as I felt the ship with the wheel and held her in the wind, even as I watched shore and opening river-mouth, I was aware of Gunner Basil and that devil-eyed little cabinboy, talking together near the foot of the main; and I wondered vaguely of what they were speaking.

"Keep it, Polly!" came Langton's gasping voice. "All for you — swear — promise me!"

The girl sobbed out something. Without looking at him I was aware that Langton's head lifted, and his eyes leaped to Ned Low.

"Ned, Ned! You'll not take it from her? Aye, you were always on the level — met on the level with us, parted on the square — Ho there, Tyler! Out sword, Tyler; run the knave through! Damn your eyes, Tyler, you missed him! Netting's up and we can't board —"

For a moment he raved, then fell suddenly silent, gasping and sobbing for breath, coughing up the black blood. I stole a glance, and his face was white as beech-ash.

"Call Russel, Ned!" came his voice again. "Where's Russel; John Lopez that was, John Russel that is now?"

"I'm here, Dennis," said the dark mate, bending over so that Langton knew him.

"Swear to me then," gasped the latter. "Swear you'll give my share to Polly — swear you'll be true to her, not cheat her — swear!"

"Aye," said Russel, whose real name seemed to be Lopez. "I swear it, Dennis, and take the cap'n to witness!"

"Swear it, Ned!" cried out Langton, looking up.

Ned Low, his face set and mournful, inclined his head.

"I'll be true to you and her, Dennis, and will protect her, so help me! I swear it by the oath that you and I know — the oath of the book and compass and word!"

"Where's Roberts, the Virginian?"

Langton's head lifted.

"Call him! Good man, Roberts; true man — stand by him, Ned! I liked that man. Call him — swear him —"

Ned Low strode over to me.

"Give me the helm, and go to him. Quick, man, before he passes!"

I obeyed. Although I was in the dark as to this oath, it appeared honest enough and would soothe the passing of a dying man. As I knelt before Langton, recognition came into his eyes, fighting the fear of death that was filling them.

"Swear, Virginian!" he panted out. "Stand wi' Polly — her share —"

"I swear, Dennis Langton," was my response.

His head dropped back, and a cry came from the girl's throat — then, with a furious and frightful effort, Dennis Langton swept Polly aside, wrenched himself to his feet, swayed there and shook his fist toward London. Laughter and blood came from his lips, and one last wild cry.

"Cheated you, Jack Ketch — cheated you first and last, Tyburn Tree! Sink me to hell if I haven't the laugh o' you after all! Zounds!"

He rattled on the word, and died, and pitched forward with a laugh terrible on his lips. Thus passed the first of our company aboard the *King Sagamore*; and as I watched Russel take the weeping girl to the companionway I wondered to what oath I had sworn myself, in the hand of a dying pirate.

III

While we pitched and rolled down-Channel that night I was below with Ned Low, seeing that Dennis Langton was properly sewed up for burial. Gunner Basil brought a shot for his feet and then, touching his forelock, respectfully enough addressed us; in the light of the swinging lantern his parchmenty face looked more yellow and wolfish than ever.

"Beg pardon, masters, but who's a-goin' to say the prayer over him?" he asked.

"I am."

Ned Low glanced up.

"Why?"

"It ain't fittin', sir," protested the gunner with an air of earnest, stubborn conviction.

His pale, deadly eyes were fastened upon Low.

"He died in sin, most like, but it ain't fittin' for you to say no prayer, sir. It's the spirit movin' me to protest."

Ned Low straightened up.

"Now, sink me! I'm master o' this ship —"

"We that has a higher hope don't hold wi' no blasphemy; beg pardon, master, what be you but an ungodly, unregenerate sinner? Blasphemy it is, no less. More'n one of us aboard ha' heard tell o' 'Bloody Ned,' cap'n. Tha' ain't here nor there; but when it comes to sayin' prayers, I speaks up! It's the spirit movin' in me —"

Bloody Ned! Well, there it was, like a slap in the face. I had heard of Bloody Ned, too, but had not connected the name with my good friend Captain Ned Low.

For a moment I thought Ned would strike the man down. Eyes clenched with eyes, and in the obscurity behind Gunner Basil I perceived more than one dark figure lurking. Then in time I recalled the tale that Bosun Pilcher had told me, and pushed forward with a nudge in Low's ribs.

"What's all this?" I demanded. "This is fine talk from you, Basil, who were on the Account with Avery and served as his gunner! And what about that French pirate you sailed with — the one who pistoled you and marooned you after the big fight, eh?"

There was dead silence, broken only by the groan of stanchions and the creak of blocks. My knowledge of his past took Gunner Basil all aback; he gaped at me from a livid and stricken face. Ned Low uttered a soft oath of astonishment. A murmur began to rise from the listening men. I struck again while the iron was hot.

"A prayer would come with ill grace from you, gunner — as lief from Bloody Ned as from Avery's gunner, if I'm the victim! Who was it nicked the lobe off that ear of yours with a pistol ball, eh?"

Gunner Basil staggered again at that thrust. I felt a swift stab of fear as I met those pale eyes of his; then he began to shake his long head and whine.

"When a man repenteth him of the evil and turns to godliness, the scornful make mock of him! Aye, sir, you ha' the right of it; a sinful man I ha' been, and taken part wi' men o' blood. And now that regeneration ha' come upon me, by the works o' the blessed Tom Deveney o' Houndsditch —"

"Regeneration your eye, ye damned lousy swab of a liar!" broke in a roar, and Bosun Pilcher lurched forward. "Who was it a-throwin' oaths so free and fine but a half hour ago? You, ye scabby sojer, thinkin' no one was by to hear! Now out knife if ye dare, and I'll show ye summat —"

It looked like blows and hot breath, for Pilcher had hand on knife and Gunner Basil was clutching under his arm; but Ned Low stepped forward and stood between the two men and reasserted his command.

"Damn me, d'ye think we're on the Account, to settle quarrels wi' the steel!" he cried out. "Out o' this, bose! You, gunner, give me no more of your sanctimonious lip, d'ye hear? You'll taste a dozen of the cat next time. Get this boy made ready, and five bells in morning watch call all hands for burial. Mr. Roberts, it's hard on eight bells — you'd better step up and stand by to take the deck from Mr. Russel."

"From Portugee Lopez, ye mean," shot a voice out of the shadows. "Lopez, the bloody pirate what scuppered three Deal craft last year!"

"Who was that?" snapped Ned Low, hand dropping to belt. "Out of the dark, you rat! Who was it?"

None answered him, however, and the darkness proved empty to the swing of a lantern. So I went on deck again, wondering not a little. That voice had held an odd twang, not unlike the tones of the impish cabinboy, but that was impossible. The child stood in deadly fear of us all and was seasick to boot.

With a fair wind, ballast trimmed anew and one of our brawny dissenters at the helm, we bore down-Channel into the darkness; while I, after lighting my pipe in the lee of the pilothouse, reflected a while upon my situation. It might have been worse, what I knew of it, and it might assuredly have been bettered. Certain outstanding things looked dark.

One certainty was that in London town I had run foul of three fine rogues, and like a blockhead had been hooked. Langton's end spoke for itself. Russel, or Portuguese Lopez, obviously had something of a reputation as a pirate. Of

Bloody Ned I had heard, and was grieved to find it was my own Ned Low, the man whom I so liked. As to the girl Polly, I had not seen or heard of her again, but she seemed to be some relation to Langton.

Why had these three men outfitted and chartered — as they must have done — the *King Sagamore*? To get gold from the Cape Verde Islands, Ned Low had said.

All very fine; but how? There was the puzzler. They had not meant to run away with her and go on the Account.

Langdon in his capacity as a city merchant had probably given bonds for her, and he had most certainly picked the crew himself. These men were godly rogues, and I did not like them in the least — but they were honest men. Langton would never have picked such a crew to ship as pirates.

Then again there was the question of Gunner Basil. Captain Low had been utterly astounded at learning the gunner's record; he had known nothing of it. Ergo, Dennis Langton had known nothing of it and had shipped the gunner at face value.

But why the hell had Gunner Basil shipped aboard us? I took no stock in his "regeneration" — one look in the man's eyes clapped a stopper on all that. He could fool the men up forward, but he could not fool me, much less Bosun Pilcher.

And what was that oath I had taken? It disquieted me.

I had reached this point, and two bells had just been struck, when the tall figure of Ned Low approached. He glanced at the compass, lighted his pipe, then took my arm and led me to the lee rail, where we could speak without being overheard.

"Roberts, I've been talking with John Russel, and I'm worried," he said frankly and bluntly. "This morning, standing on the quay, you as good as told Russel you'd been on the Account yourself. Tonight you flashed some information on Gunner Basil that staggered him — and me with him. How came you to know it, lad? If you've lied to me, then let's have it out sharp and quick, and reach an understanding."

This was a stiff jolt, and I let him know it.

"About Russel, that was said in jest, to taunt him. As to the rest, Ned — well, I learned tonight that you are Bloody Ned. It grieved me, but I didn't come running and whining to ask if the news was true. Zounds! If I'm such a fool that I can't read a man's eye for true or false, it's a queer thing. And I'll stick by my guns, swing me if I don't!"

Low caught my hand and gripped it hard.

"Spoken like a man, George Roberts!" he said warmly. "Aye, and with a bitter back to the words that I deserve! Your pardon, lad. We'll have a meeting in the cabin tomorrow morning after breakfast, all four of us, and you'll know then why I'm anxious."

"Who's the fourth, then?" I asked.

"Polly Langton, niece and heir of poor Dennis. That was a stiff loss to us, George! Dennis had a head worth any two going."

"He'd not much when he shipped our gunner," I said acidly.

Ned Low whistled.

"Perchance. But the scoundrel may ha' told truth after all, lad; there's a chance of that, d'ye mind! Men have reformed ere this, and will again. Why, look at me, myself!"

He was silent for a moment, then took me across the deck again and under the weather rail, where we sat down in comfort. I think he had been much moved by my challenging answer to his doubts; at least he spoke with a refinement and feeling in his voice that I had not previously heard.

"Roberts, y'have never seen or heard, I suppose, of a man calling himself Trunnel Toby, having a long face like a horse, and sad eyes, and a gold ring in his nostrils, and the likeness of a bleeding heart tattooed upon his breast, just above his own heart?"

"Not I," was my answer.

"I have sought that man going on five years," said Ned Low. "Once I knew that his ship lay in Carlisle Bay, and I sighted her plain; but there was a gale blowing, and we were short of men, and before we could hand the small sails and luff for the bay we were driven past, and the gale held us, and when I came back again he was gone. Oh, but I ha' tried with heart and soul to find that man, all up and down the dark bowl of the sea!

"And once I was within an hour of him. At Madagascar that was; aye, missed him by a scant sixty minutes, though I caught three of his men left behind, and hanged them! He had heard of Bloody Ned, and he ran for it. And off the Zanzibar coast I met a ship that had spoke him two days before, and north we ran and passed him in a hurricane, and he came over to the Brazils for fear o' me. Now and again, and every way, I found men who had sailed with him, men who had partnered or traded with him, and I hanged them all as I came on them.

"But I never found Trunnel Toby, and ha' lost hope of finding the man now, so I am off to recoup my wasted fortune again, and search some more. The last o' my guineas are in this ship, Roberts; and a big sum from poor Langton, and a share from John Russel. And I am afraid to ask Gunner Basil if he knew the man, for if he did I would hang him, and we have need of a gunner aboard. Besides the man may have reformed, as he says; I'd put it past no man to turn righteous.

"For look you, George! There is a reason behind all of us. Aye, there's a reason back of each man who dares this wine-dark sea and listens to the rigging as it sings the slumbering song o' night up above! Lord knows I've earned the name of Bloody Ned, earned it with hangings of men alow and aloft — but all of them men who had known Trunnel Toby, d'ye mind that!

"And I've naught to repent of at all, either. I've touched no man's life but for this cause; I've touched no man's money but mine own, honestly made.

"And poor Langton, to whom that gunner laid his tongue, had become an honest man. D'ye know why, George? Because of the girl down below, his niece Polly; and she's a rare lass, I tell you! Bred of the Devon blood, she is, and can hand sail with any man or read the card or steer by the wind. So when I came and said that I was for the gold and had given up the search for Trunnel Toby until we had the guineas again, Langton knew it was an honest word and came in with me; and John Russel made up the sum we lacked, and we bought this ship, George."

"Bought her!" I said in some wonder, for that would have taken round money.

"Aye, just so. A company venture for the gold. We'll have it again soon enough, and then I'll buy out the other shares and keep the *King Sagamore* and go again after Trunnel Toby. Sure y'have never heard of the man?"

"Never," I said. "But there's Bosun Pilcher come to look at the helm; call him, for many a thing he has heard and seen, and an honest man to boot."

Ned Low lifted his voice, and the dark shadow of bose detached itself from the pilot-box and came over to us on the sloping deck. So there Ned Low asked his question again, and described the man he sought. Bose turned the quid in his mouth and chewed upon it and spat over the stern rail, and then made careful answer.

"Why, sir, there be many a man wi' face like a horse, and one or two aboard here, but not that man. Seems like I've heard tell of he, too; let's see now — was it aboard the *Merry Thought*? No, 'twas not; yet 'twas not so long ago —

"Ha! Damn me eyes, sir, if 'twas not two v'yages back, on the *Pricket* brigantine, wi' Cap'n Baxter out o' Bristol town! I mind it well enough now. We were lying at Lisbon, and a supra-cargo there was tellin' me of such a man, bleedin' heart and all! Mate on a London trading-brig, he was, and had got into trouble wi' the Portugee folk, and had skipped between two days. That's where I heard the name, and more'n that I can't bring to mind."

"Then let it pass," said Ned Low, sinking back against the rail.

"Aye, sir," said bose. "Four bells it is, sir."

"Make it so, bose," I told him, and he went off into the darkness.

The brazen tinkle of the bell had died away before Ned Low spoke again.

"And what think you, George," he said, "of sailing mate with Bloody Ned?"

I laughed a little at that.

"What else but your own words, Ned? We're not on the Account, but for honest gold, you say; and enough said. There's a reason behind every man sails up the sea, you say; and enough said. For the rest, I like you, I have two fists, and if I go to the devil it's my own fault and no other man's leading."

"Well said, George. What reason is behind you?"

"Ruined fortunes, a girl who jilted me, and lack of ties to keep me ashore. Those in the first place. In the latter place, love of good ships, work to do and strength to do it with, and knowledge of my profession. For I hold the sea to be a profession, Ned, in despite of all men! I sailed a small sloop with two boys from the Azores to Barbados once to prove the fact. What was more, I built the sloop before sailing her."

"You're a philosopher, George, and damn me if I don't wish I might be one too!" he responded, and sighed. "Work to do, and strength and knowledge to do it with! What more could any man ask of fortune? But my work's undone as yet, and when done it's only a man hanged after all, and small joy of it to me!"

With this he rose, and was gone down below.

I wondered much about his words and his curious tale of Trunnel Toby, and what reason must lie behind his strange pursuit of that creature up and down the waters of the earth. Reason in plenty there must be, but I could not evoke it from his words. It began to appear, however, that he was not the black pirate he was painted, and this was something to cheer me.

So the night wore through, and the wind held fair, sweeping us steadily to the southward on our course, and with the dawn or a little while after we gathered all hands in the waist. Now all the world was shut away from us. We aboard the *King Sagamore*, bounded by those walls of English oak and India teak, were in a little world apart, devils and angels and men together. There was the dead man, shrouded decently; and by him Ned Low, book in hand, and dark, quick-eyed Russel, dirk and pistol in belt, and Gunner Basil, pale, terrible eyes flaming and stabbing about. Little love those pale eyes bore me, either!

There, too, Bosun Pilcher, gold earrings bobbing beside savage brown cheeks, and back of him the men, making a full score of us, all told. Some I had come to know by this time. Dickon the cabinboy, gray with the sickness and mouthing vile oaths; Simon Blake and Ezra Blake his brother, gaunt, hard-jawed fellows who could prate psalms by the hour; and Philip the cook, a black man who was very joyful about his work and always grinning. Humphrey Stave was chips and sail-maker, a bent gnarled figure with deep eyes behind spectacles, and a bit deaf; Stave was the only other man forward who was not a man of religion and godliness, so that he companioned much with Pilcher.

The others were all hard men, devout enough and good seamen, but given to exhorting each other with prayer and advice. Dennis Langton had picked them for this very reason, having no mind to ship pirates on this voyage.

None the less, he had made a mistake. One of the men, Thomas Winter, was long in the face, a real horse's face indeed, seeming but little short of a halfwit, nor ever raised his eyes to meet those of another man.

Well, we buried poor Dennis Langton there, sliding him off into the rolling seas; and after reading the proper service Ned Low softly asked the gunner to speak a prayer. Gunner Basil did so, praying a good ten minutes in a long, whining singsong, the other knaves all joining in with their nasal "Amen" when the spirit moved.

Then breakfast, and then to the cabin for the promised meeting, while Gunner Basil held the deck. And in this meeting I had sight of Polly Langton and likewise got a bid from fortune.

IV

We gathered in the stern cabin, and the new sunlight streamed down through the small skylight above and illumined the cabin with a glory of radiance as the ship rolled. Between stern window and skylight we had plenty of light.

The cabin was not ornate. It was our mess cabin aft, and was meant for use, not for ornament. Along the stern wall under the window ran a long file of muskets, locked in their rack by an iron bar and padlock. A locker for charts, another for instruments; a huge cupboard that held dishes and wine and other things; table and chairs and iron lantern slung in gimbals — this was all. Under the table was a trap leading to the lazaret below.

With the traces of grief gone from her cheeks Polly Langton sat down, and we after her. For lack of mourning she wore her gray gown; a kerchief about her throat fastened by a gold brooch; and what a head was this rising above! All a glory of yellow gold hair, and a red-cheeked, west-country face that was filled with sweetness and ability, browned by the sun and air, with skin delicately textured as any court lady's!

Yet the splendor of her face lay in the eyes; gray with golden flecks were they, level and meeting a man's gaze fair and unafraid; deliberate eyes, not to be hurried or overborne. Through these windows one perceived the fine woman's soul within, shrinking a little, yet meeting the issues of fate with a certain cool poise that was almost disdain. Could this girl ever be waked into hot passionate anger or emotion, I thought, she would stop at nothing!

Painted and powdered, patched and gowned, Polly Langton might have been no beauty; but in her simplicity she was beautiful enough. I did not miss the grip that was in Russel's eyes as he watched her; nor did she; for she gave him a slow look that made him change countenance.

Ned Low, when we were seated, put on the table before him that little black snuffbox which I had brought him from Langton. Then Russel spoke up, civilly but with a thrust to his words.

"One minute, cap'n! This is secret company business. Why does George Roberts sit with us?"

"At my bidding," and Ned Low smiled a little, taking no offense. "He is my friend, and I trust him to the full. Also I propose that he is to have a full third of my share of the gold when recovered —"

"I want no gifts, Ned," I intervened.

"No gift at all, George Roberts," he returned, a somber look in his eyes. "We don't know what lies ahead of us, but I think you are going to be a great man in this enterprise, and here you, a captain like myself, are serving as mate. Zounds, man! Was it not agreed between us that first night we met?"

"As to that I can't say," was my response, and Ned uttered a laugh.

"It's a company matter," spoke up Russel, an ugly note in his voice. "Put it to the vote, I say!"

"It's no company matter what I do with my own," snapped Low angrily, a dark color rising in his cheeks. "But the deciding voice lies with Miss Polly, and I put the vote. What say you, madam?"

All this while the girl had been looking at me with appraising eyes. Now she leaned back in her chair and spoke as if she had no interest in the affair.

"I agree," she said quietly, "though it is your own business, as you say."

So Russel sat back and bit his lip.

"Now," began Ned Low, "let us inform Captain Roberts of our quest. You've heard of the pirate Franklin, George? Some time since, I was in company with him when he took a huge amount of moidores out of a Portugee Indiaman from Goa."

He broke off, for the girl was holding his eye. He flushed a trifle once more.

"Then it is true," she asked coolly, "that you and Mr. Russel were on the Account, as they call it?"

"That is true," said Ned. "It is also true that I would touch no penny of the loot, my lady. Then I had no use for it. Now I have use. Captain Franklin buried a great share of the gold, which he swore belonged to me, on one of the Verde Islands. He and I alone knew the place. It is this gold that we go to recover.

"According to the agreement, a third share goes to me, another to John Russel, another to Mistress Langton here. Out of my share, a third goes to Captain Roberts. This is understood and agreed?"

A nod came from the other two. But now Polly Langton spoke up — cool and well-considered words; and her speech must have come as a tremendous shock to each one of us.

"Since Captain Roberts is a friend of yours, Captain Low, and is to share in your proceeds, he is evidently tarred with the same brush as you and Mr. Russel! By your own word you are pirates. How my poor uncle came to his death I know not, but I think it was through entering into this scheme of yours.

"Shame on you! He was an honest city merchant, and you bloody men tangled him in your ruthless wiles! Had it not been for you we would still be living in Lombard Street, and happy there."

She paused, coldly deliberate. Ned Low was staring at her like a man thunderstruck. John Russel was all agape, but harsh amusement was rising in his eyes. Before it could break out she was calmly continuing her speech.

"I promised my uncle to take this gold if we got it. What I do with my share is another matter, I may be penniless, but beyond taking out what my poor uncle put into this venture, I'll not turn this bloody coin to my own use.

"Very well, then. I want it understood plainly that I'm a full third partner in this enterprise, and intend to remain so. I'm not to be put in a corner and disregarded because I am a woman. My uncle picked a good crew for this voyage; if you gentlemen think you can run away with this ship or go pirating, you'll discover otherwise. We are here for a certain purpose, and none other."

Now her voice softened — perhaps from what she read in the eyes of Ned Low.

"Indeed I do not mean to speak like a shrew, but there's the fact. You're pirates. I am a woman, but I have some ability at sea. The crew are honest men. I think you mean me well, and will respect the oath which you gave my poor uncle; but I want to have things understood. Already the men are whispering that you intend running away with the ship. Be careful! That's all. I am through, Captain Low."

There was a space of silence, while we stared at her. It was easy to perceive that Dennis Langton had kept her ignorant of his past. She thought him a good, honest merchant, not knowing that he had buccaneered with the worst of them, had partnered with the infamous Spriggs. She was acting upon genuine belief, deeming the rest of us mighty insecure men.

Russel uttered a laugh and began to speak, a sneer in his heavy eyes. Ned Low turned to him, face set and cold, and uttered three words —

"Be silent, John!"

Russel checked himself, shrugged and leaned back grinning. Thus the matter passed; Ned was trying to keep from the poor girl the knowledge of what her uncle had been, was trying to leave her memory of him unsoiled. Yet he was a fool for his pains. She was bound to learn the truth eventually.

"Since I haven't known you or your friends three days, Miss Polly," I said easily, "you can't charge me with their crimes. My record is clear for all men to read, and if you'll go out to Virginia you'll find that it's not a bad record either. And as to Captain Low, I believe you'll find that he's —"

"Stow it, George!" snapped Low.

I obeyed, for he was angry.

He looked across the table at the girl, and she at him, though her gaze had softened a bit. Very handsome he was, and too proud to take notice of her words. He opened the black snuffbox that lay before him and took out the hard, folded bit of vellum, all the while keeping his eyes on the girl. And then he spoke to her briefly.

"Dear lady, you have naught to fear from us, upon my

honor! Now let us to business. I propose to lay this little chart before you — Franklin himself made it — and then destroy the thing. We shall keep the position of the moidores in our own minds. If by any chance of the sea we do not reach the Verde Islands, then whichever one of us can first come to the spot is at liberty to take the gold."

There was a little silence while he opened up the vellum. It was not easy, for the whitish skin was hard and dry and promised to crack at the folds. As he opened it slowly, I saw that on one side of it was writing, and that over the ink there had been wax laid on and polished, keeping the ink waterproof.

Then abruptly the voice of the girl leaped at us. Soft it was, but uttered in broad Devon that betrayed her apprehension and fear.

"Quick! Catch mun — look to door!"

She said afterward that the door-catch had moved slightly. Russel saw it, for he was out of his chair, silent and with a stealthy agility that amazed me, and in two steps was at the door. He opened it. There came a terrific crash as a tray dropped to the floor, and we saw Dickon the cabinboy outside.

Russel had him by the shoulder and heaved him inside and swore at the ale that spattered his feet.

"What means this, lad?" demanded Ned Low angrily. "Who bade you listen at doors?"

The little imp was no whit in awe or frightened, he faced us in stiller defiance. He could not have seen fifteen years, yet the debased evil of his features would have done credit to any pirate, and he glowered at us with all the hatred of a man for men.

"It bain't so," he said stoutly. "I weren't a-listening, Master Low! Cook Philip sent me wi' breakfast for mistress — and now look at un! Pewter bent, ale gone —"

Russel gave him a hearty cuffing and threw him out into the passage. As the boy picked himself up I saw the look he flung at Russel — a deadly, vicious look such as comes from the eyes of a disturbed and angry snake. Then Russel slammed the door shut and came back to his chair.

"I was mistaken," spoke up Polly contritely. "I thought perhaps someone was listening — I'm sorry if little Dickon suffered for my error."

"He's not hurt," said Russel. "Now, Ned, out with it! Which one of the islands is it?"

"St. Vincent," answered Captain Low, holding the vellum spread out under his fingers. "You know it?"

"I've not landed there," said Russel.

"Franklin has it marked 16° 49' north latitude, by 7° 6' west longitude from the Cape de Verde," went on Ned Low, "but I think he's off a point or two. George, get out the charts, will you? We'll show Miss Polly just where we're going."

I got out the proper chart, by which time the others were ready to relinquish the bit of vellum to me, though Russel

watched me keenly while I handled it. Upon it was rudely scratched the outline of St. Vincent, one of several uninhabited and rocky islands to the northwest of the Cape Verde group. On the northeast tip of the island was marked a cross, with the bearings below. I uttered an exclamation.

"Upon my word, gentlemen! I remember this place; I was there for turtle while we were making salt at the Isle de Sal! Aye, the very spot — and we had best lay up the ship in the cove at the north side of the island, which is the closest."

"It is ill spoke of on the chart," said Russel, looking up.

"Aye, for the trades blow square into it," I assented. "But a ship may be towed out by boats during the morning calm. I've seen the St. Nicholas men do it often. And the bay is so smooth that you may lay a ship ashore without the least damage."

"Memorize those bearings, George," said Ned Low. "We must destroy the thing."

That was an easy matter, the more so that I knew the exact spot. The northeast side of the island, unlike the rest, is low and sandy. A cable-length off the shore at low tide is a round, smooth rock that rises like a broken column out of the water to the height of ten feet; Franklin had marked it "Tower Rock," and there could be no mistake. Bearing from this due west a quarter mile were a group of dragon-trees.

Now I recalled these trees quite clearly, since they were the only group of this species which had escaped destruction, and I was interested in their singular nature and had even visited them, getting some of the gum. Half a cable-length to the west-and-by-north of these trees was a large boulder jutting out of the sand, and the gold was buried on the north side of that boulder.

So said the vellum, and you may judge of my interest in the matter, and of how the others were interested to hear me tell of the place as I knew it, though I did not recall that boulder. Franklin had been a few points amiss on his bearings of the island, but that was nothing. He certainly was not astray on his local features.

"Do you think," Polly Langton asked me, a sparkle in her eyes, "that anyone might have come there and found the treasure?"

"Not unless he were looking for it," I told her. "No one comes to that island except for turtle, or to shoot wild goats, or to fish. The black island men from St. Nicholas come there often, but they make no stay. There is fresh water in a large bay on the northwest side the island — Porto Grande it is called."

"Aye, it is marked."

Ned Low rolled up the big chart.

"Russel," he went on, "have you finished with the bearings? And you, George? And you, Miss Polly?"

We had it all in our heads, well enough. So Captain Low struck a light, and presently the white vellum curled and crumpled and became a black ash on the table. Then Low looked up at us, and laughed in his gay manner.

"And now, comrades, a sneaker to our good luck and fortune!"

He brought wine and flagons from the cupboard, and we pledged Franklin's gold, the girl with a flash to her eye and color to her cheek. Then, since Polly Langton had not yet broken her fast, I went to hasten Dickon with his second tray, and so took charge of the deck. And this ended our conference.

We had now no further talk among ourselves of the gold, for it was a dangerous matter, and would keep well enough until we arrived at the spot. With the next morning indeed foul weather came upon us; not contrary, but heavy gales that swept us on our course yet kept all hands on the jump. Day after day they continued unabated, and the *King Sagamore*, for all her battering and straining, leaked no more water than could be got rid of in an hour's pumping of mornings.

During those days we were too busy to have much time for mischief, which in the light of after events I think was most fortunate. There was indeed some preaching and ranting up forward, but since it gave the men an outlet we made no objection, even when Gunner Basil made long-winded discourses of a Sabbath.

What with the ship's roll, few of us were not seasick at times, and I saw little of Polly Langton these days. What little I did see, however, woke in me admiration for her bearing and character and spirit. I think she had ceased to class me with pirates, for she was smiling and merry when we met, and sometimes took the wheel during my watch on deck, fighting it with the skill of any man among us.

Dickon the cabinboy was quite sick during this period, which was another fortunate thing in my opinion. We replaced him for the time with Thomas Winter, the long-faced halfwit of whom I have spoken. A curious man was that, who seldom spoke, never met the level look of an eye, and mingled not at all with the other men. He had been long at sea; his hands and forearms were much tattooed; yet none could get him to speak of his goings and comings. He had a vacancy in his aspect that surely belied his wits.

This fellow Winter, also, seemed to be taken with strange spells. One day at noon we had a fleeting glimpse of the sun, and after shooting him with Low I hastily left the deck and jumped below to make calculations and verify our reckoning. As I came into the cabin I found Gunner Basil there, and the man Thomas Winter was speaking to him. I had chance to hear only a few words, but those were spoken in a new voice to me — a sane and sound and bellowing voice.

"Why, damn your eyes!" Winter was roaring at the gunner. "Who are you to tell me what to do, you whelp of Satan? You stow your jaw, blast you! I'm the one —"

He broke off at sight of me, and cringed. I was the more astonished, for Gunner Basil seemed to be taking his oaths with shamefaced manner.

"What's this?" I broke in upon them. "Winter, was that you I heard? What d'ye mean?"

"Pardon, sir," he mumbled. "They roarin' winds do fetch gusty words out o' me at times, sir, and all o' seven devils a-perched up aloft!"

He shambled away out of the cabin. Gunner Basil looked at me, wagged his head sorrowfully and tapped his skull. He let out his nasal whine.

"Bear with him, sir; bear with him! The poor afflicted fellow deserves the patience of all men. If he is a bit daft, he is also a good seaman — can hold her by the wind wi' never a flutter o' canvas from hour to hour!"

With an impatient word I settled down to my figures. Afterward I remembered again the complete change of voice and language which had been effected in the daft man, and how he had cringed at sight of me. This wakened my pity, and I thought no more of the incident.

V

Fair weather came back to us as suddenly as it had departed, and found us well advanced on our course, though much strained and battered about. Within two days all our sick were recovered, and we fell to work overhauling the rigging as we sailed, for the new cordage had stretched abominably and must be re-pitched into the bargain.

Hardly had we come into clear skies, however, than trouble let loose aft, as if it had been waiting for fine weather before breaking.

We were heeling smartly along under a spanking breeze out of the northeast-and-by-east, everything drawing well, and four bells of the afternoon had just struck. Old Humphrey Stave was seated by the for'ard water-butt, working with palm and needle at a spare topsail when the bosun appeared and talked for a little with his crony. Then Pilcher came aft, touched his forelock, begged some tobacco from me and fell into talk. He had something at the back of his mind, but was slow in leaching it.

"Cook be heatin' of some pitch in the galley," he observed, "when you're ready to get that for'ard rigging painted, sir."

Simon Blake was at the wheel.

"When it's ready," I said, "send a man aft to relieve Simon here, and let him and Ezra Blake take up the buckets. They're good careful men, and I don't want the deck spattered."

"Aye, sir."

Pilcher shook his earrings, then gave me a queer look.

"There be some wild talk for'ard, sir," he went on.

"What about, bose?"

"That you've been on the Account, sir, and I give the lie to it. But that bain't all. I don't like them there godly men, nor they me; but I've heard whispers. They do say as you and Mr. Russel and Mr. Low ain't doin' right by the lass, and that she's mortal afraid o' you gentlemen. Then there's summat about Mr. Russel bein' one Portugee Lopez, and it bain't no secret that Mr. Low is Bloody Ned —"

"Who's doing this talk?" I demanded, frowning.

We were beyond earshot of the helmsman.

"That I don't know, sir; just driftin' it is. These godly scum for'ard seem to think they'll be made turn pirate."

"We'll work it out of 'em," I said cheerfully. "Run along and attend to that pitch now."

He swung forward. Barely had he gone when from below came Polly Langton and Captain Low. They flung me a bare nod, then resumed some talk they had started below decks, and I saw that the girl was flushed and earnest, while poor Ned Low was cold and set and hard in the face. They paused by the windward rail, so that their words came to me and to Simon Blake, at the wheel.

"And have you no shame for it?" demanded the girl hotly.

"Shame?"

Ned uttered a curt, bitter laugh.

"By the Lord Harry, no! If I'd hanged twice a hundred men, and knew that twice that number would yet die to my hand, I'd go on to the end and be proud of it!"

"I am sorry to hear such words on your lips," and she spoke gravely, her anger held down. "I had thought you a gentleman, and I find you glorying in your bloody deeds, in your piracies and murders! Go on to the end, you say. Do you dare admit that your share of this enterprise is to be used in the same fashion — that if the venture succeeds, if you buy out this ship from our company, you go on the Account once more?"

I cursed under my breath, for Simon Blake was drinking all this in, as his dour face testified; yet I dared not intervene.

"Aye," said Ned Low. "I'll not lie to you, Miss Polly."

"Oh, shame on you!" she cried out. "To think that you and your precious friends so inveigled my poor uncle! You and they, to take this money and use if for more piracy and murder — how do I know you and they will respect that oath to my uncle?"

"Why, take us on trust!"

Ned broke into a laugh, half vexed, half of whimsical exasperation.

"As for my friends, I care not and know not what they'll do with their share. My share puts Bloody Ned on his feet again, madam, and that's my own affair."

She gave him a long look, eyes angry, bosom heaving.

"Then I am minded to draw out of this venture, sir."

"You can't."

Low turned on her, pressed beyond endurance.

"This is a company matter, my girl — don't try to make trouble! There's more behind it all than you know. There's more hangs on it than you know. We'll see you safe in London again with your share; and beyond that — have a care! This gold o' Franklin's belongs to all of us, mind, not you alone."

Now, whether she had meant her threat I know not, but Simon Blake caught his breath sharply, and his face was set in grim lines. But the girl laughed out right merrily under the angry gaze of Ned Low — perhaps she had only meant to tease him, after all. Then she turned and went below without more speech, while Ned fell to pacing the quarterdeck.

It was a moment after this that Thomas Winter, who was in my watch, came shambling aft to relieve Simon Blake from his trick. A few words passed between them. I stepped up, and Winter repeated the order to go for'ard and tar the lines. Blake nodded assent and obeyed.

I followed forward, as Simon and Ezra Blake secured their buckets and brushes, and came to a pause beside the water-butt, where Humphrey Stave sat and sewed.

"Do those buntlines and the forelift first," I told them, "then work in along the yards from each side, and do the shrouds as you come down. Simon, overhaul that loose foot-rope at the strap, on the fore-yard; tighten it up and watch your seizing."

"Aye, sir," responded Simon, passing the lanyard of his bucket about his neck.

The two men mounted, and a moment later I turned to find Ned Low at my elbow. He gave me a whimsical glance, and chuckled softly.

"Caught the bastard, and no mistake, eh? You heard?"

I nodded.

"Aye, Ned. So did Blake, at the helm. The men for'ard are talking already about things."

"Oh, trice up a couple and give 'em a dozen apiece," he said carelessly, "and there'll be no more gossip. Somebody's been talking to the lass, though, and I don't like it. John Russel has his eye on her. You watch sharp, lad."

"Well, Humphrey Stave, how goes it with the palm? Man, that's as neat a patch as ever I saw laid!"

Old Humphrey squinted up over his spectacles.

"Aye, master, and thankee! You'm be good judge of un, sir."

For a moment Low stood glancing around the deck. What he saw in that swift, eaglelike glance of his, I never knew. But suddenly his hand fell on my arm, and his voice sounded in my ear. Ah, the urgency, the repressed fury, of that voice!

"Quick, for the love of Heaven! Loaded pistols in the chart locker. Get Russel and the gunner. Don't run aft, now — easy does it —"

My blood jumped. I turned and walked aft, seeking as I did so what had caused his abrupt alarm and caution. Except that most of the port watch were on deck sunning themselves I could see nothing out of the ordinary. The men seemed to eye me hard as I passed aft, but that might have been imagination. The quarterdeck was empty, save for the long figure of Thomas Winter at the helm.

Once at the companionway I was down the ladder with a leap, and darted aft to the cabin. Russel was doubled up in my cabin; I paused to fling open the door.

"John! Up and arm — quick, man!"

He had his own arms, and usually wore them, so I darted on into the main cabin and in the chart locker came upon two pistols, loaded and pinned. I ran back, found Russel sitting on the edge of his bunk and blinking at me, and swore at him.

"On deck! Swift about it!"

I ran on down the passage and came to the companion ladder. As I started up it, something flew out of the darkness below — a knife, that whanged into the wood beyond my ear with a vicious song. Who flung it I could not see and dared not pause to ask, for I was in fear of what might be happening forward.

Up the ladder and to the deck again, and just in time to see it happen!

They thought me gone below, of course, thought Ned Low alone there among them, the dogs! As my head came up, I saw the thing fall — saw the bucket, heavy with pitch, leave the hand of Simon Blake and go hurtling down from the topsail yard. Low did not see it, but he saw Bosun Pilcher gape upward and heard Pilcher cry out and leap aside blindly.

There was a terrible dull sound, and old Humphrey Stave threw out his arms and bent forward across his sail with his skull stove in. Another and more frightful cry burst from Pilcher; I saw the bosun lean back, saw his arm curl and straighten, saw his knife go flaming up through the air.

"Take it, ye damned murderer of old men!" he yelled out, and Simon Blake took it fair in the throat, and pitched off the yard clear of the ship's side.

Now there was a heave of men over Pilcher; and I, running forward, saw Ezra Blake lean over from the futtock shrouds and drop his own heavy bucket toward Ned Low. The latter, warned by my shout, leaped aside once more and the bucket missed. I flung up one pistol and shot the treacherous hound, and he fell straight at the foot of the foremast, where men were rearing cutlasses from the rack.

Then Ned Low was into them with both hands, and as one man swung at him with a blade I fired again and that man fell. All this, and the body of Ezra dropping among them, and the sight of me running forward, with John Russel behind me and the gunner also on deck, gave them pause.

Pilcher broke loose and stood beside the captain, and I joined them. Then came Russel leaping like a hound across the deck with a pistol in one hand and knife in the other, and a wild grin upon his dark face. Behind him came Gunner Basil, long hair flying, pale eyes darting about.

"Up with those cutlasses again, ye dogs!" shouted Low, and they obeyed sullenly. "So it's mutiny, is it — murder and mutiny, ye swine of righteousness! You there about the arms rack, stand fast!"

Four of the men there were, still half determined to fly at us, and Low held out his hand toward them.

"Gunner Basil! Trice up those four devils. Bose, pipe all hands and give those rascals two dozen."

One of the other men stepped forward defiantly and stretched his arm at Pilcher.

"There's the man o' blood, cap'n!" he shrilled forth. "Flung his knife, he did, and murdered poor Simon Blake, as godly a man as ever walked —"

"After Blake tried to stave in my head, eh?" said Low, pale with fury. "After he'd murdered poor chips, eh?"

"It was an accident!" cried out the man. "I seen his lanyard break and —"

"You lie," said I angrily. "I saw him fling the bucket. You liar, go and join those four scoundrels and take a dozen yourself for your lies!"

"Approved," added Ned Low curtly. "Bind these five men, you dogs, and do it swift! Where's the gunner?"

"Here I be, sir."

Gunner Basil came to the front. He gave an order, and for a moment I thought there would be open mutiny. Then as John Russel grinned and lifted pistol the men obeyed. The five about the mast were bound.

"Now, men," said Low sternly. "I want an explanation of this. Pick your spokesman and send him aft to me as soon as the lashing is over."

He turned and walked aft. Then came Polly Langton running, and joined Pilcher, who was holding the head of poor old Humphrey Stave in his arms, tears coursing down his savage brown cheeks. Humphrey blinked up out of the blood, and saw the girl there, white and feared.

"Oh minny, minny!" cried the dying man. "Here's your lad Humphrey coom home again! Oh, minny, I ha' cried for 'ee! Home from sea, minny, wi' presents for 'ee —"

His head sagged over, and that was all save that Pilcher broke into a storm of sobbing and wild cursing grief. Then the girl's voice thrust in.

"What — what is all this?"

She saw the five men being led aft to the main.

"What have those men done? I heard shots —"

"Murder and mutiny, lass," said John Russel, smirking at her. "But for George Roberts here they had murdered Ned Low and taken the ship."

"Aye, and they killed poor old Humphrey," I added. "Bose, go and do your duty, man."

Tears unwiped, Pilcher leaped up and ran aft for his lash. White-faced, the girl stared about, saw the five being triced up and knew the purpose of it. I called to the other men about us, and at my order they laid out old Humphrey and Ezra Blake. Simon was gone into the deep already. The other man whom I had shot was but wounded across the scalp.

"Take charge here, John," I said to Russel. "I must see to a matter below."

I went aft, passing Ned Low, who stood white and stern at the rail of the quarterdeck, his eyes glittering fiercely.

How far this mutiny extended we could not tell, of course; whether all the crew were in it, or only the two Blakes. Perhaps indeed Simon Blake had merely seized the chance to kill the captain without premeditation.

Going below, I looked along the ladder for that knife which had so narrowly missed my head. The knife was gone, and I swore roundly to myself over the fact. Either Gunner Basil or Russel had flung it, I felt convinced, and I suspected the former. As I looked, Dickon the cabinboy came sleepily to the foot of the ladder, rubbing his eyes.

"What be the fuss, sir?" he asked. "I was asleep down yonder —"

"Get up and see," I responded. "And let the flogging of better men keep you from evil courses, younker! Up with you."

He went to the deck above, and I after him. And there I saw a thing that was bad for discipline.

Pilcher had begun laying on the lash, and the first man under his whip was bloody, for the bosun was in savage mind. But Polly Langton had stopped him and now was standing by, looking aft at Ned Low and demanding that the men be given fair trial. Poor lass! She little dreamed what her intervention was going to mean in the end!

"Dear girl," replied Ned softly enough, yet with steel in his voice, "these men ha' tried to murder me and take the ship. They ha' done murder already. They're getting off light with two dozen, lass. Stand aside, and interfere not!"

"I'll not have it!" she stormed back at him. "You bloody-minded pirates, this is past endurance! These poor men —"

"Bose!"

Now the voice of Ned Low thundered out like a trumpet across the deck.

"Lay on, I bid ye!"

Pilcher shook his earrings, and the cat swung, and the man under it screamed out. At this, Polly Langton turned about, and held out an arm to the men who watched the scene.

"Help me stop it!" she cried wildly enough. "Take the ship from these pirates, these murderous brutes — come, men! Stand by me; don't let your comrades be lashed like dogs —"

Well, the words died on her lips as she saw the uselessness of it. John Russel, all again until his teeth flashed white in the sun, stood to one side, and the hearts of the men sickened in them under his look. So Polly knew that her plea was futile, and with a little groan that hurt my soul she turned again to Ned Low.

"Well do they call you Bloody Ned!" she said in a slow and deliberate voice that carried far. "Never dare to speak to me again, you or your friends — I wash my hands of you and your filthy gold and all your doings! Go on; do your worst to these helpless men, but never speak to me, I command you!"

With this she bent her head and, tears on her cheeks, went aft and so below. While Bosun Pilcher, tears likewise on his own cheeks but from different cause, brought down the cat with all his brawn in the blow, so that the hurt man screamed again.

Presently it was done, Gunner Basil standing by and counting the blows to each man. Then, the groaning dogs staggering forward, Ned Low summoned the spokesman from the other men. All this while Thomas Winter had stuck to the wheel, wagging his long face vacantly but keeping the ship close to her course.

The spokesman came aft. A young, hard-faced fellow he was, by name David Spry, and he poured forth a long and whining plea, full of pious sentiments. The gist of it was that none of the men had intended mutiny; that they believed Bosun Pilcher had murdered Simon Blake and had so acted; that they were repentant and heartily sorry for their misdoing, and humbly begged forgiveness. All in all it was a moving and earnest plea, full of arrant hypocrisy and a lie from start to finish. Ned Low told the man as much.

"What's got into you godly rogues I don't know," he concluded. "But I know who's master o' this ship, and you'll know it, every man of you! Go for'ard. All hands stand by to bury the dead at two bells in the next watch. That's all."

David Spry went forward, and we shifted the men about so that the watches were again balanced. But Bosun Pilcher sat up in the forechains and cried like a baby over the passing of old Humphrey.

That evening after the dead were gone and it was again my watch Ned Low came up to me as I was having the lights filled and placed. We were alone upon the quarterdeck save for the man at the helm, and we were out of hearing.

"George," said Low quietly, "what the hell can I do with her? She won't join us at mess, won't so much as speak to any of us aft. Her attitude has already had an effect on the men. Damn me, I can't take the girl by the neck and throttle her!"

"If you did, Ned —" and I checked myself.

A low laugh came from him.

"Oh, aye! You'd be at my throat. Well, lad, much joy to you of the vixen if you win her. An honest lass, with the courage of her convictions — but oh, good Lord!"

The words came from him in a groan.

"Five years ago this night I was a man in hell, George. Look ye, now! I'm suspicious of this Gunner Basil. Philip, the cook, came to me tonight, and, says he, Basil and our halfwit Winter met outside the galley, and Winter drew a knife on the gunner, cursing him most vile.

"'Now see what you've done, you bastard!' says Winter. For tuppence I'd cut the rotten heart out of you for not waiting, you dog, you!'

"That's strange talk for the daft man, George. And the cook says that Gunner Basil was in mortal fear. This Winter may be harmless, but like most daft men he may have dangerous spells."

"I don't doubt it," I answered and told him of that day when I had come on Thomas Winter down in the cabin. "Excitement seems to send the poor madman's wits flying. But what's all this got to do with five years ago tonight, Ned?"

"I don't know," said he shortly enough.

For a moment he laid his arm across my shoulders.

"Oh, lad," he said softly, "don't you see that the lass is raising hell with those honest fools up for'ard — and herself all honest, too?"

"Aye," I told him. "But how to prevent it?"

"Ask the stars, George," and he drew away with a laugh. "Damn me if I know! Good night."

VI

All this while I had not seen a great deal of John Russel. The little we saw of each other, however, intensified the feelings that had arisen between us that morning on the quay below London Bridge. I heartily detested his smooth, sneering ways, and I think he was unable to puzzle me out — had not the honesty to take me for what I was, yet could not quite fathom me for a knave like himself. Ned Low, I felt certain, distrusted the man on general principles.

Fools that we were! We might better have directed our suspicions elsewhere, had we known it — but how were we to know it? Thus moves life itself, toward some vain objective, only to find itself suddenly directed toward othersome. For now, looking back at it all, I really believe that Russel was square enough in his intent toward the rest of us; but our mutual dislike ripened into distrust, and the distrust rotted into maggots of hatred, all quickly and suddenly.

It happened one day when the wind was fitful and changing, and the air heavy with brooding storm, so that all hands were kept bracing about the yards and men's tempers were apt to fly out at nothing. Not that I make any excuse of this for my own part, since through several days Russel and I had been approaching a crisis.

This came about in some degree through the attitude of Polly Langton. Ever since that day Humphrey Stave was slain she had kept to her word and held no intercourse with any of us aft. Her meals were served in her own tiny box of a cabin, and she treated us with a stony silence as if we did not exist. When she walked the deck, it was forward; and often she talked with the men, and sometimes would relent a little when I saluted her, though she spoke not.

Because I perceived that she thus softened a little toward me, her manner irked me not at all; but John Russel it infuriated, I observed that after some meeting with her he would walk the decks like a devil incarnate, raging among the men; and once he beat David Spry so furiously with a belaying-pin that the seaman bore the marks of it a fortnight.

Not that he had cause, either. The men were tamed, were obedient and lively and had given no further sign of any trouble.

Between me and John Russel, however, the hot tropic sun quickened ill-feeling. On the morning in question we had a sharp exchange of words when watches were changed. Having lost three men, we were short in each watch; added to which, one of the men was ill with the ague, passing from a quotidian into a tertian, and being too weak to move. So Russel desired to shift Bosun Pilcher out of my watch into his own, which offer I very bluntly refused. We nearly came to blows over it, yet did not.

At eight bells in the afternoon I turned over the deck to him and went below at once to get some sleep; storm was brewing and the heaviness of the air had given me a head-ache. As I came below I met Dickon in the passage and ordered him to fetch me a mug of ale into the main cabin. There I sat down to the table to pick our course on the chart, as we were getting close to the islands and had need of care.

Hearing someone enter, I spoke over my shoulder without looking up, thinking it Dickon.

"We're past the Canaries, and I would we had some of that wine aboard! Go you and tell Philip to get a fresh butt brought up for'ard, for the water in that is foul, and to have it well lashed in place at once."

"Damn your impudence!" said the voice of Russel. "Run your own errands, you cursed Virginian."

I turned to see Russel at the cupboard, pouring a cup of wine.

"Hark 'ee, Russel or Lopez," I told him, "a little more civility, if you please! I took you for Dickon —"

"The devil sink you and your takings!" he broke in with a sudden access of fury, turning at me and snarling like a wolf.

Just then Ned Low came into the cabin, and Russel gulped at his wine. Ned perceived nothing amiss, but came and glanced at the chart and chuckled merrily.

"Ha, good and well done, George! By the Lord Harry, we've a record to boast of this voyage — hardly a ship spoke, not a head wind nor a calm, and a course fair and straight as an arrow to the islands! Gunner's on deck, John? I must speak with him."

He passed out and was gone. Russel looked after him with a dark sneer.

"Aye, you'll speak wi' Gunner Basil once too often!" he growled. "I've warned you against that pale-eyed devil, you poor fool of a gentleman, you —"

"Keep your tongue off Low," I snapped. He whipped out an oath, and I saw murder in his eyes; his hand dived down to the pistol in his belt. At that I was out of the chair and at him and knocked the pistol into the corner.

His fist took me under the ear and smashed me against the wall. As I rose I caught sight of Dickon, ale-mug in hand, standing in the doorway and staring out of his evil eyes. Then Russel was atop of me, and his knife was out; but I met him with a blow from the shoulder that tapped the claret, and got out from the wall. He came on, cursing and letting drive with the knife, but I evaded him and got home another blow. Then sanity began to crowd into my brain.

"Let be, you fool!" I cried out, parrying his stroke. "More of this and well all find ourselves —"

He stopped short in his stride like a man paralyzed, and for an instant I thought that my words had checked him. It was not my words or my fist, however. He stood there with the knife held out toward me, and slowly his fingers loosened, so that it dropped and tinkled on the floor. His eyes widened on me and his mouth opened, but no words came forth.

Then a bubble of red froth broke on his lips; he dropped to his knees and rolled down on the floor, and I saw the haft of a knife sticking out from his back.

Even while I stared at him in blank horror and wonder I caught the shrill voice of that devil's spawn Dickon from the companionway.

"Ahoy, cap'n!" it cried out. "Cap'n Low! The mate ha' killed Mr. Russel, cap'n!"

John Russel, dying, heard that lifting, piercing cry. He heaved upward, raised himself to one elbow, wrenched up his head, and looked at me. A ghastly, twisted smile curled his lips as he slobbered the blood from his pierced lungs. He tried to speak, and could not — then sudden words burst from him.

"Now 'ware of them, Roberts, or you're snared! Tell Low — that the man — man Thomas Winter —"

He strangled in his own life-stream, and died on the word.

Now came Ned Low running, with the imp Dickon pointing and crying at his heels, and behind them Gunner Basil and the bosun. Some of the men were following; but Captain Low sent back an angry shout that checked them and ordered Pilcher back to keep the deck. The bosun obeyed with an ill grace and waved his hand to me before he went. Ned Low came on into the cabin.

"I seen it done, cap'n!" shrilled that little devil Dickon, pointing at me. "Took un in the back, 'e did —"

"You little liar!" I burst forth angrily. "It was you flung that knife —"

I started for him; but Gunner Basil whipped out a pistol at me, and I checked myself. A dying man does not waste words. John Russel had spent his last breath in warning me, and those pale, murderous eyes of the gunner's told me who was back of this snare. I think Gunner Basil would have pistoled me then, had not Ned Low knocked up his weapon.

"What in the devil's name is all this!" he cried out. "Dickon stow your jaw! George, what happened?"

"Why, Russel and I were fighting," I said bluntly. "In the midst of it Dickon there threw a knife and struck Russel in the back. That's all."

"A black lie!" screamed the boy, flying into a fury of rage. "It was you stabbed un as 'e leaned over the table — never give un a chance! And —"

"Do not cast the stain o' murder on the innocent boy, Mr. Roberts!" spoke out Gunner Basil in his best preaching manner. "A sanctified vessel is the lad —"

I plunged at him, but Ned Low caught my arm and flung me back. He turned a cold face to the gunner and ordered him on deck.

"It's your watch, and see that you keep it," he finished. "This is none of your affair. I want no more words from you, mind that!"

Basil looked him in the eye, and dropped his gaze.

"Aye, sir," he said, and departed to the deck meekly enough.

Ned Low took a step forward, leaned over the body of Russel and pulled forth the knife. He rose up and gave Dickon a keen glance.

"Dickon," he said in a kindly tone, "keep this matter to yourself. You understand?"

The little devil was no more astounded than I was, and could only stare and mumble something about Portugee Lopez. Ned Low nodded thoughtfully.

"True, Dickon. The man was pirate and outlaw. Tell the bosun to bring two hands here and remove the body. And no talking, mind."

The imp gave me one exultant, diabolical grin, and departed. No sooner was he gone, however, than Ned Low turned to me, a blaze of eager vehemence in his face.

"George, never mind talking!" he burst out softly. "Forgive me, lad. Don't ye see, the little fiend is not alone? Gunner's with him, and more besides. When the call came cook Philip was just yammering to me about some trouble for'ard, and there's a gale breaking within the hour and the sails to be handed. Let this matter pass for the moment; we'll make the boy confess his lie later on."

"You're right," I assented. "And, Ned! When Russel died he was trying to tell me something. He heard the boy shouting at you and warned me of a trap. He tried to send you some message about the man Winter but could not get it out."

Low's eyes narrowed speculatively.

"Winter! That proves my point; John had guessed the trouble for'ard — thought the daft man was in it, eh? John was no fool in such things. Well, slip a pistol into your pocket from the locker, George, and take the deck.

"Or, stay! You're weary. Go sleep, and bar your door; there's deviltry afoot somewhere. I'll take this watch. We can't trust Gunner Basil."

I nodded and went to my own cabin. There came a tramp of feet as a number of the men descended the ladder; also I heard Polly Langton's voice and knew that the girl was aroused by the noise. Like a coward I flung myself on my bunk and left Ned Low to do the explaining to the lass.

After perhaps an hour of sleep I wakened as the *King Sagamore* keeled over almost on her beam ends — wakened to the trampling of feet, the shouts of men, the pipe calling all hands. Getting hurriedly on deck, I found that the blow had come.

Except for a rag of sail forward we were stripped to meet it. The first blast of the wind had sent us over; now there was peace for a moment. The ship righted, fell away; and then the main fury of the storm drove down. Through the darkness the huge masses of cloud to windward were lightning-shot, sending an eerie glare across the waters.

Now we beheld it coming — a white line of spray and spindrift, racing down from the horizon under the glare of lightning, I was busy amidships, getting everything lashed down anew, when the keen, cold blast of wind smote us I sang out to all hands to hold on, and we leaped to the life-lines. Then we were smothered under water and spray.

Two of our men must have gone at that minute, for we never afterward saw them.

A poorer ship than the *King Sagamore* would never have risen out of that welter, for she laid over while three heavy seas swept her. Then she began to rise; the scrap of sail forward caught and held; she answered her helm and came before the wind, and we were off.

That night the loss of those two men was felt badly, for every hand was needed; and to add to our troubles the ship was making water, a butt having been loosened somewhere forward and the leak hard to get at. None the less we counted ourselves lucky all told; particularly in this, that the gale was driving us fair on our course, and we might look to raise the islands in two days or less.

Now of the company that had left London, twenty all told besides Polly Langton, we had lost six. Aft, there remained captain, mate and gunner, and we took the bosun into our company as second mate. Forward were Dickon, Philip the cook, Thomas Winter, and seven of the sons of righteousness who were led by David Spry; ten in all. It was by no means a large ship's company, but we could take on a few hands at the islands, for the Cape Verde men are glad to ship.

So night wore into dawn again, and ever we fled south and south with the storm roaring at our heels, the *King Sagamore* picked up and hurled forward with a hissing rush by every mountain-wave. With daybreak the leak began to show so bad that I resolved to take it in hand myself, for it was beneath a timber near the well on the larboard side.

Ordering Thomas Winter down into the hold with a lantern, I followed with David Spry to help me. We got the timber cut away about the trunnel, which remained fast in the plank; the butt had started indeed, and the water shot in the full breadth of the fourteen-inch plank.

When we had somewhat checked the force of the stream with oakum we moused the trunnel, took two clove hitches about it and lashed the trunnel to a bar, just as a port is lashed, I had brought along two rollers, or screws, such as we use in Virginia to roll tobacco hogsheads; these I screwed fast at each corner of the plank and then lashed them into the bar. All this took time and energy; and, having done most of the work myself, I was half drowned and aching in every muscle of my arms when we finished.

"Now, David Spry," I said, "fetch that calking mallet and drive the oakum tight. Lay more oakum on; and you, Winter, get us a chock of wood. We'll nail battens over that, and I'll guarantee she won't weep."

"Aye, sir," said David Spry, picking the mallet out of the water. "She'll not weep a drop."

Thomas Winter held up the lantern high. I was leaning against a beam for support. In the yellow light that half-witted face of Winter's altered suddenly to a look of such wild ferocity that I was for the moment paralyzed.

"She'll not weep, David Spry!" he cried out in a bellowing voice. "Strike, lad!"

The seaman struck — not at the seam, but at me.

The mallet caught me above the ear and drove my head against the oak. So sudden, so unexpected and bitter, was the assault, that before I knew what was happening I was dazed and reeling under the blow. I went down into the knee-deep water, and Spry flung himself on top of me, fetching me another crack that knocked the sense out of me.

So there was I taken like a pole-axed bull.

When I wakened again, it was to hear my name called. I found myself lying in darkness, but on dry planks. When I moved there echoed from the blackness a rattle of chains, and I found wrists and ankles in irons. By the surge and heave of the deck, the groanings of beams and the creak of the rudder-irons near by I perceived that I was lying in the lazaret aft, down in the run of the ship.

"George!" came a voice again to me. "George Roberts!"

"Hello, Ned!" I answered. "Is that you?"

"Aye," he replied as his foot touched mine.

"Art hurt?"

"Naught worse than a lump or two over the ear. You're not taken likewise?"

"Taken without a blow, lad!"

His voice was bitter.

"They called me down, said that you needed me — and clapped a tarpaulin over my head as I came. Damn me! That halfwit Winter has the strength o' ten men! Well, here I am, and here you are."

I was slow to speak, stunned by the realization of it. Mutiny at such a moment was madness — or so it seemed. Whom had they, except Gunner Basil, to manage the ship? And he was no navigator.

"I'd give a thousand pound," said Ned Low, "to know what it was John Russel tried to say about that devil Winter!"

"You don't think that it's he who has taken the ship?" I demanded.

"No, no!"

Ned Low laughed a little.

"This is Polly Langton's doing, George."

VII

The passage of time was nothing to us as we lay in the pitch darkness amid the powder and the cabin stores. Indeed, we lay there the whole day unheeded, all hands being busy above; but the day seemed like weeks to us.

Ned Low had heard some smattering of talk while he and I were being chained in the lazaret; enough to show him that the mutiny had come about through Polly Langton. He had heard Spry swearing that they would stand by the lass and see us hanged for the pirates we were, which indeed appeared proof positive. Yet she was no navigator, though a good seaman in all else, so how could she hope to bring the ship to any port?

"Ned," I asked during the weary wait, "d'you mind that little black box I brought aboard from Langton? You've never said how it was he had the chart."

"I had left it with him to compare with a paper he had in Franklin's writing," said Ned Low. "Poor Langton! Little he guessed what was up this cruise!"

"Well," I said, "for one, I'm not so sure about Polly's being the chief mutineer. That devilish little wastrel Dickon has more infernal brain than we credited him with. I think now 'twas he tried to get me with his knife that day Humphrey Stave was killed. And Gunner Basil is a bad one for certain, though he may be holding to his pious pose. But where's Bosun Pilcher? He'll not turn against us."

"He was on deck when they nabbed me," came Low's voice. "Aye, he's true, and so is black Philip. But that cursed Thomas Winter! I'd like to know what John Russel had to say about the dog."

"Ned," I said after a long space of silence, "tell me about your chase after this Trunnel Toby. And that day Humphrey Stave was killed, you remember? You said how five years ago that night something had happened. What is it all, Ned? What reason lay behind you and the wine-dark sea?"

"Oh ho! Art quoting Homer to me, eh?"

Ned Low's laugh rang bitter, but ended in a soft word.

"George, sometimes I think the waves are weary with weeping — but pshaw! Five years ago I had everything in life, George; university honors, a home and family, and the promise of a girl I loved."

These words had tumbled out of him as it were; jerkily to the flitting of his thought. Now for a little he was silent and finally spoke. His voice was hoarse, whether from the thirst that we had or from the tumult of his spirit I know not.

"Why, George, that is a lengthy recital, and I am no teller of tales; but since we have a quiet watch below, shall out with the yarn and appease your curiosity —"

"It is no such thing," I broke in. "It is interest and friendliness, and you know it!"

"Aye, and your pardon, lad," he answered and sighed. "I have grown cynical of men, George, and belief comes hard to my lips; but my heart is sound enough and loves you.

You've never been in the west country, by Wrexham and Marchwiel and the Brondeg Hills, and Wat's Dike, along the Welsh country?"

"No nearer than London town," I responded.

"Then take my word for it, no lovelier country may be found, George! My father was a magistrate and a knight, and of latter years had grown wealthy through his shares in the Company of Hudson's Bay. And one day he gave sentence to a poacher for killing a hare. A seaman it was, who had wandered riotously up from Bristol, spending guineas by the way. Guineas gone, the seaman headed for Bristol again, trapping the hedges for meals, and so fell foul of the law and was taken. My father sentenced him to transportation.

"Even the man's name was not known. He was a man with long face, they say, and melancholy eyes and a voice like a roaring wind when he flung out curses; a gold ring fast in his nostrils, and over his heart was tattooed a crimson bleeding heart. That, and the name he went by, was all the picture I could gain of him.

"Well, into jail he was clapped, cursing and swearing bitter vengeance upon my father, who had sentenced him. Two days later came travelers, shipmen going to Bristol, and they heard of the man and viewed him as he lay in jail. They recognized him for one Trunnel Toby, a man famed for foul deeds and piracies. Word of it came to London, and he was sent for to be hanged at Tyburn as a notable example to other pirates.

"So they took him away, chained him like a beast. How he did it I know not, but he slew both his guards and escaped clear away. And on a Sunday night he came, bringing other rogues with him, to Ravenscroft Hall where my father lived."

Now the hoarseness gained upon Ned Low, so that for a little he sat in silence, and I could hear his dry mouth working. I had by this time caught the drift of what was afoot, and guessed whither his tale led. The telling of it would ease his heart, so I kept still and let him go his own gait. He resumed presently, speaking soft and low.

"There was a lass I loved, George, and since my parents were lonely, often she would come to the hall and spend a day or two. She was spending that Sunday so when this foul Trunnel Toby and his mates arrived. They picked their time, knowing that few of the servants would be about.

"Well, they broke in and slew like dogs gone mad in Summer's heat! They slew and robbed, plundering Ravenscroft as they would ha' plundered any ship on the high seas. Two of the dogs fell under my father's steel ere they pistoled him — Toby himself fired the shot, and that same bullet slew my mother. The dear lass they murdered likewise, and fled with their booty, having horses in waiting.

"And the devils got clear away, George; clear away! They had a ship waiting by Bristol, and Trunnel Toby was captain of her.

"To this I was called home from Oxford. One of the two

whom my father slew, lived long enough to tell who and why, and then died. For a fortnight I was like a man out of his wits, and then I fell to work. I raised what money I could, sold off what lands were free and went to London.

"There I bought a stout sloop, armed her and manned her with the scurviest knaves could be picked up. There was a devil in me then, lad; for all I was just turned twenty-one I made those knaves fear me most bitterly. So we put to sea, and since that day I have never lessened in the search for Trunnel Toby.

"A year, and I was captaining my own ship, a fine, fast ship that we took from a French rover off Brazil. They had little ease who sailed with me, I promise you! We were on the Account sure enough, but we molested no innocent trader, George — only hunted up and down the seas whatever ship Trunnel Toby might be in.

"He heard of it, and others heard of it, for I hanged every man that had sailed with him or shared with him. More than once, as I have told you, I came close to him, but the hound was wary. I made the seas so hot for him that men were afraid to ship under him, and he was forced to take lesser berths. Always he fled from me; for he knew why I was after him, although no one else knew the reason, and he was afraid to face me.

"Ah, but he is a man of blood past reckoning! A fiend in human form, George; I've heard how he has dealt with captive men and women, so that your blood would freeze to imagine it.

"And he's no coward, either. Only last year with some small boats he boarded a Portuguese Indiaman in the very harbor o' Funchal, slew every soul aboard her and with the remnants of his men worked her out from under the shore guns, I was there a week later and heard the tale, and tracked him to the African coast.

"Indeed, I found the ship in the Guinea River, up a bit from the English factory at Sierra Leone, and I took her. Every man aboard her I hanged, but Trunnel Toby himself got ashore and fled among the blacks up the river. There I lost him, for I pursued with boats and discovered that he had doubled back to the coast again and escaped me in a ship bound for Virginia with slaves. And since then I have been able to obtain not the slightest trace of him.

"Most like he is in Virginia now. With my share of Franklin's gold I'll buy this ship and start out anew, and I think I'll find him in Virginia, for he's poor and without followers, and even the brethren of the coast are afraid to sail with me for fear I'll trace them down and hang them. And that's the reason behind me, George Roberts."

"You've told it to Polly Langton?" I demanded.

"The Lord forbid!" exclaimed his voice, startled. "I've told it to none save you."

"Then no wonder she deems you a common pirate," I said thoughtfully.

"I forbid you to mention it, George."

"Oh, I'll not! I thank you for the confidence, Ned Low, and if it's ever in my power to aid you, count on me. But for the present — zounds! Here we are chained up like felons, and what's to come of it?"

He made no answer to this. Presently, for all my pondering on that sad story of his and the wreck which had been made of his life, I fell asleep from utter weariness.

It was after night when I wakened, for the trap to the cabin above was open, and David Spry was coming down with a lantern and food and mugs of ale. Ned Low was asleep, and Spry stirred him with his foot until he sat up, then gave us the food and ale and watched us make way with it. His dour, gloomy face was saturnine.

"Wind be falling," he announced, "and we're like to raise the islands tomorrow."

Ned Low glanced up at him.

"You'll raise nothing but the coast of hell, you mutinous dog!"

"Aye, by your guidance."

David Spry grinned, and then sobered. He sat him down on an ale-keg and regarded us while he played with his knife in one hand.

"Harkee, masters! The ship's ours. Mistress Polly be in command of she, and Thomas Winter the cap'n —"

"Winter!" I said, choking on my ale. "Are you mad?"

"Nay, un can navigate right well," said David Spry, and grinned again. "Now, Master Winter bain't a man of God, not he! Nor Gunner Basil neither, for all his pretended repentance; for did we not hear un swearing great oaths? Aye. Nor Bose Pilcher neither. And they all say to hang the two of ye and take the ship. We'll not abide this, masters."

We listened to him in stark amazement. He was in deadly earnest, and we realized that he was speaking for the hands forward no less than for himself. But Pilcher —

"Need not call us mutineers, masters," he went on. "We'm be honest men. You be rogues and scoundrels belike; and for the lady up above we've took the ship over, and save the blood of honest men from your hands. Ye unregenerate sons o' Belial, take shame to yourselves! We'm be honest British men and sail not wi' murderers and pirates and suchlike."

"Yet you're going to murder us," put in Ned Low.

"Not us, master. Set un ashore, maybe."

The man rose and took our mugs.

"Think o' your sins now, and do 'ee spend the night at prayer. It won't hurt ye none."

He climbed up again through the trap, which he left open, perhaps for convenience. We remained in the darkness. Presently I heard Ned Low chuckle.

"George, sink me if this isn't the richest joke ever perpetrated! Here that lass has taken my own ship from me, Bloody Ned — and is mistress of the ship herself!"

"The joke will end as it began — with death," I said broodingly. "These long-noses have seen through Gunner

Basil at last, it appears — that's one good thing! But what d'ye think about Thomas Winter, eh? Who dreamed that the lout could navigate — or is he lying to the others about his ability?"

A whistle broke from Ned Low.

"Damn me, George, I'd give a thousand pound to know what it was John Russel —"

"Make it five thousand," I said, "and Russel might come back from hell to tell you."

He laughed at that.

"I doubt it. So those devils are figuring on hanging us, eh? I'm surprised that the bosun is with 'em."

"He's not," I said. "I know Pilcher, Ned, and he's a true man. But listen! There's a light above —"

Through the open trap we saw a light in the cabin above. It darted down, a square of radiance, and with the roll of the ship illumined our prison-chamber by flashes, now here, now there. Both Ned Low and I were ironed wrist and ankle, and chains ran from the irons to ring-bolts in the deck, so that we had freedom of movement but no liberty. Between us was a small keg of excellent port, laid aboard for cabin use; and I knew we would not die of thirst or suffer from it again.

Now a voice came to us from the cabin. The words we could not catch, although by the tone it was the voice of Gunner Basil. Right after it came the clear, high tones of Polly Langton.

"Nay, I will not! I am weary, I tell you, and shall do no talking until tomorrow. Let the two men lie in peace — look to it, gunner; and you, bosun! If harm comes to them you both hang, I swear it! Time enough tomorrow for a talk."

Pilcher made roaring response, perhaps in order that we might hear.

"But, mistress! The men want to know if you be with 'em or no! It's for your sake we have taken the ship —"

"You and the gunner and that man Winter can talk with me at eight bells in the morning, and not before," came her response, and after this, nothing. Presently the light vanished from above.

A bowl or porringer in which some food had been fetched, remained with us. I took this and set it under the spigot of the keg and drew some port. After drinking I passed it along to Ned Low.

"I have a pipe but no tobacco, Ned —"

"Here's 'bacca and a tinder-box."

Neither of us spoke until I had managed, with some trouble, to get the good brown weed alight and had passed the pipe to Ned Low.

"Did you get the catch in her voice, Ned?" I asked. "And she's sparring for time, d'ye mind! Come, Ned, things are not quite so obvious as we thought. The lass is having hard work of it somehow."

"Bah! Nothing of the sort," growled he. "The jade has come to realize that neither she nor Winter can navigate,

that's all. She's afraid. By morning, George, they'll make us an offer if we'll navigate for 'em. Wait and see!"

I was not so sure about this, and events proved my doubts well founded.

"Who keeps the keys of these irons, Ned?" I asked suddenly.

He laughed harshly.

"The gunner. There's a spare set o' keys in the chart locker, but small use they are to us here."

By the movements of the ship we soon perceived that the sea was going down, but the night wore away intolerably for us, and the thought of being thus chained like slaves for any longer time was past endurance.

We had worse than thoughts to torment us, however — worse even than the rats which scurried about and over us until movement frightened them. It was, I think, with the midnight change of watches when the filtered rays of a tiny iron lantern came about the ladder, and then a sound of maudlin cursing and swearing. Down the ladder tumbled the boy Dickon, by some miracle preserving the lantern unhurt as he fell, and picked himself up with more oaths. He was, to put it bluntly, drunk as a lord.

He set the lantern on the ladder and turned to us, cursing and reviling us with the tongue of an arrant pirate. A vast change had come about in him; he had knotted a red kerchief about his head, wore a shirt looted from my bag and had donned my sea-boots which came nearly to his knees. About his waist were belted pistols, though unloaded, and in his hand he held a deadly little gimlet dirk — a round handled weapon, the blade protruding from the fingers of his clenched fist.

"Pirates, is it?" he maundered, coming toward us. "Sink me, but I ha' been cabinboy to Avery, and this is a poor pack o' thieves and woolsack rogues — there, ye lousy dogs! Wake up and give tongue. An I had my way ye'd walk the plank come sunup; aye, and if the old gunner had his way too!"

With this he fetched me a kick and stood regarding us drunkenly, the devil in his face. Cabinboy with Avery indeed! Avery had died before the young rascal was breeched.

"Stare at me, dogs!" He leered at us as he spoke. "Aye, damn ye for cowardly curs! Silly old Langton never dreamed 'twas all cut and dried, eh? Nor you, called Bloody Ned — I'll blood ye, and a pox take ye —" With this he leaned forward and jabbed that little dirk of his into the calf of Ned's leg. The same instant my foot took him in the waist, all my weight back of it.

"Woof!"

The air burst out of him; he went back head first among the boxes, dropping the dirk as he fell. Groaning, holding his hands to his middle, he rose up; then Ned flung the pewter porringer at him and caught him across the eyes. A howl broke from the imp. Catching up the lantern, he scrambled back whence he had come, and his groans died out overhead.

"Sickened him, and well done too!" said Ned, laughing.

He leaned forward, and with his foot raked in the dirk.

"Here's the first symptom of hope we've had, George — aye, I have it. A good little weapon."

"Did the pup hurt you?"

"A scratch. He'd have murdered us if he'd been let alone. Did ye mark what he said about Langton, George? 'All cut and dried,' quoth he!"

I recalled now how Dickon and Gunner Basil had been thick from the very start. It was clear enough that they had fooled Dennis Langton into shipping them; yet we vainly sought a reason until I recalled the tale Pilcher had told me and laid it before Ned Low with some further details that I had forgotten when I first confronted Basil.

"That must be the right of it, Ned!" I concluded, "Gunner Basil served under Avery, d'ye mind? And this talk about knowing where Avery's gold was hid — d'you think it's the same gold we're after?"

"It's not," said Ned stoutly, "I was at the taking of this hoard; none but Franklin and I knew where it was hid. It may well be, however, that Avery buried some other gold about the islands, and that the gunner knew of it. Avery's been dead long years. Yet I don't like the smell of it all, George; to me it looks like a plan ready laid. All cut and dried, said he! I'd give a thousand pound if I knew what it was John Russel wanted to say about Winter —"

"Hist, below!" came a sudden low voice.

We fell silent.

"Below, cap'n! Art well?"

"Aye," responded Ned Low. "who's there?"

"Me — Philip! What can I do for you, master?"

Lord, but how my heart leaped at those words! The black cook!

"Get the keys from the chart locker and loose us from the irons!" snapped Ned swiftly.

Hope thrilled in his voice, and I felt eagerness surge through me. Philip was a true man, and —

A curse, a shrill cry, the sound of trampling feet came to us, and the voice of Gunner Basil poured forth furious oaths. He had come upon Philip, had discovered him aft, and now drove him forward with blows and beery revelings; evidently a cask had been broached forward. And so our hopes died even more swiftly than they had arisen. All became silent up above.

"Well," quoth Ned philosophically, "better luck next time, lad! And at least I have the little dirk."

It was small consolation, to me at least.

VIII

With the morning, suddenly and most terribly, there was laid open before us the whole book of villainy which those above were writing. No, not the whole book either; one page of it was still hidden from us!

David Spry came down to us again, left us food and ale and went his way without saying a word, hurriedly. A little while afterward voices came to us through the trap, which remained open. The first voice which reached us was that of Spry himself.

"I am come to speak for them for'ard," he said, "The bosun is a child o' darkness, and we who be honest men will ha' naught to do with his decisions. I say to your face, Gunner Basil, that we ha' doubt of your regenerate state; and I demand to be heard among ye."

The gunner's whine rose, but with an ugly note to it.

"I accept the burden which be laid upon me; aye, the burden o' doubt and mistrust! For my sins —"

"Stow it," commanded a new voice curtly and with irritated contempt. "Stow it, ye swab! As for you, David Spry, ye are dead right, lad. Aye, sit among us, and welcome."

Light came filtering down to us through the open trap. I stared at Ned Low, and he at me, with open wonder and astonishment. What voice was this? It was new to us; we could not place it. Then even as we stared came the answer to our wondering. Polly Langton's voice floated to us.

"Well, Thomas Winter? Where is the bosun?"

"On deck," returned Winter. "One of us must keep the deck, miss. Will ye sit?"

From Ned Low broke a low ejaculation. Winter, indeed! There was no daft vacancy in this voice; it was the full-throated growl of a seaman, as different from the man's usual tones as day from night. The sickening conviction broke upon me full force.

"Ned, it was a plot from the very start!" I said softly with an oath at my own past blindness. "He and the gunner and Dickon, perhaps others! The man was no halfwit at all."

"We're a trifle late discovering the matter," and Ned Low smiled whimsically.

"Now let us have an understanding once and for all."

Polly Langton spoke up coolly, quiet command in her voice, and I could imagine her level eyes sweeping from man to man.

"You have taken this ship from her officers and owners, claiming to do it on my behalf, but without any orders or bidding of mine. Thus far I have consented to the matter, for the ship was in storm and distress. Now speak out your purposes flatly. What mean you to do?"

There was a moment of silence. Ned Low looked at me and made a grimace; here was a morsel of news indeed! We thought that the lass had been a party to our captivity, but now the matter appeared otherwise. As for me I felt a glow of warmth and joy, since it had been hard for me to lose faith in her.

"Mistress," began Gunner Basil, "it be in the purposes of Providence —"

"Stow it!" commanded Thomas Winter. "David Spry, do ye answer the lady."

There was something grim, something significant, in the

way this man spoke to Gunner Basil. I remembered how I had overheard him addressing the gunner formerly in the cabin, and instinctively I began to feel a cold chill at thought of the man. Gunner Basil was no baby, but a murderous scoundrel himself; yet the gunner obviously stood in blank fear of this man Winter, whom we had accounted a daft person! Ned Low must have felt something of the same sense, for he murmured to me:

"Mark, 'tis Winter who gives orders! Winter who captains the ship! Winter who navigates her —"

"Why, mistress," broke in the cold voice of David Spry from the cabin above, "we be honest men — some of us at least. Do 'ee mind how, that day Simon and Ezra Blake were murdered, and men lashed, ye cried to us to stand by 'ee against they pirates and bloody rogues? Well, we ha' done so, and that be all."

"All, you say?" spoke out the girl. "What say you, Winter? And you, gunner?"

"Aye," they answered together.

"And what is your purpose now, David Spry?" she demanded. "Do you know why we sail to the Verde Islands?"

"Aye, mistress," he responded. "We ha' heard talk o' gold. We stand with 'ee, I say, and we be honest men. We want no gold but our pay. We'll not see they pirates do no more robbery an' murder, nor take the ship from 'ee, mistress. We'll ha' no more to do wi' they sons o' Belial an' darkness! Do 'ee say the word now, and we stand with 'ee."

"Oh!" said the girl's voice. "What say you to that, Winter? And you, gunner?"

"Aye," they answered again.

Then her voice leaped out at them.

"Very well. If you be minded to obey me, Winter, go above and take the deck, and send Bosun Pilcher down here."

Ned Low gave me a shove with his foot, and grinned admiringly. I awaited the answer. It came with a scrape of feet, and the heavy tread of Thomas Winter leaving the cabin. Immediately afterward, the girl spoke, but softly, so that we could hardly hear her.

"Gunner, what and who is that man? Since the day we left the Thames, he has been known to all aboard as a man of poor sense, no better than a fool. Now he is lucid, and you obey him, and he navigates the ship!"

"Why, mistress, 'tis the dispensation o' Providence!" replied Gunner Basil in oily tones. "I know him no more than you, but praise be, in the hour o' need he has been lifted up as a horn o' salvation to us! What 'ud we ha' done, else, for a navigator, mistress? If it be not a plain case o' Providence, I know naught!"

Now Pilcher made his appearance evidently, for Polly Langton addressed him bluntly.

"Bose, these other men have declared that they have taken the ship on my behalf, will stand by me and take my orders. What say you?"

"I say now, as I said afore," said Pilcher, "that Cap'n Roberts be no pirate! But as for standing by 'ee, mistress, I say aye to that. What's done is done. I obey."

"Very well; then we are agreed," said the girl. "These are my orders! First, that we complete our voyage and get that for which we have come. Second, that the treasure be divided among those to whom it belongs — me, and Cap'n Low, and Mr. Roberts. Third, that these two gentlemen be kept confined until the division is made, then be given their shares and free passage ashore at the first port we make. Now, lads, speak out! Yes or no?"

"That's fair, mistress," said David Spry. "I agree."

"As righteous men," said Gunner Basil, "we ought to hand they over to the law; but I say aye your orders, mistress. Aye."

"And you, bose?" she asked.

"Aye," said Pilcher.

"Very well. See that it be so done. Who among you elected Winter captain?"

"It was agreement, miss," said David Spry. "He could navigate."

"Very well. It is understood."

The sound of feet and the scrape of chairs told us that the conference was over. I was about to speak when Ned Low, his head cocked on one side, made a gesture of caution. I waited. A moment afterward we caught a soft sound of laughter and the voice of Gunner Basil — shorn of its whine.

"Ha, Dickon! Here's a mug o' wine, ye devil's imp! Now run and tell our cap'n, blast his soul, to step down here and finish the bottle with me. Move, ye damned pup!"

A mocking retort from Dickon, and the boy fled on his errand. I sat motionless and stared at Ned Low. We waited expectantly, and were soon rewarded. Winter's heavy tread jarred the deck, and Gunner Basil greeted him with another laugh and an invitation.

"I ha' no time to drink, ye black dog," responded Winter's suddenly masterful voice. "It went well?"

"Aye," said the gunner. "She's after the gold, right enough."

"Good! Then we'll not have to squeeze the location out of her," said Winter. "Play it fine and slip not, or I'll carve the heart out of your carcass, d'ye mind that?"

"But, lad!" cried the gunner, "When this be done, will ye not run to the other island and pick up that gold I told ye of? The gold that Avery buried, his own share it was! No man alive but me knows the place, now that Cap'n Avery be burnin' in hell! What say?"

"Like enough," answered Winter indifferently as if postponing a matter on which he were none too eager. "But, mind ye, we have to make the rendezvous first, lad! We ha' not enough hands to work ship, and will have less. Obey the lass, mind ye! Let her put her gold aboard afore we act. And take good care o' Cap'n Low now; good care! I'll carry him along of us to the rendezvous. There's yet a fortnight afore the *Rose Pink* can be looked for; so, Gunner Basil, bide patient. If ye spoil my work I'll spread-eagle ye!"

Now both men apparently left the cabin. I drew a long breath and met the gaze of Ned Low, for the moment wordless. But it seemed as if new life had come into him; as if these staggering disclosures had invigorated and heartened him. All the old reckless gaiety back in his eyes, he gave me a grin of sheer, delighted amusement.

"Ha, George! Now we have the right of it, now we have the whole scheme unfolded, sink me else! Damn me, but the rogues were smart! D'ye see, George, they were stranded in London town most likely or else were waiting for word from their friends. So they shipped aboard us and made a rendezvous with the *Rose Pink* at one o' the islands —"

"Who's ship is she?" I demanded. "Who's this devil Winter, anyhow?"

"Damn me if I can figure it, George! The *Rose Pink* is a right good ship o' twenty-two guns; Spriggs had her, but sold her to a Frenchman before he was taken and hanged. Whose she is now, I know not."

"Perhaps Winter knew all along of our errand," I mused.

"Not so. More likely he and the gunner and Dickon shipped with us, meaning to betray us as a prize to the *Rose Pink*; they did not look for so quick a passage as we made, which explains why a fortnight still lacks to the time appointed. Ye see how they ha' made use of these honest fools for'ard? On the way they learned o' what we were after, and Winter is handling the matter so Polly Langton will uncover the gold for him. Cursed clever rogue, ain't he?"

"Too cursed clever for us, Ned. We'd better acquaint the lass with the truth —"

"Tut, tut! She'd never believe us; it would be taken as a ruse to get clear of our irons, lad. Make no mistake, George, the devil is loose aboard here! Bose Pilcher knows it. You heard how meek he spoke, assenting to all that was said! Take cue from him, George, and bide patient."

Ned Low was aroused now and no mistake, and I began to see the man of energy, below that gay and almost insouciant exterior. There was a bite to his words. I verily believe he was enjoying himself, was scenting the battle. Perhaps indeed he had some prescience of that which was to come.

"Damn it, I don't intend to stay in this hole a fortnight!" I cried angrily.

"We'll not. Philip will be back when he gets a chance — perhaps when watches are changed and Polly takes the deck. Trust the black man, George!"

"But what the hell can we do even if free?" I demanded. "We've no arms."

Ned Low laughed out at this.

"Ha, George — what'll we do? It'll be a sweet play, I'll warrant you! Mind now, have patience! Leave the business to me."

His tone of confidence irritated me.

"You're damned cocksure about it, Ned. What'll you do

then? Out with it!"

"Why, hide honor under necessity, as Falstaff has it!"
He chuckled again.

"When needs must, lad, I can play the pirate very well, I do assure you! Ha' faith, and wait."

"I'm no pirate," I said sulkily, "and sha'n't go on the Account for any man."

He laughed at that, then drew a dismal sigh.

"Heigh ho! Times aren't what they were, George, even in the good old days when Kidd and Avery were in their prime! If we'd lived a few score years ago! What ruffing, bold times they were, eh? Sink me if there's any romance at sea these days! Ships in the new fore-and-aft style, all the galleons rotted out, and the brave buccaneers degenerated into rascally thieves who'd slit your weasand for a shilling rather than risk a fight for a thousand pound!"

"Well, a few hours more and Bloody Ned will be walking his own deck again — then hey for villainy! I'll slit weasands my own sweet self, and a kerchief about the head will vastly transform, you, George; should take to earrings, like the bosun."

Realizing that he was only playing on my ill humor, I made no response to this.

The hours dragged past most unbearably, for it was stilling hot down in the lazaret; we both waited impatiently for noon to arrive, but it came on leaden wings. At length we heard cries and the stamping of feet on deck, though what had happened we did not learn at once. A little later Dickon came into the cabin and began to arrange it for the meals of those who were now aft. The little Imp had either forgotten the loss of his dirk or else dared not mention it. Instead of closing the trap, over which he moved the table, he began to shy oaths and hard biscuit down at us. In the midst of this he gave us news.

"A pox on ye, dogs! Tomorrow morning we'll have the hanging of ye," he shrilled most venomously. "We've raised the land, and by night we'll be hook down. Tomorrow we'll string ye up to a merry tune!"

His head vanished from the opening, and we heard Gunner Basil's voice.

"Ha, Dickon! Make no talk of hanging where the lady can hear, ye imp o' Satan! Out with ye now and bear dinner. Here's Pilcher, what's second mate now, to eat wi' me. Ho, Pilcher! Be it true that land yonder be the islands, hey? What says cap'n?"

"Cap'n be ciphering and changing course to make the right island," said Pilcher's voice. "Harkee, gunner! I ha' heard tales of ye afore this, man. Mark, I said no word this morning afore the lass — but I know well enough that you, and the cap'n likewise, aren't no chickens. What's i' the wind, man? Are ye for the Account? If so, here's my hand on it!"

The two men fell into low-pitched talk, little of which we could overhear, until the half convinced tones of Gunner

Basil lifted in argument.

"Do 'ee listen, Pilcher! There be an article to which all the company, like all companies on the Account, be sworn; and that is not to force no married man to join us; d'ye see? I ha' heard that you be married, Pilcher. The cap'n might be glad of ye, for you know they coasts o' Virginia, whither we'll be bound; but if ye be joining from fear —"

I listened in no little amusement while Bosun Pilcher swore by teeth and toenails that he was not married, hated women as the devil hates holy water and desired to go upon the Account of his free will. He convinced Gunner Basil too, and only a master-liar could have done that thing, especially as the two men disliked each other.

It was obvious that Pilcher was trying to get into the confidence of the rogues and was stopping at nothing to do it. We heard no more, for the gunner discovered the open trap under the table, and with an oath slammed it shut; but we had caught enough to be of great heart to us.

About an hour afterward the trap was hauled open again. That imp Dickon had secured some rock ballast and now began to heave the lumps of stone at us with many foul curses; he would assuredly have worked us some damage had not Thomas Winter come into the cabin and kicked him out. With Winter was David Spry.

Both of them were in huge glee, and no wonder! For by some miracle, since Ned Low was not at all sure of having run out his easting, the island which had been sighted was no other than St. Vincent itself, the very one for which we were bound. The two men discussed this, from which we learned that before sunset the ship would be anchored, then entered up the log and departed again.

"I'll lay you two to one, George." quoth Ned exultantly, "that they'll go after the gold — take the boats and go — this very night! If they do, we're free."

I would not take his bet, however. Unless we were freed before Polly Langton left the ship I feared that the imp Dickon would pistol us where we lay. And such indeed was his intent, for the lad was bloody-hearted as Winter himself.

IX

Notwithstanding our hopes of the black cook, Philip, we saw nothing of him then, until later in the afternoon, by the stamping and singing above and by the change of motion in the ship, we understood that all hands were at the braces and the *King Sagamore* was beyond doubt heading up for the harbor.

"They'll pick the northeast haven, that being closest to the treasure," said Ned Low coolly. "Is it rocky about there, George?"

"No; all sand-hills, and two long spits of sand protect the cove," I told him. "Indeed they might go across the end of the island to get the gold, since it cannot be over a mile and a half or two —"

"Not they!" And Ned laughed heartily. "They'll row ten mile to avoid walking one. Wait and see!"

"If Philip uses that woolly head of his," I observed, "he'll come aft, get the keys, and free us the minute the anchor goes down. All hands will be busy up above for a spell."

The anchor did not go down in a hurry, however, for the ship tacked about more than once before she was in shape to make the entrance to the bight. Gradually she came to an even keel, we could hear the thunderous roar of Thomas Winter as he bellowed orders, and presently we were at rest.

Our voyage was done.

Almost at once we were aware of a soft-footed scurrying up above in the cabin. I was minded to call out, but Ned Low restrained me; excitement was upon both of us at thought of Philip there, getting the keys and coming down to let us free.

Philip it was, but in mighty fear, since he had no legitimate business aft. We heard a sudden ejaculation burst from him; then like a blow the voice of David Spry reached down to us.

"What be doin' here, ye black man? Ha, in the cap'n's chests —"

A cry broke from Philip, then the furious thud of a blow. Spry uttered a shout, which must have passed unheard on deck. The two men now began fighting across the cabin, and in the midst of this something fell between me and Ned Low, tinkling on the boards.

"The keys!" cried Ned eagerly. "Grab them, George —"

I found them and closed my fist on the precious things.

Up above the two struggling men came to the deck with a crash, and their legs showed in the opening of the trap. From Philip a choked cry of despair and fear rang out; a moment they lay fighting there at the opening, then came gradually through, and at length fell precipitately, crashing down atop of us headlong.

I saved them from broken necks, but at the cost of being knocked well-nigh senseless. When I had writhed clear, so far as the length of my chains permitted, I saw David Spry kneeling on the chest of the black and whipping out his sheath-knife.

"Enough o' that, Spry!" commanded Ned Low.

Spry looked about and found that gimlet-dirk at his back. He was paralyzed.

"Drop the knife, now! George, George, throttle him, lad!"

Even as the fellow raised a wild yell in his throat, I lunged forward and got him with both hands, dragging him to the deck with me. Now he was beyond reach of the dirk, and knew it, fighting furiously to get at me; while black Philip, twisting to his knees, added his strength to mine.

With never a sound out of him, David Spry fought on until he was black in the face as Philip and then suddenly collapsed.

"Quick, George! Give Philip the keys. Now, cook, loose my wrists, then get back up to the cabin and make all straight, and get for'ard," commanded Ned swiftly. "Look alive, lad; look alive! Not a minute to lose. We'll take care of all here."

Under the spur of his tongue Philip fumbled about for the keys, where they had dropped out of my hand. Panting like a blown horse, he found them and worked at the ironed wrists of Ned Low until a sharp word broke from the latter.

"Done! Enough, lad — up with ye! Leave all to us. Wait for word from us. Quick now!"

Obeying in his blind fashion, Philip leaped for the ladder, planted a final kick in the ribs of the senseless seaman and made the best of his way above.

When he had freed his ankles Ned Low knelt before me and worked on my irons with the keys. Blessed relief! In another moment my wrists were free, and I was rubbing at the torn skin, while Ned freed my ankles likewise.

"Now," I said grimly, "there'll be a reckoning alow and aloft —"

"Softly, softly!" said Ned, and laughed quietly in his throat. "First give me a hand with this godly rogue — thus! Good. Now strip the shirt from him and truss that jaw of his all shipshape."

In no long time we had Spry ironed in Ned Low's place, and so well gagged that nothing but a stifled moan could come from him. He would not soon recover his senses, however.

"Give us a sneaker of that port, lad," said Ned, handing me the bent pewter bowl. "Aye, a good one! Now look 'ee, George, be not hasty to wrath, as Master Spry might say. They'll not miss this rascal, what with the excitement and all. They'll leave an anchor-watch and turn in all hands soon enough."

A few swallows of wine made us both sense our freedom more acutely.

"You'll try and take the ship tonight then?" I asked.

Ned Low grinned. He was getting my pipe alight, and had trouble with the tinder; but at length he got it drawing, and shook his head.

"Not a bit of it, George! Mind now! We have the run of the ship here below, if we want it. We've all the cabin stores here to hand. Let's eat, drink and be merry, lad! Let's have a sound night's sleep, keeping alternate watch lest anyone comes down, and be ready for the morrow.

"Figure it out for yourself," he went on with an eager earnestness. "They'll take the longboat to row around the point o' the island after that gold, and they'll go at the break o' day. Who'll go? Polly, for one; Thomas Winter, for another. Winter will take the six honest lads from up for'ard to row the boat. He'll leave Gunner Basil here to keep the ship with Pilcher. Take the ship while he's gone, George, and when he comes back we'll have the dog at our mercy! Eh?"

There was sense to this; I was forced to admit it, though somewhat against my will, for further waiting was both dangerous and irksome.

"If things go as you expect," I said, "that's the best plan. Agreed! Then let's get some food broken out before the light fails. Lord, but it's great to be free to stretch again! What if Dickon comes down here, Ned?"

"Clap him in irons."

Ned Low grinned.

"I'll hang that little bastard, George! I'd sooner fling him overboard, but he'd not drown, mark me! Well, I'll not hang him either, for he's only a lad. Wait and see, George; the rascal may yet hang himself."

"And so save Jack Ketch a job," I said. "All right, Ned! I agree. Now to dine."

We were not disturbed again all that evening, for it appeared that owing to the heat and the calm of the bay dinner was served on deck. We ate our fill, luxuriated in our freedom and let our captive snore. From the silence above, all hands were sleeping.

Ned Low had curled up and gone to sleep, and I, on watch, was beginning to nod, when a slight noise sounded above, and then came the voice of Polly Langton softly.

"Are you there, Mr. Low — Mr. Roberts?"

I touched Low's face, and he sat up.

"Aye, mistress!" I responded. "And we are like to stay here a while, thanks to you!"

"Oh, you must not — you don't understand!"

There was a break in her voice.

"If I had done anything else they would not have obeyed me! Don't you see, I had to act as I have done, in order to keep where I am? When we get back with the treasure, I shall have you released at once, and then —"

"You've been badly fooled, Miss Polly!" I spoke out, throwing off Ned's warning hand. "Winter and the gunner have a rendezvous at one of the islands with a pirate ship; they are using you to get the gold, then they mean to take this ship and join their comrades. Go with them and bring back the gold, and trust all to us. Make them take the bosun with you, and do you have a talk with Pilcher, for he knows the whole game. He can give you proof enough of everything. But be careful! Don't let Winter suspect that you know —"

"Ah — I hear someone — I dare not stay!"

She was gone again, and what effect my words had upon her we could not tell. Although we listened for a while we could hear nothing. Finally Ned Low whispered to me.

"Why the hell did you tell her to take Pilcher?"

"We don't need him," I responded. "She may."

"True enough," mused Ned Low. "Sink me if I don't believe her, George! Aye. She's handled things well enough, all considered. She's none of your patched and powdered fools who cry, 'La, la!' and fly into hysterics at the sight o' blood; but an honest Devon lass, with hard good sense and sober wits. George, I take back all my harsh words and thoughts about her!"

"Then go to sleep again," I bade him. He obeyed,

laughing softly to himself.

The remainder of the night passed quietly. David Spry came to himself and tried to shake off his irons, but soon relapsed into immobility. The more I thought about Polly Langton's words to us the more I admired the girl's good sense in acting just as she had done. I could see now, in the light of those few sentences from her lips, that she had done the best possible thing for all of us.

She had of course played into Winter's hand without knowing it. Those poor "honest fools" up forward, panicky over being led astray by bloody pirates and murderers — as they considered me and Ned — had undoubtedly been prodded and urged all along, ever since we weighed anchor, by Winter and the gunner; in dealing with those fanatics the girl had been walking in slippery places and was aware of it. So all in all I felt greatly heartened by her few words; and when I waked Ned and laid myself down to sleep it was with the feeling that we owed a large debt to Polly Langton.

Morning came at last. Even before the first break of day, we were roused by the activity overhead. Obviously Winter intended to be off and away with the light, and our only fear was that he would visit us to make sure of our safety. As we later learned, we had been placed in the keeping of David Spry, and all hands were too filled with thoughts of gold to waste worry over what had become of Spry. Even Winter could not be blamed for supposing his prisoners well ironed and stowed; for he, playing a deep and desperate game — deeper even than we yet knew — was that morning on the verge of success, with the gold all but his.

Ned and I broke our fast very pleasantly; and though poor Spry's eyes besought us to have pity on him we dared not loosen his gag, promising to take care of him after a bit. Nor did we have any particular desire to ease his lot, since he had certainly made ours hard enough when he had the mastery.

The stern window of the cabin above was open. We heard the men embark as soon as there was light enough to pilot the boat from the harbor. Water and provisions were placed aboard the boat, and the deep voice of Thomas Winter penetrated to us with his final orders. Then at length silence ensued, and we knew the boat had departed.

"Now, George!"

Ned Low drew a deep breath, and then laughed out gaily.

"The question remains as to how many went along! Be quiet a while, lad. Give 'em a chance to get out o' the harbor. Beshrew me if I don't pistol that cursed Gunner Basil, and we do not want them to hear the shot."

"First get your pistol," I reminded him dryly.

He caught my arm. Steps sounded above, and immediately after, the voice of Gunner Basil himself, evidently addressing that imp Dickon.

"What's that ye want, Dickon lad — wine? Well, well, fill your cursed skin if ye will! Hast deserved it, ye limb o' Satan! Here, pour me a drink likewise; I'll wash my mouth clean o'

that damned sanctimonious talk. This time tomorrow, lad, we'll ha' the gold aboard, and hey for the Indies!"

"Here's luck, damn yer eyes!" shrilled the boy's voice.

"Sweet lad!" murmured Ned Low.

Now Dickon vomited a volley of oaths, demanding to know why he had not been taken along with the others.

"The black scum of a cook must go," he swore roundly, "and that dog Pilcher, and they six godly fools from for'ard; eight sons o' dogs at the oars, wi' the cap'n and his lass in the starn — and me left here! Damn their eyes, I hope the damned boat sinks with all hands!"

Gunner Basil fell a-laughing at these oaths and valorous wishes.

"You and me, younker," he responded, "got to stick here idle while they work. Aye, the cap'n knows Gunner Basil can lay a gun! Guzzle away, ye varlet, and I'll go set me a fish-line for'ard. There be mighty fish in these waters."

For a while there was silence. Ned and I conferred together, being in no haste, and were delighted by the news we had gained. Those two were alone on board, which made things so much easier for us. Basil alone was sufficient to guard the ship, and Winter had wanted all the hands possible along to work out the treasure, as well as to row the longboat, which was a heavy craft.

All of a sudden we heard a satanic chuckle from above, and then the head of Dickon appeared in the trap. The boy was half drunk, and I looked up to see a pistol in his hand. Staring down into the darkness, he could for the moment see no details.

"Now, ye dogs!" he shrilled at us in maudlin tones. "Now ye have it, Bloody Ned! I'll bleed the both of ye, blast yer damned souls!"

Ned and I must have realized at the same instant that the little devil was run amuck. We sprang up together, but collided and fell back. He, weaving the pistol about in his unsteady hand, uttered a wild laugh and more curses.

"I'll bleed ye, ye dogs!" he went on. "I'll show ye who's the best pirate aboard this damned ship, damn ye! Take that! And there's more for ye where it come from —" The roar of the pistol, volleying smoke and flame in our very faces, proved his words. Only that collision with Ned had saved my life, for the thing bellowed not a yard above my head. I was already heaving for the ladder again, and this time made it, and was up at the murderous little wretch while he still peered through the smoke.

He uttered a strangled cry and rolled aside, but I was through the trap and had him. And how the drunken rascal fought me! He gouged and bit with the venom of a very fury, until I got hold of his fallen pistol and slashed him over the head with the barrel. That laid him quiet at last, knocking the senses out of him.

I rose, and then found that Ned had not followed me.

"Ned!" I cried. "Ned! You're not hit, lad?"

His head rose through the trap, a grim look in his face.

"The bullet slew David Spry," he said, and came to his feet, looking down at the boy. "Sink me, but I could hang this little murderer —"

"No time," I broke in. "That shot will fetch the gunner, Ned! Get your pistols!"

"Right," he cried, and whirled about.

Even as he started toward the lockers, Gunner Basil came running down the passage with a shout to Dickon. There was nothing else to do; I went for him with the empty pistol, and he stopped short in the doorway, his pale eyes popping at sight of me and Ned. His hand flew to the pistol in his belt, but I was ahead of him, and sent him staggering with one shrewd blow in the face.

He tried to run for it, with me at his heels, and got to the companionway. Then as he started up for the deck I had him by the leg. He drew his pistol and fired down, and the bullet actually nicked my cheek and cut the skin of my shoulder, so that he pulled free of me.

None the less I got him, for I reached the deck only a step behind him and gripped his shirt, and he whirled at me with knife up. I caught his wrist, and we went to the deck together, while Ned Low seized the pistol I had dropped and waited with butt reversed. His chance came as we rolled into the scuppers, and under the smash Gunner Basil relaxed in my grip.

I rose, panting, and regarded the man. His face was smeared with blood, and though the eyes were closed that yellowy parchment face was evil to see. Ned Low touched my arm.

"Get a coil o' light line for'ard, George. We'll tie up him and the boy."

Breathing heavily, yet mighty rejoiced to be free, I went forward and got the line. There I paused to glance around, and the pause cost us dear in the end. The *King Sagamore* lay in the quiet, landlocked bay with nothing in sight but the long sandspit to seaward and the sand-hills around. We were but a cable-length from the shore.

A sudden shout from Ned Low roused me. I caught sight of Dickon, just risen from the companionway, and Ned leaping at him. The boy ran like a hare, evaded Ned and got to the rail. With one clean plunge he was overboard.

Ned jumped to the fife-rail, caught out two of the teak pins and flung one. It drove within a foot of Dickon's head as he came up and struck out for shore. The little fiend twisted his head and looked up at us.

"I'll bleed ye yet, ye dogs!" he screamed shrilly.

Angered, Ned loosed another pin, but Dickon saw it coming and dived. Escaping it, he came up again and struck out for shore. Then I perceived something else, and flung a shout at him.

"Quick, boy! Sharks astern!"

True enough; a black fin was cleaving the water, and another after it. Dickon redoubled his efforts, and made so great a splashing that he got into the shoal water safe, and a moment later staggered up on the sand. He paused there only to shake his fist at us, then turned about and ran across the sand, and presently was gone over the nearest hill.

Ned Low and I bound Gunner Basil hand and foot, gagged him and lashed him to the foot of the mainmast. The ship was ours again.

"And what about Dickon, Ned?" I demanded.

He shrugged, reading my thought.

"The chances are ten to one, George, that he'll not find Winter and the men. And if he does, what of it? We have the ship."

X

In the course of the day Ned Low and I got David Spry decently buried and reoccupied our own cabins. Likewise we noosed a huge turtle swimming alongside, for the season was just beginning and the island waters were thick with the creatures, and we dined famously.

We laid out loaded muskets and pistols with which to receive Winter when he came, and all the while the pale eyes of Gunner Basil watched us. We left him bound and gagged all day, then fed and watered him and took him below, ironing him where we had lain. He had not a word to say.

It was late in the afternoon when we descried a boat, under sail, coming up the bay. The glass showed it to be one of the island boats, with four black islanders aboard; at sight of us they were fearful, but I stood in the shrouds and signaled them, so that they came on and rowed alongside. I could speak their tongue to some extent, and when they came aboard we had a conference.

They were simple fellows, come hither after turtle. I told them that our men had mutinied and gone off in a boat but would return, and that we wanted a dozen islanders to ship aboard us as far as Lisbon. They were suspicious until I gave them what money we had and told them my name, and that I had visited their island of San Nicholas more than once.

"Your governor knows me," I told them, "also Senhor Gonsalvo, the former governor. They will tell you that I am an honest man of my word. How soon can you get the men here?"

They talked together, and decided to return at once to San Nicholas, saying that they could be back the day after tomorrow in the morning, barring bad weather. Ned Low made me a sign of delighted assent, and so we agreed upon it. Before sunset the blacks were rowing out of the bay, and so departed.

Although Ned and I kept watch and watch that night, we saw no signs of Winter coming back. Sunrise was at hand, we were getting breakfast in the galley, when Ned stepped to the rail, then called me and ran aft for the glass. Sure enough, there was a blot out between the sandspits.

When we had inspected that blot through the glass we stood staring one at the other in blank amazement. For the tube showed us that this was the longboat indeed, with a figure stooped aft, bailing the water out of her, which we took to be that of Polly Langton; only two others were aboard her, and these at the oars — cook Philip and Bosun Pilcher. They were rowing her slowly and wearily, as men who had been long hours at the task, and the boat was low in the water.

"Stove in, George," said Ned Low, wrinkling up his eyes perplexedly. "Now what's it mean, I wonder? Where's Winter and the other six?"

So slowly did they come on that it was after sunrise when they drew near, and Polly waved to us. The two men were too exhausted to wave, although we caught a faint grin from Philip and saw the bosun nod his head to us as the faces strained upward. The boat was half filled with water, and we saw that she was badly stove in the bows.

In fact, so weary were all three of them that they hardly made any comment upon finding us two alone there and the ship ours. The two men crawled over the rail and sank down, gasping for breath. Polly leaned against the rail and looked at us with a tremulous smile upon her lips. Her hair was fallen about her cheeks, and she was very lovely.

"Where's Winter?" I asked.

She nodded toward the sand-hills.

"Coming. We ha' been rowing most o' the night —"

"Rest then," said Ned. "Come, George! I'll be cook. You bring ale."

I fetched some ale, and Ned produced biscuit and turtle-steak. We asked no questions, but waited, and when she had eaten a little the girl suddenly looked up at us.

"Gentlemen, I ask your pardon, for — for everything," she faltered. "I ha' learned the truth —"

Ned took her hand and smoothed it, looking into her eyes.

"Dear lass," he said gravely, "why speak so? Sure, we owe our lives to your wit and good sense. Had you not taken the head of things —"

Her eyes widened and came to me.

"But — but they used me as a tool!" she said. "Bose Pilcher has told me all, as you told me last night, Mr. Roberts! It is all true about that man Winter —"

"Does he suspect that you know?" I demanded.

"No, no! He was glad enough when I offered to come back in the boat and bail her —"

"Then where's the gold?"

Ned broke out in a laugh.

"Come, lass, forget all else and tell us what's happened?"

"Aye, he has the gold," she said, color coming into her cheeks. "We found it just where the directions said. But in coming ashore we ran on a sunken rock that hurt the boat; to fetch back the gold in her was impossible. So Winter remained to bundle it into canvas and carry it across the headland to the bay here. He was too excited over the gold to protest my departure, and sent Pilcher and cook Philip with me. He is sure that bose has joined in his schemes, you see.

He'll be here some time today."

"Good!" cried Ned joyfully. "You, lads, get for'ard and sleep while you can. First, however, help get the boat hauled in, and I'll go to work on her. Canvas and pitch will make her tight enough to use in a pinch."

When the boat was hauled aboard Pilcher and the cook stumbled off to sleep, and Ned fell to his task, whistling blithely.

I got a spare sail rigged aft for a sun-shelter and remained talking with Polly Langton, who refused to go below. She was much concerned to have matters set right between her and us — but no more anxious on this head than was I myself.

From Pilcher, I discovered, she had gained a very accurate understanding of the whole situation — including her worthy uncle's past history, since the bosun had held back nothing. However it must have shocked her, she was now facing too stern realities to spend much thought on the past.

Now I went over with her the varied details of the voyage, pointing out how this and that had come about; and, having the perspective of distance and an awakened mind, Polly could clearly enough discern the right and wrong of things. Of Ned Low I could say very little, but I told enough to make her see that he was not altogether the bloody pirate he had been named.

In an hour we were talking and laughing together as friendly as ever or perhaps more so, and there came up mention of her native Devon. At that she cried out bitterly:

"Oh, if we could only get away from here before the men come back! I want none of that gold. I would it were all at the bottom of the sea! And I am afraid of Winter. If you had heard and seen him when they brought the gold up out of the hole you'd have thought he was more devil than man! Can't we work the ship out now, at once?"

"It might be done," I said, casting an eye at the bay. "There's a light air off the land — Oh, Ned! Ned!"

Ned Low had finished his work on the boat and came at my call, pipe in one hand and mug of ale in the other. Very merry and laughing he was, too.

"Ned, the lass fears Winter. And I am none so sure that it were wise to lie here all today and tonight. He took a brace of muskets with him, and pistols. What d'ye say to letting the gold go hang, slipping the hawser, and —"

"Not by a good deal!" exclaimed Ned coolly.

He regarded Polly with a smile, his brown face very frank and cheerful to see.

"I don't blame ye, Polly, for wanting to be rid of it all and away from here; but, lass, gold is mighty useful in the world. Once away from the *King Sagamore*, once back in London or Devon or where ye will, a few thousand guineas is a mighty fine thing wherewith to fight the world, the flesh and the devil! If the clergy had each a pocketful o' money there'd be less talk of hell and more of heaven — I'll wager ye never heard a bishop talk of hell now! Nor ever will. We see the world quite different through gold spectacles, lass —"

"A brave dissertation, Ned," I broke in dryly, "but come to the point!"

He pointed overside with his pipe, to where several large black fins were slowly cleaving the water.

"There y'are — come to pick the leavings of our turtle! What better guard could we have against Winter tonight, George? Without a boat he can't reach us, and a musketball or two will do us no harm. So fear not; we are safe from him and all others!

"As for the gold, I mean to have it from him; that's one reason for not leaving. The second is like unto it — I'll not leave him wi' that gold in his paws, d'ye mind? I need the gold, and I'll not see him rewarded with it. Nay, leave him ashore for a day or so without fresh water or food or strong liquor, and hear how the dog'll whine to us! We'll give him bread for gold, and when the last red round piece is down below I'll slip the cable and set our black island men to the braces and leave Thomas Winter here to think on his sins.

"For your sake, lass," he continued, "I'll not try to hang him, since that might make or lead to trouble. We'll leave him marooned and be content wi' the gold."

Leaving him to argue the matter with Polly, I took his mug and went forward to get some ale. While I was there, Pilcher came yawning on deck. I paused for some talk with him, and he told me what had finally and terribly convinced the girl. Under the jubilant excitement of finding the gold Winter had momentarily flung off his mask, telling the lass that he meant to have her as well as the gold; he had charged Pilcher to watch her closely and to lock her into her cabin on reaching the ship.

What Winter had said to Polly Langton was enough to set any man's blood to boiling. Then and there I changed my mind about leaving the bay.

"Bose, who's this fellow Winter?" I demanded. "He's no riffling jack playing in luck. There must be a name to him that men would know."

"Aye, sir, but I could never come at it."

Pilcher shook his gold earrings.

"Gunner Basil knows him, I be certain; no one else. Where be gunner and Dickon, sir?"

I told him of Dickon's escape.

"Gunner's ironed down below. You must have deceived them all finely, bose! Winter really thought you'd go on the Account with him, eh?"

"Gunner be an old fool," Pilcher grinned at me. "Yet there's murder in the heart of un, mark that! The tales he's poured into me would shiver your soul, Mr. Roberts! If he be not a liar he ha' seen and done such things as 'ud melt a Turk!"

"Go down and talk to him," I suggested. "Perhaps you can get something out of him about Winter. That man's a pirate, a known man, I'm certain of it."

"Be goin' to hang 'un, sir?"

"Aye. You might get the line and block ready now, too."

I went aft with the ale and informed Ned and Polly bluntly that I was for staying until the men returned. Then Ned Low saw what the bosun was doing at the main and questioned me about it.

"Making ready for Winter," I said. "The man hangs."

"Why so changed?" said Ned, laughing. "Would you jeopardize us all?"

"He insulted the lass here," I said. "Make no more talk about it now."

Polly Langton looked at me, and the color came into her face. We must have looked mighty humorous, for Ned Low began to laugh again and went forward. When he was gone, the little lass spoke softly.

"You must not bear him such ill, Mr. Roberts —"

"No protests if you please!" I told her frankly. "Pilcher told me what was said, and I'll give that rascal what he deserves if it kills me! But it won't. Before we leave here the rogue hangs."

She looked troubled, but made no more mention of the matter.

All this while we were keeping a sharp eye upon the sandhills, but in vain; and since Winter and the six men could not come near the little bay without being seen, we were safe in taking our ease.

After a little Philip appeared and came aft. We were prompt to thank him for his loyalty, and for those keys which had near cost him his life to obtain. The Negro was delighted with our words of praise, and Ned promised him more substantial reward later, when occasion offered.

I had never seen Ned so full of good spirits as this morning. Polly began to take all in jest his announced purpose of buying out her share of the ship and going forth once more on the Account, and small wonder; no man ever looked less like a pirate than Ned Low that morning. Even when he stated that he would transship her at Lisbon she thought him joking.

So came noon, and Philip brewed us a mighty stew of green turtle in the regular island style, which we hugely enjoyed. Pilcher had held some conversation with Gunner Basil, but it was all one-sided. He reported that the gunner would utter nothing save oaths, and those unfit for repetition.

We had just lighted our pipes, and cook Philip was clearing away the meal from the shelter aft, when Polly Langton looked up and changed countenance suddenly. I followed her gaze, and came to my feet.

"Stand by, Ned! Here they are."

We stood at the rail, watching the seven bowed men coming over the crest of the sand toward the bay. Seven? No, there was one more following them; eight in all, and the eighth was the cabinboy, Dickon.

XI

Foremost of the eight came Thomas Winter. He and the six men after him had flung away their arms, even to pistols; they bore each of them a rude canvas sack, some on shoulders, others in arms, and by their weariness under that dragging weight of wealth we knew how great was the treasure they had unearthed. Dickon alone carried no burden.

"Dickon has told them his tale — yet they come!" exclaimed Ned Low, watching the scene with frowning perplexity.

We shared his uneasy wonder, all of us. We had expected anything but this open coming. It could not be doubted that Winter now knew we held the ship, and he probably thought the gunner dead; he could have had little hope of Pilcher and the cook having subdued us. Yet he came on openly, the six men behind him, bringing their golden treasure down to the shore of the bay! And all unarmed, too, except for knives.

"I looked for them to attack us tonight somehow," I observed, "but not for such a coming. Watch out for tricks, Ned!"

"Yes, yes!" added Polly earnestly. "Don't let him trick you!"

"Fear not," said Ned Low quietly. "I want but that gold of him, and he can have the island! And let him try his tricks, now that we know him for what he is."

The eight came filing down to the sandy shore of the bay, a scant cable's length from us.

"Way enough, lads,'" cried Thomas Winter, dumping his load into the sand. In the hot stillness of the bay, with not a breath stirring aloft, each sound reached us plainly; the hot panting of the men, as one by one they added their burdens to the pile; the oaths and curses of Dickon, toiling in their wake; the dull sound of clinking metal as the pile of gold grew complete. More than one of the godly rogues vented himself of profane words as shoulders and arms were rubbed.

"Gold makes a change, even as I told you, in men," commented Ned Low. "Mark those rascals, George! A day or so ago they were pious, regenerate dogs — and now look at the flame in their faces, the passion in them!"

"More like thirst," commented the girl practically. "The water in the boat's cask was foul. And they have thrown away even the provisions in order to carry the gold."

That was true. The group of men stood there staring at us, and even in the face of Winter we could lead the hopeless despondency of a beaten man. They had neither water, food nor arms. We, who held the ship, held everything.

At length Winter came down to the water's edge and hailed us.

"Ahoy! Pilcher, are you there, bosun?"

"Aye," roared back bose. "Here and with the cap'n, ye damned dog!"

Winter stared at us from his long face.

"I hadn't thought ye'd go back on us, bose," said he, and shook his head. "Be you with 'em too, Miss Polly?"

She would not answer him. Ned Low made laughing response.

"Come aboard, Thomas Winter! Come aboard, with the men. Swim, lads, swim! The ale is warm, but hearty, and here fine fresh turtle, and fish for the taking. Come aboard, lads, and never mind the sharks."

The other men and Dickon were by now sprawled in the sand in various attitudes of despair. But Thomas Winter stood and stared at us.

"Master Low, ye'd never see us starve an' die o' thirst?" he cried.

"Aye, and with a good heart!" said Ned cheerfully. "There's water to the south end of the island, lads. Take up your gold and go for it."

Sullen curses from the men showed how his words bit, and how they themselves had changed from their former godliness. Ned Low laughed at them.

"Come, come, regenerate hearts!" he derided. "Shall I have up Gunner Basil out of his irons to give you some godly exhortation?"

"Master, we be poor, unlucky men," returned Thomas Winter mournfully. "There be no gettin' around it, you ha' beat us. We ha' throwed the main, and you ha' beat us despite all. Will ye not ha' mercy on us?"

"Not I," said Ned Low blithely. "What about your rendezvous with the *Rose Pink*, Master Winter? Do you still think to pick her up, and carry these good honest lads off to a life o' piracy?"

I watched the men at this, hoping to find that this was news to them; but they clustered about Dickon, merely glared at us. Evidently they had thrown off all restraint. The very sight and touch of the gold had corroded their souls. Thomas Winter only wagged his long head and wiped sweat from his brow.

"You ha' beat us," he said again. "We ha' no water, no food, and will die like dogs out here i' the hot sun. Take us board, master, even if it be in irons!"

"Not I," quoth Ned Low, tamping tobacco into his pipe. "I want ye not. You have gold there in plenty. Eat it, drink it! Make a canopy of it to shade yourselves from the sun! We'll be gone from here tomorrow morning, and ye can enjoy the gold to the full."

A sudden transport of rage shook Winter.

"Gizzard and guts! Will ye have no mercy, damn ye?" he roared out.

"Should have thought of that yesterday," I broke in, and he stared at me as if he had never seen me before. "You dog, Winter! I'll see you hanged for what you said to the lass. Mind that! I'll see that the island men know you for pirates, and the first king's ship we speak will come to take you off."

"Master Roberts, you'll never do that?" he returned as if

struck aghast by the possibility. "We didn't do no harm to you, sir — only put ye in the bilboes, so to speak, for a day or two. We be main sorry for all we ha' done, masters; aye, we be main sorry! We be naught but poor sailormen, masters. Ye'd not bear malice against us? And now you ha' the ship and all's well, you'd never go off and maroon us here?"

"Aye," said Ned imperturbably. "Like the dogs you are!"

"Do 'ee speak to un for us, mistress!"

Brazenly Winter addressed himself to Polly.

"After all, mistress, we be Englishmen! Maybe we ha' been tempted; aye, it's true enough, the yellow gold tempted us, mistress! But we be not all bad. Do 'ee speak a word to cap'n, and he'll hear it. We'll work ship good and faithful, we will. Aye, he can have us in irons for the mutineers we be, so he don't leave good men here to die o' thirst! Do 'ee speak a word to 'un, do now!"

Polly stood and looked at him, her eyes inflexible. Ned Low laughed again.

"She'll not speak the word, Winter, nor would I listen. Ye'll set no foot on this ship again."

Thomas Winter stood desolate, with head hanging, for a long moment. Then he heaved a great sigh and looked up.

"It be main hard on us, masters!" he said slowly. "Will ye make no terms?"

"Not with you, Winter," answered Ned, who by this time had his pipe alight and stood puffing calmly. "I'll take the men aboard and will hand them over for trial; that's their wages, if they want to come."

"Where be David Spry, cap'n?" spoke out one of the men.

"Dead," I responded. "Murdered by Dickon, there —"

"A foul lie, mates!" screeched young Dickon. "Spry were murdered like poor Mr. Russel — knifed un in the back, Master Roberts did! Don't believe un! It's but to murder us he wants us aboard!"

I disdained to answer this. Among the men there arose a violent altercation. Some were for accepting Ned's terms, anxious to get away from the island at any cost; others called Ned and me bloody murderers and would not allow it. Then one of the men leaped up hotly.

"We all stick or we all go!" he cried out. "Who says stick?"

He and three others voted to stay. Two of the men cried that they would come aboard, and he turned on them angrily.

"No, ye don't!" he cried. "All or none it is. We stick with ee, Winter!"

Ned frowned at this, for I think he had counted on some of the men helping to work ship, and this attitude of theirs rather took him aback. Winter, who had listened to them in silence, now faced us, again and spoke.

"You ha' the whip hand of us, master," he said resignedly. "But if ye will have no pity on us, will ye not barter us even for the gold? Give us biscuit and some rum, and water enough to last until we ha' found the springs, and set a price on it!"

Now I perceived by the light in Ned's eyes that it was for this he had been waiting all the time, for he was intent upon getting that gold aboard. One of the men cried out for shoes, since the sand blistered their bare feet, and another for hats.

"It might be done, lads," rejoined Ned Low, not too eagerly. "Ye have seven bags o' gold there. For the top four of those bags I'll set ashore all the things ye desire; and for the bottom three bags I'll leave the longboat behind when we sail i' the morning. What say ye to that?"

"The boat's stove!" said Winter.

"Aye, but I've patched her, and ye can clap another patch over. What say ye now?"

Winter turned and stepped back to the men. There was a hoarse discussion for and against the offer, since certain of the men had no mind to hand over all the gold. Winter, however, argued with them at length, showing them the hopelessness of their condition.

Polly and I came back under the awning of sail, and Ned joined us.

"Winter has enough sense to know he's beaten," he observed complacently.

"Be careful of him," said Polly slowly. "Be careful! Let the gold go and put to sea now, or he'll play us some trick yet."

"Not he," and Ned chuckled heartily. "Hark to 'em arguing about it! Why, lass, they haven't so much as a pistol among 'em! It'd be a sin and shame to leave all that gold behind; your gold, that your uncle died to leave you his share of, honestly bought; and the gold poor John Russel died for, and his share ours too! Eh, George? Why so solemn?"

"Gold gets paid for," I said. "Oh, I'll be glad o' my share, Ned — but gold gets paid for. Some pays in work and sweat and gets little, like I've done these years at sea; but I've got better things than gold. Some pays in roguery and gets much, and think it the biggest thing in life; but the gold decays on 'em, and they find it's not so big after all."

"Gold don't decay," said Ned briskly, and clapped me on the shoulder. "Ha, George, so art still a philosopher, eh?"

"And I think George has the right of it," said Polly, then blushed red. "I mean Mr. Roberts —"

"Na, nay!" said Ned, laughing. "It's George and Ned and Polly among us three, lass, why not? Aren't we friends and comrades together? If we be free and easy, it's all in good comradeship."

"What about Dickon?" I demanded. "You'd not take him aboard, even if the men come?"

"No. I had meant to leave him out of the offer," said Ned, and knit his brows, "I want those two men if they'll come; we'll have need of them. We must work the ship around to the south end of the island and take on fresh water, too. We need those men, George. But Dickon stays here, the foul little beast! Gunner Basil we'll take with us —"

"Ahoy, cap'n!" called out the deep voice of Winter.

We went to the rail, and found him ankle deep in water, staring at the ship.

"Agreed, cap'n," he called, "on one condition — that ye let Gunner Basil come free to us. He knows where there be more gold. We can get it i' the boat and join the *Rose Pink* if we ha' no bad luck. That's our best offer, cap'n, and I ha' sweat makin' the agree to it."

"Done with you, Winter," said Ned Low promptly. "Now listen well! Those men o' yours shall retire a hundred feet to the top o' that little sand-hill. You wait for us where you are. At the first sign of treachery, you'll be shot, and those men with you. Understand that, do you?"

"Aye, sir; but why talk so?" Winter looked astonished. "I be not treacherous, master! It's mortal good o' you, says I, to be so main kind to us — wi' boat and all! Bain't that so, lads? Come, lads, gi' the master three cheers!"

Not they; the six men were again vehemently discussing Winter's offer to them, two begging to be let go aboard the ship, the other four dissenting violently. Dickon took no share in that talk, but sat chewing on a stick to ease his thirst, glowering savagely at the ship.

"You're going to make the barter now, Ned?" I asked.

He nodded, beaming gaily.

"Aye, lad! Get the gold aboard and stowed. Then by morning, most like, all six of those rogues will beg to be took away on my terms. We ha' the sharks for watchdogs, mind ye! It's all safe enough. Wait now, and you'll see; I'll take no chance of that dog tricking me."

Under his assuring confidence, Polly's uneasy look vanished, and I gave over all protest. Indeed, the thought of that gold coming aboard us had a sort of necromancy that bewitched us all with its wizard light.

We turned to in the waist and got the boat into the water. Winter sang out to know when we would release Gunner Basil, and Ned told him in the morning before we sailed; with which Winter had to content himself, taking our word on the matter.

Finding that the boat was well patched and worthy, we got into her some bags of biscuit and other stores, with rum and a breaker of water and everything that could be useful to the rascals save firearms. Winter anxiously demanded if we would leave the boat in the morning likewise, to which Ned assented.

"Boat and gunner together, Winter! Now get your men up the hill."

Ned turned to us.

"George, you and the bosun take pistols and row the boat ashore, Philip, you stop here at the rail wi' the muskets handy, and let fly if you see anything amiss."

His scheme was safe enough, it appeared. Pilcher and I got down into the boat, put out an oar each with pistols at our feet, while Ned sat in the stern with two more pistols, so if need were our pistols could account for six of the rascals.

Meantime Dickon and the six men had retired as commanded to the crest of a little sand-hill a hundred feet back from the water.

"Give way!" said Ned, seating himself.

He looked up and waved a hand laughingly.

"Fare you well, Polly! We'll bring you gold when we come again."

"Be careful!" she warned once more.

We headed the boat for the shore and heaved her slowly through the water. Presently her nose scraped, Thomas Winter caught her by the bow, and as Pilcher and I stepped out, gave a tremendous pull that brought her a quarter-length up on the sand.

"Now," said Ned Low, cocking his pistol, "watch yourself, you dog! Take out the stuff and throw in the gold. Pistols, George, and watch him!"

Thomas Winter, his long horse-face adrip with sweat, gave us a reproachful look.

"Can 'ee not see when a man be playin' fair?" he said, and stooped over his task.

Indeed it seemed a bit ridiculous that three of us should wait there with our pistols in hand while one man labored. Winter put his giant strength to work with a will and heaved the stuff ashore until at length he had the boat cleared. Then, wiping his brow, he dropped in the sand for a brief rest.

At this instant we caught a cry from the men on the sand-hill.

"Ho, master! Ho, cap'n! Wilt take me and Jeff aboard?"

"Aye, that we will!" sang out Ned Low, who still sat in the boat's stern.

We heard a cry from Polly. Among the men on the hill arose something of a scuffle. Two of them were trying to break away, the others were restraining them. Winter paid no heed to this, but lay panting, his eyes closed.

Then the two men got free and began to run, the others hot after them as they leaped down the hillock. The two struck at their pursuers, who followed at their heels, cursing and struggling. Ned Low heaved up his pistol.

"Let 'em go, you rascals!" he cried.

At that Thomas Winter heaved himself up and looked. Then his stentorian voice roared.

"Stand back, ye villains! Back, or I'll break your blasted heads —

The two foremost came running to us, the others still at their heels. Ned hesitated to fire, as did Pilcher and I. From the ship Philip let fly with a musket, the ball going high. A cry broke from one of the men running to us.

"Don't let un stop us, cap'n! We're coming —"

Winter roared at them again, but the rout of men came rushing at us. At a little distance Dickon and the four pursuers paused. The other two came panting up and dropped on their knees beside the boat.

"Wilt take us, cap'n?" they begged together.

"Aye, but you'll stay in irons until we sail," said Ned Low, then looked up at the others. "In with you, lads. You there, stand back! Back!"

Sullenly the others began to obey, while Winter roared at them again. One of the men clambered into the boat — and then went sprawling atop of Ned. The other was up and at me before I realized his intent. Winter whirled and flung himself at Pilcher.

And the others came bursting at us.

XII

I cut a sorry figure in this mishap, for my pistol went off in air, and I was on my face in the sand with two men plunging on me. Ned Low blew out the life of his assailant, but could not get rid of the body before another was on him. As for the bosun, he went down like an ox under the fist of Winter and stayed down.

And cook Philip dared not fire for fear of hitting us.

A cruel trap it was, well sprung and full of guile, and we were in truth snared in our own folly. I was bound hand and foot and left lying, but wrenched myself about so that I could see what was happening. All this took place, not as I give it here, but so swiftly that it were hard to realize at once.

Ned Low was struggling both with dead and living, trying to get his other pistol free, in the stern of the boat. She had careened as the load was taken out of her, and now Thomas Winter, an ugly grin showing his fangs, leaned forward and bore down on her with his weight. As she gave, Ned Low and his assailant were tumbled into the water.

"That takes the bite out of his pistol!" quoth Winter. "At him, lads — and alive, mind ye! Any man uses his knife, I'll spread-eagle!"

Why he was so anxious to take Ned alive was by no means clear, and it came very near to costing him all that he had gained. For Ned was on his feet, knife in hand and standing knee-deep in water; twice, with knife and fist, he broke clear of the men and was trying to swim for it to the ship, taking the chance of sharks. He could not get away, however.

At length one of the men got a grip on his knife-arm, and the others piled in. All went down in a turmoil of water and spray, and they haled Ned ashore with a man hanging to either arm, and so bound him.

Winter turned, shot out a long arm and seized Dickon by the shoulder.

"Boy, bide ye here and watch un, and if ye murder un I'll flay the hide off thy back!" he said, in so deadly a voice that the boy shrank back.

Then, loosing Dickon, Winter roared at the men:

"Pile in, lads; pile in! To the ship, afore they lay a gun on us!"

He shoved out the boat and leaped in, the five remaining men after him. There were only two oars in the boat, but with two men to an oar they sent her through the water.

From the *King Sagamore* began to bang muskets; both Polly and the black cook were firing from the rail, but quite failed to stop the boat. Two of the men were wounded, and no other damage was done.

A groan broke from Ned Low as the boat swept in under the ship's side and the men began to go up. Dickon, who had picked up one of Pilcher's fallen pistols, echoed the groan in a demoniac chuckle.

Not quite so easily done, however! The first man over the rail went back to feed the sharks, with a ball through him. Winter and the others piled aboard and beat the black cook down; we could hear Winter roaring at them not to kill him, for they would have need of every man to work ship.

Polly had fled to the quarterdeck with a pistol, and now Winter ran at her. She would have killed him then, with luck; but the priming flashed in the pan. Winter tore away the weapon and picked her up and took her below. A moment later he reappeared, having locked her in a cabin.

Upon that, having secured the ship, the men began to go over her like famished wolves. Gunner Basil was found and let loose. The ale-cask was broached and our turtle was made way with; one and all were so keen for food and drink that they forgot all else.

Dickon stood on the shore and bawled curses at them unheeded. So he turned to the pile of stuff we had brought ashore, broke out some biscuit, opened the rum and the water and began to get himself into a fine condition of drunkenness. Ned and I looked one at the other, but I could not reproach him.

"You were right, George," he said, and swore bitterly.

That was all, but it showed how keen was his self-blame for what had happened.

After a little Dickon came to his feet, staggering, for the rum had shot to an empty stomach and he was drunk. Plucking out his knife, he made his uncertain way to the form of Bosun Pilcher, who lay as Winter had stretched him out. Squatting down, he began with deliberate deviltry to cut the gold earrings from the ears of the bosun.

Naturally enough this treatment revived Pilcher, who sat up cursing. Dickon hiccupped, fell way and retreated. I cried out to Pilcher to kill the young devil and free us, but as bose came to his feet Dickon picked up his pistol and let fly. Pilcher reeled to the shot, and a staining smear of red leaped out across his face; turning around, not knowing what had happened, Pilcher ran for it, Dickon with the second loaded pistol staggered after him and fired again, but missed.

The bosun disappeared over the crest of the sand-hills, whether dying or dead we knew not, and Dickon came back again uttering oaths. A roar of maudlin approbation came from the men watching the ship's rail. He shook his fist at them and returned to his rum.

With all these things the afternoon was passing quicker than we knew; but to me and Ned Low, lying there on the open sand, the time dragged like an eternity. Dickon gave no heed to us, but sat maundering over the pistols, trying to recharge them with futile fingers until his potations and the hot sun sent him fast asleep. The pile of goods we had fetched ashore lay where Winter had flung them. Beyond the pile of canvas-sacked gold lay gray and hideous, at least to my eyes; since for this gold had Polly's liberty and our own lives been bartered. The men aboard ship were still drinking and feasting.

The sun was fast westering when Ned Low turned a white, strained face to me.

"I ha' almost got it, but not quite," he said in a low voice. "When I roll over, see can you put your fingers on the cord." A chorus of drunken song lifted to us as he wrenched about in the sand and got his back to mine. Of Pilcher we had seen nothing. Either the bosun was dead or lying hurt and unconscious like a wounded animal.

Instinctive hope rises in all of us. Now as I fumbled with blind fingers for the cords at Ned's wrists I perceived Dickon asleep in the sunlight of the dying afternoon, saw the pistols at his feet, realized that we might yet have a desperate chance to win. And as the thought came to me I heard the rattle and clatter of men getting into a boat, and turned my eyes to the bay to see the longboat shoved off from the ship and sent toward us by half drunken oarsmen, with Winter in the stern.

"Give way, ye dogs!" came his voice. "Lively does it!"

"No time to lose, lad," said Ned coolly. "I've been all afternoon working 'em loose."

"There y'are then."

I could not see him as I lay, but I heard him curse softly. His hands were too stiff and bloodless for his fingers to work on his bound feet. Meantime the longboat was coming in to the shore, Winter standing in the stern and roaring at his rowers to lay back. Drunk as they were, they brought him in with a rush.

He leaped out of the boat and was at us — just as Ned Low rose up free. For a long moment the two men looked at each other; behind Winter, the four men tumbled ashore and stood gaping, too fuddled to know what was going on. But I, looking up at Winter, perceived that he seemed cold sober. Behind Ned, Dickon was stirring and staggering to his feet, wakened by the voices. Winter and Ned Low stood motionless, a grin upon the horse-face of Winter, who realized that Ned's feet would scarce bear him as yet.

"Why, here's Bloody Ned the pirate!" said he, and guffawed.

I had never before known, as I knew now upon looking up at him, the indescribable villainy of the man's face; perhaps he had never before let himself go free of restraint. Now, with the mask off, the furious and inhuman cruelty of him was all evident.

"I'll fight 'ee barehanded, Bloody Ned!" he went on. "Dost remember the fight ye had wi' Francis Spriggs on his own quarterdeck, eh?"

Ned started.

"Zounds! How in the devil's name d'ye know of that, Winter?"

"I heard tell on it."

Winter took a step forward, his huge hands clenching and opening again at his sides. His mirth vanished. He showed his yellowed fangs in a snarl, as does a dog to frighten an adversary.

"Fight, ye bruiser! I ha' looked a long while to get my fingers around that windpipe o' thine; gizzard and guts, but I'll tear it out afore I finish ee!"

A spasm of ferocity crossed his face. He lunged forward and dealt a powerful blow with his fist.

Ned avoided it, stumbled a little on his numbed feet, evaded the huge Winter and so came around in front of me. There he faced about and put up his hands, and for a moment I saw the old reckless gaiety in his face.

"Fall to, ye bastard!" he called out — and then drove in a right-hander that rocked Winter's head on his big shoulders.

Now they fell to in all truth, Ned's recklessness vanished; before half a minute was gone he knew that Winter was coming in to tear the throat out of him, literally. After the first few blows all Winter tried to do was to grab with those steel-hook fingers of his. Once he got a grip on Ned's shoulder, and nothing but a full-weight smash on the point of the chin loosened it. And as he came, Winter began to curse.

It was no ordinary cursing, but the foulest outpouring of rottenness that could be spawned in tavern or forecastle. That volley of filth drove Ned white with sheer fury, for there was a venomous madness in it that burned. As for me, I wondered what reason there could be back of it, for Winter's rage was no ordinary battle-anger.

"If you want it, take it, you dog!" panted Ned suddenly.

He opened his arms and let Winter come into a clinch. Both men gasped under the impact, then Winter set himself and made as if he would tear Ned Low asunder.

Instead Ned sent him headlong over the hip in west-country fashion, and when he rolled over and leaped upright, half of Winter's shirt was torn away. And over his heart there was tattooed a crimson, bleeding heart!

I saw it, and Ned saw it in the same instant.

Ned Low took a step backward, and his face was ashen. For a moment he stood powerless, absolutely paralyzed by the realization of whom he faced. Winter grinned and snarled, and then cursed him anew.

"Aye, it's Trunnel Toby!" he roared out furiously. "Trunnel Toby it be, ye spawn o' hell, who have chased me these five year! And now it be Trunnel Toby a-chasing of you —"

Ned seemed to shiver. Then a frightful cry broke from his lips, and he hurled himself forward, and the other came to meet him. No less was the hatred of the hunted than that of the hunter.

But now Ned Low was as a very flame of fire. Not a word

came from his lips, and his face was a gray mask; his arms wrought upon Winter like the rods of an engine, and all the brute power of the other man was helpless before him. It was an awful thing upon which we stared in that moment — a man taking bitter and utter vengeance for such wrongs as few men have suffered.

For Ned Low was taking vengeance in red and running measure. He moved about Winter like a dancing corposant, and left the fiery mark of his fists wherever he touched. Not once could Winter reach him. He drove in without mercy or pity, until Winter was backing helplessly before him, roaring in fury yet unable to fight back. Then Ned began to utter sharp, panting words.

"Take that — for the girl — ye murderer! And that — and that — for the old man — for the two ye killed — wi' one bullet — and that —"

"I'll tear out the throat of ye yet!" roared Winter, even under the blows. "I've saved ye up — till I could hang ye —"

He tried a kick. Ned parried it and drove out with his own booted foot. Winter gave a horrible grunt and doubled up, and Ned smote him full in the face, so that he jerked backward again and fell in the sand. He tried to rise, and could not.

"Up with ye, murderer!" cried Ned, kicking him. "Up, and take —"

Something flew over me, catching the last rays of the dying sunlight in its course; something that curved above me against the sky, like a blue flame. I heard Dickon's wild, shrill cry, and saw Ned Low stagger and throw out his arms. Then he set one hand to his side and pulled out the knife.

Ned plunged to his knees. Even then he tried to reach the figure of Winter, stabbed down at it with the crimsoned knife, but the blade only dabbled the sand. Ned fell to his hands, and then slowly rolled over and lay still.

Then there was a silence. Even Dickon stood aghast before his deed.

Upon that silence broke a storm of oaths and curses and orders from the ship. Gunner Basil stood on the rail, shaking his fist and trying to waken the staring men.

"Aboard with ye! Aboard wi' the gold — aboard!" he yelled frantically. "Aboard, ye drunken fools, afore night comes!"

They awoke, stirred, broke into movement. I could say no word, for the tears that were blinding my eyes, until Dickon came and took the knife from Ned's relaxed hand. Then I cursed him, and cursed him so bitterly that he could not answer me, but ran to the boat.

Me they hove into the stern, and the groaning figure of Winter above me. Then the gold was stowed aboard, and, leaving poor Ned where he lay, they ran out the boat and set her for the ship.

So the day died, and the swift twilight of the tropics merged into night almost by the time I was carried over the rail and flung into the scuppers; and the buckets of sea-water that they flung over the quivering bulk of Winter came running down past me in reddened streams.

XIII

Lanterns were lighted above the deck, dimly lighting the planks and coiled ropes and sea gear strewn about. Besides Winter, Gunner Basil and Dickon, there remained four men, two of them wounded; I, who lay bound in the scuppers, and cook Philip, who had been beaten into a mass of bruises and now went groaningly about his work in abject terror. Polly Langton had not appeared on deck, being still locked below.

Winter was a long time in being brought to life, for Ned had near killed him, I lay watching in bitterness of soul. So this man was Trunnel Toby! That explained much — his crafty dissimulation, his plotting, his venomous hatred of Ned Low, his anxiety to take Ned alive. Gunner Basil and he had shipped aboard us, with Dickon, with the twofold intent of pirating us and murdering Ned Low.

And they had won. Despite all, they had won. Pilcher was dead, and Russel, and Ned Low; they had the ship, the treasure — and at thought of Polly Langton down below I kept back a groan.

Gunner Basil brought dry clothes, which Winter donned, his face all puffed and bruised out of shape. Dickon brought him a great flagon of rum, which he gulped down neat. With this to hearten him Winter was soon on his feet and ordering things. Gunner Basil, who knew what arrangements I had made with the black islanders, told him that he might look for a crew in the morning, but Winter was more interested in learning just what had happened ashore. He sent for Dickon, who faced him jauntily at first, but soon changed in demeanor.

"So it was you knifed Bloody Ned!" said Winter heavily. "I have a mind to hang 'ee, lad."

He meant the words, too. Dickon shivered under his baleful stare.

"It was to save your life!" cried the boy. "He had 'ee down —"

An oath burst from Winter.

"Stow yer jaw! I'd ha' broke his cursed neck in another moment, ye swab! Get out o' my sight afore I gut ye! Ho, gunner! Is the boat made fast?"

"Fast, but not hauled up," responded Gunner Basil. "I had thought to go ashore later and turn some turtle —"

"Turtle be damned!" growled Winter.

"Where be the gold? Fetch it here, lads, on the deck. Fetch it here, my bullies!"

Dickon slunk into the background, stumbled over me and kicked me savagely, uttering a flood of curses whose malevolence was directed rather at Winter, I thought, than at me.

The roughly sacked gold was brought up and chunked down on the deck. Winter called for a knife and then stooped down — painfully, since he was bruised and sore from head to foot. With the knife he slit the canvas of each sack, and let all the gold come out into a ruddy yellow stream over the planks.

"There y'are!" he roared. "Dickon, more rum! There y'are, lads — fill yer pockets! That's what braw lads gets on the Account — gold! Take it, bullies!"

Though I was across the deck from them, I could see all that took place there beneath the lanterns. Everyone flung forward at the gold. Those four seamen, who a short fortnight previous had been exhorters to righteousness, and honest enough about it too, had now been turned completely to the rightabout. They matched the eager oaths of the gunner and Dickon in the scramble for the gold, until it dawned upon them that there was more gold here than they could well stuff into pockets, so that they all fell to laughing and jesting hideously.

The rum entered into it too, for a keg was brought up and broached, and all hands fell into a wild saturnalia. Each man decked himself to his fancy with plundered stuff from our after cabins; pistols and knives were brought forth and donned; in the midst came a flash and a roar as Dickon's pistol went off and came near to killing one of the men. The answer was a blow, and the two fell to fighting until Winter flung them apart with a bellowing laugh and made each of them down a mug of rum.

I soon saw where this would end. Presently Winter cocked one bunged eye at the main yard, and roared at the gunner.

"Ha, Gunner Basil! Be that block an' tackle rigged to hang me?"

"Aye," hiccupped the gunner, who was reeling. "Master Roberts rigged un."

"Ho, ho!" laughed Winter, and flung a knife across the deck that passed over me and slapped into the bulwark. "Shalt hang at sunrise, Roberts, ye dog! Shalt go to hell to join Bloody Ned, damn ye both! Dickon! Where are ye, Dickon? Go unlock the lass' door and bid her come hither, else I'll come down and fetch her!"

He added a jest to this that fetched a howl of maudlin laughter from the other men. Dickon slipped away aft.

Just here I heard a faint sound, and twisted about to see the black cook Philip come crawling along the rail toward me cautiously. He was in mortal fear, and his teeth were chattering from terror; none the less, he reached up and took from the wood that knife Winter had flung, and then set it to my bound wrists.

"They'll murder us all," he whispered. "Swim for it, master! I'll wait."

Then he went crawling away again into the darkness, and I realized that my hands were free, and the knife left beside them. That was the act of a brave soul!

So numbed was I that it was some time ere any feeling crept into my fingers, and I was as helpless as if still bound, though my arms could move freely enough. While I lay trying to get some sense of touch into my hands, in order to take the knife and free my ankles, Polly Langton came quietly into the circle of lantern-light, followed by Dickon.

The men gaped at her in shamed silence. Winter was seated on the keg, and met her look with a bold stare. Then he spoke.

"Dickon! Draw rum for the cap'n's lady!"

Dickon moved about the task. As for me, I found the knife with my fingers, and inch by inch moved it in front of me and toward my ankles, fearful lest some eye catch the motion. None did, however, and presently I was parting the hemp that bound me.

Not that this new freedom of mine gave any hope. I lay at the starboard rail of the ship; across from me, near where Winter and the men were grouped, the ropes ran down to the longboat. Gain that boat I could not. All I could do would be to go over the rail and swim for the shore.

Help Polly Langton I could not, unless I attack and kill the whole band of those rogues; and that was an impossibility, even had I firearms. At best she might leap the rail and chance sharks in a swim for the shore. Even then Winter would pursue. And if we got away in the darkness, what remained? A lingering death from thirst and hunger and misery of the hot sun.

I had not forgotten Ned Low, however. As I felt the cords give under the blade, it came to me that I might at least finish Winter, give the lass a fighting chance to reach the shore and perhaps work damage on the other rogues ere they killed me. And this I resolved to do, for I was mad to get a blow at that devil Winter.

My ankles free, I began to rub them cautiously.

Dickon came with the pewter flagon, but Polly took no heed. He shoved it at her, and, grinning, laid his hand on her arm. At that she snatched the flagon and struck it over his head, so that he staggered from the blow and cursed as the rum went over his face. Aye, and his hand went to the knife at his belt, whereat Winter came to life suddenly.

Rising, he swept forward an open-handed blow that knocked Dickon sprawling.

"None o' that, ye spawn of hell!" he roared. "Get up!"

Dickon rose with so black a look that I thought he would let fly at Winter. But the latter only broke into a laugh at the boy's aspect, in which the other men joined.

"Lay hand to the cap'n's lady again, and I'll hang ye!" he said, then turned to the lass with his bold regard. "Gi' me the cup, lass! I'll fill it again for 'ee. Shalt have silks and jewels, diamonds and pearls! Trunnel Toby's lass ye shall be — give it to me!"

She dropped the flagon on the deck.

"Murderers!" she cried out, "Oh, I saw it all from the cabin window! What have ye done with Master Roberts?"

"We be going to hang un at dawn," said Winter, and grinned. "Come, lass, come! What wilt offer for his life, eh?"

"She be soft i' that quarter," spoke up Gunner Basil with a hiccup. "Main soft, I tell 'ee, Toby! Look out she don't knife ye, Toby. Dost remember the Spanish jade that slipped a knife into Cap'n Franklin, hey? Damn my eyes, but she split his weasand! Look out ye don't go the same way, Toby."

Winter laughed — broke into a hearty guffaw. He stooped for the pewter cup, bent it into shape again and held it to the spigot of the keg. When he had downed the rum he wiped his swollen lips and tossed away the flagon.

"Come, lass!" he said in a maudlin jocularity that might turn at any instant to a raging madness. "Come, lass! Wilt give a kiss to spare thy Roberts a day, eh? A kiss for a day — a day for a kiss, lass! Rot me, the rum ha' got my tongue.

"Bloody Ned be dead, and the bosun dead, and Trunnel Toby's loose. Here be a fine ship, and the *Rose Pink* yonder be waitin' for us, and Trunnel Toby be commodore. Aye! Ye shall be commodore's lady, sweety lass, wi' diamonds an' rubies from the Indies, and fine silk to wear! Come, lass — a day for a kiss!"

No one was watching me; all eyes were on the lass, standing there straight and slim and defiant before the brute who taunted her. I had no skill throwing the knife, or I might have sunk it into him then. I gathered myself together and waited, ready to shout to Polly and leap forward at them.

"I will ha' naught to do with you, ye murderers!" she spoke out bravely. "Aye, and if ye hang Master Roberts I'll never rest until I see each one of you brought to Tyburn Tree and laid there!"

At this, Winter guffawed again.

"Sink me, but I like a lass o' spirit! So ye'll bring me to Tyburn, eh? Well, many another ha' said that, lass. Ned Low said it five year gone, when I pistoled the doddering old rogue who called him son, and when I put my knife into his lass! Aye, and where's Bloody Ned now, tell me? Call him up from hell to help ee, lass! Here, give us a kiss and we'll leave Roberts' hanging until sunset instead o' sunrise!"

He lunged forward, his hand outstretched to grip the lass.

She drew back a step, then, swift as light, threw her weight into a ringing blow. Her fist took Winter squarely in the mouth, where Ned Low had battered him sorely; and, no less from the pain than from the surprise, sent him staggering and stumbling sidewise until he tripped over a coiled rope and came to hands and knees.

A wild howl of laughter and mirthful oaths surged up from one and all. Winter recovered, swayed on his feet, then uttered a roar of anger. I gathered myself for the leap, and a shout to Polly was upon my very lips — when it was checked.

For the girl took a step backward, staring at the rail. So great was the fright painted in her face, that the men turned to see what she was staring at; and so did Winter. And, over the rail, they saw the face of Ned Low rising.

Terror froze me, no less than them. Ned was dead in the sand, and Bosun Pilcher was dead, yet there rose the head and shoulders of Ned Low, and beside him those of Pilcher, whose earrings glittered yellow in the lantern light. Ghastly and terrible were they, heads and faces streaming with water, and drew themselves over the rail to the deck. From the one side Winter gaped upon them, a frightful honor in his countenance, from the other, the group of men, sitting there paralyzed.

"Back from hell to help the lass, Thomas Winter!" said Ned.

At sound of his voice I ceased to shiver, for that voice of his was alive and no ghost. I rose and stepped forward to join them, but no man heeded me.

A sudden howl, an awful thing to hear, shrilled up from the men. They fell backward, rolled on the deck, stumbled over each other, trying to get away. Pilcher, empty handed like Ned, grinned and started toward them. But Ned Low stepped forward and faced Winter, who was trembling there as he stood.

"Bloody Ned!" he gasped. "Back to hell with 'ee, I'm done with 'ee!"

"You're not done with me till I see ye hung!" shot out Ned, and started forward.

"Ghost or no," rang out a thin, drunken scream, "I'll kill ye over again!"

It was Dickon. He darted out of the shadows, mad with fear and rum, and his arm swung in an arc. I shouted at Ned and, hearing the shout, Ned turned. The knife went past him, singing viciously — and thudded into another mark. The sound of it hitting was plain to all of us.

From Winter broke a furious, gasping shout. He put hand to belt, and a pistol broke the silence with its roar. Then he tried his second pistol. Through the smoke I saw Ned go plunging forward, bringing him down to the deck with raked hands. And through the smoke I saw the boy Dickon, rent and riddled by those bullets, fall across the rail and gasp out his life.

One of the seamen ran at me blindly and struck with his knife, and I loosed at him. We had it hot and thick for a moment, the man stark mad with fear, until the steel went into him and he sank blubbering away. Out of the shadows reeled two figures — Gunner Basil and the bosun, locked breast to breast and fighting like mad. Aye, and there was the black cook, Philip, swinging an empty musket and yelling as he ran after the frightened men. Looking back to Ned, running to help him, I saw him swing an empty pistol and then come to his feet. I had him by the hand, and cried out at the good grip.

"Man, man, I thought you dead there ashore —"

"Zounds, there's not much life left in me!" he said, and laughed out with so gay a note that I wondered. "Had not Dickon's knife spoiled Winter's aim, I'd be gone. But he's taken care of — see that he's bound fast, George —"

He staggered and would have fallen, but that I caught him. There was a bandage about his body, beneath his shirt, and the blood was seeping out afresh from his wound. Polly Langton ran to us, crying and laughing all at once, and as Ned sank down on the deck I turned to her.

"Polly — take care of him, quickly!" I cried. "I must see to things —"

I left her kneeling over him and started forward, wild with easiness to clinch this astounding turn that had flung the ship into our hands again. Bosun Pilcher rose up from the dock before me, a dripping knife in his hand, and I looked down to see Gunner Basil writhing out his life on the planks.

"Quick, bose! Go tie up Winter unless he's hurt to death. I'll see to all for'ard —"

I ran on, and in the bows found the three remaining seamen, partly recovered from their mad panic, roiled in a furious encounter with Philip, who had pursued them there. When I came up and the men knew my voice, they flung down knives and yelled for mercy. I shoved a coil of light line into Philip's hands and told him to bind them.

"You shall have what punishment Cap'n Low metes out," I told them. "Stay bound until morning, ye dogs, and if you're not hanged, thank your fortune. Philip, make 'em fast! Then haul each to a gun-carriage and lash 'em there. When you're done, report aft. We must have the ship cleaned up before those islanders come aboard in the morning, else they'll take us for pirates and not ship."

"Aye, sir," sang out Philip with a laugh. I went back aft and found Bosun Pilcher just mounting to the main yard with a line. He grinned cheerfully and paused long enough to tell how he had been scraped by a bullet over the head but not greatly hurt, and how that evening he had found Ned Low crawling over the sand; and the rest was not hard to guess, though I shrank at thought of their swimming out to the ship through those shark-infested waters.

And so to where Polly Langton knelt weeping beside Ned, who sat up and caught at my hand with the shadow of his old gay laugh.

"Polly!" I exclaimed. "Why the tears, dear lass? Here Ned is hurt, but not badly and the ship and the gold are ours, and yonder goes bose to reeve the line that will hang Trunnel Toby — why the tears?"

"That's why, George," she said, and laughed through her tears.

ASTROPHOBOS

by H. P. Lovecraft

In the Midnight heaven's burning
Through the ethereal deeps afar
Once I watch'd with restless yearning
An alluring aureate star;
Ev'ry eve aloft returning
Gleaming nigh the Arctic Car.

Mystic waves of beauty blended
With the gorgeous golden rays
Phantasies of bliss descended
In a myrrh'd Elysian haze.
In the lyre-born chords extended
Harmonies of Lydian lays.

And (thought I) lies scenes of pleasure,
Where the free and blessed dwell,
And each moment bears a treasure,
Freighted with the lotos-spell,
And there floats a liquid measure
From the lute of Israfel.

There (I told myself) were shining
Worlds of happiness unknown,

Peace and Innocence entwining
By the Crowned Virtue's throne;
Men of light, their thoughts refining
Purer, fairer, than my own.

Thus I mus'd when o'er the vision
Crept a red delirious change;
Hope dissolving to derision,
Beauty to distortion strange;
Hymnic chords in weird collision,
Spectral sights in endless range. . . .
Crimson burn'd the star of madness
As behind the beams I peer'd;
All was woe that seem'd but gladness
Ere my gaze with Truth was sear'd;
Cacodaemons, mir'd with madness,
Through the fever'd flick'ring leer'd. . . .
Now I know the fiendish fable
That the golden glitter bore;
Now I shun the spangled sable
That I watch'd and lov'd before;
But the horror, set and stable,
Haunts my soul forevermore!

WILDSIDE PULP CLASSICS: PULP FACSIMILE SERIES

Series editor: John Gregory Betancourt

#1: *Spicy Mystery Stories* (August 1935)

Includes Robert Leslie Bellem, Atwater Culpepper, Ellery Watson Calder, Carl Moore, E. Hoffman Price, Arthur Wallace, and more.

#2: *Ghost Stories* (June 1931)

Stories by Conrad Richter (author of The Light in the Forest*) and E. & H. Heron featuring psychic detective, Flaxman Low.*

#3: *Spicy Mystery Stories* (February 1937)

Features Robert Leslie Bellem, Lew Merrill (Victor Rousseau) Hugh Speer, Justin Case (Hugh B. Cave), & many others!

#4: *Strange Tales #7* (January 1933)

Features Hugh B. Cave's classic "Murgunstrumm," as well as stories by Robert E. Howard, Henry S. Whitehead, and many more.

#5: *The Black Mask #2* (May 1920)

2nd issue of classic mystery mag, where hardboiled fiction was born!

#6: *Tales of Magic and Mystery* (February 1928)

Legendary rare early fantasy magazine!

#7: *The Phantom Detective #1* (February 1933)

The premiere issue of the detective-hero pulp!

#8: *Submarine Stories* (March 1930)

Rare pulp magazine, stories and articles about (what else?) subs!

#9: *Sinister Stories #1* (Feb 1940)

The first issue of this "weird menace" pulp!

#10: *The Thrill Book* (Sept. 1, 1919)

The facsimile reprint from this legendary rare pulp magazine!

#11: *The Spider* (March 1940)

Includes the "Spider" novel Slaves of the Laughing Death!

#12: *Spicy Adventure Stories* (Dec. 1939)

- -

Please send me the following books, for which I enclose payment. (Or order online with a credit card at www.wildsidepress.com, or through your favorite online bookseller or pulp deather.)

☐ *Spicy Mystery Stories* (Aug.1935) - $19.95
☐ *Ghost Stories* (June 1931) - $19.95
☐ *Spicy Mystery Stories* (Feb. 1937) - $19.95
☐ *Black Mask #2* (Jan. 1920) - $19.95
☐ *Tales of Magic & Mystery* (Feb. 1928) - $19.95
☐ *Phantom Detective #1* (Feb. 1933) - $19.95
☐ *Submarine Stories* (Mar. 1930) - $19.95

☐ *Sinister Stories* (Feb 1940) - $19.95
☐ *The Thrill Book* (Sept 1. 1919) - $19.95
☐ The Spider (March. 1940) - $19.95
☐ *Strange Tales #4* (Mar. 1932) - $15.00
☐ *Strange Tales #7* (Jan. 1933) - $15.00
☐ *Spicy Adventure* (Dec. 1939) - $19.95

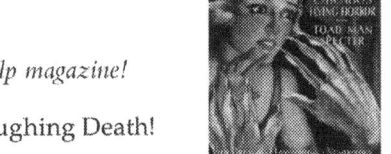

Mail to: Wildside Press
9710 Traville Gateway Dr. #234
Rockville, MD 20850
Online: www.wildsidepress.com

Name: _____

Address: _____

Address: _____

U.S. shipping: $3.95 for 1-2 books, $1 per additional book.

Other countries: please see www.wildsidepress.com